"Intelligent, laugh-filled. . . . This is a novel even mystery purists can enjoy."

—*Mystery News*

❧

"Reminiscent of Hugh Pentecost's Hotel Beaumont series but with greater humor and more appealing characters."

—*Armchair Detective*

❧

"Russell shows glimpses of greatness. . . . His plot is unpredictable and fresh. . . . Like Tony Hillerman and Sue Grafton, Russell has created characters we care about, whom we want to visit again."

—*San Diego Blade-Citizen*

❧

⇔

"Just plain fun. In addition to providing lively characters and a delicious plot, Russell knows just how to combine humor and mystery in a perfect blend."  —*Ocala Star-Banner*

⇔

"A lot of fun . . . replete with double entendres and raunchy humor. . . . This witty novel is the next best thing to spending a weekend in a posh hotel."
—*The News* (Southbridge, MA)

⇔

"A laugh-out-loud telling of the helter-skelter pursuit of a brazen murderer. . . . This is one mystery that deserves wider investigation."
—*La Jolla Light*

⇔

**Alan Russell** was general manager of a luxury hotel in the San Diego area. He is the author of *No Sign of Murder* and *The Forest Prime Evil*. He lives with his wife and two children in southern California.

# THE HOTEL DETECTIVE

## Alan Russell

**THE MYSTERIOUS PRESS**

Published by Warner Books

A Time Warner Company

MYSTERIOUS PRESS EDITION

Copyright © 1994 by Alan Russell
All rights reserved.

Cover design by Rachel McClain
Cover illustration by Tom Nikosey

The Mysterious Press name and logo are registered trademarks of Warner Books, Inc.

 Mysterious Press books are published by
Warner Books, Inc.
1271 Avenue of the Americas
New York, NY 10020

 A Time Warner Company

Printed in the United States of America

Originally published in hardcover by The Mysterious Press.
First Printed in Paperback: April, 1995

10 9 8 7 6 5 4 3 2

To Sully—who laughed too hard at my hotel anecdotes. And to Marc and Kirk, good friends for a long, long time.

And to everyone who has ever worked in a hotel especially to those who worked at the Sea Lodge at La Jolla Shores during my tenure there as manager.

# Introduction: Check-In

There was a part of Am Caulfield's consciousness that knew this was Scrooge time, a time when the spirits took him to his past. The vision came to him as more than a dream. It was as if he lived once more through his entrée into the hotel world. Am's dreamscape always brought him to 1972 and the Pelican Inn, when he was eighteen, and life was the next wave, and immortality was a good set.

"Graveyard's usually quiet," said Mr. Wells, the general manager.

The GM's body was fifty, but his eyes were more bloodshot than not and looked a little older than Methuselah's.

"You just gotta stay awake," he said. "You'll take bags, answer the phone, do rounds. Whatever. Just show up. The night auditor will tell you what to do."

Third person, Am watched his head do a "red, red, robin," but Mr. Wells was more interested in scratching his beard than in acknowledging any posturing. The GM's five o'clock shadow belied the half-past-noon time. Only his world-weariness matched the time frame of his beard.

"No drinking. No drugs. You'll be gone faster than a hotel towel if I even suspect you. At night you got a lot of rope to play with. Don't hang yourself."

Wells tossed a brochure at Am. In his dream, Am tried to

will himself to catch the brochure this time, but again he missed.

"Read," the GM said. "Tells you about the place. Guests are going to ask you questions. Nothing I hate more than the answer 'I don't know.' Our guests don't pay to hear a stupid parrot imitation. You got any idea of what a room goes for here?"

Am caught himself just before doing that parrot imitation. "Plenty," he ventured.

"Damn right," said Wells. "But that's not something I'll have to remind you about. They'll remind you."

If Hitchcock had made the movie of Am's dream, he would have echoed those words, probably put organ music around the "they'll."

Wells closed his eyes and for a minute didn't talk. When he finally broke his silence, his eyes remained shut. "One hundred and twelve rooms, kid. Couple hundred people staying the night sometimes. This is called the hospitality industry. Contradiction in terms, I've always said, but what the hell. Home away from goddamn sweet home."

Wells lifted one eyelid, looked at Am, then said, "Welcome to the wonderful world of hotels, kid."

There was a shifting in Am's dream, a slight awakening, an acknowledgment among some of his synapses that he was looking back. Am had never pictured himself as being a part of a historical photo, of looking—quaint. Everyone wants to think they're the latest model—not a Model T. In 1972 there was a naiveté to the hotel business, a ma-and-pa sensibility to the trade, at least in San Diego, which was still a backwater city then. Nixon and the Republican National Convention were set to come to town that year, or were before somebody who could count realized that San Diego didn't have enough hotel rooms and facilities to handle the event. That changed the course of history. Watergate would never have happened in San Diego. Back then the city was on military time and was used to letting its sleeping sacred cows lie.

The window of Proust passed. Am Caulfield, again submerged back into Scrooge time and his first night on the job, remembered how he had reported to work a half hour early. The night auditor knew better than that. He made his entrance at 10:59 P.M., grunted out something that might have been a greeting, then started counting the cash drawer. Bill was about forty, had a pallor that a ghost would have envied, thick glasses, and oily hair that called out for a premium shampoo. While he punched in figures, the clerk and the PBX operator were silent. He commanded that kind of respect. They knew they were in the presence of a maestro of the audit, of someone who knew more about hotels in his unconscious fingers than they could ever imagine. Or would want to imagine. Everyone watched as Bill's fingers danced over the ten-key. In less than a minute he had his tallies finished. He looked up to the expectant clerk and nodded his head once.

"Nothing to report, Bill," the clerk said, already halfway out the door. "Except you got a new night man."

In his bed Am stirred uncomfortably, felt the spotlight turn on him again.

The clerk gave Am a sympathetic glance, said that he hadn't caught his name, but then he didn't stay to hear it, either. Bill apparently wasn't keen on introductions. He held up his hands before Am could speak.

"Stay here six months and then I'll learn your name," he said. "This last year I trained five new people. I'm tired of learning goddamn new names." He scowled. "Ever work in a hotel?" he asked with the slightest bit of hope in his voice.

Am shook his head.

"Christ," said Bill. "Another virgin."

There is no harsher word than "virgin" to an inexperienced young man. The embarrassment traveled through the years, through the dream. Am was still grateful that Bill didn't observe his red face. The auditor was already immersed in his work, pushing buttons on a large machine that the clerk had introduced as the 4200. *Ker-chunk*, went the 4200. Bill fed it folios and hit more buttons, while Am listened to *ker-chunks*. Bill's speed with the machine made the front desk sound more like a canning factory than a hotel. Between his postings, he finally deigned to talk to Am.

*Ker-chunk*. "Take this pager and take a walk," he said. *Ker-chunk*. "Familiarize yourself with the hotel." *Ker-chunk*. "Find a bellman's cart, and if you get a check-in, pretend you know your ass from a hole in ground." *Kerchunk.* "Come back in an hour. I'll have finished posting room and tax by then."

There wasn't much difference between dream rounds and what had been actual rounds. Am again felt like a big shot. This was a real job, with real responsibilities, not like mowing lawns. His footsteps sounded loud, important. One hundred and twelve guest rooms, he thought, and in them all sorts of people. At eighteen, hormones are usually more active than brain cells. Am imagined that within all those rooms lurked women who wanted him desperately. His hour away from the desk passed quickly. When he returned, it was clear Bill hadn't missed him.

Sighing, Bill drew himself away from some figures he was scrutinizing, then pointed to the switchboard. The Japanese hadn't microprocessed the world back then. The Pelican Inn had a cord board. Bill grudgingly started to explain its workings. His teaching methods wouldn't have gotten him nominated for educator of the year.

"Use the inside cords for incoming calls," he said, "and use the outside cords to connect them to the extension they want. Before connecting calls, check to see if the extension is busy. You do that by testing the line. It makes a little static sound if it's busy. Got it?"

Bill's thick glasses magnified his hard snake eyes. They captured Am, mesmerized him into nodding. The phone rang, and Am reached for a cord. Wrong cord. He was pushed aside and heard Bill mutter something about God and brains and trains before he answered the call, "Good evening, the Pelican Inn."

When Bill explained the routine a second time, he exaggerated his speech in a slow and sarcastic manner. Bill asked Am if he knew his ABCs and said that most of the staff didn't. Then he showed Am where the phone rack was and how to look up the guest names. When Am returned to his work he felt a little more confident. With each call handled successfully, Am's assuredness increased exponentially. After half an hour's work, Am felt ready to lecture Alexander Graham Bell on telephones. It was about that time the guest came to the desk.

He was white and perspiring, exhibiting textbook signs of shock. He looked at Am, stuttered a few unintelligible words, then managed to light a cigarette with shaky hands.

"The p-phone," he said.

Even in his dream, Am remembered the feeling. It was something akin to when a plane encounters turbulence and your stomach drops with the vessel. Am desperately looked for Bill, but the auditor had moved to the side of the front desk, out of sight of the guest. He was watching what was going on with interest. Later, Am was to learn that Bill was fascinated by car crashes.

"What about the phone, sir?" Am asked.

The guest took a long pull on his cigarette, but it didn't help relax him. "I was talking with my girlfriend," he said. "She was ready to come over here. We were giggling and laughing. And then suddenly my wife was on the line.

"My wife."

He looked to Am for an explanation. Self-preservation camouflaged Am's face. Too late Am remembered about checking the lines to see if they were busy.

The man inhaled on his cigarette again, sucked for dear life. "It was my worst nightmare," he said. "My wife, my girlfriend, and me, all on the same line. I started yelling that we must have a crossed connection. I told everyone to hang up. And then I hung up."

Am sneaked a look at Bill. He wanted to believe that the worst was past. But Bill's rapt expression, and the way he was settling in, clued Am that there was to be more. Bill knew his pileups.

The man tried to smoke, but his hands were shaking so much that he had trouble bringing the cigarette to his lips.

"I picked up the phone a few seconds later. I was going to call my wife. I was going to explain. But she was still on the line. And so was my girlfriend. They were talking. It was like a nightmare out of hell. I couldn't get them to stop talking. I couldn't get them to hang up. For all I know, they might still be talking."

The man looked at Am, the pain clearly on his face. Like Job, he wanted an explanation for his suffering, for having to pay the penance of being human. "What happened?" he whispered.

Another Am came out then, a person he didn't know existed. With a pained face, Am said, "Who knows? That damned phone company. That goddamn phone company." Am shook his head in disgust and offered the guest a reassuring look of sympathy. The man took Am's alms and echoed his curse.

"That goddamn phone company," he said. He finished his cigarette in silence, stamped out the butt in an ashtray that Am offered, then left the desk. As soon as he was out of sight, Am disconnected all the active cords at the switchboard. He didn't care that he was terminating several conversations. He knew the callers could ring back and also knew that this time he'd check for a busy signal.

There are some long breaths you take in your life that suck in everything around you and make a photograph forever on your viscera. Am took one of those breaths. The bullet had missed him.

Or had it? Had a spell been struck then? Had he been enchanted? Am almost awakened. But the play wasn't quite concluded.

Am heard strange sounds. It took him a few moments to identify them as laughter. Bill wasn't used to laughing. The auditor started choking, but that seemed to please him all the more. When he finished, after he wiped away some tears, he looked at Am with true admiration.

"Kid," he said, "I think you were made for hotels."

That's when Am awakened from the dream. As always. And he wondered his usual Scrooge-time muse: Was that an anchorite night auditor talking, or was that the fates?

# 1

Damn fine knife, was David's first thought as he cut into the filet. If they ordered in a few more times, he just might try to collect a set of the cutlery and slip them into his luggage to take home with him. Hotel life. There was nothing like it.

He cut into the meat again. Not for the first time, David thought he should have been a surgeon. Except that doctors had to pay too much for malpractice premiums. He should know. He had sued enough of them.

"This is a great hotel, Deidre," he announced. "At great hotels they don't give you the usual butter knife with a hint of a serrated edge. They give you a real steak knife. A cutting instrument."

David demonstrated for the woman, sliced off a particularly rare and juicy morsel, and then dangled it in front of her face, unmindful of its dripping on the bedspread. From the oversize bed, she leaned over and opened her mouth, took a bite, and let the juice dribble down her chin. Deidre's robe fell open, and the man reached for her breasts. The couple hadn't—except to raise themselves for room service—risen from the bed since they had arrived the night before. It was now late afternoon.

The knocking at the door stopped their groping. "The be-

lated bubbly," the lawyer announced. A minute before, a
bellman had made a surprise delivery of wine and cheese, no
doubt from his secretary. He rose, stretched languidly, then
reached for a towel. "Hold that thought," he said to Deidre.

She reached over and swatted at his bare bottom. The
knock came again. He postured for her for a moment, then
wrapped the towel around his waist, positioning the blue-
and-gold Hotel California logo directly in front of his pri-
vates. As he walked out of their bedroom, David paused at
the full-length mirror and admired himself. There were lots
of mirrors in the suite, but not too many for his taste. That
damn personal trainer cost him a fortune, but he sure delivered the goods. Forty-five years old, and he had the body of
a twenty-year-old athlete. You swim with sharks, he thought,
and you better look like you can bite. Business had never
been so good. Clients liked his bait.

He had worked up a thirst, and was looking forward to the
Dom Pérignon. There was nothing better than ordering a
hundred-and-fifty-dollar bottle of champagne, especially
when someone else was paying for it. These were billable
hours, he thought. When Deidre got her settlement, there
would be enough zeros in it that she wouldn't object. The
room was registered under his name, of course, but for all
practical purposes everything would eventually be part of her
legal expenses. For consultation, he thought. And for services. Especially that. The getaway was their little secret.
Their precelebration.

David took a breath and pushed out his chest before opening the door. There were more and more women room service waiters these days, and he always liked to look his best
for the ladies. Head lowered, he motioned the cart inside,
waving his towel like a matador leading on a bull. "Olé," he
said. But when he looked up, he could see there was no room
service cart, no display of Irish linen and crystal glasses, no
rose in a vase, no iced champagne. There was only a man.
Given a choice, David might have preferred the bull.

The man stepped inside the suite. He was of average
height and had thick glasses. Over the years his red hair had
grown thinner, while his waist had grown thicker. For once
the lawyer was short on words. "C-Carlton . . ."

The man didn't answer. He started walking toward the bedroom. David was at a loss as to what he should do. He was too surprised even to articulate a threatened lawsuit.

In the bedroom, Deidre waited. She didn't know anything was amiss. The suite was well insulated, the walls designed to keep the noises of the world at bay. She was laughing to herself at what David had said. "Hold that thought." She was holding more than that. He liked her vamping, but that wasn't what he said he liked best. The door opened, and Deidre raised her lashes in her best come-hither look. Then she screamed.

The scream moved her lover to action. David didn't like it that their privacy had been violated and that his client was upset. He felt wronged, transgressed upon. But he chose to ignore one salient point: the man who had entered their hotel room was her husband.

"Get the hell out of here," David said.

Carlton took a swing at him and missed. David was almost amused. His assailant was lumpy and slow, already red-faced and puffing after just one attempted blow. David figured he could beat him with one hand tied behind his back, and he was glad of that, because his left hand was holding up his towel. With his right, he shoved.

Carlton was not particularly nimble. His last fight had been in the sixth grade, over thirty years ago, and he hadn't done very well back then, either. He fell into the room-service tray, landed on the floor with all the remains from the half-eaten plates: the filet mignon, the lobster thermidor, the wilted dandelion greens, the curly endive with bacon dressing, the celery braised in white wine, and the mushrooms florentine. There were also all the condiments and utensils and the melted butter. When Carlton raised himself up from the floor, Deidre stopped her screaming and started laughing instead. It was probably hysterical laughter, but Carlton only heard the scorn.

The lawyer apparently wasn't a believer in not kicking people when they're down. He kicked Carlton in his dirtied pants and sent him sprawling to the floor a second time.

"I told you to get out of here," he said, then took a few

moments to try to readjust his towel. It was difficult to do that and keep his chest inflated at the same time.

When Carlton rose from the floor for the third time, he didn't come up empty-handed. He turned on David and struck at him. The lawyer was still fussing with the towel. Counsel proved right about one thing: it was a good knife. It found the lawyer's heart.

Deidre was still laughing. She hadn't noticed the red stain appearing on her lover's towel or the knife in her husband's hand, only saw the food and goo dripping from Carlton. It was so like him to appear the buffoon.

A moment later, and her laughter suddenly stopped.

# 2

A geologist had once told Am that earthquakes didn't frighten him as much as the aftershocks. Am felt the same way about his dream. It always seemed to presage some momentous event in his life. The changes hadn't been all bad, but at the moment Am did not feel like embracing flux. When you work at a beach resort, the end of summer is like the bell sounding the end of the fifteenth round. You've survived, and you're not anxious to leave your corner.

Damn dream. It had Am on edge. He wondered why, at certain intervals in his life, that vision of things past came to him. Am thought his dreaming about hotels was unfair. Wasn't it penance enough that he worked in one? He had once read about a psychologist who studied the dreams of murderers. The shrink had discovered that most murderers remembered their dreams as being beautiful, and he had said their nightscapes were much more sublime than those of the general population as a whole. Am had always wondered if that was an endorsement for insomniacs to commit murder.

The fantasy wasn't unappealing. In hand Am held a memorandum from the general manager, Raymond Kendrick. The memo addressed personal effects on the office walls in the Hotel California. It described, in Kendrick detail, what was appropriate and what was not. The GM had apparently nominated himself Miss Manners. Diplomas were appropriate. Pinups were not. Quotations or aphorisms were allowed, but none that exhibited bawdiness or profanity. Wildlife animal photography was acceptable, but wildlife human shots were out. The memo's concluding paragraph stated the rule of thumb was that nothing should be displayed that might be objectionable to others, *especially* to any guests who might visit. Am would have chosen to ignore the memo, save that Kendrick had handwritten on his copy: "Your drawing and your cartoon must go."

Am's office was not rife with mementos and memorabilia, as were those of so many others. On display were the Bill of Rights, a picture of Am surfing, an old photograph of Harry Houdini pulling off an incredible escape, and the drawing and cartoon in question.

He reached for the ink drawing first. Cassie had made it for him, had signed it with her trademark artistic "Cassandra." They had lived together for two years in Ocean Beach in a funky little cottage on Voltaire Street. Cassie had been a bohemian artist then. He hadn't seen her in a dozen years but heard she'd been married, had had two kids, had gotten divorced, and now ran a preschool. Cassie's preschool would be full of colors, he thought. She liked vibrant yellows and reds. He remembered how she had painted her VW with flowers, and he had had to fight off her trying to do the same thing to his Dodge Dart. Crazy Cassie.

Am acted like a visitor to a museum, viewed his own piece of art from a number of angles. Devoid of colors, the sketch wasn't typical of Cassie's work. She had created it in a matter of minutes, inspired by one of his hotel stories. Cassie was like that. In some ways she had opened his eyes to his own profession. "Your hotel's like *Canterbury Tales*," she said. "People all going on that one important pilgrimage. And the characters!"

Cassie's drawing wasn't titled. Over the years Am had kept coming up with his own titles, descriptions that had become more cynical with time. The picture showed a happy Procrustes leading one of his guests to a bed. According to Greek myth, Procrustes was a giant who enjoyed putting guests up, though he did have an odd way of accommodating his visitors. Procrustes lopped off the feet of those who were too tall for his iron beds and stretched the limbs of those who were too small. Unofficially Procrustes was a hero to the innkeeping world. Whenever Am came home feeling he had suffered enough guest abuse to last him a lifetime, he would announce to Cassie, "Procrustes had the right idea." There were circumstances and guests, he said, that called for procrustean solutions. Cassie had drawn him a giant who had a "*mein* host" exterior, a welcoming arm and a smile, but whose gimlet eyes were taking a measure of the guest.

Was there a hint of Am's visage in the Procrustes? He supposed there was. But Cassie had also known his working in hotels was more than just a paycheck. She had labeled his vocation Am's "noble quest," words spoken only half-sarcastically. And sometimes she had called him "Myron," after the hotel man in Sinclair Lewis's *Work of Art*. Am touched Cassie's drawing but couldn't bring himself to remove it from the wall. He figured taking down the cartoon would be easier. It wasn't.

Capitulation is usually done in degrees of swallowed pride. Complying at the point of a gun didn't settle well with Am. When he finally took down the framed cartoon from the wall, he saw how its removal left a dark rectangular patch and revealed how faded the rest of the wallpaper had become. Like my principles, he thought.

How long had the cartoon been hanging? Eight years? No. Nine. Am wiped an accumulation of dust off the cover plate. It was a gift from his last hotel job. The cartoon, or one like it, was on the walls of most hotels in the country. It showed a beleaguered-looking front desk clerk trying to cope with a domineering guest. Clearly the clerk had been put through the wringer. The caption read "Suppose we refund your money, comp your stay, send up a fruit basket, close the hotel, and have the manager shot. Would that be satisfactory?"

Am put down the cartoon, then traced his finger around the rectangle of where it had hung. He thought back to when he had first arrived at the Hotel California, popularly known simply as "the Hotel." That first day he had felt drunk, a good drunk. His senses were heightened, aware as never before. It was as if he were in love. He had walked around the Hotel, had breathed its rich air and been giddy. He was the assistant general manager (AGM in hotel parlance) of San Diego's landmark hotel, *the* Hotel, and life was good.

For a moment Am remembered the feeling, but the high didn't last. Now he felt only the hangover.

After a few minutes' thought, Am arrived upon a solution. It wasn't exactly procrustean, didn't cause him to lose a limb, but it did allow him to save face. When he returned the cartoon to the wall, he reversed it. He did the same with Cassie's drawing. Guests couldn't possibly be offended by the back of a frame. Even Kendrick would have to concede that.

As if to contradict that thought, Am's phone rang. The telephone display showed the call came from Kendrick's extension. Reluctantly Am picked up the receiver.

"In my office," said Kendrick. A dial tone followed. Kendrick never bothered with salutations or closings.

The executive offices were located well away from the front desk, out of sight and hearing of any of the front of the house operations. Insulated from reality, thought Am, not for the first time.

Kendrick's secretary, Maria Ortiz, gave her usual sign language of support to Am. She had large brown eyes, sympathetic beacons to those who entered Kendrick's office. Am paused for a moment before speaking, but his presence had already been detected: "Mis-tah Caw-field."

The summons came from Kendrick's inner sanctum. Kendrick was originally from Georgia. In front of guests he played the southern gent to perfection and came off even sweeter than pecan pie. But at the moment he sounded as though he were a long way from whistling "Dixie."

Kendrick had an enormous desk. He had brought it with him, must have had it custom-made somewhere. He looked down on all visitors to his office, which was the point of his desk. You could fit three Kendricks there. He was about five feet seven and slight but had a talent for making people feel about sixty-five inches shorter. Since he had taken over the GM's job a year ago, browbeating his assistant had proved one of his favorite pastimes. Am took a chair but didn't even attempt to get comfortable. The staff was convinced that Kendrick had selected reconditioned electric chairs for office seating.

The two men looked at each other, and neither appeared happy by what they saw. Both were about forty, but any similarity between them ended there. Kendrick came across like titled southern gentry, looked as if he had been born with a riding crop in his hand. He was sharp of features, sharp of dress, and sharp of tongue. He had light blue eyes that were closer to permafrost than sky blue. He parted his short salt-and-pepper hair in the middle, and there was never a hair out of place.

Am was a native Californian. His hair was on the shaggy side, lightened from the sun but dark at the roots. He was about six feet tall and permanently tanned, had grown up before the words *skin cancer* sent people running from the sun. He had never lived more than half a mile from the Pacific and had been raised under its influence. Am had yet to meet the tie that didn't look more like a noose on him than a neckpiece, and none had ever lasted around his neck more than six seconds away from the workplace.

Kendrick cleared his throat. "Mis-tah Caw-field," he said, "Mis-tah Horton has decided to end his employment at this company."

Gary Horton was a former cop and the director of security and safety at the Hotel. Over Horton's objections, Kendrick had fired his entire security force and contracted with Brown's Guards, a rent-a-cop outfit. The staff called them Brownshirts. Kendrick had justified his decision by saying that although security was a necessary evil, he didn't think it had to be a necessary and *expensive* evil. The Hotel now had minimum wage mercenaries. The Chief's leaving didn't surprise Am.

"Effective when?" asked Am.

"Five minutes ago."

Kendrick picked up his Montblanc Meisterstück fountain pen and started to write on a piece of paper. While he was scratching away, the implications of his statement belatedly struck Am.

"I don't know anything about security. . . ."

Kendrick stopped writing, but just for a moment. "This is the Hotel California. This is not Al-cah-traz."

"I wouldn't know what to do. . . ."

This time Kendrick continued to write while he spoke. "I don't imagine the post will be yours for long," he said. "Just until we find a suit-ah-ble replacement."

"I am not qualified."

"I certainly won't argue that point," said Kendrick, "nor will I argue any further. This is not a matter open to discussion. You will assume the security director's position along with your other duties. As there ahl-ready is a security force in place, you will merely have to review their reports and be someone they can intah-act with."

For a moment Am considered following Chief Horton's lead and quitting. The vision was more than satisfactory in his mind but didn't play so well with his wallet.

"And to make things easier for you," Kendrick added, his tone and manner regal, as if dispensing a boon, "I have someone whom you may call upon to assist you with your new duties. An intern."

That generosity delivered, the GM returned to his scribbling.

"An intern," said Am, not trying to hide the anger in his voice. Bill's words came to him—Bill, the night auditor, who had been resentful of always having new employees foisted on him; Bill, who haunted him still in his dreams: "An intern doesn't know his ass from a hole in the ground."

Kendrick didn't bother to look up. "Then I'm sure, Mr. Caw-field, that the two of you will get along famously.

"Mrs. Ortiz," he said into the intercom, "send Miss Baker in."

# 3

One of his mother's favorite proverbs had been "Act in haste, repent in leisure." She had frequently used the words to hector his father, whose forays into business always showed little in the way of forethought. Carlton Smoltz was glad his mother hadn't lived to see his disgrace but wished he could rid his thoughts of her proverb. The words had never sounded so ominous. Repent in leisure? If he didn't get the death penalty, he supposed he would have a very, very long time behind bars to do just that.

He wondered at how his life could have changed so quickly. The night before he had come home, expecting the usual. Deidre was in the habit of leaving a TV dinner out for him. She liked the ones with French titles and low calories. But instead of chicken divan, there was a note. Deidre wrote that she had begun divorce proceedings, and that any communication should be made through her lawyer, David Stern.

Admittedly, they did not have a marriage for the poets, but Carlton was still shocked. They had been married for almost eight years, and during that time Deidre had never complained about their relationship. He worked long hours and rarely took a day off, a situation she accepted all too readily. In his heart of hearts, Carlton knew that Deidre wanted the leisure and luxuries his job afforded her more than she wanted his companionship. He had bartered for a pretty woman, she for a meal ticket. Apparently her appetite had changed.

Carlton vaguely knew her lawyer from several of the fund-raisers Deidre had dragged him along to, the see-and-be-seen social events that benefited good causes almost as much as they did egos. Divorce lawyers rarely get mistaken for marriage counselors, but Carlton figured David would at least do him the consideration of passing on his fervent desire for reconciliation. By his heart's accounting, the call had a 911 priority. David Stern's secretary said she could take a message, as the lawyer would be away taking depositions for several days, and no, he couldn't be reached.

Carlton thought it bad enough that he had to go through a middleman to speak his piece, but to be denied that one outlet for a period of days was unacceptable. What if he wrote a letter? Carlton asked. Couldn't they fax that to him? He pushed Stern's secretary all the way into a maybe, then wrote that letter and hand-delivered it to the firm. Face to face with the lawyer's secretary, Carlton tried to secure a commitment but instead received ill-suppressed ennui. Incensed spouses weren't anything new to her. An attempt would be made to fax Mr. Stern, she said, but that was all she could do.

It wasn't enough.

He wasn't comfortable with making a scene. That wasn't his way. Carlton had an analytical mind. He had created his own successful software company, not because he was a brilliant programmer, but because he was willing to work harder than anyone else and attend to all the details. The lawyer was supposed to have been his pipeline to Deidre. That her counsel was derelict in his duties forced Carlton to act in a manner quite unusual for him.

He set up a surveillance of the law firm, and waited outside the office until Stern's secretary took her lunch break, then he stole back inside. Rifling through her papers, he found his letter to Deidre. Attached to it was a fax cover sheet addressed to David Stern at the Hotel California.

The hotel's name sounded familiar. Carlton had some vague recollection of the property, remembered it as one of those posh resorts that had been around forever. But that wasn't why it stuck out in his mind. Carlton hadn't been on a vacation since his honeymoon. It was Deidre who was always mooning over one brochure or another, who was always planning her next trip. She had said his busy schedule forced her to vacation by herself. That was her word: "forced." Odd how she had been forced so often. Every other month or so she was always going somewhere. And then Carlton remembered the connection—just a few days back he had seen Deidre looking at a Hotel California brochure. She had put it aside after noticing his attention, and rather hurriedly, now that he thought about it.

Maybe Deidre was with David, consulting on the divorce. Then something else occurred to Carlton. He didn't like the thought, but he found it hard to put aside.

The staff at the Hotel California was apparently as well trained in obfuscating as Stern's secretary. When Carlton called to ask whether the lawyer was registered, he was told, after only a short pause, that he was not. Deidre Smoltz wasn't registered, either. Carlton didn't ask about a Mr. and Mrs. John Smith.

The flight from San Jose to San Diego takes little more than an hour, but Carlton felt he could have walked the five hundred miles just as fast. He took a cab from the airport but stopped to pick up a bottle of fine wine, a wheel of gourmet cheese, and a card. Spurred forward by a twenty-dollar gratuity, the cabbie happily made the deliveries to the front desk, where a busy desk clerk accepted the tagged items.

It was only after the cabbie left that the clerk seemed to have second thoughts. He consulted a timid-looking man with glasses, who seemed to throw the decision back to the clerk. With a shrug of his shoulders, the clerk beckoned for a bellman and handed him the wine and cheese. What Carlton hadn't calculated on was the service elevators. He almost lost the bellman, had to walk by two Employees Only signs, and jumped in just ahead of the elevator's closing doors.

"This place is a maze," Carlton said to the surprised bellman.

"This is a service elevator, sir," he was told, but the car was already moving.

The bellman got off on the sixth floor and Carlton the seventh. He ran down a flight of stairs and, from a cracked-open stairwell door, watched where the bellman made his delivery. The room revealed, Carlton suddenly found himself reluctant to go forward. It wasn't only that he chanced looking foolish; part of him wanted to embrace denial. But a greater part of him had to know.

He remembered knocking. . . .

Memory and reality blurred and merged. There came a loud knocking at that same door, but Carlton wasn't outside now. He was inside. Someone had heard what happened, he thought. It's the police. It's all over. He was relieved and afraid at the same time.

Murderer. No, twice as bad. A double murderer. No one would believe it. He could barely believe it himself.

Carlton walked to the door. He felt it was a tune-up for the last mile. He noticed the blood on his hands, and without thinking, or without trying to think, he picked up a towel and wiped them clean. He still looked a mess, but he supposed it didn't matter. The loud rapping came again. The police. He opened the door.

"Good afternoon, Mr. Stern. Where would you like the champagne?"

In front of him was a short, smiling Hispanic man. He was about sixty years old, and his dress resembled the livery of a beefeater. Carlton blinked his eyes. This was the strangest-looking cop he had ever seen.

Augustin Ramirez had been a room service waiter for over forty years. His lilting Spanish accent rivaled Ricardo Montalban's. He had been at his job long enough to not require an answer. He had a long repertoire of rehearsed words. Some of his favorites were "Very good," or "As you please," or "If you will excuse me . . ." When Carlton didn't say anything, Augustin employed the last phrase. Gently guiding Carlton out of the way, he carried a tray into the room and then went about setting up.

"Strawberries on your glasses, Mr. Stern?"

Again Carlton did not answer. "Quite right, sir," Augustin said. "Better to let the taste of Dom Pérignon stand by itself. I'll put them on the side."

Displaying two chilled glasses, Augustin asked, "Would you like the champagne served at this time, Mr. Stern?"

This time Carlton remembered to nod.

With a flourish, Augustin popped the cork. Not a drop spilled out. He poured a thimbleful into the champagne glass and presented it to Carlton.

For a moment Carlton considered putting down the glass. He wanted to confess. He was ready to spill his guts. But somehow it didn't seem right confessing to a room service waiter, especially a room service waiter who was waiting with such an expectant look. He sipped. He nodded. Almost magically the glass was filled.

"The other glass, Mr. Stern?"

Being addressed by the dead lawyer's name was disconcerting to Carlton. He didn't know that the staff at the Hotel California was instructed to use the names of the guests whenever possible, and that the room service waiters always tried to address the recipients of their deliveries.

Carlton nodded. White gloves lifted the bottle. Augustin served with fine technique and flourish; four fingers supporting the bottle, thumb pressed into the mold, bottle raised high above the fluted vessel. The second glass was filled.

"May I be of any other assistance, Mr. Stern?"

Carlton shook his head.

"If you will be so kind as to sign this," said Augustin, presenting a gilded leather folder that housed a restaurant check and a Cross pen.

This is ridiculous, thought Carlton. For a moment he almost signed his own name, but then he remembered to write "David Stern." He also remembered to sign for a tip.

Augustin retrieved the folder, offered his thanks with a bow, then walked out of the room. Only after the door closed behind him did he check the amount of the gratuity.

Forty dollars. Much better than he had hoped for. Mr. Stern might not talk much, and he might look a mess, but he sure knew how to tip. And few things in life were more important than that.

Carlton stood at the door, the champagne glass in his hand. He didn't know what to do. It was bad enough that he had murdered his wife and her lover. For that he expected immediate and horrible retribution. But to be delivered champagne when the corpses weren't even cold—why, that was unthinkable. It was almost as though he were being rewarded. Carlton took a sip of the champagne. He needed some bolstering. He was surprised at how easily the first sip went down. And then the glass. And finally the bottle.

**4**

Sharon Baker wasn't typical of most interns. She was older, around thirty, and professionally attired in a gray business suit, a far cry from the high school or college kids who usually interned at the Hotel. Sharon was about five and a half feet tall, with a light complexion and dark, short hair with finger waves running through it. Her face was angular, but her full lips softened the sharp lines. Her eyes were dark and intelligent and rather regal.

The riddle of her internship grew as Am listened to Sharon and Kendrick talking. She wasn't a homemaker entering the work force or someone looking for a career change, but a graduate in the Master of Professional Studies program at Cornell University, Kendrick's alma mater. They didn't do a Masonic handshake for one another, but Am felt a certain clubbiness in the air—whether it was there or not.

Sighing, Am waited for old home week to end. Because he knew that theory was so different from practice, he liked to tease hotel school graduates, saying that hotel programs thrived in those schools that emphasized major collegiate football. He had learned the trade while on the job, working in hotels for the six years it took him to earn a degree in philosophy, and in that time not one guest had asked him about nihilism or existentialism or logical positivism. They cared more about a clean room, a comfortable bed, and soft towels.

While at the university, Am thought of his hotel jobs as way stations between more important ventures. It was only after graduation, when he took the grand tour around the world, that he began to see innkeeping in a different light. There were times in his travels when nothing mattered so much as the haven of a well-placed bed. A good inn, Am discovered, was a sanctuary, a godsend, and with that epiphany he returned to San Diego, a born-again believer in the hotel trade.

Sharon's talking to Kendrick gave Am the chance to observe her. And the more he looked and listened to her, the more he kept thinking she arrived with the caption "What's wrong with this picture?" Finally she took notice of his scrutiny and turned away from Kendrick to return Am's gaze.

Kendrick noticed their eye contact. "Mr. Caw-field," he said, "will be seeing to your work program."

She tilted her head slightly. Her brown eyes weren't as deferential as the movement. They challenged, and behind them was almost a smugness. Am had noticed that Kendrick hadn't mentioned a word about her helping him with security. Of course not. He had the feeling that Sharon wouldn't be jumping for joy when she learned about her duties.

After thanking Kendrick for his time, she left him with all the right parting words. The GM wasn't oblivious to her charms; he looked about as contented as a dog getting his hindquarters scratched. Turning to Am, Sharon motioned with waving hand, inquiring, "Shall we?" Am fell a step behind as she led the way out of the office and down the hall, moving forward as if she knew the path better than he did.

"You have an unusual name," she said. "Am."

Kendrick never called him Am. His "Mis-tah Caw-field" was indictment enough. Am wondered where she had heard it spoken.

"It's an abbreviation of sorts," he said.

"For what?"

"Long story," he said, "and I'd rather hear yours. So far it doesn't make sense."

"What doesn't?"

"Your interning. People like you are supposed to step out into high-powered jobs."

She arched one eyebrow. Am had always been envious of those with that talent. "Haven't Cornell graduates ever worked here before?"

"Sure. They come in here thinking they know everything, and then we go about training them. Generally they take just a little bit longer than high school grads to learn."

His words were light, joking, but Sharon wasn't anywhere near a smile. "I also have an MBA," she said, a hint of superiority in her voice.

"In that case I'll speak slower," Am said.

"Maybe," she said with false sweetness, "you should consider not speaking at all."

"Partners in crime need to communicate."

"Partners in what?"

"The hotel security director just quit. We're the replacements."

"I don't think my talents will be best utilized," she said, choosing her words carefully, "by having me walking around saying 'Ten-four' into a walkie-talkie."

"With so many talents," said Am, "I still find it hard to understand why you've chosen to intern at all."

"Have you ever spent a winter in Ithaca, New York, Mr. Caulfield?"

"No. I'm a born-and-bred Californian."

Sharon gave him a knowing, if not very complimentary, look. "Ithaca gets more snow than most of Alaska," she said. "I promised myself to go to a place that was warm, a place where there wouldn't be any snow."

"Ever consider a vacation?" he asked.

"I expect to be enjoying myself while I am here. I also figure two or three months of operational experience will look good on my résumé."

"Two or three months," said Am. "Gee, by that time you should know everything."

She ignored his sarcasm. "Security holds little interest for me."

Her attitude, Am realized, echoed his own of just a few

minutes past. Instead of explaining, he had acted like
Kendrick. Belatedly he tried to appeal to her. "Sometimes
management is filling in," he said.

"Ever hear of delegating?" she asked.

His reasonableness vanished. "Thanks for volunteering."

Her jaw tightened. Then she relaxed. Somehow Am knew
she wasn't capitulating, though, merely reformulating her
plans, whatever those were.

"It couldn't be short for am-enable," she said.

For a moment Am wasn't sure what she was talking about;
then he remembered that Sharon had asked about his nickname. She wasn't easily distracted.

"No," he agreed.

"Amoeba? Amentia?"

He stopped her, doubting seriously whether she would
come up with anything flattering. He had forgotten he had
another name. Even his parents called him Am now. The re-
naming had occurred over fifteen years ago.

"No. And it's not some exotic name."

"So, what is it?"

He opened his mouth to tell her, then held back. There was
something about Sharon that wasn't forthcoming. He decided he should be the same way with her.

"You're a hotel dick now," Am said. "Figure it out."

# 5

Carlton wandered aimlessly around the suite. Nothing in his life had prepared him for being a murderer. Other people did things like that. Terrible people. Evil, awful people. Not him. He finally settled in front of the wine and cheese that he had purchased only a few hours, and another lifetime, ago.

I won't get this kind of thing in prison, he thought, suddenly maudlin. Unconsciously he began to gorge himself on the cheese, his motivation akin to an animal's instinctive preparation for a long winter. After retrieving a corkscrew from the nearby wet bar, he opened the wine and started drinking from the bottle. It didn't dull his senses as much as he hoped it would.

Carlton caught a look at himself in the mirror. He was a mess. His clothes were disheveled, and his thin, stringy hair was matted in little unkempt clumps. There were stains on his shirt, telltale marks of the horror he had committed. He stripped off his clothes and walked into the bathroom.

The fragrant smell of potpourri welcomed him inside. Strains of Brahms sounded, so restrained as to be almost subliminal. Carlton looked around the enormous bathroom. It had a separate shower and an oversize sunken spa. Both were marble. The ceramic tile floors, he noticed, were heated, warm to the touch. It was the first bathroom he had ever seen that had its own television and telephone. There were even headsets in the spa. Five kinds of soap were displayed, one seashell-shaped, one in a box, one scented, one with a designer label, and one that was even functional. There were two sinks and two amenity baskets. Among the offerings were bath salts, bubble bath, hairspray, hand cream, shaving cream, razors, a sewing kit, body lotion, conditioning cream, cologne, toothpaste, and toothbrushes. A lump came to Carlton's throat. The Hotel had been so thoughtful. It was almost as if they had anticipated his dilemma.

He filled the spa, poured in a little of the bubble bath, and turned on the churning jets. His conscience still troubled him, but as he descended into the suds his other senses were soon overwhelmed by pleasure: the gentle music, the bubbling water, the lilac scent. It had been a long time since he had indulged himself. The thought brought on a twinge of self-pity. In his lifetime he had never taken time to smell the roses. Now it was too late.

After twenty minutes in the spa, Carlton regretfully raised himself out of it. All good things must come to an end, he thought darkly. He reached for a towel. It was thick, more like a mink stole than a towel. While drying off, he took a moment to examine an item new to him: an electric towel warmer. He was tempted to warm some towels just for the novelty of it but decided instead to wrap himself in a terry-cloth robe. The blue-and-gold Hotel California crest was emblazoned on the robe. He felt it with his hands, touched the stitching that stood out proudly like a royal signet. Then he picked up the cologne and sprinkled some on his hands. It was Old Spice. He patted his red cheeks and dared to peek into the mirror. He looked better now, no longer resembled one of those post office Wanted posters.

Trying not to think, Carlton walked into the bedroom. It wasn't in his nature to leave a mess. He went to the bed and stripped off the bedspread, then used it and the extra blanket to wrap the bodies. The bedroom's large walk-in closet provided ample space for their placement.

The strewn food, scattered room service trays, and spilled blood weren't as easy to tidy up, but Carlton's work was simplified by the thick, stain-resistant carpet. When he finished, he felt an almost desperate need for fresh air. He opened the curtains and the sliding glass doors and stepped out to the suite's double balconies. Breathing deeply, he took in the panoramic expanse of La Jolla Strand. Six floors below was the sandy beach. From where he stood, everything looked like an interweaving mosaic. Couples walked arm in arm along the boardwalk. Weaving between bodies were skateboarders and roller skaters. Beyond the seawall were the volleyball games, half a dozen or more being contested. The center of the strand was taken up with Frisbees, and paddleballs, while joggers pounded along the surf line. Even the ocean had its territories, with waders, then the divers, and finally the boogie boarders and surfers.

The sun was setting, and everyone was trying to get the most out of the waning light. How long has it been since I've watched a sunset? thought Carlton. He settled onto a balcony chair, front row to the blue Pacific eating fire. When the sun set, he heard clapping from below, San Diegans applauding the colorful end of the day.

The vermilion sky gradually gave way to darkness, and Carlton's mood followed the colors. He thought about his life. His thinking was mostly in the past tense. He was full of regrets, the enormity of his crimes overwhelming everything else.

A light suddenly came on behind him. He blinked, confused, lost for a moment. A young woman was standing in the bedroom.

"Excuse me," she said very deferentially. "I knocked, you see, but there was no answer. And there was no Do Not Disturb sign on the door."

She was wearing a black outfit with white buttons and a lace collar. The outfit looked like a modified French maid's uniform. It went well with her dark hair and eyes. Her name tag read Teresa. Teresa's eyes still asked for forgiveness. Carlton wondered if his did the same.

"I came to do turndown," she explained.

"Turndown?"

The room attendant extended her uniformed arm toward the bedspread, only to notice it wasn't there. Carlton saw her look of confusion.

"The bedspread got wet," he explained. "I had to hang it up in the bathroom."

"I can get you a new one—"

"No," he interrupted. "That won't be necessary."

"How about your good-night goodies, then?"

Teresa seemed anxious to please, Carlton thought. But that didn't help him to understand what she was talking about. She took his silence as assent, though, and said, "I'll get them from my welcome wagon."

She was gone before Carlton could refuse, returning a few moments later with a tray that had two covered bowls of strawberries, some packets of brown sugar, and a creamer.

Carlton still looked confused.

"Strawberries and cream tonight," said Teresa. "Or if you prefer, I can get you cookies and milk."

"The strawberries are fine," Carlton said.

When she finished setting up, Teresa turned to Carlton and asked, "Would you like Teddy tonight?"

Teddy, he thought. What was she talking about? He raised his hands, signaled that he wasn't sure, and Teresa smiled. She had yet to meet the man who could come right out and make that admission. "Why not?" she asked.

"Why not?" repeated Carlton.

Teresa went to her welcome wagon once more and this time returned with a teddy bear. Its arms were closed around a heart-shaped chocolate that bore the words Suite Dreams. She placed the stuffed animal in Carlton's hands.

"Thank you," he said, albeit a bit uncertainly.

"Will you be needing a second one?" Teresa knew that two people were registered to the room.

"No, thank you."

She offered a bright smile. "Good night, then, Mr. Stern."

Carlton almost winced at the name. "Good night," he said.

Teresa closed the door softly behind her.

People keep coming to the room and giving me things, thought Carlton. He had never been religious, but he thought that if there were a heaven, it should be a place like this. For a moment he was happy, but then he remembered what he had done.

He gave his teddy a troubled squeeze.

# 6

She was an ant, Am decided. Definintely an ant.

As a child he had watched a cartoon version of Aesop's fable of the hardworking ant and the devil-may-care grasshopper. Am found the grasshopper a much more appealing character than the self-righteous prig of an ant. What might have played in Peoria didn't translate to the Golden State. He figured the grasshopper's big mistake was not living in San Diego, where winters equated to an occasional sweater, not a grim outlook on life.

At least Sharon wasn't an ant masquerading in grasshopper's clothing, a condition Am feared was overtaking him. It had been months since he had waxed his surfboard. And he couldn't remember the last time he had downed a margarita in Old Town, or cracked open a lobster in Puerto Nuevo, or unpacked a picnic basket in Balboa Park, or taken in a sunset off Sunset Cliffs. A friend had once told him that not having fun in Southern California was a felony charge, and if convicted, you were sent to live in New Jersey. Maybe he could plead temporary insanity.

He doubted whether Sharon would disagree with that assessment. Am sneaked a glance at his passenger. She was less than pleased to be accompanying him to the security hut.

When he had commandeered a utility motor-cart and announced their destination she had responded, "I can hardly wait to learn the anatomy of a missing hotel towel." Am was pressing the cart forward at full speed, all of fifteen miles an hour, causing enough wind to push a few of Sharon's hairs out of place. The sight wasn't unappealing. He could almost picture her in dark glasses, ornamenting a convertible. Maybe she was an ant who given a chance could be a grasshopper, sort of like that thin person who was always supposed to be screaming to get out of a fat body.

"Annual event tonight," said Am.

Dumb, he thought. I'm even beginning to sound like that goddamn ant.

Sharon looked over, the slightest interest in her face.

"Staff party," he said. " 'Come as a Guest.' "

"Come as a guest?"

Am nodded and decided to give her a tame description. "We dress, and act out the characterizations, of our most memorable guests. You might consider coming."

A smile breached Sharon's solemnity. "I'm afraid I don't know your guests."

"I can help you in that," said Am. "I was in charge of the sign-up sheets and know which guests were taken and which are still available. A couple of plum roles are still open."

"And you say this is an annual staff party?"

Am nodded. "One of two. We also gather for the Feast of St. Julian the Hospitaller on January twenty-ninth."

She looked suspicious. Nothing she had seen so far indicated any piety in hotel life. "St. Julian?"

Am looked incredulous. "You mean Cornell didn't teach you about the patron saint of innkeepers?"

She shook her head, and then Am shook his, feigning great sorrow. "I suppose I shouldn't be surprised. Why advertise to students that their professional patron saint was a murderer? Might make you wonder about your chosen field."

"What are you talking about?"

"Saint Julian, to whom I frequently pray."

"What's this about him being a murderer?"

"That happened in his pre-saint days," said Am. "One day Julian was away when his wife received a tired couple at their door. The man and woman asked for food and board, and Julian's wife gave them both. She left them in the one household bed and went to market, and in her absence Julian returned.

"When he saw the man in his bed, Julian assumed the worst. He grabbed a knife and stabbed the couple to death. Then he ran from his house, only to meet his wife on the road coming from the market. To atone for what he had done, Julian decided to spend the rest of his life tending to the needs of strangers."

"Saint Julian," Sharon mused.

"Our remembrance isn't exactly reverential," admitted Am. "Hotel staff being what it is, you can imagine the menu for our St. Julian feast: ladyfingers, Bloody Marys, and dev-iled-made-me-do-it eggs."

Her smile grew. "What's the menu at tonight's party?"

"Everything but the usual eating crow. Coming?"

She was clearly tempted but didn't answer immediately. Then, as if determining what her boundaries should and should not be, she finally shook her head. At least she didn't offer a lame excuse.

"If you change your mind . . ." But Am knew that she wouldn't.

He pulled the cart into a well-worn path. Guards didn't walk except at the point of a gun. The security office was about as far from the gardens, and marble, and ocean as anything on the Hotel California's forty acres. To call it unprepossessing would have been an overstatement. The office was a surplus World War II Quonset hut hidden behind shrubbery.

The guard on duty was more interested in the sports section than in greeting visitors. He put down the paper reluctantly. Am noticed it was three days old. He wondered if the guard had made that discovery yet.

"Control post," said Am. "We try to maintain a presence here twenty-four hours a day. The guard stationed on this post acts as a dispatcher to the rover on patrol and also checks pass keys in and out."

Sharon was already taking her own tour, her attention captured by a wall lined with dozens of photographs. "Rogues' gallery?" she asked.

"Mostly vagrants," said Am. "Everyone up there was found trespassing on the property and warned not to return. They were given the speech usually reserved for the sheriff in westerns: Get out of town by sundown or else. If you want the rogues' gallery, just keep walking."

Three steps brought her to a bulletin board. Dossiers were attached to the mug shots. As police blotters went, there wasn't anything too bloodcurdling. The crimes ranged from credit card fraud to drunk and disorderly.

"Welcome to the Hotel California?" she asked.

"Knock wood," said Am. He looked around to follow through on those words, but none was at hand. "We've been damn lucky in the past few years to have only experienced the penny-ante stuff you see in front of you. Not like what some other hotels have had to deal with."

He pointed to another bulletin board that featured investigative reports, police bulletins, and FBI posters. "Visitors we hope never to host," he said.

Sharon started reading aloud from the reports. What began as a cavalier tone quickly changed. The crimes that had been committed were anything but trivial. Together they examined the faces that had murdered, and assaulted, and raped, and burgled. Most of the criminals specialized in hotel crimes, foxes all too familiar with the ways of their hens.

"Not the stuff of hotel brochures," Am admitted. "This industry has its mean streets, even if they are flower lined."

Next to the criminal corner was a large display map of the Hotel California. Am started tapping at the many red marks on the map, enough so that his finger sounded like an out-of-control flamenco dancer. "Entrances and exits," he said. "Security is a matter of control, and this place is a security director's nightmare. Controlling access and egress is difficult, and the guests usually don't make it any easier. They don't like their midnight walks on the beach impeded, or some polyester figure questioning their right to leave their doors or windows open. Who the hell are we to deny them their ocean breeze?"

Realizing how impassioned he sounded, Am reddened

slightly. Chief Horton had used that same sermon a number of times, but Am had only half listened. Funny how when someone else has the responsibility, the priority doesn't seem as pressing. Still, he didn't like sounding like Chicken Little. To his surprise, Sharon looked more engrossed than amused.

"I didn't realize the property was so—immense," she said.

"Four restaurants, six lounges, fourteen meeting rooms, seven hundred and twelve guest rooms, and over forty acres of worries," Am recited.

"And Visigoths at the walls," she said.

They both allowed each other a small smile. "Would that the enemy was so defined," said Am. "On a busy day there are more than ten thousand visitors to the Hotel, clientele we have little control over. The Civil Rights Act of 1964 tells hoteliers that they can't discriminate against any guest desiring accommodations. That means if Charlie Manson ever gets paroled and comes to the Hotel asking for a room, by law we have to rent it to him. And while Charlie hasn't come a-knocking yet, we've had a few guests who probably would have fit in real well with his family."

They walked by several storage closets that housed emergency supplies that seemed sufficient to handle everything from flood to famine. Beyond the disaster relief area were the key lockers and cabinets. Just to get to some of the keys you needed a key. Sign-in and sign-out sheets marked the comings and goings of the keys.

"Key control," said Am. "Did Jack the Ripper stay in one of your rooms and neglect to return a key? Is there a master key that hasn't been accounted for? I keep pressing for electronic locks, but Kendrick has declared those an unnecessary expense. Not that he's the only GM who thinks that way."

Smiling to himself, Am shook his head. Sharon asked for an explanation.

"The other day," Am said, "I heard about a couple celebrating their golden anniversary. As part of their trip down memory lane, they visited their honeymoon hotel.

"They asked for, and got, the very same room where they had begun their married journey half a century ago. As a memento, the honeymooners had kept their key to that special hotel room.

"Imagine their surprise when they found their keepsake key still worked fifty years later."

Sharon's laughter, a sound Am found very much to his liking, was interrupted by his beeper. Roger, in a panicked voice, wanted him to call.

Roger Gifford's alarmed tones weren't anything new. The front office manager was always in a panic over something. Most of the staff referred to him as Casper, which was short for Casper the Friendly Ghost. Roger disappeared whenever there was trouble.

"What's up, Roger?"

"There's been a theft, Am."

For a moment Am experienced amnesia. "Why call me?"

"Mr. Kendrick just announced that you are the acting security director. And you know how Chief Horton always liked to visit the scene of a crime in person."

Am sighed. "What was taken?"

"I didn't ask."

"And I suppose you didn't happen to mention hotel liability laws?"

"That slipped my mind," Roger said.

"What a surprise," said Am, hanging up the phone.

In California an innkeeper's liability for stolen or damaged goods is limited to a thousand dollars. That doesn't mean hotels are obligated to compensate guests for their losses but merely refers to the property's liability. As a rule, hotels don't pay for any items declared missing from guest rooms. From experience, Am knew that was the last thing guests ever wanted to hear. They expected the hotel to admit blame, then hand over the money for their loss.

"I hope it's not jewelry," he said. "Women always cry when it's jewelry."

# 7

"A hotel thief," Chief Horton had often said, "is as sneaky as a fart in church."

Am had never pursued that conversation with the Chief, had always let his remark stand, but now that he was confronted with a potential theft, he was almost tempted to make that same announcement to Sharon, mainly because he didn't know what else to say. The Chief (staff called him that—his real title had been security and safety director) had enjoyed colorful metaphors. Most of them, Am realized belatedly, revolved around flatulence.

"The job's not easy," the Chief had told anyone who would listen. "Sometimes you're given a choice between taking a crap in public or going blind. So you gotta learn how to close one eye and fart."

Reality stepped on Am's muse in the form of one closed eye. At the front desk, T.K. Washington was offering him a none-too-subtle wink. There are more winks offered in movies and on the tube than are played out in real life. This was one of those Hollywood suggestive "we've got a secret" winks. Am didn't try to divine T.K.'s wink. T.K. was the Hotel comic who aspired to a larger forum. Every week he tried out new material at the Comedy Store's amateur night.

His real name was Cornelius, T.K. being an invention of his own, a setup for guests to ask him what his initials stood for, a chance for him to say, "Toooo Kool."

And the funny thing, he said, was that most guests believed him. "Hello, Tooquol," he'd mimic in what he called "white voice." "Good afternoon, Tooquol."

Am made brief introductions, then asked, "Who, what, when, and where?"

T.K.'s astigmatism reappeared. "Kris Carr," he said, showing all of his teeth. "Don't know what was snitched, don't know when, but do know you can find her in room four forty."

"Where's Roger?"

"Left for the night."

Am sighed. It figured. Roger's escapes were legendary. He was the Teflon front office manager, never letting anything stick to him.

"If you want," T.K. said, "I'll be glad to go up and take the report from the lady in distress."

Again that wink. Something was supposed to be obvious to Am, but it wasn't, and he didn't feel like showing his stupidity by asking. Besides, Sharon already had the floor for questions. She was asking T.K. about the front desk operations, and he looked as if he were ready to go into his P. T. Barnum mode. It was evident that Sharon would be happier learning at the front desk than helping with a hysterical guest. Who could figure her preference?

Am didn't hurry up to the room. Too many times guests had cried wolf. They were quick to claim losses, quick to point a finger at a suspected maid or lurking hotel employee, until they remembered how they had hidden the item in question under the mattress, or in the corner of the closet, or in the lining of their coat. On several occasions Am had had to restrain guests from acting like prosecutors at the Spanish Inquisition. There was usually an inverse correlation of the loudness of their entreaties for justice and compensation with the quietness of their admitting fault, even after the "stolen" property turned up in their room.

Am knocked on the door. Kris Carr. There was something familiar about the name.

"Who's there?"

Clenching his teeth, Am said, "Hotel security."

The door opened. Kris Carr was wearing a terry-cloth robe. It didn't fit very well, and Am suddenly remembered who Kris Carr was. Whenever she visited the Hotel, her halter and bikini top exhibitions paralyzed a good part of the male work force. If she hadn't made some plastic surgeon rich, she was in the process of redefining Newton's laws of gravity. Just the day before, one of the Hotel painters had fallen from his ladder and broken his collarbone. Guess who had been out at the pool?

"My name's Am Caulfield," he said, doing his best to maintain eye contact. "I'm the, uh—acting security director here."

"Kris Carr," she said, extending her hand. "Did you say your name was Am? That's an unusual name."

"Nickname," he said, reluctant to say any more.

She motioned him into the room, and he followed behind her. There was a pleasant perfume smell in her wake. "Am," she said, giving his name a special deep-throated intonation, "I feel a little silly for having called you, but I'm missing some articles of clothing."

Clothing. Thank Julian, he thought. At least it wasn't jewelry. "Which articles?"

She gave a wry smile. "Some of my brassieres were taken."

"Your what?"

"My bras."

Am tried to maintain a stoic face. Not knowing what else to do, he pulled out his notepad and made an entry: Missing Bras.

"Anything else?" he asked.

She shook her head.

"And how many bras are missing?"

"Four. Two were left."

Am stopped writing. The strange disappearance was getting stranger. "If," he emphasized, "your bras were stolen, why do you think four were taken and two left behind?"

"I think he liked the frilled models."

"Frilled?"

"He took the ones with embroidery and lace. They weren't exactly Frederick's of Hollywood, but they were sexier than the plain ones that were left."

Am kept writing. It seemed like the safest thing to do. "Anything else distinguishing about the missing bras?"

She laughed, and Am felt stupid. Was there anything distinguishing about the World Trade Center?

"They're not padded," she said.

This time Am laughed. Few males on the staff had ever really talked to Miss Carr. They had just gawked.

"Would it be presumptuous," he asked, "if I were to ask the size of the missing bras?"

"Why? Do you plan to put out an all points bulletin?"

Am tried to regain control of the interview. "The size would help for identification purposes."

Kris smiled. She had a pretty face. It was probably the least noticed part of her anatomy, which was a shame. Am guessed she was in her early thirties. She had long lashes, and her chin had a slight cleft. Her tinted hair reached down just past her shoulders.

"Fifty-eight double F," she said.

Am forgot about her face for a moment and peeked southward. He made another entry on his notepad, remembering not to include an exclamation mark.

"Whoever stole my bras," she lamented, "probably doesn't realize what a pain it is to get them replaced."

"When did you notice they were missing?"

"Just now."

"And how did that discovery come about?"

She laughed at Am's attempted seriousness. "The discovery came about when I walked out of the shower naked and found most of my bras missing."

"How long were you away from the room?"

"Most of the day. I was at the beach. I come here twice a year just for the ocean. That's what I miss most in Las Vegas."

"What do you do in Las Vegas?"

"I'm a brain surgeon," she said, then laughed at Am's look of surprise. "Actually, I'm a topless entertainer. Don't knocker it."

It was his fault for having asked the question, Am thought. "How much longer will you be with us, Miss Carr?"

"Four more days. Then back to the grind. And bump."

She was determined to unstarch Am's collar, but he still tried to maintain a formality between them. Am usually lectured his staff that they should be friendly, but not familiar, with the guests. He walked back to the door, examined it, and determined that there was no sign of forced entry. The Hotel California guest room doors had automatic dead bolts, adequate protection but by no means state of the art.

"Are you in the habit of closing the door behind you?" he asked.

"Self-preservation runs deep in me," she said. "I made sure the door was locked, and I didn't leave any windows open, either."

Having ruled out the obvious, Am tried to downplay the situation. "I'm certain that housekeeping inadvertently took away your underclothing with the dirty linen," he said. "It's happened before."

"They just thought they were sheets, huh?"

Am acted as if he hadn't heard. "As a precaution, though, I am going to have your door rekeyed. I'd also like the name and address of your undergarment company. I'll try to get them to overnight a shipment to the Hotel."

She wrote the name down on a piece of Hotel California stationery, and when she handed him the paper, he offered his business card. "I'm sure there's some reasonable explanation," he said, "but please call me if I can be of any help."

They walked to her front door, and Am paused a moment before saying anything else, thinking about the best way to proceed if there wasn't that "reasonable explanation."

"In the odd chance your bras aren't found," he said, "I might consider salting the replacements."

Kris looked more amused than incredulous. Men were in the habit of offering her unusual suggestions, but this was a new one to her. "You want to salt my bras?"

Am felt the heat rise in his face. "Salting" was a term he had picked up from the Chief. "Police lingo," he explained. "By chemically marking your bras, we'll be able to tell who has come into contact with them."

"Salted bras," she said, "and me on a low-sodium diet."

"The tracer dust," said Am, "is invisible to the eye, but under an ultraviolet light the dust casts quite a glow."

"So we can catch the bra thief red-handed."

"Lime-green-handed," said Am, then added quickly, "Not that I really think there is a bra thief."

Kris shrugged. "Anything to share in the bust," she said.

She waved good-bye while closing the door. Am stood there a moment. First the dust, he thought, then the bust, then the lust. He wasn't sure if the order was accurate, but he didn't much care.

# 8

Carlton had never been an introspective sort. Even with two bodies in his closet, he was reluctant to make any personal decisions.

He felt comfortable at the Hotel. It was old and grand and reassuring. If he didn't think too hard, he could almost relax. He had spent most of his evening reading a booklet detailing the Hotel's history. In 1982, one century after it first opened, the Hotel had been entered into the *National Register of Historic Places.* In California that kind of honor was usually reserved for old missions. But more than saints had stayed at the Hotel. It had attracted sinners aplenty. The gangsters, pony players, painted ladies, and playboys were as woven into the lore of the property as were the visiting emperors, heads of state, and fabled actors and actresses.

The Hotel. That's what Southern Californians called it. There was no need to elaborate. There were many pretenders to the throne, but only one Hotel. Its standing was perpetuated by the staff. The switchboard operators were instructed to answer calls with, "The Hotel. May I help you?"

The Hotel had grown in reputation over the years, even gained a dignity that wasn't there in her youth. Such is the case with many a biography. As the seaside resort became more popular, as La Jolla established itself as a playground for the rich, the Hotel had added, and expanded, and gilded upon the original lily.

Carlton read about the hotel characters, personalities as big as the property. He marveled at the anecdotes, all the tales and tragedies, never stopping to think that he himself was now a part of that history. There was everything at the Hotel, he thought, even a ghost affectionately known as "Stan." Ladies be warned! the booklet cautioned. Stan wasn't a malevolent sort, but he did like to show off for pretty women.

Before putting the booklet aside, Carlton read about the guest who came to stay. He envied Wallace Talbot, the artist who had checked into the Hotel in 1942. Half a century later he was still there. "I could never bring myself to leave," Wallace said.

I know just how he feels, Carlton thought. The Hotel was seductive, a world unto itself. It offered an ongoing soap opera. He could almost pretend that nothing bad had ever happened, that it was all a dream and he had awakened to this beautiful place.

I don't ever want to leave, either, he thought.

# 9

The faces, thought Am. If he squinted just a little, he could almost believe. And if he drank just a little more tequila, the resemblance would get that much closer. He took another swill of to-kill-ya.

Come as a Guest. And they had. A thousand employees worked at the Hotel, and probably half of them were at the party. It was an outdoor affair, perfect for a balmy September evening. One of the staff had family in Rancho Santa Fe, an exclusive retreat north of San Diego, a place where horse stables are as common as Mercedes. The gentleman's ranch was an ideal place for the peons to stage their one-night revolt, a proper theater for the staff to transform themselves into the demanding and eccentric gentry they served. In Rancho Sante Fe several million dollars bought you several acres. It was a good thing there were no nearby neighbors; the revelry quickly got loud.

It was like a Halloween party, thought Am, but instead of Frankenstein and Wolfman and Dracula, there were the Guests from Hell, figures as familiar to the staff as the monsters. Am tried to put names on the caricatured guests as the bodies swept by: there was Mr. Parker, who somehow managed to cop a feel of every woman on the staff; and there,

there was Dr. Jamison, who always patted his pockets and told every server and bellman that he'd "catch them next time." The Reverend Mr. Forbes and his nephew were in attendance, walking around arm in arm. The reverend and his kin were always close enough that they shared a king-size bed, even though he somehow had a different and younger "nephew" every year.

Through blurred eyes, Am looked around for other familiar figures. There was no mistaking Dr. Ann Walters, the platinum-blond self-proclaimed "shrink to the stars." The staff called Dr. Walters the "stopwatch doctor." She had never been known to go more than a minute without using her title of doctor.

Someone stumbled into Am. Or was it Am who had done the stumbling? He was surer of his identification than he was his own feet. Judge Franken, as played by purchasing agent Tad Phelps, bounced away from him. Silverware was falling out of the judge's pants, a reminder that he never failed to leave the Hotel without taking everything from his room that wasn't nailed down.

Am grabbed a chair and seated himself rather unsteadily. He looked around at his table mates. Gary Zabrinski, the assistant front office manager, had come as Mr. Jeffries. He had brought along a prop telephone and, like Jeffries, was carrying on risqué conversations for all to hear. Jeffries was an audioexhibitionist. He always used a lobby telephone for the lewdest of discussions, the louder the better.

Kim Yamamoto, the convention and sales director, had come as Sally Simmons, better known as Superstitious Sally. One of Sally's many phobias was her aversion to walking on cracks. The Hotel had acres of Mexican tile, so it was doubtful if Sally ever got the chance to appreciate the Hotel scenery. Her attention was always focused downward so that she could painstakingly avoid stepping on cracks. Kim was keeping in form. She never raised her head.

Am heard his name called. A crowd was gathering around him. "Speech," they were yelling to him, "speech!"

"Who are you dressed as, Am?" Greg Tipatua was the crowd's shill. The cashier was dressed as Mr. Thorpe, known by the staff as Mr. Goldfinger because of his propensity for golden chains, rings, and bracelets. Greg was awash in golden jewelry.

Everyone laughed at Greg's question. They knew who Am was dressed as. But they laughed even more at Am's answer: "The hotel dick," he announced.

"Speech," they called again.

This time Am obliged them.

# 10

Am caught a glimpse of himself in a mirror while walking into the executive offices. He would have described his sorry-looking state as the morning after, except that his night had never really ended. It was almost seven-thirty, and he had the distinct feeling he wasn't going to look any better as the day wore on.

Kendrick stared at him critically. "Mis-tah Caw-field, you look ah-ful."

"I was supposed to have the day off, sir."

"As you are aware, situations ah-rise which preclude management from having time off. Such a situation has ah-risen. This is a testing occasion, and from appearances I find you woefully lacking."

Am knew better than to respond.

"We had an ah-pparent suicide last night. As you are supposed to be the ass-istant general man-ah-ger, and as security is now supposed to fall under your purview, I thought you might be interested in your job. Are you interested in your job, Mr. Caw-field?"

"Tell me about the suicide," said Am.

By his glare, it was apparent Kendrick would have preferred another response, but after a few moments of silent rebuke he responded anyway. "A man jumped from the balcony of his seventh-floor room. I was ah-pprised of the facts at about three o'clock this morning. Ah-pparently you could not be reached."

Three o'clock, Am thought. If memory served him, he was pissing into a very large fountain at about that time. It had seemed the logical thing to do. There were about a dozen people waiting at all the restrooms. Of course, that particular fountain had been on the first floor, and he had taken aim from the third. Am decided that wasn't something the GM needed to hear.

"But then we didn't have too much trouble tracking you down," said Kendrick. "You were at that party."

He made it sound like an orgy. Not that he was off the mark by much. Nonetheless, Am tried to imbue the party with a dignity it didn't deserve.

"It's an annual event," he said.

"It's a tradition I undah-stand you started."

"End of summer," said Am. "A full house every night for more than two months. It's a safety valve for all the staff, a way for everyone to blow off the pressure."

"It's a disgrace," said Kendrick, "an irreverent display that I fear our guests might hear about."

Everyone agreed it had been the best Come as a Guest party yet. Character assassinations had reached new heights.

"I noticed your sign-up sheets," said Kendrick. "Half the staff or more must have ah-ttended your party. And they registered under the names of some of our most prestigious and influential patrons."

And some of our biggest assholes, Am thought.

"I didn't notice your name on the list, Mr. Caw-field."

Am looked distinctly uncomfortable. "As the unofficial master of ceremonies," he said, "I didn't find it necessary to dress up as a guest."

Kendrick stared at him. "Nevertheless," he said, "I'm curious as to whom you did dress up as."

Am started sweating and made minor medical history. As dehydrated as he was, perspiration should not have been possible. He wiped his brow and changed subjects with about as much finesse as a semitruck moving through city traffic.

"I'd really like to hear about that suicide," he said.

Kendrick let him sweat a few more seconds, then slowly passed a manila folder his way. "A guest noticed the body on the beach a little before three this morning," he said. "The front desk assumed it was just some drunk but called security anyway."

Am read the report. The deceased was identified as Tim Kelly. He was part of a contractors group staying at the Hotel. He had been staying in room 711. That was the extent of the security guard's report. Am thought it was better than usual.

"Have we gotten any background on the leaper?" Am asked.

Kendrick shook his finger in Am's face. "Sir," he said, "I expect you to expunge that word from your vocabulary. I will not have anyone on the property use the word *leaper*. He is to be referred to as Mr. Kelly, or the deceased. We will be especially sensitive in the presence of the media."

Leapers don't enhance a hotel's PR effort, and the Hotel California constantly preened its public feathers. The worst thing about leapers is that they attract other leapers, and while hotels love walk-in business, they're not too keen about the walk-out trade. Am had heard how one San Diego high rise had dealt with a rash of suicides. The staff had requested a suicide hot-line number be posted on all guest room phones, but the GM had instead decided to have new room service menus made up. Employees called them the "Don't Kill Yourself—Call Room Service" menus.

"Do we know anything about the le—man?" Am asked.

"Yes," said Kendrick. "He's dead."

"I asked because there have been instances where hotels have been held liable for suicides."

Kendrick shook his head and gave Am a baleful look. "Mr. Caw-field, I am asking you to be neither a lawyer nor a policeman. Mr. Kelly is dead. We don't need any legal hysteria. Detective McHugh is handling this case. He has agreed to meet with you this morning at ten-fifteen."

Am looked at his watch, then stood up. His scheduled meeting was almost three hours away, but it seemed as good an excuse as any to leave the office. Am had learned it was never wise to linger around Kendrick.

"But even without that unfortunate death," said Kendrick, "it would have been necessary to call you in anyway. Developments have occurred which will force me to leave town and be incommuni-cah-do until Sunday. The owners have arranged for a two-day retreat. I will neither be able to make any calls nor to receive them."

The Hotel was family owned. The principals usually only got together for a three-day annual meeting, time enough to renew old hatreds and supply vitriol for the rest of the year. It was highly unusual for them to be gathering other than for that meeting.

"Anything up with the owners?" Am asked.

The GM chose not to answer. "Regret-ah-bly," he said, "my absence leaves you in tit-uh-lar charge of the Hotel for the next three days. I hope it will still be standing uh-pon my return."

Kendrick knew only too well that Am had been the acting general manager for the two months prior to his getting the job. He also knew that Am had aspired to his position.

"You needn't worry," said Am, walking toward the door. But he didn't escape so easily.

"I understand I am your role model, Mr. Caw-field."

Am froze. "I don't understand," he said. But he did.

"I heard you didn't dress up as a guest last night. Instead you opted to portray me."

Am had made him a cross between Hitler and Attila the Hun—with a southern accent, of course, and preppie attire.

"Uh, as southern hospitality is renowned, and as you could not attend the party, I thought it might cheer the spirits of the staff to represent you in an, uh, jocular vein."

Kendrick let the silence build, let Am twist for the longest time. Then he smiled, and Am's stomach became acquainted with hitherto unknown biles.

"You made," said Kendrick, "some rousing speeches on my behalf. You gave, I understand, new meaning to 'the South will rise again,' equated my management techniques to those used to operate Auschwitz, and said that I was giving serious consideration to turning the Hotel California into a hot pillow joint."

"Uh, sir, you did say that you were looking at new revenue-enhancement possibilities."

"Yes, I did, didn't I? So you interpreted that to mean I would turn a historical landmark into a no-tell motel. Is that correct?"

"I was attempting a form of levity. . . ."

"You are supposed to be the ass-istant general manager, Mr. Caw-field. I don't remember having made you my comedic spokesman."

"No, sir."

"This insubordination will be noted in your file. Included will be a full account of what transpired last night. That might be grounds for dismissal. It is a matter I will have to consider at my leisure over the weekend."

"Yes, sir."

Kendrick looked at his nails for a long moment, then returned his eyes to Am. "Don't forget your appointment with Detective McHugh, Mr. Caw-field. Let me reit-ah-rate that you're to leave the matter entirely to him. Your only involvement should be ah-sisting the bereaved, and working with the Contractors Association group leader. Send a fruit basket or two if you feel it necessary."

Fruit baskets, thought Am, the ultimate hotel weapon. If a guest is unhappy, send him a fruit basket. If a couple is celebrating an anniversary, send them a fruit basket. Got a VIP coming in? Send up a fruit basket. And now Am had learned that if someone dies, by all means, send a fruit basket. The only question was, where to?

# 11

Am sipped at his third cup of coffee, hoping to find a few operational brain cells. Employees did not drink the coffee for pleasure. The staff brew was a different blend from that offered to the guests. The Hotel's four restaurants featured haute cuisine in oceanfront dining rooms that were constantly being displayed in slick magazines, while the staff meals were served in an employee cafeteria that had last been remodeled during the Harding administration. Employees were frequently offered fare the chef no longer deemed fit for guest consumption. On a good day, the employee meals were referred to as "road kill." Usually the raging debate was whether it was fresh road kill, hit by some car that day, or whether it was road kill that had been left to stew in its own juices on asphalt for a few days.

"Ham, Ham."

Am knew the accent, even if he cringed at the executive chef's interpretation of his nickname. Marcel Charvet was in his late sixties but was the antithesis of Southern California mellow. You can take the chef out of France but, *Mon Dieu,* not the French out of the chef. If that were possible, French chefs would be a more popular export item. Am faced Marcel reluctantly. He knew he was in for an oral shower. Marcel had been in America for thirty years but still struggled with the language. What he lacked in words, however, he made up in spray. He enthusiastically spat out his broken English, and he always did it at close range. There was also his ever-present aroma. It was quite clear to Am that Marcel had been preparing bouillabaisse all morning. That, or bathing in it.

The chef's chief claim to fame was that he had served meals to four presidents. His kitchen crew also knew he had served two years in jail. Marcel had once decisively settled a difference of culinary opinion by thrusting his chef's knife— a Sabatier, no doubt—into the stomach of a dissenting cook. His time in jail hadn't tempered his opinions.

Am was surprised that Marcel didn't immediately start in with his talk/spray. He motioned for Am to follow him into the kitchen, which for once was relatively quiet. All Hotel meals were created out of the central kitchen. On a busy night, with all the Hotel restaurants and banquet rooms full, thousands of entrées were turned out. It was always an amazing sight, organized chaos reigning for hours on end, scrambling servers, flying plates, orders shouted out in half a dozen languages, and food with continental names and flowery descriptions being tossed on plates like Big Macs to go. The magic was that the trick usually worked. The food came out and almost lived up to all its cedillas.

"What's the road kill today?"

A busboy with his back turned to Am and Marcel shouted the question to one of the line cooks. The cook pretended not to hear but gave an almost imperceptible signal that alerted the busboy that other ears were present. Marcel might not be making his points with steel anymore, but his temper was still legendary. So was his hearing.

"Ham," he said, "what is zis road keel I keep herring about?"

"It's just, uh, slang," Am said.

"Slang," said Marcel, apparently satisfied. He had worked with Southern Californians for long enough not to be worried about slang. Am hid his relief, glad that yet another Gallic war had been averted.

Marcel's office was his private domain, a holdout from

days of old when to enter a chef's lair was to risk the wrath of a butcher's knife. Urging Am inside, Marcel shut the door behind them, then looked around suspiciously.

"I just talk with Mis-teer Kendrick," said Marcel. "He tell me our food costs are up. He wonder if zee employ-eze are stealing."

That figures, thought Am. Any of a dozen factors could have accounted for the food costs going up. But the easiest scapegoat was always the employees. Employ-eze.

"Mis-teer Kendrick said I should talk with you. He say you now are in charge of ze-curity."

Am nodded reluctantly. He suspected Kendrick had encouraged Marcel to seek him out as a way of having a proxy spit at him. "You have a suspect, no doubt," Am said.

"Yes," Marcel said conspiratorially. "Ted."

Am wasn't exactly surprised. Ted Fellows had the title of sous chef, but he actually ran the kitchen. He worked with a computer more than he did a whisk, much to Marcel's disdain. Ted was reasonable and steady and could turn out consistently good plates while maintaining organization in the kitchen. He was the first to admit he was not a culinary artiste and not the person you'd want to create a repast for heads of state. When it came to the pièce de résistance, that was Marcel's domain. He was the oohs and ahhhs department. Ted was the kitchen's glue, and Marcel always got stuck on that point.

"You've seen something?"

"Two nights ago, he carry a big bag out. Everyone zee him."

"But no one saw what was in the bag?"

That point didn't mean much to Marcel. He was more interested in describing the special he had created on the night in question, going into rapturous descriptions, and giving out the kinds of details that only Nero Wolfe would have considered germane to an investigation. The upshot of his narrative was that truffles, " 'eavenly and divine" truffles, had been the key ingredient in his special, a risotto made with white truffle and pork kidneys. Marcel claimed that his stock of truffles had disappeared the same night Ted had walked out with the bag.

"The spezal was saved," he said, "because zee rice always needs to breath in zee ezzenze of zee truffles a day before you make zee risotto. But zee bag of truffles I not put in zee rice iz gone."

Am was only half listening to Marcel's story until he heard how expensive the missing truffles were. The fungi cost more than most illegal drugs. Promising to look into the matter, Am began easing away from Marcel's theories and fish cologne, but the chef followed him.

"I will zave you a taste of tonight's spezel spezel," Marcel said. "I know how you love zee spezel spezel."

Every night Marcel made a special, but he only made his "spezel spezel" on auspicious occasions. Am tried to think who was in house to merit such a spread, then remembered that one of the country's leading food critics had flown in from New York just to dine.

"That critic's coming a long way to try your fare," Am said.

Marcel's chest expanded. "I know," he said. "He will not be dis-a-ppoint-tid."

Marcel was his own Michelin guide. He had decided a long time back that he was three-star material. Having tasted his creations, Am couldn't disagree.

If you've got it, Am thought, flaunt it. Or better yet, flambé it.

# 12

Carlton felt guilty about having slept so well. It would have been more proper if he hadn't slept a wink. But there was something about the Hotel that lulled and soothed. He hadn't meant to sleep, had stopped just to listen to the ocean, then had sort of naturally worked his way over to the bed, all the while telling himself that he would only be unwinding for a few minutes. That was ten hours ago.

It would have been the proper thing, he decided, to have never slept again, to have walked around like Lady Macbeth, doing a lot of hand rubbing and making lugubrious speeches. His contrition should have been such that he shouldn't have noticed earthly things, like being hungry. But he was hungry. That embarrassed him, but not enough for him to forget about the untouched basket of dinner rolls he had put out with the room service trays the night before. For a time, at least a minute, Carlton resisted the urge to seek out the rolls. And even when he did, he was convinced he at least felt guilty about it.

Discovering the trays had already been collected provided him a perverse pleasure. Serves me right, he thought. But his penance was short-lived. Walking back into the room, Carlton noticed the portable bar and soon discovered it offered possibilities far beyond alcohol.

There was orange juice, and mineral water, and tonic water, and club soda, along with dry-roasted almonds, and macadamia nuts, and Swiss chocolate, and crackers, and cookies, and pâté, and cheese spread. Carlton figured if this was to be his last meal before prison, he could do worse, although he was somewhat disappointed in the pâté.

The thought shocked him. Was he that uncaring? He wondered if his amnesia was a way of coping. Or maybe he wasn't that different from a cockroach. He had read that cockroaches didn't have a memory span that went beyond thirty seconds. A half minute after almost being stepped on, they were ripe for another heel. But was mankind so different? No. He did care. He was sorry. But he still wasn't quite ready to give himself up to the police. He started pacing, tired of it, then sat down on the sofa. On the coffee table was the Hotel's guest information directory.

At first thumbing, Carlton knew he had unveiled something better than the Home Shopping Network. He could get a massage in his own room or a mud bath in the spa. There was a tennis pro available for lessons (I always wanted to take up tennis, he thought) or an aerobics class. The Hotel had gift shops of all sorts. He could call for a book from the library (twenty-five thousand titles—so much for the Gideon Bible) or get a video. There was everything. The directory progressed from A to Z, with every letter receiving multiple pages of listings (except for Q, which only had two entries— quahogs, available daily in the seafood salad bar, and the Queen's Tea, an English high tea served every afternoon in the Royal Room).

It was the letter *T* that Carlton lingered over the longest. A score of tours were listed. The Hotel tour interested him the most. He was curious about this place, this temporary sanctuary. He wanted to know more about its history, wanted to walk its grounds. But he couldn't, of course. He was just avoiding the inevitable, and besides, his clothes were an incriminating mess. Anyone who saw their condition might guess at his crime. Missing the tour, Carlton decided, was the metaphor for his life.

Sighing, he started to close the directory when a boxed entry caught his eye. While the Hotel didn't allow any advertising in the booklet, it did highlight some of its own services. He saw that on-property dry cleaning was available, and that for an extra fee, one-hour service was even offered.

Dare I? thought Carlton. He wasn't behaving as he knew he should. Sackcloth and ashes were the only appropriate garb for him now. Clothes couldn't, or shouldn't, hide his sin. Yet Carlton dialed the boldfaced extension.

"Say," he said, "I've made an awful mess of my suit. I had a bit too much to drink last night, and I suppose you can guess the rest.

"What's worse is that it's the only suit I brought along, and I've got a meeting this morning. . . . Could you? . . . You're a lifesaver. . . . How much? . . . That's fine. Thank you very much."

For a price at which some retailers sold suits, the Hotel California promised to clean Carlton's. The dry cleaner said they were good at spot cleaning and getting out even the most difficult stains. Carlton stuffed his soiled suit in a laundry bag provided by the Hotel, and less than five minutes later a bellman knocked on his door. The bellman gratefully accepted Carlton's generous tip along with his bag and promised to return the suit within an hour.

While waiting for his dry cleaning, Carlton studied the guest information directory a little more thoroughly. There was a men's clothing shop in the Hotel. A crazy thought entered his head.

Maybe I could use another suit.

# 13

The turned-around pictures greeted Am on his return to his office. He wouldn't have minded turning around himself and going home. The incoming already had him ducking: the suicide, the perilous state of his employment, and the truffles. Well, not the truffles, at least not as much as Marcel's spitting. He wondered who had snitched on him to Kendrick. Useless to conjecture, he thought. Or was it? Wasn't he the Hotel detective?

The hotel dick. It was a term half a century out of date, a description that brought to mind a smarmy sort, someone as likely to be looking through a keyhole as protecting a guest from someone doing the same. The title conjured up an image of contraband hooch, poker games, and smoke-filled rooms. The biography of a house dick would have to be a history gone bad and a position by default, not a post to which anyone would aspire. Hotel detectives were the sorts thrown off their police force for petty theft or brutality. Houses of sin were just the place for them, sordid operations where they could supplement their income by running call girls or blackmailing the unwary.

Kendrick had made him the Hotel detective. So be it. There was one place Tim Kelly was still alive. Am turned on his computer and pulled up Kelly's account. At first glance, the display didn't tell him much. Kelly had checked in two days ago as part of the Contractors Association group. His convention had been given a special rate, if you could call $172 a night a special rate. Am scanned the charges. There was nothing unusual about Kelly's bill, except that booze accounted for about half of it, and that certainly wasn't uncommon. The Hotel California wasn't as generous in camouflaging charges as were other inns. Boozing businessmen on company expense accounts usually frequent those hotels that magically convert their bar bills into restaurant charges. "And how was your olive, sir?"

Kelly had closed out his ample bar tab at 1:50 a.m. the night before, had beaten his hangover in the only way possible. His server had been Katherine "Cat" Ross. Kelly had signed a twenty-dollar tip to her. She'd remember him.

A groundswell of noise at the front desk interrupted Am's study. The chaos in progress sounded even louder than usual. Sneaking a peek out at the check-out line, Am saw what looked like rush-hour traffic. He wanted to ignore the pileup but immediately threw himself into the fray. Guests didn't take kindly to having to wait for the privilege of paying over two hundred a night for their rooms.

"Where's Casper?" he whispered, referring to the front desk manager. "Where the hell is Casper?"

Am had Roger paged, but once again Casper's timing was perfect. He appeared just when the last guest had been helped.

"Roger," Am said in a voice only he could hear, "I don't have time to run your desk this morning."

Casper was all innocence. "What? Were there check-outs?"

Am tried to match his Academy Award–winning performance. "Yes."

"Well," Roger said indignantly, "all they had to do was beep me."

Casper's famous retort. The clerks heard his remark, not for the first time, and rolled their eyes, also not for the first time. Whenever Casper was beeped it took him five minutes

to respond to the page, and by then most situations had re-
solved themselves.

"No doubt you were doing something important," Am
said.

"There was a complaint about pigeon dirt on one of the
balconies," Roger said. "I was checking out the situation."

Am gave him a look that said he thought Roger's explanation was full of—pigeon dirt. "Look," he said. "I want you to
stay at the desk and shield traffic. Okay?"

"Of course, Am."

Casper much preferred disappearing to arguing. If guests
were disappointed with their room assignment, he always
sent out the reservations manager. If anyone wanted an ad-
justment on their rate, he invariably deferred to another manager. Staff meetings for Casper were Quaker meetings.
Kendrick never got anything more out of him than everything was going "fine, just fine." Maybe that's why Kendrick
liked him.

If anything, Casper was predictable. At least he was, up
until last night. He had surprised Am by showing up at the
party. Casper lived with an invalid aunt and rarely associated
with any other employees outside of work. Now who had
Roger come as? Am thought for a moment but couldn't remember. He turned to ask him, but Casper was already gone.

Tim Kelly's bill was still flashing on the computer screen
when Am returned to his office. He did a printout, then methodically went through all the charges. There didn't seem to
be anything extraordinary about Kelly's account. Maybe
that's what didn't feel right to Am. It all seemed too normal—the long-distance calls, the greens fees, the restaurant
tabs, even the bar bill. Am would have expected him to have
gone out with more of a splash.

Sometimes you get a feel for guests through their hotel
bills, but two days of charges didn't tell Am all that much
about Tim Kelly. Besides, sometimes hotel bills deceived
more than enlightened. When people escaped from their rou-
tines, they frequently allowed themselves freedoms they
wouldn't indulge in on their home turf. They watched an
adult film, or drank too much, or took a nocturnal swim
without clothes. "Guests," said one of Am's former GMs,

"act like Mormons out of town." Not that religion had anything to do with it. Just human nature.

Tiring of looking at the bill, Am accessed the guest history data base and entered Kelly's name. This visit hadn't been Kelly's first. He had stayed at the Hotel the two previous years, both times with the Contractors Association annual convention. Curious, Am called up the group history. Hotels were getting to the point where they could almost crank out their own TRW credit reports. At the Hotel, group expenditures were tracked more faithfully than baseball scouts analyzing batting averages, and group bookings were prioritized by their spending habits. The Contractors Association was evidently "A" team material. They liked to spend money.

Let me count the ways, thought Am. He scrolled through the file, paying close attention to both individual and group requests. Everything was documented, from room setups to banquet menus. High rollers are catered to, and the guest rooming assignments had been prepared carefully rather than slotted in the usual block of rooms. As a repeat group, many of the conventioneers had known what they wanted and hadn't been shy about making those desires known. The usual litany of requests were indicated, from bed size to location to type of accommodation, with the usual petitions for everything from feather pillows to special lighting. Kelly hadn't been among those with requests.

Had he known he was going to commit suicide when he'd checked in? Am started speculating, then chastised himself mentally. It was a moot point, not to mention a waste of time. Maybe Kendrick was right, as much as that possibility hurt him. Maybe he could best serve the dead by "ah-sisting" the bereaved, sending those all-important fruit baskets. Condolence calls on behalf of the Hotel were also in order. Sighing, Am assembled a list of people who should be contacted. John Leonard, the Contractors Association group leader, was his first call.

"I'm sorry to bother you, Mr. Leonard," said Am. "My name's Am Caulfield and I'm the assistant general manager here. On behalf of the Hotel, I'm calling to express our deepest sympathies."

Am's attempt at sorrowful sorries didn't get very far. "I really didn't know Tim very well," Leonard said.

And by the tone of his voice, Am didn't think Leonard was going to be starting a retrospective any time soon.

"Well," said Am, "might the Hotel be of any assistance to your group at this difficult time?"

Leonard thought a few moments before answering. To Am, that wasn't a good sign. "Steve Daniels is the one you should talk to," he finally said. "Steve's in five twenty-two. He was a friend of Tim's, so he's pretty much handling everything."

Daniels's line was busy, which was excuse enough for Am to walk up to his room. A small man who looked like a depressed version of Harpo Marx answered his knock. Am barely got the chance to utter a few platitudes before the guest swept him into his room. Maybe it was the face-to-face, or maybe Daniels just needed someone to talk to. "I still can't believe it," he said. "Tim's the last guy I would have figured for this."

Am sat down on the sofa and let Daniels talk. He heard that Kelly had walked out on a good life. The deceased had run a successful development company in Menlo Park and had a family he adored. Daniels had known him for almost ten years, and this was the third consecutive year they had attended the convention together. It was an excuse for them to play golf and drink, the best tax write-off either of them could think of.

Tim was forty-four years old, Daniels said, and he'd left behind a wife and two small children. Phyllis Kelly was understandably very upset. She couldn't accept that her husband had committed suicide. Self-murder went against their faith, was a sin.

Mrs. Kelly was too distraught to fly down, he said. In her absence she had authorized Daniels to take charge of all her husband's possessions. The police had released them with alacrity, no doubt grateful to free themselves from dealing with the logistics of a long-distance death.

"You want a drink?" asked Daniels.

Am shook his head.

"Guess it is a little early," Daniels said. It wasn't even nine o'clock.

"Tim insisted upon buying the drinks last night," he said mournfully. "I wish I had bought him his last drinks."

"Were you with him the whole night?" Am asked.

"From ten until about two. We closed down your bar."

They had done their drinking at the Breakers Lounge. Four- and five-star hotels never referred to their drinking holes as bars.

"Was he morose?" Am asked.

"Nah," Daniels said, first giving Am a glance, then giving him a story. Am wasn't a police notebook; he was a sympathetic face. "He was horny."

"Horny?"

"As a toad. Tim tried to put the make on the cocktail waitress, but she just played him along."

"Was he having marital problems at home?"

"Nothing more than usual. It was just that he was out of town, away from home. He said he was ready for an adventure."

"So there was no crying in his beer?"

"Chivas. No. And like I told the police, I just don't see Tim as a suicide. My guess is he fell."

"Very hard balcony to fall from," Am said. "It's about four feet high."

"Yeah, I know. That's what the police said."

"How can we help?" Am asked. Translation: Who can we send a fruit basket to?

"Geez, that's nice of you," said Daniels. "I'm pulling my hair out figuring out what I'm going to do. I told Phyllis I'd bring home Tim's personal effects. What am I saying? Personal effects. I'm sounding like a cop. This is Tim I'm talking about."

Am made some reassuring sounds. Harpo looked sad enough to cry. "Problem is," Daniels said, "his golf clubs alone are going to give me a hernia."

"We can help," Am said. "Our concierge can arrange to have everything shipped out."

"That'd be great," Daniels said, then gave Am a sideways look that asked for more help.

Am had seen that delicate but desperate expression before. About a million times. "How else," he asked, "might we assist you?"

"What about shipping the body?"

Daniels interpreted Am's silence as repugnance, not surprise. "I wouldn't even ask," he said, "except that almost the first thing Phyllis asked me was how she was going to get the body up to Menlo Park. And she was crying and everything, and I said, 'Don't worry about a thing, I already got everything handled.' Only the thing is, I don't have anything handled. The cops won't even tell me when I can get the body. They said they were going to have to perform an autopsy."

Am made sympathetic noises while Daniels told him how the police had advised him that under California law the coroner had to inquire into any violent, sudden, or unusual deaths. Kelly's demise was apparently at least one of those.

"I wouldn't worry, Mr. Daniels," Am said. "I'm sure we can make arrangements to have a mortuary ship the body whenever the medical examiner sees fit to release it."

"You're a lifesaver," Daniels said, then winced at his choice of words.

Am wrote Patrice Rushton's name and extension on the back of his business card, and an eager hand accepted the offering. "Our concierge can work out the details with you," he advised.

And after she learns how I volunteered her, Am thought, she'll probably kill me and work out a two-for-one with the mortuary.

"If there's anything else I can do, please call," he concluded.

Or thought he had concluded. When Daniels smiled, Am could see he was still holding back a few teeth. For too long Am had been practicing mind reading without a license. Daniels absently rubbed Am's card between his fingers. There was something else on his mind, something he wasn't quite ready to volunteer. Am wanted to walk away, but the same impulse that had made him help at the front desk, the values inculcated by his years in the service industry, prompted him to reach out.

He offered an echo. "Anything else?"

"Tim's wallet," Daniels said in a rush of words. "The police released it to me. And I noticed it's missing his cundum."

"His cundum?"

"His rubber."

"Oh, a condom."

Harpo looked a little offended. "Either is appropriate."

You say tomato . . . "Really?"

He nodded his head, and Am amicably nodded his. Agreeing on a dead man's cundum. Or condom.

"How were you so sure he had a condom?"

"He showed me his cundum," Daniels said pointedly, "while we were drinking last night. Tim said he intended to get laid."

"When did you see this condom?"

"I saw the cundum at about midnight. He thought he had a chance with the cocktail waitress."

"Couldn't it have just slipped out of his wallet?"

"I saw him put it back in."

They had closed down the bar just before two. Tim Kelly had died less than an hour later. And now Am was being told that he had used or lost his condom during that short time.

"Did you walk back to his room with him?"

"No. He had to go to the john, so I told him I'd see him in the morning."

"Did you tell the police?"

Daniels shook his head. "I didn't go through his wallet until just a little while ago. And it's not the kind of thing I'd want the police investigating anyway. Phyllis doesn't need that now."

Am agreed with him. Harpo finally looked relieved. Some of the burden of his friend's death had been removed from him. But it wasn't as if his discontent had vanished. It had just passed on to Am. Now he was the one wearing the funny expression.

In less than twenty-four hours as security director Am had come up against a suicide, a potential bra burglar, a company snitch, and a truffles thief. But this topped all.

Now he had a cundum conundrum.

# 14

So this is what cheerleaders do when they grow up, thought Sharon.

Am had advised her to take the morning Hotel tour, and a small part of her wondered if he had given that counsel out of spite. Sharon was one of a dozen people trailing behind a young, thin, athletic, beachy-blonde woman named Buffy. As if those weren't sufficient reasons to hate her, there was the guide's voice: high-pitched, exclamatory, and perpetually effusive.

"These terra-cotta tiles we're walking on were made in Tecate, Mexico," announced Buffy. "Does anyone want to guess how many tiles there are around the Hotel's grounds? Come on, someone must have a guess!"

Much to Buffy's delight, several someones did. She was even happier that the guesses were so wrong. "Well, hard as it is to believe," said Buffy, her tone of voice amazingly reminiscent of that of Sharon's kindergarten teacher, "I'm told there are over half a million of these tiles throughout the property!

"Anyone care to count them?"

Who wrote her script, A. A. Milne? But even Sharon had to concede that her group was enjoying the tour. They had gotten their fill of Italian marble, rococo woodwork, and original art, had traipsed through rooms that had troves of antique furniture, each discovery accompanied by their appreciative sounds. It was hard finding the commonplace at the Hotel. Even the ubiquitous wrought-iron fixtures, lamps, and gates were identified as special ("hand-crafted in Spain and hard as the dickens to keep up. Do you know we have four full-time painters constantly priming and painting them? That's a fact").

Another "fact" was how difficult it was to dust the chandeliers in the Crystal Room, three immense crystal chandeliers hanging from vaulted ceilings. The glass pendants shimmered like finely cut diamonds and were said to be almost as costly. No wonder Am was so jumpy about security, Sharon thought.

Her mind wandered from Buffy's rote speech. Am Caulfield wasn't what Sharon had expected. He was full of contradictions: cynical yet concerned; laid back but professional. The only thing fast about him seemed to be his wit, but he got things done. Sharon still had reservations about his appearance. He didn't look like a manager. He looked as though he should be riding a wave or just finishing up a run on the slopes. It was that casual Southern California manner, combined with his tan, that had made her immediately question his professionalism. Sharon had assumed he didn't have any gray matter to go with his sunshine look, but he had surprised her. She had to be careful around him. After knowing him for only a few hours, she had been tempted to accept his invitation to that ridiculous Come as a Guest party. But it wouldn't have been fair to go. That would have been exceeding the boundaries of false pretenses, and Sharon was already feeling a little guilty on that front.

Her group started moving again, and Sharon followed. The Hotel was different from the heads-in-beds factories she was used to. Part of the Hotel's appeal was that it was supposed to be behind the times, supposed to be a throwback to when the world was less rushed and more genteel. The Hotel offered spectacles aplenty, but its showmanship was understated. It didn't have to compete with volcanoes, waterfalls, fireworks, and all the other extravaganzas so many resorts now felt it necessary to offer.

"Now we've come to the green stage of our tour," said Buffy. She held up her thumb. Surprisingly retractable, Sharon thought.

"Though my thumb's not green," said Buffy, "we luckily have plenty of gardeners with such digits."

"How many?" asked a smiling, slightly pudgy man with thinning red hair.

"I'm glad you asked."

Sharon glanced at the questioner while Buffy meandered into her answer (abridged version: about forty gardeners). This wasn't the red-haired man's first question. His overeager interest in the Hotel made him stand out among the group. He was treating Buffy as if she were St. Peter. Come to think of it, thought Sharon, her backdrop did look angelic, a huge and spectacularly colorful floral centerpiece. The arrangements were positioned throughout the Hotel, and according to Buffy, many of the property's exotic floral displays were supplied from its own gardens.

Buffy inhaled in front of the group, exhorted them to do the same like she was Jack LaLanne. The flowers did smell nice. Next to her, Sharon found the red-haired man doing nasal aerobics. He smiled at her, and she gave a tentative smile back. Most members of their group were older couples, so she wasn't surprised that they had eventually ended up together. Still, she wasn't sure she should encourage his attention.

"Amazing place, isn't it?" he said.

Sharon agreed. He looked harmless enough, she thought. There was something puppylike about him. And something sad, she decided. He stayed by her side when they walked out to the rose garden, and there he surprised Sharon by gently lecturing her that she should make the time in her life to smell the roses.

"What about you?" asked Sharon.

He shook his head, and she saw his sadness once more. Then he let some rose petals drop from his fingers. He didn't recite for her "She loves me not," but Sharon could hear the words in the dropping petals.

They moved down the path to another garden. Sharon was about to broach a question to him, to get at his unspoken sorrow, but Buffy spoke up before she could.

"How many bulbs," she asked loudly, "do you think are planted every year in the Hotel's gardens?"

The man smiled, entranced once more. Through the Hotel trivia he seemed to forget about what Sharon perceived were his own regrets. Diverted, she never got the chance to ask her question, and a few minutes later the tour ended.

But not before Sharon learned the Hotel planted almost a quarter of a million bulbs every year.

# 15

"Patrice."

"Am, darling."

Patrice Rushton fancied herself the leading lady of the Grande Dame. She had been hired as a concierge before it became de rigueur for all properties aspiring to airs to have a French title on staff. In the French tradition the concierge was the "keeper of the keys." Am had come to believe the English translation was "extortionist." The Hotel California's concierges had trained local restaurateurs into inviting them over on a regular basis. When the restaurateurs failed in that duty, the guest referrals disappeared magically. Patrice referred to her concierge department as the "diplomatic corps." Such titles, Am thought, begged for an international incident.

"Patrice," Am said, "I need to enlist the skills of your diplomatic corps."

Patrice beamed. She might have even attempted a blush, but only X-ray vision could have penetrated the layers of her generously applied makeup. Patrice was around sixty, but she let it be known she was in her forties.

"Guest services is our middle name, Am," Patrice said proudly.

If that was true, then gratuity had to be their last name.

Patrice had her hot lines to what she called power people, those who could get her the window tables, the tickets to popular events, the eight o'clock dinner reservations, the golf course times, and the seats on sold-out airline flights.

"You'll be hearing from a Mr. Daniels in room five twenty-two," he said. "I told him we'd help him ship some belongings."

She nodded confidently, gave the barest touch to her short, well-coiffed hair. So far so good. Am cleared his throat. "I also said you'd assist him in a delicate matter."

The touch of the hair again. "That's what we are here for."

"You might have heard about Mr. Daniels's friend," Am said. "Former friend, that is. Tim Kelly. He was in room seven eleven."

It was undoubtedly a popular name that morning. Patrice suddenly didn't look so comfortable. Kelly, she knew, wouldn't be wanting tickets to the symphony.

"I told Mr. Daniels you'd take care of arranging the shipment of Kelly's body."

"Am . . ."

He knew better than to stop speaking. "You'll probably have to work out the release of the body with the medical examiner or the police department. Apparently it's in the morgue now."

"Am—"

"Mr. Daniels will be finding out who's handling the funeral services up north. That's where you'll need to send Mr. Kelly."

"You must be—"

"If a local mortuary can't help you ship out the body, I'm sure some airline will be able to assist in its transportation."

Makeup always looks out of place when plastered to an angry face. In Patrice's case, she looked like a hateful clown. "I am a concierge," she said. "I am not a ghoul."

"I'll be putting you up for employee of the month, Patrice."

And if she won, her picture would be posted in an area where even bored guests never nosed around.

"I am not happy about this, Am," she said.

Probably because dead men aren't the best tippers, he

thought. "Delegation, Patrice. We don't have marines, but we do have our concierges."

Patrice stormed off. She looked ready to take Iwo Jima single-handedly. From behind him, Am heard clapping. Jimmy Mazzelli was his audience.

"Lady's got a stick up her ass," he said, then minced around in an amazingly accurate parody of Patrice's walk.

Am didn't let his amusement show. Jimmy didn't know it, but he was due for a lecture. Besides, Jimmy didn't need the encouragement. He had been a bellman at the Hotel for the last dozen years and always managed to straddle that fine line between being crudely funny and being fired. Sometimes you couldn't be sure whether Jimmy was hustling a guest or just working a tip. He was in his mid-thirties, had lived the last half of his life in Southern California, but his formative years had been in New York City, and that showed both in his accent and in his manner. When Jimmy wasn't running a comb through his long, slick hair, he was running the Hotel betting pools. The surest bet in the Hotel? That Jimmy had a *Racing Form* somewhere on his person.

"Got an interesting note yesterday, Jimmy," said Am. "It was from a Mr. Edward Bell. Does his name ring a bell?"

Jimmy's blank face was perfection, his innocent and arched eyebrows making him a candidate for some cherubic order. "Can't say it does, Am."

"Mr. and Mrs. Bell checked in a few days ago. You helped them up to room four sixty-five."

Still no overt glimmer of recognition. Jimmy liked to play poker, too.

"They were honeymooners."

Jimmy produced a thoughtful lip. "Lots of honeymooners, Am. Must help twenty, thirty a week."

"Do you remember taking their luggage?"

"Four sixty-five? Coupla days ago?"

"Woman wearing a white dress?" Am said in his most sarcastic voice. "Man in tuxedo? Sparkling new rings. Maybe some wedding cake crusted around their noses. Honeymooners, dammit."

"Yeah, yeah, I remember, Am. Now I remember."

"Let's test your memory a little more, then. Mr. Bell

thought he should fulfill the tradition of carrying his bride over the threshold, but he didn't want to ruin his wedding night, either. He has a bad back. So he turned to you and asked for a helping hand. He wanted you to assist him in carrying his wife over the threshold. And you did."

Jimmy remembered. He remembered very well.

"Mr. Bell gave you a tip, a generous tip. That's usually a signal for the bellman to leave. But for some reason you chose to linger around long enough to say, 'I'd be happy to help out in any other marital duties you can't perform.' Is that an accurate quote?"

Jimmy started rolling his eyes around. "It was just a joke, Am."

"Mr. Bell didn't like your joke. He said you were leering at his wife when you made your comment."

"I was smiling at her, Am. And she was smiling at me. That's probably why he didn't like it."

Jimmy thought most women had the hots for him. They exhibited this desire in a number of ways, all of which only Jimmy could discern.

"You were asked to pick up a bride, not put the make on her, Jimmy."

"Just a joke, Am," he repeated.

"Verbal warning," Am said in his sternest voice, then added the lamest words in management's vocabulary: "It better not happen again."

The worker response, in time-honored litany: "It won't." Then, changing subjects or, more likely, already having forgotten the warning, Jimmy said, "Package arrived for you, Am. I stuck it on your desk."

The large box Jimmy had left on his desk was plastered with "Rush" labels. Am couldn't think of anything that would have necessitated so much postal signage, not to mention postage. Cautiously he lifted up the box. The contents were light. Am did some mild shaking and couldn't come up with a guess. After opening the box, he became acquainted with some very visible reminders of one of his open cases. Memories of mammaries: Kris Carr's bra shipment had arrived.

Am punched housekeeping's extension, and the executive housekeeper answered. "Any bras turn up?"

Barbara Terry laughed. "None the size of which you're looking for. You sure you're not pulling my leg, Am Caulfield?"

"No. Cross My Heart bra and hope to die."

Cradling the phone, Am dropped his gaze to the opened box. Curious, he hoisted out one of the bras. It wasn't weight lifting, not exactly. He felt the fabric, ran his hands along it. They lingered for just a moment, a stretch of time almost imperceptibly brief, but long enough for Sharon to walk into his office and observe the placement of his hands.

Am dropped the bra as if his fingers had been scorched. Then he picked it up again, his face red and defiant. "It's the Carr case," he said, trying his damnedest to sound official.

"Looks like you have your hands full," she said.

# 16

Partly to save face, and partly because it was a good excuse to act like one of the Hardy Boys, Am drove Sharon over to the security hut and hunted down the fluorescent tracer powder. Using gloves, Am started sprinkling the dust on the oversize bras. Sharon was as hard-pressed not to laugh as Am was to ignore her twitching mouth. While he powdered, Am brought up the strange case of Tim Kelly's suicide.

It wasn't the first suicide the Hotel had experienced. There had been a handful of others, but not during Am's tenure. He was interested in the death, not because of a morbid curiosity, but because nothing about it seemed right. Am told Sharon about Kelly's family and business. He had come to the Hotel to have a good time, a golf getaway. With some trepidation, Am even told Sharon about the missing condom.

She didn't laugh. His death sounded more and more senseless to her, even if the disappearance of the condom didn't strike her as an important clue. "Maybe it just fell into his pocket," she said.

Am shook his head. "His friend saw him slip it back into a fold in his wallet."

"Then he probably got rid of it on the way back to his

room. Maybe he was afraid his wife would find it on him when he returned home."

"That's possible," said Am. "But he wasn't due to check out until tomorrow."

"You think he used it?" she asked.

"Pretty unlikely, isn't it?"

"More than pretty unlikely. He leaves the bar a little before two, he's dead a little before three, and somewhere during that time he has sex. It doesn't even happen that way in soap operas."

"Soap operas are one thing," said Am, slightly petulant, "hotels another. Stranger things have happened."

"So he finds some woman and seduces her in a half hour or so?"

"He's drunk, she's drunk," said Am. "They meet on the elevator. Both are away from home. It's possible."

"And in the space of forty-five minutes they have sex, and the man ends up killing himself. Explain to me, then, why anyone contemplating suicide would wear a condom in the first place?"

"Maybe it was on the instigation of his partner."

"That still doesn't explain why he killed himself."

"Maybe he couldn't perform."

"Kill yourself over something like that? Come on."

"It can be very debilitating to a male," said Am, then added quickly, "Or so I've heard."

It was Sharon's turn to shake her head. "The more we conjecture, the more plausible his suicide sounds. What kind of a woman would allow herself . . ."

They looked at one another and saw the same idea forming. "Wait a second," said Sharon, walking over to the wall of police bulletins. Bra in hand, Am followed.

"Here," Sharon said, pointing.

The bulletin wasn't new to Am. It described prostitution-drugging crimes that had taken place in major hotels in Southern California. He took a close look at the mug shot of Conchita Alvarez, the woman wanted in connection with the crimes. Conchita was twenty-five years old and managed to look good even with a countdown of police inches behind her. She topped off at the sixty-five-inch level. Conchita's

MO was to approach affluent-looking men, usually in a hotel bar. After striking up a conversation, she invariably wangled an invitation to their hotel room for a drink. Then it was Mickey Finn time. But Conchita Alvarez didn't have her chemistry down very well. One of her victims with a heart condition had succumbed to her fatal nightcap. Now there was possibly a second victim.

Sharon read from the pharmaceutical list: "Scopolamine hydrobromide, chloral hydrate, lorazepam, diazepam, benzodiazepine, Halcion, and Placidyl. This lady mixes a mean drink."

Conchita had a long list of druggings to her credit, and it was suspected that most of her victims hadn't even reported the crime because they had been too embarrassed to come forward to the police.

It was Am's turn to read from the fine print: "The drugs are administered in high doses. Typically, victims are rendered unconscious for periods of six to twenty hours."

"Or forever," said Sharon, tapping her fingernail on the description of the victim who had never awakened.

Neither Am nor Sharon spoke for several moments. Both were taking a measure of the possibilities. Am broke the silence: "He could have walked out to the balcony and been disoriented."

"He literally might not have known which way was up," said Sharon.

They looked at each other, and neither tried to hide their excitement. "I'm supposed to be meeting with Detective McHugh in half an hour," he said.

"We are," said Sharon, pulling down Conchita Alvarez's police bulletin.

Detective McHugh was the lone occupant in room 711. He was seated on an easy chair and didn't bother to get up when Am and Sharon walked into the room. McHugh looked like an old fifty, world weary without apologies. His eyes were a washed-out blue, the color you see in a pilot light.

Am offered introductions, and McHugh stirred ever so slightly. "That's right," he said, motioning them to come closer, as if ready to offer a secret. "I've been wanting to talk to you."

Am and Sharon leaned forward eagerly. "Got an anniversary coming up soon," McHugh said. "Just how much would a room like this go for?"

McHugh's question surprised Am. It took him a moment to reply. "The rack rate is two seventy-five."

The detective whistled. "Is that your best suicide special?"

"How do you know it's a suicide?" Am asked.

The pilot light in McHugh's eyes activated and showed a harder blue. "I don't," he said. "I only know someone took a long walk off a short balcony. Maybe the booze was speaking to him. Maybe he thought the drop was just a shortcut to the beach. But I got to figure a four-foot balcony isn't an easy obstacle to overlook. My call is suicide."

McHugh pushed his words out, as if daring someone to challenge them.

"Quite possibly," said Am, "but I thought you might be interested in some discoveries we made this morning."

"By all means," said McHugh, his sarcastic tone belying the words.

"Mr. Kelly never asked for a room on this top floor. He could have just as easily gotten a room on the first floor."

McHugh shrugged his shoulders.

"Doesn't that seem odd to you?" Am asked.

"No," said McHugh. "You mix some booze and mix some melancholy, and strange things have been known to happen. Maybe he got a sudden urge. Maybe he clapped himself on the chest like one of those gladiators and announced, 'Today's a good day to die.' "

"Did he leave a suicide note?" asked Sharon.

McHugh yawned. "Most suicides don't leave notes," he said.

"But there is going to be an autopsy?" Am asked.

"Standard procedure for a case like this," said McHugh.

"Then you'll know if any of these drugs have been administered," Sharon said, handing him the bulletin.

McHugh took his time digging out some glasses from his shirt pocket, then unhurriedly scanned the circular. When he finished, he handed the page back to Sharon.

"And what makes you think this woman had anything to do with his death?"

Am and Sharon had another eye conference. "We think Mr. Kelly might have been entertaining just prior to his death," said Am.

"Entertaining?"

"Having sex."

"What makes you think that?"

"Mr. Kelly was carrying a condom in his wallet," Am said, "a condom that was apparently on his person less than an hour before he died. The condom was not among the remains in his wallet."

"And you think there might be some connection between safe sex and his death?"

Am was getting a little tired of being the rube. "I'm not making any claims," he said. "I'm only being curious. I thought that's what detectives were supposed to do."

McHugh evidently thought differently. "What do you got besides your smoking condom?"

"Nothing much," Am admitted.

McHugh sighed loudly. "Tell me more about the missing raincoat," he said.

Am and Sharon went over the story again. When they finished, McHugh made it clear he didn't buy any of their theories. He had already talked with the bartender on duty, as well as with Steve Daniels. Kelly had left the Breakers Lounge by himself. There was nothing, he said, that indicated Kelly had received company in his room. No extra glasses, or pulled-out chairs, or mussed bedspread. Not even a condom wrapper.

"Would the medical examiner be able to determine if Kelly had sex just prior to the time he died?" asked Am.

McHugh rolled his eyes, then nodded.

"Could you have that checked out?"

McHugh gave a repeat eye-rolling performance before reluctantly nodding his head again. Neither Am nor Sharon felt reassured. McHugh's parting sarcastic words weren't meant to encourage, either.

"Without a used rubber," he said, "there's not much hard evidence for me to go on. But bring me that soiled condom and I'll muster all the manpower possible."

# 17

"That arrogant jackass!"

Sharon made her announcement just outside room 711 and punctuated it by shaking her fist. Realizing there was a certain measure of temper tantrum in her response, and that Am was watching her, she forced herself to be more collected.

Am was having second thoughts about his partner. She was actually human. Her personality seemed to have blossomed under the California influence. Or maybe it was the potential murder that had brought out the best in her.

"He wasn't exactly encouraging, was he?"

"He was horribly condescending," she said, "and that's something I find intolerable."

They stepped into an elevator and started their descent. "But he did leave us an opening," said Am.

"What are you talking about?"

"McHugh said it: Bring him the condom, and he'll put people on this case."

The elevator doors opened. They walked out to a hallway of people, so Sharon lowered her voice to a whisper: "But the condom wasn't in the room."

"Which means what?"

"I can assure you, Am Caulfield," she said, "that I am no

expert on these matters, but I assume the thing was probably flushed down the toilet."

"Wrapper, too?"

"Presumably. Where else would it be?"

"You'd be amazed at what people throw from their balconies," said Am. "Absolutely amazed."

Sharon considered his implication. "But that would be like—like finding a needle in a haystack."

"Depends," said Am, "on where the condom landed. The Hotel uses a bulldozer to clear seaweed from the beach every morning. But the stretch of sand just beneath the rooms gets raked by the grounds crew every day. They manicure the sand, give it a special look, do everything but imprint the Hotel logo in it. Even a used condom wouldn't escape their notice."

The glamour of their enterprise, Sharon thought, was dulling rapidly. "Not exactly a treasure hunt," she said, screwing up her face slightly.

Even Am had to concede that hunting for a used condom didn't rank anywhere near searching for a missing weapon. It might have been evidence, but it was hard to envision it as desirable evidence. "Just think of it," Am said, trying to put the best light on the object, "as looking for a clue."

Sherlock Holmes never solved any cases this way, thought Sharon, but Am was right. A clue was a clue, wasn't it?

Am could see her doubts and decided he should quote Chief Horton: "You don't look a gift horse in the mouth," Am said, "and you . . ."

He stopped himself before finishing with the Chief's, "And you don't fart into the wind." The man truly wasn't quotable. The break in his own wind wasn't noticed, though; another voice had stepped in.

"Am! Oh, Am!"

Only Mary Mason could sound that excited. Am groaned. It wasn't that Mary was a bad person. It wasn't that she didn't try hard in her job. But her Pollyanna demeanor would have driven Norman Vincent Peale to take a poke at her. The word *perky* had been invented to describe Mary. A television game show hostess didn't have anything on her, but if ever the right person had been mated to the job, Mary was it. She was the Hotel's social director. Mary was the one who led Hotel guests in limbo lines and sing-alongs. She organized clam bakes and passed out the wood for the beach bonfires. As she was quick to tell everyone, her job was "so much fun!"

"I was just about to page you, Am!" she bubbled. Mary was the only adult Am knew who really bubbled.

Am introduced Sharon to Mary and in the same breath tried to explain their need to run, but Mary wasn't about to be denied an audience.

"I just heard about Chief Horton," she said, "and I can tell you that news threw me something terrible. Did you know the Chief was supposed to talk to one of my groups today?"

"No, I didn't Mary. Look—"

"Then I heard that you were serving in his place, and you know what I thought? Why, Am could give the same talk."

She was more Valium than human, Am thought. "What talk, Mary?"

"Hotel security."

Am's first impulse was just to say no. His second was to protest that he hadn't even had the job for twenty-four hours. He settled on his third response: What group would possibly want to hear such a speech?

"Murder Mayhem Weekend, Am!" exclaimed Mary. "It's upon us."

Shit, he thought. Murder Mayhem Weekend. Of all the artificial events the Hotel sponsored, and there were hundreds of them, murder mystery weekends were the worst. Imagine a high school pep rally going on for two days, and you had some idea of what a hotel staff endured during such goings-on.

"Mary . . ."

"It's important, Am. These things are so much fun, but sometimes they do seem a teensy bit unreal. This time we agreed to inject a little reality at the onset of the event. Besides, it's in their contract. Hotel security talk. See?"

Mary stuck a paper under Am's nose. He purposely didn't read it. "You'll have to get someone else, Mary," he said. "Kendrick's gone, and we've had a theft, and there was the suicide . . ."

"Don't you think that suicide will fit marvelously into your talk?" she asked.

"Marvelously," Am replied, deadpan. "Why, maybe we can even have a body thrown by the window when I'm referring to it."

There were some people sarcasm shouldn't be attempted upon. Mary clapped her hands. "Oh, that's a great idea, Am! I'll see if I can get a dummy."

"I was just—"

"The talk is scheduled at one o'clock in the Spindrift Room. You should see how they've set up for the luncheon! We've got a bunch of Art Deco props. It's very twenties. The actors will just love it."

From what Am had been forced to witness in the past, the actors were about as subdued as Gilbert & Sullivan performers. They went around reciting their speeches in mock operatic form and were as subtle in their posing as a troop of flashers.

"In fact, I'm going to help pick up the Murder Mayhem participants right now. They're coming by train. We're going to meet them with a hearse caravan at the Del Mar station. That should be a scream!"

Lily Tomlin once remarked, "I hate to imagine what the creator of Muzak is thinking up at this very moment." Am was certain that same genius had come up with murder mystery weekends. The plots changed frequently, but the outcome was always the same. A mock murder occurred at the onset of the gathering, and the guests had to figure out who the murderer was. Various clues were offered during the course of the weekend, some valid, some red herrings. Sometimes the episodes were structured like great scavenger hunts, with each clue leading the would-be sleuths to actors, who furthered them along in the puzzle. Am had had to deal with the aftermath of misinterpreted clues and faulty detecting, had been forced to apologize for those would-be detectives who had made nuisances of themselves to guests who weren't participating.

Amateurs, he thought. Walter Mitty complexes every one. He almost said that aloud before remembering that he himself was in hot pursuit of a soiled condom. But this was different. This was real murder.

"But it wasn't only your speech that I needed to talk to you about, Am," said Mary. "I just realized that there was something else I should tell you."

Am didn't like the tone of Mary's voice. She wasn't a deep thinker. Mentioning the advent of a nuclear war would be an afterthought to her. "What?"

"The Murder Mayhem group is taking up a hundred and twenty-five guest rooms. Right now it's booked under the name of the Bob Johnson Society, and I'm afraid that's where some confusion might occur."

Am was watching her closely. There was something that wasn't ringing quite right in her "Up with People" act.

"You see," she said, "I booked all the rooms under the name Bob Johnson."

That wasn't unusual. Sometimes getting individual names out of groups was as easy as pulling teeth. Conventions often committed to guest room space long before knowing the names of their attendees. Since time immemorial, hotels have been imploring groups for their rooming lists, but more often than not the individual names are turned in late, sometimes at the last minute. It's not uncommon for hundreds of rooms to be blocked under one name. In this case it was Bob Johnson.

"And there might be one eensie little problem."

Am's eyebrows asked the question.

"The Bob Johnson Society is just that," she said.

"Just what?"

"Everyone in it is named Bob Johnson."

Mary kept talking. She didn't see Am's face changing. It looked something like Lon Chaney turning into the Wolfman.

"As I understand it, a journalist named Bob Johnson founded the society," she said. "Bob Johnson thought there ought to be an annual gathering for people with his name. I guess it's about the most common name in the country, even more common than John Smith."

Am knew only too well that hotels had enough problems when two people with the same name were registered. Now

he was facing a situation where one hundred and twenty-five
rooms were to be registered under the same name. The confusion promised to be horrendous. The Hotel was projected
to have six hundred and twenty-five rooms occupied that
night. That meant that one in every five guest rooms would
be registered to a Bob Johnson. The potential for Bob Johnson chaos couldn't be underestimated: messages, and deliveries, and charges, and reservations were all waiting land
mines. A plan had to be drawn up to mitigate the Bob Johnson effect.

"Gotta run, Am," said Mary. "Remember, one o'clock."

Am was thinking desperately. At Mary's retreating figure
he had time only for a diversionary vision: murder. And not
one that had anything to do with the mystery weekend. Am
turned to Sharon. She took in his despairing glance and offered sympathy in return. The solace gave Am some
strength. He found his voice.

"Find the condom," he croaked. "Ask for Enrique. He's
the head groundskeeper. I'm going to . . ."

He made a feeble motion, searched for the appropriate
words, then waved his hand in disgust and walked off. Ran
even. Sharon felt sorry for Am. But then she also felt a little
sorry for herself.

Find the condom, he had told her. Nothing like being left
holding the bag, she thought.

# 18

While he was rifling through the remains of the dead, Carlton came to the sobering conclusion that in addition to being a murderer, he was now a grave robber. The thought was almost enough of a deterrent to stop his plundering, but not quite. Carlton justified his actions by reasoning that he wasn't really disturbing the dead. They were still in the closet. He was just going through some of their hitherto untouched belongings that had been left in the room. David had strewn his wallet, and his Breitling watch, on the bedstand, while Deidre's pocketbook and her nylons had been thrown on top of the dresser. The items looked as though they had been dropped rather hurriedly. That thought hardened Carlton to his search.

David's wallet was full of green, and credit cards, and the telephone numbers of half a dozen women. As wallets went, the inside contents were much like Carlton's (except for the telephone numbers). There were no secret pictures, no surprises.

Deidre's purse held more interest for him. Women and their handbags had always been a mystery to Carlton. At another time he would have derived pleasure from doing just such a surreptitious search. What was in purses that pro-

duced so many bulges and made them look so weighty?
Carlton had never seen anything useful, like a Swiss Army
knife, emerge from a purse. His observations had yielded
him glimpses of lip-stained Kleenex, fuzzy key holders, and
appointment cards. Trembling slightly, Carlton dumped the
contents of Deidre's purse on the bed. She had been traveling
with a cosmetics counter. There were also tissues, gum, jewelry, hair bands, tampons, pictures (none of him, just of her
sister and parents), pens, combs, lotion, sunblock, and a
checkbook/wallet.

Carlton knew where Deidre carried her mad money. She
had dug through her purse on more than a few occasions in
search of her hoard. He had never understood her logic. Why
hide money away when you know it's there? He opened the
compartment and took out her store of mad money. Usually
there were a few bills inside. This time there were a number
of Ben Franklins. He counted ninety-six, almost ten thousand
dollars.

Hundreds (or was that thousands?) of ideas popped into
Carlton's head, plots and snippets from every hackneyed police show he had ever seen. He could flee with the money
and end up in Mexico. It was only a half hour drive south,
and there was enough money to keep him in margaritas for a
long time.

Or better yet, he didn't even have to flee. He could bury
the dead, and no one would be the wiser. There was plenty of
room on the Hotel grounds. Or in the sand. People were always digging holes in the sand for one reason or another. Or
what if he just flew back home? The police would have a
hard time proving he was a murderer. Wouldn't everyone
say he was the last person in the world who could have done
such a thing?

Enough, he thought. Carlton told himself the schemes
were too repulsive to consider. He had never been the type to
root for the bad guys. When good didn't triumph in the films,
he got downright annoyed. It wasn't right that the bad guys
should ever win. In his estimation the movie business had
gone downhill ever since John Wayne had died. But that was
Hollywood, always twisting things, and thighs, around.

He would give himself up. That's what he would do. But

when Carlton left the room, he made a point of posting the Do Not Disturb sign on the door. He also didn't leave empty-handed. He took Deidre's wallet, and all of David's money, with him.

# 19

Enrique Albanil had been tending the Hotel's grounds for twenty years. He was a swarthy man, his naturally dark complexion baked an even darker brown from the long hours he had spent out of doors. All of Enrique's workers were Latino, as he was. His English was minimal, which was why Enrique had kept repeating, and amplifying, upon this strange woman's request. What she was asking didn't seem to make sense in either Spanish or English, though.

The lady, he could see, was in considerable distress. The more he tried to understand what she wanted, the more red her face had become. They were repeating the same words to each other, each trying different variations of the same linguistic formula. Their lingua franca seemed to center over one word: condom. Just getting that far had taken some interesting pantomiming.

"Am Caulfield," Sharon said, uttering the name with considerable vexation, "wanted me to find out if any of your grounds crew found—it—while cleaning the beach."

Why wasn't she saying it now? Could he have misinterpreted? *"A condone?"*

"A condom," said Sharon, struggling in her attempt to be a dispassionate diplomat. "Yes."

Enrique spoke in Spanish to her, his words slow and deliberate. Why had she taken French? Let's see, thought Sharon, concentrating on what he was saying. *Playa* meant beach. She knew that. Everything in San Diego was Playa this and Playa that. And *día* was day. Even the gringos went around saying *Buenos días*." And she knew the other word. By this time she knew it only too well. "Yes," she said, answering in English to his Spanish. "A condom on the beach this morning. It was probably dropped from room seven eleven."

Ennrique pondered the situation. There was a lot going on here that he still didn't understand. He'd been asked to have his crew look for many things before, such as watches and wallets and keys. But nothing like this. There was much to think about.

Sharon alternated between embarrassment and anger. A condom, dammit, she thought. It wasn't like Galileo had been doing a test on falling objects. Or condoms.

*¿Cómo se dice. . . ?* thought Enrique. How do you say . . . ? He searched his mind for the English. "Was it broken?" he finally asked.

"Broken?"

He could see she didn't understand. That wasn't the right word. "The *condone*—new or used?"

He was looking at her as if she should know. As if she had been a participant! "I don't know," said Sharon, stifling an urge just to walk away. She held her hands up and out, the universal sign of incomprehension. Then she reconsidered her body language and nodded. "We think so."

Enrique was more confused than ever. But he pulled a walkie-talkie from his belt and paged Angel Jimenez. Angel had done the beach cleaning that morning. In staccato Spanish, they discussed the situation.

Sharon was able to make out one word during their conversation. It was repeated a number of times. *Condones*.

# 20

His change felt like a metamorphosis, thought Carlton. He had gone to the Hotel haberdashery and bought some new outfits, and now he felt like a new man. The colors were vibrant, much richer than the browns he had traditionally worn. He felt like an emerging butterfly.

He was also glad to be rid of his other suit. Not that the Hotel dry cleaning hadn't done a good job with the cleaning, but there were too many bad memories associated with the suit. He had thrown it away, had dropped it into a trash can, and immediately felt better for doing so.

The shopping had made Carlton hungry, and he had selected the Courtyard Cafe as his dining spot. The cafe was just off the lobby. He could look at all the guests coming and going, could wonder about their activities and their plans. It was a pleasant morning, sunny and warm. The cafe was trellised with flowers, red bougainvillea, and pink mandevilla. Jasmine snaked around the supports and scented the air. Carlton sniffed appreciatively.

Wouldn't it be nice to start over, he thought. To take on a new life just as he had his new clothes. He wouldn't make the same mistakes again. He would enjoy life, just like those around him.

The daydream swept into a pleasant reality. Everyone was on vacation. They were laughing, and eating, and looking content. They were alive.

The word echoed in Carlton's head. It made him ashamed. If only he could take back those few crazed moments. If only he could just be a guest at the Hotel California, be someone else, be free again.

He could get cash advances on his credit cards. Maybe he could even clean out his bank accounts. La Jolla was to plastic surgeons as Silicon Valley was to computers. He could put on a new face. It could be as vibrant as the teal sports jacket he was wearing. He could have hair plugs and liposuction, a new body to go along with his new thoughts.

In the bright cafe, with the aromas of espresso, and jasmine, and the Pacific, with the rainbow colors and his own peacock plumage, these thoughts were possible.

Like all the other guests, Carlton was vacationing from reality.

# 21

The best definition for a hotel that Am had ever heard was "a circus without a tent." He knew his role at the moment was to be the ringmaster to the clowns, the performers, the wild animals, and all the acts. Even the high-diving one, he thought ruefully.

Kim Yamamoto, convention and sales director, met him at the door of her office. "I know," she said, cutting short his tirade. "We're working on Bob Johnson right now."

"How did it happen?" asked Am.

She shrugged. Kim didn't like to levy blame on others, even when they deserved it. "It just fell through the cracks."

For the last four months Kim had been on maternity leave. Her absense had been a daily demonstration to the Hotel of her value. Even though Kim had been back for two weeks, enough land mines had been set in her absence to make damage control an almost daily event. "The cracks," as Kim had put it, were closer in Am's mind to the Grand Canyon.

"Because of the Murder Mayhem Weekend angle," Kim explained, "the group was sloughed off on Mary. No one even thought about getting a rooming list until yesterday. I told Mary we needed one right away, and she turned it over

to me about half an hour ago. Needless to say, I was discon-
certed."

Am wondered if the rooming list had come with one name
and a bunch of ditto marks. When even Kim sounded exasperated, you knew the situation was serious. She was unfail-
ingly polite, had a tiny voice, but always managed to make
herself heard when the situation called for it. Some middle
linebackers could have taken notes from her.

"We've decided to cross-index the Bob Johnsons, Am,"
she said. "There are one hundred and twenty-five rooms in
the Johnson block, with one hundred and seventy-five Bob
Johnsons scheduled to attend. Almost half of the Bob Johnsons are coming with a spouse or girlfriend, so we'll try to
register those rooms under the women's names. We're also
going to try to get a middle name from every Bob Johnson
who registers. That should help the operators clarify which
Bob Johnson the caller wants. And finally, we're going to be
listing all Bob Johnsons under their cities. We expect that
will make for very little duplication."

Am didn't say anything, just tried to figure if there were
other ways of separating Bob Johnsons. Kim misinterpreted
his silence.

"It could be worse," she said. "All the Bob Johnsons are
scheduled to eat their meals together. That should eliminate a
lot of the confusion."

Kim tried to be motherly. "I'm writing out the instructions
for their check-in," she said. "Don't worry. Everything will
be fine."

Thousands of groups booked into the Hotel every year. If
they weren't the gamut of humanity, they were close enough.
Work at any hotel long enough, and eventually you see
everything. Sometimes the fates conspire with the bookings.
The previous year two conventions had overlapped: the Tree
Toppers and the Little People of America. Membership in
the Tree Toppers required overactive pituitaries, while all the
Little People were four feet eight or under.

Both groups were apprised of the other's booking, and
neither saw any conflict. Their respective memberships were
used to being viewed as spectator sport; dimorphism on a
more extreme scale didn't matter to either group. Their con-

ventions proved that opposites attract. The big people and the little people got along famously, peas of the same oversize and undersize pod. Events were suddenly combined, seven-footers and four-footers gathering for picnics, sporting activities, and tours. They even had a farewell dance together, where there was more dancing cheek to stomach than cheek to cheek.

Am let Kim reassure him. He didn't believe a word of what she said, of course, but he enjoyed her soothing tones. Maybe she was right in saying the Bob Johnson Society would end up being just another good parlor story. The thought appealed to Am's mind, even if his stomach didn't buy it.

What's that noise? thought Carlton as the repose of the courtyard was shattered by chanting. The clamor drew closer. Most of the noise makers went straight into the lobby, but a few decided to march through the cafe.

It was the arrival of Bob Johnson, plural.

Everyone was wearing the same name tag: "My Name is Bob Johnson." The Bob Johnsons came in all sorts of shapes, sizes, and colors. They even came in different sexes. There were several Bobbie Johnsons.

The boisterous group started milling around the lobby, announcing themselves to the Hotel California with the refrain: "Bob John—Son, Bob John—Son, Bob John—Son."

Bob Johnson, Carlton thought. What a nice name. So different from his. He was probably the only Carlton Smoltz in the country, if not the world. How convenient it would be to join a ready-made fraternity just by having the right name. And they seemed like such a fun group, too.

Finishing his coffee, Carlton decided to walk through the lobby to get a closer look at the curious gathering. As he stepped through the double glass doors, one of the Bob Johnsons bumped into him.

" 'Scuse me," said Bob. "Little too long in the hospitality car."

He winked at Carlton conspiratorially, patted him on the shoulder, and rejoined his milling brethren. It wasn't until he left that Carlton noticed the man's name tag had fallen off.

He picked it up and looked around for his Bob Johnson. Spying him, he set off to return the name tag.

The main goal of any front desk is to make order out of chaos, but on any given day the objective sometimes is less lofty. There are some days where staving off anarchy is a major accomplishment.

Am could see that Casper and his crew were clearly overwhelmed. They resembled actors in the throes of stage fright, Kim's instructions forgotten in the face of the onslaught of the Bob Johnsons. The staff was prepared for fire, theft, and earthquakes; could deal with the loud, the obnoxious, and the drunk; were versed in evacuation procedures, CPR, and hospitality law. But nothing had prepared them for the Bob Johnsons.

Entering the fray, Am stepped behind the front desk and took a deep breath. He had friends who got their thrills from parachuting and bungee jumping, but Am had always found hotels free-fall enough.

"Bob Johnsons," he yelled, "form seven lines."

Am shouted the instructions several times, and gradually the Bob Johnsons heard, or chose to hear, and began forming lines. Carlton was in the middle of the lobby when the queing up began, and he found himself gradually being herded into a line. His search for the elusive Bob Johnson interrupted, Carlton took a few moments to study the name tag he was holding. It comforted him somehow.

"My name is Bob Johnson," whispered Carlton, reading, and thinking. Could he do it? he wondered. Wouldn't he get caught? But wasn't he going to be caught anyway?

Carlton stuck the name tag on the lapel of his new sports coat. I am Bob Johnson, it announced. Ahead of him, a dozen Bob Johnsons were waiting to check in, and behind him were a dozen more.

"Remember Kim's instructions," shouted Am to the line of shell-shocked desk clerks.

He welcomed the first Bob Johnson: "Will you register, please?"

To the staff, in sotto voce: "Middle names. Everyone get middle names."

Am heard the staff voices start up around him, autopilot taking over for them. In his lifetime Am figured he had checked in around fifty thousand people. He had speculated that one day his larynx would surely break like a worn elastic, stretched thin over the words "Enjoy your stay."

"Am," said one of the desk clerks, her voice strained, "this Mr. Johnson doesn't have a middle name."

A moment of thought, a loud announcement: "Are there any other Mr. Johnsons without middle names?" A few hands. Am repeated himself, this time even louder, which resulted in more hands. "Any Bob Johnson without a middle name please come to the front of the line."

There were seven, prompting Am to a quick decision. He announced the need for the Hotel to have middle names for all Bob Johnsons and quickly christened the seven as Happy, Doc, Dopey, Sleepy, Grumpy, Sneezy, and Bashful. "Ignorance is bliss," announced Bob "Dopey" Johnson. Everyone but Bob "Grumpy" Johnson appeared amused with their new middle names.

Whistling "Heigh-Ho" (until Am shot him a critical glance), T.K. finished checking in Bob "Sleepy" Johnson and signaled for the next man in line. For a moment Carlton considered bolting. This was surely the time he would be discovered. It wasn't too late to walk away, as the lobby was noisy and full of people. Even though half the Bob Johnsons had already registered, none of them appeared to be in a hurry to leave.

An alarm sounded. Carlton certainly would have run then, save that he found himself pressed in on all sides, the milling about at a momentary standstill. Heart racing, he turned his head. It wasn't an alarm, he saw, but a cow bell being clanged vigorously by a woman.

"Hospitality room's open," shouted Mary Mason.

Her announcement was met with cheers and was followed by a minor stampede. It was his chance to escape, but . . .

"Sir," said T.K., offering Carlton a fountain pen and pushing forward a registration card.

Writing "Bob Johnson" was the easy part for Carlton. Then he had to come up with an address. He remembered a street and city from his youth, then filled out a few more boxes before pushing back the card to the clerk. He almost expected to be graded.

"How many in your party?" T.K. asked.

The inquisition begun, Carlton tried to keep his voice firm. "Just myself."

"We need your middle name," said T.K.

After a long pause, or at least it seemed that way to him, he said, "Carlton."

"I'll just need a credit card imprint, Mr. Johnson."

Carlton had been afraid of that moment. "I'm afraid I don't have one," he said softly. He was ready to give an explanation about how he didn't believe in plastic, but T.K. was already mouthing his rote reply.

"In that case, we'll need you to pay for the room and tax in advance, as well as leave a two-hundred dollar deposit. Any incidentals are to be handled on a cash-only basis."

Carlton offered up the money, his deposit paid in crisp hundred-dollar bills. Normally the clerk would have asked Carlton for a driver's license also, but not when there were another dozen Bob Johnsons waiting behind him to register. T.K. handed him a receipt, a room key, and a map of the hotel. He quickly drew an arrow and circled Carlton's room location. "Room two oh eight, Mr. Johnson. Enjoy your stay."

Here it comes, T.K. thought. Can't you get me a room higher up? But that whine didn't occur. The man accepted the key and thanked him. T.K. didn't have time to contemplate the miracle. "Please register," he said to the next Bob Johnson in line.

Carlton left the desk in a daze. He was in possession of a new name, and even better, he was on vacation. He let out a long breath. Then he was almost knocked over. Snaking through the lobby was a rumba line, the participants chanting in rhythmic beat, "Bob—Bob—Bob—Bob—Bob—Bobbbb, John—John—John—John—John—Sonnnnn."

Laughing faces were pulled along. Carlton didn't have long to play the spectator and admire the spectacle. Grasping arms pulled him into the promenade. He didn't resist. Shimmying and shaking and shouting, the Bob Johnsons, and Carlton, danced their way forward. In the lead was Mary, her cow bells clanging, the call of the pied piper to the hospitality room.

Within fifteen minutes of Carlton's departure, Hurricane Johnson totally passed, leaving no Bob Johnsons in the lobby. The front desk crew was left to deal with their aftermath, but at least the room assignments had been made. The hard part was supposedly over, even though for the next hour the clerks tried to make sense out of what they had done.

When Am finally left the desk, he was relatively satisfied that the Bob Johnson situation was under control. Only one thing nagged at him. A preliminary guest room printout showed that the front desk had exceeded the Johnson room block by one room. Mary had been adamant about only one thing: there were one hundred and twenty-five Bob Johnson rooms and one hundred and seventy-five Bob Johnsons. She claimed to have checked, and double-checked, her rooming list (the same list with one name on it). That still didn't jibe with the desk having given out keys to one hundred and twenty-six rooms, and the one hundred and seventy-six Bob Johnsons who had registered.

It was a minor detail, Am was sure. Mary might have miscounted. It was also quite possible that one of the Bob Johnsons had decided to pick up an extra room. It really wasn't anything to worry about, he told himself.

All things considered, the check-in had gone much more smoothly than he would have imagined, rumba line and all.

# 22

Am returned to his office, hoping for a little peace and quiet. He had been too busy to realize how tired he was from the night before. Paul Revere was beginning his horseback ride through his head, crying, "The headache is coming, the headache is coming!" Am liked to call major headaches "mythological encounters." He knew that the aspirin he was taking would ultimately fail him, just as his rotating his head, and rubbing his temples, were measures designed only to stave off the pain, not to conquer it. The reckoning would come, and when it did, Am would think of Zeus, who had found headache relief in a manner unique to the gods. To stop the pain, Zeus had called for lightning to split open his own skull, and out had popped Athena, the goddess of wisdom.

Not that a goddess of wisdom would pop out of his head. Far from it. Am wondered what would. Maybe his vision of the ultimate hotel, the carrot that was always dangling in front of him. With a few mirror tricks in his mind, the Hotel California could almost be that place.

He wanted that, wanted to be part of the world's greatest caravansary, an oasis where mankind could stay and be refreshed. Every large hotel announces itself a city within a city, but the Hotel was more than that. It was a country within a country. Much like at the United Nations, the flags of the world flew in front of the Hotel, the flagpoles planted between the swaying palms. The staff enhanced the international flavor. Someone in human resources had told him that the thousand Hotel employees hailed from over sixty nations. And then there were all the international guests. His landlocked ship took him everywhere, and every day was a new voyage. Some days the seas were rougher than others.

Sharon walked into the office, saw the aspirin bottle on his desk, and picked it up. Without water, she swallowed two of the capsules. Neither one spoke. Two sets of eyes looked at each other, and there was the recognition of battles fought and lost.

"Let's get some road kill," Am finally said.

"What?"

"Nothing. Come on."

In the employees' cafeteria they were both served heaping platefuls of spaghetti. At first they didn't say anything to one another, just went about eating methodically. Am was interrupted periodically by other employees who came by to clap him on his back and say, "Great party." He found it difficult to believe the Come as a Guest party had occurred only the night before.

"Two condoms," Sharon said at last, breaking the silence between them.

"Two condoms," he repeated.

She nodded. "If I understood correctly, and I'm not making claims that I do, Angel raked up two condoms from the beach, both near to one another."

Sharon pronounced Angel's name as if he were a winged messenger instead of using the Spanish pronunciation, but Am didn't bother correcting her. Back in the days when only doctors wore pagers and most hotels summoned their workers by intercom, Am had worked at a hotel that had hired a temporary worker from the Bronx to handle the switchboard. In her one day on the job the woman never mastered the pronunciation of "Jesus," which in Spanish is "Hey-SOOS." All day long the intercom had blared, "Jesus, you're wanted in housekeeping," and "Jesus, go to room three-two-two for a check-out," and "Jesus, I need you." Guests and staff had laughed uproariously at those periodic New York calls for Jesus.

Jesus, thought Am, two condoms. That complicated matters. It was like having two guns. Well, sort of.

"Where were they found?" he asked.

"Angel said they were around rooms one oh five or six."

As the crow flies, not that far from room 711, thought Am. Or as the condom drops.

"How far apart?"

"Not more than a few yards." She paused, unsure as to whether she should continue, then, with red face, said, "I asked him if he noticed the condition of the condoms." She hesitated, pride interrupting her speech. "He seemed to find that amusing."

"I'm sorry," Am said softly.

Sharon shook her head as if it didn't matter, but she was pleased that he wasn't laughing. "Angel didn't look closely at either condom, but apparently one was shattered and the other—more intact."

"Used?"

She nodded. "Angel seemed to be of the opinion that he died a happy man. That is, if I judged his pantomime correctly."

"Sure he wasn't propositioning you?"

"Not at all sure."

They both offered the other a little smile. "You can't say I didn't try to bring Detective McHugh his smoking condom," she said. "I did some sifting through the Dumpster that Enrique said usually got most of the beach garbage, but I didn't come up with anything."

Am gave her a look of disbelief, which she misinterpreted. "Don't worry," she said. "I did wash."

"That's not it," said Am. He thought of this patrician presence sorting through garbage. "I was just overwhelmed by your going that extra yard."

"I wish I'd had better luck," she said, then reconsidered and made a face. "Or maybe not."

Both faced their spaghetti again and did a little more eating and a little more puzzling over their cundum conundrum.

"Are we going to let a sleeping suicide lie?" Sharon finally asked.

Am shook his head. "Not yet. This whole thing is playing on my mind. It's tickling me like—like . . ."

"Like a French tickler," she said.

The Breakers was the Hotel's racier lounge. It exploited the ocean view, and the view of calf and thigh, more than the other drinking holes. Tim Kelly had spent his last hours there, reason enough for Am and Sharon to go there with questions. To Am's surprise, Cat Ross was already working on the floor. Usually she didn't come in until five o'clock.

Cat believed in big smiles and friendly hands. She usually patted her male customers on the arm after they gave her an order or after saying anything that approached cleverness. Pavlovian reinforcement. There hadn't been a complaint from a male guest yet. Cat had a nice figure and knew it better than anyone. Her hemline challenged company standards. Am had once heard Cat announce to some customers that she was a "high-stepping hussy." Apparently she prided herself on her strut. Most of the time she looked as though she were carrying a baton instead of a cocktail tray.

She approached Am without acknowledging Sharon, gave him a big smile, then touched his tie lightly. "Haven't seen you in a while, stranger."

Am felt slightly uncomfortable. He and Cat had attended several company events together. Cat had teased him into agreeing that he would take her out on a real date some night, an outing Am had avoided. She was reminding him of his promise by standing uncomfortably close to him. Feeling awkward, if not compromised, Am made introductions, then asked if Cat had a minute to sit with them. The three found a booth, and Am found himself sitting in the middle.

"You closed last night, didn't you, Cat?"

"Yeah, but they called me in early today because they needed LeAnne to help out with a banquet. Don't worry, Am. Overtime's already been approved."

"I'm not here about overtime, Cat. I wanted to ask you about last night. You were waiting on two men, a Steve Daniels and a Tim Kelly."

"I was waiting on lots of deuces," she said. "What'd they look like?"

"Kelly was hitting on you," Am said.

"So do half my customers."

Cat's smile appeared as much for Sharon's benefit as Am's.

"Kelly and his friend closed the bar. He left you a twenty-dollar tip."

"Bingo," she said. "I remember. Good Time Charlie in search of a better time."

"Did he find it?" asked Sharon.

Cat gave her a look of umbrage, and Am quickly interjected, "Mr. Daniels told me that Mr. Kelly was under the impression that you might visit him for a drink after your shift."

"That's what Mr. Kelly wanted to believe," Cat said. "Before he left, I made it clear I wouldn't be seeing him."

She patted Am's knee, glad of the chance to clarify matters. "Did Mr. Kelly seem sad to you?" Am asked. "Despondent?"

The waitress did a double take at the question, shook her head to emphasize the ridiculousness of it. "Far from it."

"He wasn't disappointed that you weren't coming up to see him?" asked Am.

She laughed and shook her head. "He told me I didn't know what a good time I was missing. If I had a dollar for every man who's ever said that to me . . ."

Sharon's editorial comment could be heard in her cough behind her hand.

"Your impression of him," said Am, "wasn't that of a man ready to kill himself?"

"Kill himself?" Cat sounded surprised.

"Yes," Am said. "The police believe Mr. Kelly jumped to his death from his balcony shortly after he left the lounge last night."

"Wow."

"That surprises you?"

"Sure does."

"Why?"

"It seemed like all he wanted to do was make love. Not make death."

"He didn't say anything," Sharon asked, "to make you believe he was contemplating such an act?"

"There was only one act he seemed to be contemplating." Cat gave her answer in such a way as to imply that Sharon might not know anything about that.

"Did you notice any professionals at the bar?" Am asked.

Cat gave a sidelong glance at Sharon. "They don't *usually* let them in here."

Am hurriedly produced the police bulletin that pictured Conchita Alvarez. "Was this woman at the bar?"

Cat took her time looking at the picture. "No," she said.

Am tried to hide his disappointment. "Was Tim Kelly talking with any other women last night?"

"He didn't seem to feel the need," said Cat.

She patted his knee again.

# 23

Because they shared a name, declared one of the Bob Johnsons, they were brothers. Loud agreement came with his pronouncement and loudest of all from Carlton. The rumba line had solidified his feeling of belonging. A few drinks hadn't hurt, either.

"It's the best name in the world," said a skinny, and rather sentimental, Bob Johnson.

"The best," said fat Bob Johnson, holding up his glass for yet another toast.

"The best," agreed Carlton, who was rapidly forgetting that he had another name.

There were rules to the fraternity that Carlton had already learned. You didn't greet your brother with "hello": you shouted, "Bobby boy!" Everyone was "Big Bob." And when two Johnsons were together, it was "Johnson & Johnson" time.

"I've got two boys," said tall Bob Johnson. "And I think it's a damn shame only one of them could get my name."

There was commiseration and maybe even a tear or two. Then there was another toast and more contemplation on that great name of Bob Johnson.

"Did you ever stop to think," said fat Bob Johnson, "that Bob spelled backward is Bob?"

They contemplated the wonder of that palindrome and drank to those special three letters. No one observed that "Boob" worked the same way. Carlton found that his glass was empty. Again. He wandered over to the bar. Ahead of him, pouring herself a healthy tumbler, was one of the three Bobbie Johnsons (though this one spelled her name "Bobbi") and the prettiest, to his thinking. Four years ago the Bob Johnson Society had opened their doors to Bobbie Johnsons. He thought of offering a greeting, but he decided that it wouldn't do to shout "Bobby boy" at her. There wasn't anything boylike about her.

She was around thirty-five, Carlton guessed, and nothing at all like Deidre, for which he was grateful. Bobbi was a big woman, tall and heavy. She didn't put on airs. She might have had a few extra pounds, but not an ounce of that was artifice. He watched as she mixed her drink with her finger. Then, with evident satisfaction, she sucked on her flesh swizzle stick and finally pulled it free from her lips with a Jack Horner yank.

Carlton found himself getting aroused, and that surprised and horrified him. The passion had mostly disappeared from his marriage years ago. There were times he wondered if it had ever been there. Carlton had been consumed by his work for so long, he had forgotten his feelings, his needs. He had heard some psychologist explain it on the radio once. What was the word she had used? His drives had been—something. Then he remembered. Sublimated. That was the word. But he didn't feel sublimated now. And he knew that was terribly wrong. But there was something about big Bobbi that attracted him. Maybe it was her open manner. He had noticed her talking with others, had immediately liked her friendly and homey ways. Bobbi was a bit like Dolly Parton, at least before Dolly got thin. Like the singer, she wore a loud blond wig, and her lips were painted a garish red. So intent was Carlton on staring at her that he didn't avert his eyes when she turned around.

"Why, hello there, big bad Bob!"

Usually Carlton was tongue-tied around women. But he

felt a welcome in her words, an adrenaline shot from her address. By gum, he felt like big bad Bob.

"Ah, the belle of the Bobs."

Her big, red lips opened, and a horse-laugh came out of them. "I kinda like the sound of that one."

"I kinda like the sound of you."

"Fast on your feet, are you?"

"Just so long as I'm not so fast when I'm off of them."

Was he, Carlton, saying those things? And was she laughing so hard at what he was saying? Was she patting his shoulder? She was.

"Didn't see you last year," she said.

"Didn't know you were going to be in attendance," he said.

"These things are so much fun I wouldn't miss them," she said. "Only problem is, now I got myself a beau, and his name's not Johnson. It's Gresham."

"I'd break it off right now," said Carlton.

"Would you? I'm thinking I could be one of those liberated women and keep my name. That way I could keep coming to these soirees."

"Ol' Gresham probably wouldn't let you out of his sight. I know I wouldn't."

"Do talk," she said, then managed an all-too-obvious look at Carlton's left hand. "So why is it that all the good men are either married, gay, or not named Bob Johnson?"

"I'm not gay," Carlton said, then added thoughtfully, "and I'm not married, either."

He was suddenly somber, reminded of the terrible thing he had done. Bobbi noted his downcast face. "Didn't mean to get you blue, darling," she said. "It's just that I noticed the gold on your hitching post." She tapped one of her thick red fingernails on his ring finger.

Surprised, Carlton looked at the ring. He had worn it enough years that he never noticed it anymore. The ring was an indictment of his crime. If only he could shed it, he thought, shed it the way a snake shed its skin. "My wife died—recently," he said.

For once, Bobbi's smile left her. "I'm sorry."

Wasn't it the height of hypocrisy to still be wearing a wedding ring? "I suppose I should retire this," he said.

Almost ceremoniously, Carlton removed the gold band. Then he poured himself a few fingers of Scotch. Bobbi stepped next to him and raised her glass to his. "To new beginnings," she said.

They clinked glasses, then ambled off together. Behind him, Carlton left his ring at the bar.

# 24

The quiet continuity of rust-colored guest room doors was broken by the yellow Do Not Cross police tape in front of room 711. The mustard marker of tragedy was out of place among the trappings of the Grande Dame. While the barrier could easily be removed, its presence was reminder enough to make Am and Sharon pause before proceeding. They regarded each other silently. Little had been said between them since they'd left the Breakers Lounge. Sharon figured Am was angry at her for rising to that cocktail waitress's bait. Or was it the other way around? She didn't like women having to truckle to men, didn't like it that some women felt it necessary to be provocative and competitive. Women in business had it twice as difficult as men. They were supposed to play by male rules and yet act like women. If that wasn't enough to make any woman schizophrenic, there were also the male egos to deal with. Figuring out what was right or wrong could be a full-time job if you let it. Sharon had decided it was easier to be like her male colleagues in that regard: act and think about the consequences later. Damn the torpedoes, full speed ahead.

"Shall we?"

She pointed to the yellow tape. Am looked at her cocked

head and her extended pose. It was almost as if she were asking him to dance. He nodded. Together they removed the
strip-taped barrier. Am used his pass key to open the door,
and this time it was his turn to motion. Sharon entered the
room first.

It was somehow different without Detective McHugh
being its centerpiece; that, and they had arrived with new expectations. On their prior visit they had been swept along by
their theory and had expected the grateful police to act
quickly on their pearls of wisdom. Now they came a little
humbled, hoping for no more than a clue.

From appearances, the room was little changed from when
Tim Kelly had taken his long drop, the only ostensible difference being that his luggage had already been removed. Sections of newspaper were scattered over the carpeting.
Yesterday's news, thought Sharon, checking the date to
make sure. Towels had been dropped, one in the entryway,
another balled and crumpled on a chair, and a third on the
bathroom floor. A long trail of dental floss had been left in
the sink.

"Is it de rigueur for suicides to floss before dying?" she
asked.

"It's not without precedent," said Am.

Sharon raised an eyebrow.

"Socrates," Am cited. "He bathed before he drank his poison to save someone from having to wash his body."

Where did this guy, who looked as though he should have
been cast in a Frankie and Annette film, learn about things
like that? But instead of asking, instead of allowing their
conversation to take a personal turn, Sharon said, "Looks
like Mr. Kelly might have taken his bath, too."

There was a large puddle of water on the tile floor, but the
liquid pool was closer to the sink than the bathtub.

Am rubbed his chin thoughtfully. "Over time drainage
takes care of most runoff or spills," he said, "so either this
happened recently or there was a lot of water on the floor last
night."

He examined the faucet, then looked for leaks under the
sink. Nothing appeared amiss.

"Maybe he didn't make it to the toilet," Sharon suggested.

The speculation offered, she didn't appear inclined to reach any definitive conclusions.

"Be my guest," said Am, nodding his head to the floor.

"I'm only an intern, remember?"

Sighing, Am bent down and sniffed the puddle. "Water," he said.

"So maybe he was just messy."

"Quite possible," said Am. "Some guests don't feel like they've gotten their money's worth unless they leave as much mess as possible."

They walked out of the bathroom and made their way to the middle of the room. Virtually every accommodation in the Hotel was designed to take full advantage of the ocean, with the rooms opening up to the west. The walls were covered with sea scenes, and the room motif was an interior designer's version of the Mediterranean. Am thought the ten thousand dollars it cost to decorate each room was largely superfluous: center stage always had been, and always would be, the Pacific.

The ocean was a magnet that both of them tried to ignore. Officiously and diligently, they looked through trash and under the bed. They stuck their heads in the closet and scouted all the bureau tops, but their efforts only prolonged the inevitable. Within five minutes Am and Sharon were standing on the balcony and looking at the ocean.

"Clear day," said Am, scanning the blue horizon. "We might get a green flash."

"Is that anything like a hot flash?"

He shook his head, remembered that she wasn't a local. "Sometimes a green flash bursts on the horizon right after the sun sets into the ocean. People are afraid to blink, because it only lasts an instant."

Suspecting a tall tale, Sharon said, "And I suppose at the end of the green flash there's a pot of gold?"

"It's not a myth. It's a natural phenomenon that has something to do with a prismatic effect and the reflection of the sun. But it isn't the science that's fun, it's the looking. You can watch a hundred sunsets and not see a green flash, and then boom, one day it's there."

Am had heard some old-timers claim the green flash

didn't occur as often anymore. Rose-colored (or was that green-colored?) glasses might have had something to do with such sentiments, but drifting L.A. smog couldn't be helping the green show. The flash only occurred when the horizon was clear; it couldn't be seen under conditions of cloud or smog cover. If pollution worsened, Am wondered if the green flash would become a myth, would be the snipe hunt for future generations of Southern Californians. Time to start a committee, he thought. Save the Green Flash.

He wasn't the only one lost in ocean thoughts. Sharon had always thought that there was no real life west of Philadelphia, but in her heart she had been afraid that San Diego would be this beautiful. She wasn't used to having views, or much of anything, capture her. But for the moment, she was held.

"I keep looking out and expecting Botticelli's 'Venus' to rise from the surf," said Am.

The admission sounded too personal. Am changed the tone of his voice and suddenly played the tour guide. He stretched his arms to take in the expanse from La Jolla Cove to Scripps Institution of Oceanography. "Underwater ecological reserve," he said. "No fishing or collecting. That, and the fact that this is a placid beach, brings a lot of scuba divers."

One diving class was coming in from the sea. Out of water, the divers looked ungainly. Burdened by gravity and their flippers, tanks, wet suits, and buoyancy compensators, they were veritable fish out of water. Most of the divers crawled on all fours to get beyond the surfline.

"Watching the divers come in always reminds me of an evolution film," said Am, "man's distant forebears crawling out of the drink. The only difference is we get to see them convert to two legs and walk upright right in front of our eyes, rather than waiting millions of years."

They watched the divers struggle to their feet and shed their carapaces. Then their attention shifted back to the ocean. They let it do the talking for a minute, the boom of the surf awakening thoughts that usually slept.

"Maybe McHugh was right," said Am, his words slow and reluctant. "Maybe Kelly got the Pacific blues."

"What do you mean by that?"

"The ocean is a curative for most," he said, "but some people prefer rivers or lakes. They like being able to look to an opposite bank, knowing where a body of water starts and finishes. Psychological terra firma. Oceans aren't that way."

Am pulled at his lip thoughtfully, his eyes still looking outward. "I still don't think Tim Kelly committed suicide, but maybe he just forgot his way. Contemplating an ocean is like trying to take a measure of God. In the scale of an ocean, it's hard to find yourself. Look too long and you can get lost. It's conceivable that he experienced rapture of the depths from right here."

Did they both feel that pull? Was that what happened to Tim Kelly? Had he watched the ocean, and listened, and heard a Siren's call?

Gulls swooped down on the watchers and awakened them from the fathoms. The birds were looking for handouts. Sharon reached into her purse, but Am put a light hand on her arm.

"Throw any food to them and before long we'll feel like extras in *The Birds*."

Am was as slow to withdraw his hand as she was to let her arm drop. A languidness descended on them, an unwillingness to move. For a score of moments they let themselves bask, creatures drawing strength from the sun. The warmth kissed their faces. It felt good, too good. Am had to struggle the hardest to break the spell, had to play tricks on his mind to convince it that he wasn't too tired. There was still work to do. And the matter of a death.

Opening his eyes, he saw Sharon standing on her tiptoes, leaning over the balcony and looking down. From seven floors up it wasn't his favorite view. The sand was far away, not Waikiki far, not nosebleed high like other megalith high rises, but high enough to die.

"I hope you don't have acrophobia," said Am. Her leaning over the railing made him uncomfortable.

"Was Kelly a big man?"

"I don't know."

"I'm five six," she said, "and I'd find it pretty hard to drop unintentionally."

"Ditto," said the six-footer.

Sharon had planted her shoes inside of the hollowed clay cylinders that lined the balcony. Her momentary scrabbling caused Am to take note of the decking and her footholds. The wood was scraped, almost grooved, the indentations made along the worn surface. Near to where Sharon was standing were two missing cylinders. The decorative rounds were ubiquitous in Southern California architecture, almost as common as glass bricks. Natives called them red doughnuts. Aesthetically the cylinders were attractive, but Am would have preferred more traditional balconies. Even when plied together with generous amounts of adhesive, the doughnuts eventually loosened, and separated. It wasn't a question of gravity calling, but one of just when the calling came. A rainstorm at the Hotel invariably resulted in a small avalanche of the tiles. No guest had been struck yet, but Am wasn't taking bets for the future. Normally the top tiles loosened first; however, in this instance they had fallen from the bottom left side of the balcony. If the missing tiles weren't soon replaced, more of the clay doughnuts would drop.

Sharon raised herself from her beach viewing in time to see Am making an entry on a notepad. She looked at him hopefully, but he shook his head.

"Just another work order for maintenance," he said.

# 25

In theory, at least, guests are supposed to be able to flag their desires to the housekeeping department through their door signs. The typical makeup of these signs has one side requesting privacy, with the reverse side welcoming maid service. To further eliminate any confusion, the Hotel words its signs in five languages: English, Spanish, French, German, and Japanese. As if giving international significance to Do Not Disturb and Please Clean Room weren't enough, the Hotel's signs feature two distinct drawings: on the one side a slumbering guest and on the other a smiling maid brandishing a duster.

To some Hotel employees, these signs were about as closely regarded as the fifty-five-mile speed limit on Interstate 5. In particular, the engineering department has never regarded the Do Not Disturb signs as significant obstacles. Maintenance workers have learned to knock at the guest room doors (although there are a few engineers who think the knocking part is optional), look both ways, and then quickly turn a sleeping guest into a dusting maid. Voilà! In five languages the engineers find themselves encouraged to enter.

The human race distinguishes itself from animals by stating that we're tool users. No one could deny that "Cotton" Gibbons was a tool user, although it would have been hard to amplify on that. Cotton's neck was about the reddest in San Diego County. He drove to work from El Cajon in a jacked-up Chevy pickup that had one of the country's last "Guns Don't Kill, People Kill" bumper stickers. His sole window decal was the message "Insured by Smith & Wesson." But for all of Cotton's social shortcomings, he was a tool user par excellence.

His nickname had been bestowed early in his career at the Hotel, the result of his frequent refrain of "I don't cotton to no fools" (typically words aimed at management). What Cotton did cotton to was wiring, and plumbing, and fixing. His world was one of circuits, pumps, capacitors, and compressors. He patched and repaired, greased and lubed. His fraternity spoke a language of augers, casings, conduits, and ballcocks, joints, coil fins, valves, and sequencers. Cotton and his engineering brethren were never seen without their tool belts, ever weighing down the propriety of their pants, and their dirtied uniforms (clean at the beginning of the shift, but a sign of dishonor if still unstained more than thirty minutes into a workday).

Most maintenance workers would categorize themselves as being "independent." Their co-workers might endorse other phrases, "rogue elephants" being one of the more kindly. Engineers think themselves the embodiment of the self-sufficient man and have a hard time hiding their disdain for a damn-fool world that can't understand, let alone be able to, jury-rigged solutions out of bubble gum, chicken wire, and maybe a little chewing tabacky. To an engineer, the accepted definition for a Do Not Disturb sign, especially those that announce themselves in five languages, is "Ignore Me."

Cotton knocked at the door of room 605 (his hands were greasy, but he didn't care that he left a calling card of his oily fingerprints—cleaning was housekeeping's job). When no one answered, he reversed the sign, then used his pass key to let himself in.

Something was gumming up the plumbing, and Cotton was trying to narrow down the offending section. Old bitch of a building, he thought. Rust and rot covered up by fancy wallpaper and doo-dads. Function sacrificed to aesthetics ("horseshit" was the word he preferred).

Cotton's first stop was the bathroom, where he checked the bathtub. It wasn't full of shit like the last one he'd seen. He hadn't minded the shit half as much as the guests in 501, who had been running around like the goddamn world had come to an end. Bad piping, he'd told them. Misdirected plumbing. Which translated that a couple of crappers were taking aim on their tub. After his pronouncement, Cotton had gone on the hunt. It wasn't his job to deal with the mess or calm the hysterical. He was there to fix.

He flushed the toilet a few times, with not a little satisfaction. Taking aim, he thought. But he knew those old pipes, and from the sound he didn't think 605's crapper was a contributing factor to 501's problem. Just to be sure, though, Cotton decided to do a little more checking. Some of the plumbing was visible from the walk-in closets.

Cotton went to take a look.

# 26

Without saying it, Am and Sharon knew their case had come to a standstill. There was nothing to indicate that Tim Kelly had met up with a Mickey Finn in his guest room; there were no witnesses who could place him with a drug-administering woman; there wasn't even that accursed condom. The thrill from playing cops and robbers (or detectives and murderers) had worn off.

Am's beeper sounded and was followed by the voice of Mary Mason requesting his presence. Emphatically he turned off his pager. Sharon's eyes had followed his rather dramatic gesture. He decided to take her look as a challenge, declaring: "I am *not* going to talk to the Bob Johnson Society about hotel security."

Her hands, and mouth, and eyebrows, all opened up at the same time. She wasn't the one asking him to speak. But Am conveniently ignored her body language.

"I could, you know. But I didn't ask for this responsibility, and I certainly didn't volunteer to speak. Is it fair to work a job where they ask you to give blood every day?"

Sharon's tongue got as far as her front teeth when he announced: *"Infra hospitium."*

She waited a moment to see if she was expected to respond with a question. Apparently she wasn't.

"Latin," he said. "It means within the inn. There was a time when hotels were responsible for the loss of a guest's property, when they had an obligation to watch out for the safety and protection of guests. Inns were sanctuaries from the highwaymen and brigands. But nowadays hoteliers don't have to worry about the onus of *infra hospitium*. They just have to supply what the courts deem 'reasonable care.' Of course, that responsibility seems to change with the frequency of the flavor of the week.

"This week's ruling is that we're supposed to be psychics. We're supposed to foresee the potential for guest injury. But just how are we expected to be the Praetorian Guard? Robert Kennedy was assassinated in a hotel, and when Ronald Reagan was president of the United States he was shot and wounded on the grounds of a hotel. If a troop of Secret Service agents can't protect one man at a hotel, then how is a solitary hotel dick expected to protect a thousand guests?"

Sharon knew a rhetorical question when she heard one. It took Am only a moment to catch his breath.

"So many things can go wrong at a hotel. Every decade brings a new tragedy. The seventies had Legionnaires' disease at the Bellevue Stratford in Philadelphia; the eighties had the horror of the collapsing skywalk at the Kansas City Hyatt. And let's not forget the MGM Grand fire in Las Vegas, or the inferno in Puerto Rico. Those are only the headline stories. For every major catastrophe, there are thousands of smaller, but not less terrible disasters: guests killed by exploding hot-water heaters; murders and rapes and robberies; deaths resulting from design negligence; guests hurt as a consequence of property neglect or, worse, because no one at the hotel ever cared enough to try to make things right.

"Did you know one Las Vegas hotel lost as many as five hundred room keys a week for twenty-five years, but in all that time they never bothered to rekey their locks? It wasn't until tort cases started bringing sizable settlements that hotels began to try to see to that 'reasonable care' of their guests. They learned they couldn't mint keys like the U.S. Treasury does money, or house guests in rooms with known faulty locks or broken window latches. These days a hotel's responsibility doesn't end with handing out a room key and wishing the guest a good day.

"Not that there aren't times I think the pendulum has swung too far the other way," he added. "Like the woman who sued the Ritz for forty thousand, claiming that her contraception pills had either been stolen or thrown away by the maid, and that her pregnancy was a result of hotel negligence. What? Are we supposed to be conducting bed checks?"

Am sighed long and loud. He looked at Sharon and acted as though he were conceding to her. "All right. I'll give the talk."

Odd, she thought. Not her being quiet, and not his speech making. But just that she was beginning to think of all this madness as being totally normal.

# 27

"You see, Am?" said Mary. "Everything turned out all right."

The Bob Johnsons were noisily finding their seats, the same Bob Johnsons whose imminent arrival had wreaked panic on the Hotel. Anything short of a death, and Mary would always maintain that everything had turned out all right.

Am wasn't listening. He was intent on thinking up a speech. On the way over to the Spindrift Room he had thought of a grand theme. Everyone who worked in a hotel was a hotel detective, even if the cases they toiled over weren't the sort to make headlines. Hotel detectives tried to answer the little questions and concerns that popped up on any given day. So far Am's speech had translated into the words *Welcome, Bob Johnsons*. Maybe it wasn't such a grand theme after all. The rest of his draft was still blank.

Mary tapped on the microphone to see if it was operational. It was something she needn't have done. Herman Gerschlach was the director of meeting services. He was a nerd with a mission, happy only when he could improve upon state-of-the-art equipment. The more complicated the AV needs, the more content Herman was. Even though the Bob

Johnson Society had probably asked only for a simple microphone, Herman's setup was designed to make a mouse roar.

Mary's fingernail test didn't quite shatter eardrums, but it
did get everyone's attention. Her welcoming address was
brief but would have been even shorter had she not used the
phrase *lots of fun* at least a dozen times. She introduced Am
as "the Hotel detective," and he tried not to cringe. His talk,
she assured everyone, was "going to be lots of fun."

Am stepped up to the microphone, took a long breath, and
wondered how the hell he was going to fudge the suggested
half-hour speech out of three words. His confidence wasn't
helped by a loud critique directed at him by a man sitting directly beneath the dais: "He don't look like no hotel dick.
Probably one of them actors. I've been to a few of these
mystery things, and they're always trying to pull surprises."

The man had a name tag like all the other Bob Johnsons,
but his scrawl made his name look more like "Bull" Johnson.
Bull was about fifty pounds overweight, had a red face, red
eyes, and the sympathetic demeanor of a confirmed heckler.

"They're big on trying to pull one over on you," Bull said,
broadcasting not only to his neighbors, but to the continental
United States. "Pull out their rabbits from their hats when
you don't expect them. All part of the show."

As good as Herman's microphone setup was, Am's voice
didn't carry as well as Bull's. "Welcome, Bob Johnsons," he
announced.

Silence greeted his first, and only, draft.

"Before I begin my talk," Am said, "I should explain that
although I am currently in charge of safety and security matters in the Hotel, I am not the Hotel's detective per se, but
rather the assistant general manager."

"Told you he was no hotel dick," said Bull.

Am pretended to look at his notes. He also pretended to
ignore Bull. "Large hotels are called 'a city within a city,' "
he said. "There's some truth to that cliché. Many of the same
problems that society experiences also surface in hotels."

Reaching for a glass of water, Am made as long a production out of his drinking as he could. Herman's microphone
picked up the descent of the liquid down his gullet. Most of

the audience laughed, probably thinking it was part of the show.

"Of course," continued Am, "the Hotel California isn't exactly the downtown precinct, but nonetheless there are those situations that require the services of a host of hotel detectives."

He described how the accounting department tracked down charges, and how the front desk deciphered signatures, and how housekeeping and security tried to match up lost and found items. Am pointed out that hotels, like life, were rife with little mysteries ("the missing sock, the multiplying hangers") and related what he hoped were amusing anecdotes. In the middle of a story that involved the tracking down of a lost reservation, he paused to assess his audience. They seemed a very long way from the edge of their seats. They needed a wake-up call.

Am clung to that thought and tried to tell them about the time an operator had forgotten to record a wake-up call and how the front desk had been forced into calling and awakening half the hotel just to find the right room. They had solved their mystery, but had it been worth it? Was the guest pleased with the Hotel's diligence and concern? No. He complained that he'd been awakened from a sound sleep, and now he didn't want a wake-up call, dammit, because he'd probably be up for the rest of the night.

There were a few amused laughs from the Bob Johnsons, but Am sensed he hadn't gotten through. They didn't want wake-up stories. They didn't want human nature. They wanted true crime tales, and he was hard-pressed to provide that. Wiping the sweat from his face, Am stole a glance at his watch. He'd been talking for less than ten minutes, but enough was enough. It was time for a grand finale he didn't have.

"Being the hotel detective usually isn't glamorous," he said. "Sometimes it's figuring out which room has the pet in it. Sometimes it's deciphering who a message is for. Sometimes it's as mundane as determining whether you should be charging for a single or a double. And sometimes it's just tracing a little child's steps to find a lost stuffed animal."

And sometimes it's just boring an audience, he thought.

When he stopped talking, not too many people noticed. "Are there any questions?" he asked.

"I hear you had a leaper last night," said Bull with his foghorn voice, suddenly awakening the audience.

"An unfortunate incident," Am said. "Out of respect for the deceased's family, it is not a subject open to discussion."

Bull was sidetracked—a little. "You had any murders here?" he asked.

"Not in the years I've been here," said Am. There was a collective sigh from the Murder Mayhem Weekend participants. He realized his guilt at their disappointment was not logical, but at the same time he began to understand why performers would try anything, and say anything, to regain an audience.

"But we have had some serious disturbances. Why, recently there was even gunfire."

That drew some appreciative murmurs. And the demand for details.

"The guest was annoyed with the seagulls," said Am.

The Bob Johnsons' reaction made Am wonder if gladiator contests had drawn more charitable crowds. Their disappointment was palpable. He tried to talk up the story anyway.

"The man had called the desk a few times to complain about the birds," he said. "The gulls were interfering with his nap. He said he couldn't even step out onto his balcony without them harassing him. We explained that we would be glad to move him to another room, but he told us he didn't want to move. He said that if we couldn't help him, he'd help himself, and that's when he started shooting at the gulls."

"What happened?" Bull shouted.

"It's against the law for guests to have firearms in their rooms," Am said. "The police confiscated the man's gun and cited him for shooting within the city limits."

Bull shook his head, or at least swiveled it back and forth. He was one of those people who seemed to be missing a neck. "That's not what I meant," he said, looking rather disgusted at Am's denseness. "Did he hit any of the birds?"

The microphone amplified Am's surprised intake of breath. The sound was not unlike a birdlike squawk.

"Hard hitting birds with a handgun," Bull announced.

A number of heads nodded in agreement. Am had heard of round robin discussions, but this was a group he suspected would prefer dead robin discussions. Stiffly he asked: "Any other questions?"

Someone else besides Bull finally spoke up, a happy-looking red-haired man who was holding hands with an equally happy-looking platinum blonde. "What was your most unusual case?" he asked.

Dare he mention the bra thefts? But that was an ongoing investigation. Am tried to think of anything vaguely resembling a case that he had ever worked on. There were the times he had confiscated bad credit cards at the front desk, and there were the noise complaints he had attended to personally. He had helped separate fighting husbands and wives, and he'd once evacuated the building when there was a bomb threat. But a case?

"Most unusual case," Am said aloud, acting as if there were hundreds for him to choose from. A case indicated a mystery, something he had solved. And while at the moment he felt he was in the middle of too many mysteries, he couldn't say that he had ever really figured out a crime. Or had he?

"That would probably be the mad remote controller," he said.

Over a period of three days and nights a number of guest rooms had called to say that their televisions had mysteriously shut off on them. Most of the transmission disruptions had occurred on the first floor. Some sets had deactivated five, even six times. Maintenance hadn't found anything wrong with the televisions or electrical system. The staff began crediting supernatural explanations, pointing primarily to the Hotel ghost (Am still wasn't sure whether he believed in that poltergeist), but the culprit proved to be flesh and blood and hardly a hardened criminal.

It wasn't genius that helped Am to solve the crime. It was the woman's legs. They were extremely attractive and made him pause on a stairwell to admire them. When she also paused, ostensibly to tie her tennis shoe, Am was being more observant than usual. And that's when he noticed her surreptitiously pull out a television remote control from her purse. He watched her aim and shoot.

All of the Hotel's television sets are the same; all operate by remote control. The woman had been scouting out rooms where she could use her censor's touch. Her easiest targets had been first-floor rooms with their patio doors open.

Am explained the woman was mad at her husband. She said that even though they were on vacation, they might as well have been at home. Apparently, he didn't want to do anything except watch TV. She had stormed out of their room after they had argued, had unwittingly departed with a remote control in hand. She hadn't set out with the intention of being a vandal of the airwaves, but while walking around the courtyard trying to gain her composure, she had been interrupted by a blaring television. Before the woman knew what she was doing, she had taken aim and knocked the offensive set off the airwaves. That was the beginning of her mission, her vendetta. She was only sorry that her room was on the fifth floor, too high up to zap their television out of commission.

The woman had given up her remote control without a fight. It wouldn't have ended that way on the TV, she had told Am.

With the Bob Johnsons finally receptive, and his speaking pump primed, Am remembered a few other victories over crimes, talked about the capture of the haughty man with the epicurean stomach who had falsely signed in their restaurants at least a dozen times before being caught. He liked good food but didn't have the means to pay for it. When apprehended, the man was anything but repentant. While being led off, he had opined to Am that they should get some new menus in the Marina Restaurant.

"They're getting to be the scratch and sniff variety," he had announced disdainfully.

Everyone laughed, except maybe Bull. Am felt good. Now he had them. Maybe he could tell them about—

Jimmy Mazzelli ran into the room. How many times had Am told him not to run? Hotels were an illusion, and illusionists weren't supposed to rush or sweat. Through sleight of hand, with a flourish, hotel workers were expected to conjure up visions of beauty. No one cared how the tricks were done, no one wanted to know that to make ice displays and floral arrangements, or to feed five hundred people and bring water and then wine (or, better yet, change water into wine), there were hundreds of invisible staff working, some circulating as anonymously as possible, others toiling feverishly behind the scenes. But here was Jimmy, being anything but invisible, bounding right up onto the stage where Am was speaking and wildly motioning him away from the microphone. Reluctantly he stepped back.

Jimmy spoke for Am's ear only. He didn't count on Herman's acoustical wizardry. His excited whisper was converted into a reverberating screech: "Am, Cotton just found two fucking corpses in one of the rooms."

It would have been difficult distinguishing who looked more shocked: Jimmy, listening to the echo of his profane words, or Am, who didn't want to believe the messenger.

Unwillingly: "Two?"

Jimmy had learned his lesson. He nodded mutely.

"Hokey," announced Bull Johnson, loudly enough for the rest of his brethren to hear. "I was up in Frisco for one of these murder mystery weekends, and they started their program in just the same way."

# 28

In every life there has to be a worst day. Am was hoping this was his. What had Nietzsche said? "What doesn't destroy me makes me stronger." But then Nietzsche had never worked in the hotel business.

Two guests had been murdered in his Hotel. Detective McHugh had displayed a facsimile of the suspected murder weapon to the press, and had identified the knife as Hotel California cutlery. Because the assailant hadn't brought the knife in from the outside, the press later announced that the deaths were the result of an interrupted robbery. The burglar had entered the room while the couple was in bed, and the speculation was that he hadn't known they were in the room. There was a struggle with the male victim, a prominent Bay Area attorney, and afterward, no doubt in a panic, the knife wielder had stabbed the Jane Doe to silence her screams. It had originally been assumed that the woman was the lawyer's wife, a theory based on the one-carat-plus diamond on her ring finger, but later it was learned that the lawyer, a man identified as David Stern, was unmarried. Because it was believed the woman's wallet had been removed from her purse, her identity was still in question.

In an effort to keep Hotel guests from panicking, it was reported that the criminal had fled the scene the day before. Am wished he had done the same. There wasn't anyone else who could speak for the Hotel. No one was stupid enough. Kendrick and the owners could not be reached in their inviolable retreat, and Am knew it wouldn't be proper for the Hotel to respond to double murders with a "No comment." Melvin Carrelis, the Hotel's legal counsel, had cautioned Am to speak in generalities and appear very sympathetic. He was advised to refer as much as he could to the police, decry the basic sickness of society, and try to avoid referring specifically to what had occurred at the Hotel. The plan was for Am to read a short statement, answer a few questions, and then encourage the reporters to let the police conduct their investigation without interference. Two words into his statement, Am was deluged with questions.

There is a taint of scandal associated with even the poshest of hotels. The business of selling rooms isn't perceived to be quite as respectable as selling insurance, or groceries, or bonds, or flowers. Beyond all the sanitized-for-your-protection sealants, hotels are among the most human of all environments. They are ports of call, destinations, and offer an allure more salacious than salubrious. One manager had once confessed to Am that he could never quite shake the feeling that he wasn't working so much for a hotel as for a bawdy house.

The reporters' thoughts ran along those lines. They voiced their speculations in baying voices. Could the woman have been a prostitute? Were drugs a problem at the Hotel? Did criminal elements frequent the place? Am tried to hide behind the flag of the Hotel being on the *National Register of Historic Places,* but the media weren't visibly impressed. Their attitudes seemed to suggest that this was a hotel, and despite the purported vintage of the inn, it was just another outlet of a business that smacked of sex, and licentiousness, and a general laxness of morals. Scant hours had separated a suicide from a double murder. The reporters wanted to know what other terrible things were going on at the Hotel.

Even after Am finally freed himself from the reportorial questions, there was still the deluge of staff and guest inquiries. Extra personnel were assigned to cover the phones, and Am had Brown's Guards send as many uniforms as possible to present an image of ample security. Additional staff was also called in, with the end result of much trumpeting but little in the way of cavalry. A special room had been set up to try to handle the crisis, a place only for Hotel staff. It wasn't so much the setting for strategy sessions as a fire auxiliary.

Public Relations Director Ben Cooper had been putting the Hotel in the society and travel pages for years, but when asked by Am to try to keep the Hotel out of the spotlight, or at least to soften the lighting, Ben announced that the only thing worse than bad publicity was no publicity at all. Am's double take went unnoticed.

"The biggest knock from the locals is that we're so old," he said, "so staid. San Diegans think that nothing exciting ever happens here. This might wake them up."

Ben rubbed his aquiline nose thoughtfully and looked rather pleased with himself. There had to be a correlation between permanent brain damage, Am thought, and too many public relations releases. He could just imagine the tone of Ben's proposed piece: "The Hotel California, voted one of the hundred best hostelries in the world by the Travel Writers Association, located on the famed Riviera of the west, the La Jolla Strand, and situated in San Diego County, which American meteorologists have labeled as the only 'perfect climate in the country,' was host to an exciting double murder yesterday."

"I'd like to clear whatever you send out, Ben."

"Certainly, Am. No such thing as bad publicity, you know."

What about a hepatitis outbreak in one of the restaurants? Or a convention of child abusers? But Am let the rebuttals die in his throat. Ben had probably been repeating his catechism for forty years. It wasn't the time to tell him about the emperor's clothes.

Phones kept ringing, and staff kept yelling questions at Am, most of them unnecessary. Few people were willing to make decisions themselves. Sharon was Am's biggest help, willing to use her own judgment. When she called out to him, he knew to listen.

"I think we ought to look into this one," she said, hanging up the phone. "It's the Bob Johnsons."

Huns. Mongols. Vandals. Congress. Words that invoke fear. Bob Johnsons now had that same hold on Am.

"They've organized into what they call posses. They're going around the Hotel trying to solve the murders."

Instead of wearing silver stars, they had on their My Name Is Bob Johnson name tags. Am would have prayed to St. Julian, or even Procrustes, but he had the feeling neither was listening.

# 29

Most actors think there's little to the travails of the postal credo. They believe that delivering mail through rain, and snow, and dark of night pales when compared to delivering lines through the same. And mad dogs seem of little consequence when stacked up against chronic coughers, sadistic audiences, incompetent staging, and abysmal direction. When not on stage, journeyman actors sound much like battle-hardened marines. They've seen and lived through it all and stand proudly as living examples of perseverance. To a seasoned actor, giving up on a performance is unthinkable. But eight veteran actors, four women and four men, did just that.

From the first, their show had not gone well. The bellman had made his surprise announcement, and then the security director had excused himself hurriedly. The staging had called for the production to begin right after the hotel dick's exit. The unexpected circumstances of his departure had left everyone in the audience buzzing. Nonetheless, the company had proceeded as planned. One of the actors, guised as a banquet waiter, had spilled a glass of wine onto another actor. A loud argument ensued. The script then called for other actors to intervene, with the intended result of general chaos. There was chaos aplenty, but it turned out that little was of their own invention. The actors called out their lines, pounded their chests dramatically, and waved their hands, but the Bob Johnsons ignored them. The attention of the audience was already taken by news of the actual murders. The Bob Johnsons found that topic infinitely more interesting than their acting.

For a while, the murder mayhem production continued, the actors performing mostly for themselves. There were a few occasions when the audience actually seemed to be showing a glimmer of attention, but those moments were always dashed whenever a self-appointed Bob Johnson news courier would race into the room and breathlessly yell out the latest information about the murders. Thespians who had outroared planes and trains and thunder lost their voices, and their audience, to the murder updates. There was a Frank Capra feeling to the setting: the waiting crowd, the exciting news, the popular responses. Desperately the actors tried to continue. The show, by God, had to go on. That's what they had been taught. Those were the words to their religion. But at last they realized they were upstaged and gave up.

The Bob Johnsons started speculating aloud on what could have occurred. Tablecloths were pulled from tables and tacked up on the walls. Markers and pens were produced; table linen quickly became ink-ridden (the banquet manager walked in, saw what was going on, and ran out screaming hysterically—only the actors noticed). Information was collected and shared, and suppositions followed: it was a drug deal gone bad; the mob had done a hit; the deaths were from a love triangle. The amount of conspiracy theories began to rival the JFK assassination. Instant experts appeared, their main qualification a loud voice. There was a carnival atmosphere to the room, with Bob Johnsons circulating around and listening to the best pitchmen.

Bull Johnson quickly drew the biggest crowd, the result of his voice and his tactics. When information about the murders dried up, Bull primed the pump for more details, generously tipping hotel staff for any and all news. Jimmy Mazzelli became a favorite of Bull's. The bellman ran a table and an extension phone into the room and provided diagrams and layouts of the Hotel.

The actors, huddling together in a corner, watched the goings-on with attempted cool contempt. Every so often there were giveaways to their studied postures, quick head movements, a nervous shaking of their legs. The phenomenon going on around them was something they had never witnessed before, something almost combustible. There was a frenzy, a sensibility, that was moblike. Pandemonium occurred when a new rumor started circulating and took hold of the room. Suddenly everyone was talking loud and mean: other murders had been discovered in the Hotel. There was a serial murderer loose. He was in hiding. The mood of the Bob Johnsons turned ugly, changed to that of a lynching mentality.

"I think some western justice is in order," Bull Johnson shouted.

The crowd agreed.

"Isn't this exciting?" asked Bobbi Johnson, holding on tightly to Carlton's arm as if he were her protector. Carlton didn't demur. He found Bobbi's holding on to him exciting.

"I'm a member of the police reserve in Barstow," said Bull. "Seems to me it's time I invest in all of you the power of a *posse comitatus.*

"Latin," he said a little less loudly. "Means something about being a force of the county. Now why don't everyone raise their right hand and swear after me."

There was a rustling in the crowd and a raising of hands. Bobbi Johnson reluctantly disentangled herself from Carlton and raised her arm. Carlton did the same.

Bull cast his red eye around the room, saw that every Bob Johnson hand was up, then said: "I, Bob Johnson . . ."

The echo followed.

". . . vow that I will do my best to find this murderer . . ."

Out of synch, but gamely, the voices repeated the words.

". . . and see that justice is wrought."

Bull's sentiments concluded by all, he shouted, "Let's form into posses and get that son of a bitch!"

# 30

Being told that there were vigilante Bob Johnsons roving around the Hotel was a frightening thought for Am. He kept imagining wannabe Dirty Harrys moving around in packs, looking for a murderer.

"Now, who was it," Am asked Sharon, "who told you about the Bob Johnsons?"

They were hurrying forward in a southwesterly direction. Am hoped that most of the Bob Johnsons were still in the proximity of the Spindrift Room and could be contained, isolated the way you would a cancerous growth.

"A man identified himself as someone the bellman. I think he said Maury."

"Cory?"

"Yes, that's it."

Am groaned. Cory Corrigan wasn't exactly known for his accuracy. His nickname was "Wrong Way." He'd been a bellman at the Hotel for about twenty years, and it was a foregone conclusion he'd get lost at least once during his shift while helping a guest to his room. Cory was the Hotel's version of the United Way, a charity case, but there was a sweetness to him you rarely found in the human species. Cory wasn't slow; he was scattered. He'd ask the guests where they'd come from or what had brought them to La Jolla, and he'd be so engrossed in their conversations that he'd forget what room they were going to or exactly where they were.

"What'd he say?" asked Am.

Sharon wrinkled her brow and tried to remember his exact words. "He was excited. He said he was outside the Spindrift Room when the Bob Johnsons came out. They were talking about posses and justice, and they were brandishing forks, knives, and spoons."

Am groaned again. It wasn't as if they were storming the Bastille. He motioned for Sharon to continue with her story.

"Then Cory told me he'd followed the largest of the posses, and that they'd ended up at some room."

"What room?"

"It didn't make sense. I thought he said the T. P. Room."

Am nodded and redoubled their pace. He didn't bother to explain that the T. P. Room was the informal name for the Hotel's paper storeroom. Every hotel staff seems to think it is their duty to apply alternate names to everything on the grounds, to essentially create a second language. To help alleviate confusion, the keys were often labeled two ways, on one side the proper name and on the other the Hotel vernacular. This was done to maintain the sanity of new employees. In the presence of guests a supervisor might dispatch a new busboy to the "restaurant supply room," a location seemingly unknown to the busboy, but when handed a key the busboy would find two names, one at least familiar to him: the Roach Motel. Housekeeping storage was called the Doghouse, with spare mattresses found in the Corral. The gardeners usually ate, and hung out, in the Taco Shop. In some instances the Hotel nomenclature didn't seem to make sense, but if anyone dug deeply enough, the roots to the naming emerged. Am had never been able to figure out why the utility room was called the Smoke Shop, until resident guest Wallace Talbot told him that in the sixties half a dozen employees had been busted for smoking marijuana there.

"T. P. Room?" asked Sharon.

"Toilet paper room," Am explained. "It's really the paper storeroom. Hotels will never get an Esperanto award."

She gave Am a quizzical look, one that called for an explanation. "Just consider the word *double*," he said. "Every hotel offers a different definition. In some, a double represents two people; in others, two beds; in still others, just a double bed."

"Double trouble," she said.

"And then some," said Am.

They passed several room service trays on the way to the T. P. Room, Am clucking at every one. "They multiply," he said. "That seems to be the only explanation. In every hotel I've ever worked, the morning and evening room service waiters claim 'the other' shift shirks their pickup duties. Hotels are famous for their border wars."

"I don't think I'm familiar with that phrase."

"Every department has borders with other departments. There are always gray areas as to who should be doing what, so the departments snipe at each other. And there are always plenty of civil wars, with A, B, and C shifts doing finger pointing every which way. I think of the Hotel as a microcosm of the world; the departments are like nations, with temporary allegiances, nonaggression pacts, and surprise attacks. And just as countries sometimes sever diplomatic relations with one another, departments do the same. You should try running a banquet when the catering manager's not talking with the chef, who, in turn, is mad at the convention director."

"Do you play the role of ambassador?"

"No. Usually a more important role: fall guy."

Am held up his hand. They were nearing the T. P. Room, and he heard voices. There had been a number of additions to the Hotel over the years, and the paper storeroom was part of what was referred to as the old section, a general term that denoted about half a dozen buildings and a number of stucco structures that had once been guest bungalows.

The Bob Johnsons had ignored the Hotel Personnel Only signs, had squeezed by a chain barrier down a path supposedly reserved for staff, and were now grouped behind the T. P. Room. Two men, encouraged by the onlookers, were using their hands (their spent and bent forks and knives had been thrown on the ground) to tear apart the back wall. A plywood board had been nailed over a hole in its stucco exterior, a board that was gradually giving way. The wooden obstacle had been secured in enough places that it resisted coming out in one piece—that or the Bob Johnsons just liked the idea of breaking down a makeshift wall.

"New nails," announced Bull Johnson, holding up one of the loosened spikes for everyone to see. "No sign of rust whatsoever."

His announcement was met by excited chatter, cries, and talk that got even louder when the board gave way. One of the Bob Johnson heads breached the opening. "Give me a light," he yelled.

Am and Sharon had made their approach without being noticed. "If you'd gone through the front door," he said, "you would have found a light switch."

The Bob Johnsons turned around. Am was disappointed that they didn't even have the decency to look sheepish, appearing more annoyed than anything else.

"Besides vandalizing," asked Am, "and illegally breaking and entering, what do you think you're doing?"

Bull took the measure of his cohorts. They still seemed to be behind him. "Doing your job," he said.

"Oh," said Am. "My job is to tear holes in an old building?"

His sarcasm didn't draw the blood he wanted; the Bob Johnsons were already too awash in their imaginary blood.

"We heard about the serial murderer," said Bull. "Tell me this isn't a good place to hide out.

"Or hide a body," he added darkly.

As corpse dumping grounds went, it wasn't a bad spot. The T. P. Room was off the beaten path, secluded from view. Because of its remoteness, repairing the crumbling stucco hadn't been a priority.

"Seems strange that a bedboard was used to cover up this hole," said another of the Bob Johnsons. "Not the kind of patching material you'd expect from a fancy hotel."

"If you'd like a tour of some of our more unsightly patch jobs in restricted areas," said Am, "I'd be glad to make arrangements. But this is not King Tut's tomb."

Am touched the stucco, even got a little dramatic and

crumpled some of it in his hand. "This hole has been gradually widening over the months. There was a water leak. You don't even have to look closely to see the discoloration. So rather than leave an open invitation to vermin, we decided to stick up this board until a more permanent repair could be made."

Most of the Bob Johnsons looked deflated. Their hidden passageway, the secret burial ground, was suddenly revealed as a moldering paper room. Am led them to the front of the building and used a key to open the door. A few of the Bob Johnsons made a point of looking into every corner of the room, but most just listened as Am announced there was no serial murderer and there had been no other murders besides the unfortunate couple. The police were investigating, he said. Any other efforts would be counterproductive and would only hinder their work.

The Bob Johnsons seemed to take Am's word to heart. Heads downcast, they began to drift away. Only Bull Johnson remained defiant. Aiming a little kick at the stucco, he announced, "Wouldn't be surprised if you had something to do with this red herring."

# 31

Am made yet another entry in his notepad: "Board up hole in rear of T. P. Room, but not until Monday." The repair was deferred so as to not offer temptation to another group of roving Bob Johnsons before their scheduled check-out on Sunday.

While he was writing, Am took two peeks: one at his watch and the other at Sharon. His high school basketball coach had said that only a team that was tired, or losing, or both, looked at the clock. Whenever he acknowledged the time, Am felt he was close to defeat. It was almost six o'clock, depressingly early for the work that still had to be done. Sharon was a better sight than the hour. The intern was holding up surprisingly well, better than most of his seasoned staff. Still, she had to be tired.

"Why don't you go home?" asked Am. "Get a good night's sleep." The words were offered almost wistfully.

"What are you going to do?"

"Try to talk to McHugh and see what he's learned about the murders."

She didn't hesitate: "Count me in."

The day before, Sharon hadn't wanted to have anything to do with security, and now she was willing to work into the night. Am was torn between teasing her about her change of mind and praising her for being so conscientious. His hesitation to act conspired with the call of his pager.

"Am," said a cloying voice, "this is Mary Mason. I wonder if you could come help me out in the Spindrift Room. We have a minor situation. Thank you."

"Shit," said Am. He took off with a trot. Attempting to keep up with him, Sharon said to his back, "Mary indicated it was minor."

"And she said the Bob Johnsons were an eensie problem."

Despite his fears, Am slowed to a fast walk. "With Mary," he conceded, "it could be anything. She makes fiascoes festive, or vice versa. The staff calls her 'Typhoid Mary,' and believe me, the nickname's deserved."

"So why don't you fire her?"

Am had to think about his answer. "It wouldn't be quite fair," he said. "Believe it or not, most of the time she's just the lightning rod that attracts disaster. Unforeseen things invariably go wrong. When Mary organizes a parade, it's sure to rain. When Mary books a fishing expedition, everyone gets seasick. The way I heard it, the whole boat was throwing up their guts and Mary was trying to get them to sing 'Kumbaya, My Lord.' And you know how they have those fire-walks across coals? The organizer assured us that no one had ever gotten burned, but it was hot-foot central that fateful night, with all the Hotel limos full of burn victims. The group leader couldn't understand what went wrong. But he couldn't exactly blame Mary. Because she's so nice, people continue to like her even when everything goes to hell."

His facial expression was a cross between a smile and a grimace, and Sharon called him on it. "What brings on that look?" she asked.

"Last month's luau on the beach. Mary went the whole nine yards. There were hula dancers, and tables of food, and Don Ho on the loudspeakers. There were mock coconut trees, and banana plants. There were Hawaiian shirts and grass skirts and puka shells and leis. There was even a pig roasting on a spit. Everything looked great." He shook his head, lost in the reverie.

"So what happened?"

"She planned everything perfectly," said Am, "save for one thing. Mary never consulted a tides table. And no one noticed until too late how the water was coming in. The last anyone saw of the pig, it was floating off to sea, apple in mouth."

Sharon laughed, then considered the ramifications. "Did the group demand a refund?"

"For that kind of entertainment? They couldn't have asked for a better show. That's how it usually works for Typhoid Mary. The guests somehow leave happy.

"Maybe the staff, too," Am said, after a little reflection. "We had a pig vigil for a while. We called it our wild boar hunt. There were watchers and search parties. There were T-shirts made up and rewards offered. We kept it up for about a month. The lifeguards put out an A.P.B., an all pigs bulletin, on their towers. There were purported pig sightings everywhere. He was spotted surfing. He was seen driving a stretch limo. He was sighted dining with the mayor. The reports got more and more absurd. It was almost as though everyone expected the porker to really show.

"Who knows," said Am, opening a door into the Spindrift Room. "Maybe today's our lucky day. Maybe the pig's finally come home."

If not the pig, then at least the pigpen: the Bob Johnson tablecloths-turned-displays lined the banquet room walls. Bloodied virgin sheets were never exhibited so proudly. The felt-tip-markered tablecloths featured drawings of where the bodies had been found, diagrams of where the murders had supposedly taken place, and lists of purported clues.

"Looks like an Amway sales seminar," Am said with not a little amazement.

Near the dais were the actors and Mary. She was encircled by the thespians, who at the moment didn't look like audition material for *The Sound of Music.* Am was familiar with most of the troop, having seen them in other Murder Mayhem Weekend productions. There seemed to be two ringleaders: an older man with a handlebar mustache who usually played the British colonel and an artsy-looking younger woman with red-hennaed hair and a pageboy cut. Her chosen role at the moment was the aggrieved artiste.

"I'm afraid that's impossible," the woman said in a stage whisper. "When I wrote this play, the gestalt is what made it. It's not mix and match."

"Breach of contract," said the colonel. "Pure and simple."

Through the surrounding bodies, Mary noticed Am and Sharon. She motioned for them to come forward. "This is our assistant general manager," she said, "Am Caulfield. And this is Sharon."

The colonel stepped close to Am, but not to shake his hand. The only prop he was missing was a monocle. He inspected Am with a dubious stare, then announced, "I thought you were supposed to be the house detective."

Am considered saying, "And I thought you were supposed to be an actor," but his hotel training stayed his purer instincts. He replied diplomatically, "Like you, I am called upon to play many roles."

Good cop, bad cop time. The hennaed woman stepped in front of the colonel. Sotto voce, the playwright said, "Mr. Caulfield, Ms. Mason is asking us to do the impossible. She wants us to reconvene the production in the morning, believing that our audience's homicidal madness will have passed by that time.

"I was raised in the theater," she added, one hand raising itself majestically. "I was weaned on the commandment that the show must go on. But we can't perform for uninterested groundlings, and we can't truncate the first and second acts into some new and bowdlerized version. We're professionals. We don't do the hodgepodge."

Seven heads behind her nodded emphatically, but Am appeared unmoved. Having worked in hotels his entire adult life, he considered himself versed in theater.

"Open tab tonight," he announced, as if that were the only question in dispute. "Drinks and dinner on the house. Rediscover your collective muse. Regroup so that you'll be prepared for the early matinee."

"I suppose," the director said with grudging, albeit whispered words, "we could work on revisions over dr . . . dinner tonight. Mind you," she added, "much will have to be extemporaneous."

"That's in keeping with the theater of hotels," said Am.

The theater of the absurd.

He offered them a nod that was almost a bow. For his parting lines, he closed with his avuncular mein host: "Mary will be glad to see to all of your arrangements. Enjoy your evening."

After motioning to Sharon, they exited the banquet room. When they were out of sight of the actors, Sharon commented, "That was fast."

Am nodded, an answer not good enough for her.

"How did you know their complaints weren't of a truly artistic nature?"

"I've seen them perform before."

She digested that for a moment. "And how did you know what compensation to offer?"

"I've seen their bar tabs."

"They were quick to accept your offer. That usually means you started too high."

"Maybe," he said. "But since we have pressing matters to attend to, I knew better than to start with the traditional nickel."

"Nickel?"

"The man asking the woman if she'd go to bed with him for a million dollars, and the woman thinking about it, and deciding that for a million dollars, yes, she would. Then the man asking if she'd go to bed with him for a nickel, and she responding indignantly, 'A nickel! What kind of a woman do you think I am?' Then the man replying, 'We've already established that, now we're just quibbling over price.' Thus, the traditional nickel."

"You're cynical."

"Some might say experienced."

"I suppose," Sharon said, "we're just quibbling over semantics."

They smiled at one another. In the midst of a hellacious day, they kept discovering each other's smiles, and each other.

"Nickel for your thoughts," said Am, his voice huskier than he intended.

"You buy off the actors with dinner and drinks, and then offer me only a nickel?"

"Dinner and drinks, then."

She had encouraged him in his offer; they both knew that. But now, not for the first time, she backed away. "Maybe tomorrow night," Sharon said. But the tone of her voice sounded a more permanent deferment than twenty-four hours.

Was she a tease? Am wondered. Why her sudden ambivalence? Neither spoke to the other while walking to room 605. The quickness of their pace wasn't enough to mask their uncomfortable silence. This time they were stopped not by police tape, but by a police officer. He stood with the pose of a seasoned bouncer, his considerable bulk positioned so that the only way through the door was through him. Patton's army might have paused to consider that advance.

Approaching the cop, Am felt like a kid trying to pass off a bogus ID. He offered his business card and asked to speak to Detective McHugh. With a pointed finger, the officer directed Am and Sharon to remain outside the room until he passed on the message. Being told to cool his heels in his own place of work didn't improve Am's mood, and neither did the bouncer's reappearing with the message that it would be a few more minutes before McHugh could see them. The minutes passed, and a few more, before the detective finally emerged.

"You got some more theories?" he asked, his tone irritable, his face a sneer.

"You need some?" asked Am, upping the animosity ante.

"Not likely," McHugh said, "after your last one. Sex, drugs, and a missing condom. Them's the kind of movies I see on TV. And when two young, bright, attractive people come on so persuasively, it does make you think. So, against my better judgment, I made a call to the ME. I red-flagged the case as a priority, and I told him what I wanted looked at hard. And you know what? Just before a couple of real murders brought me back to this hotel, I heard from the pathologist. No drugs. No sex. But a blood alcohol level that was about two point four. Maybe it wasn't suicide. Maybe you were right about that. Maybe our jumper thought he was the Great Wallenda performing on his balcony. But his death sure as hell wasn't murder.

"Now," he said, jerking his thumb toward the opened door, "I suppose you're going to tell me the two bodies we took out of there weren't murdered, but committed suicide."

McHugh looked at Am, then at Sharon, with pretended interest. He opened his hands as if imploring them to respond.

"We came in the hopes of being briefed about what's going on with the case," said Am, his lips barely moving, his face red.

"You mean you didn't come to me with all the answers? You don't have a murderer for me?"

Sharon saved Am from having to respond again. "We have a hotel full of concerned guests. We have demands being put upon us by the media. And we have a lot of fear and confusion all around us. We are trying to respond to all of that with staffing, and security, and reason. Your cooperating might help us to deal with that."

An articulate woman with a well-reasoned response is a male cop's worst nightmare. He can't crack heads or go male ego *mano a mano*. Shuffling slightly, McHugh said, "I already held a press conference."

"Where your main comment was 'No comment,' " said Sharon.

"That, and his brandishing a Hotel California knife as if it were Excalibur," said Am, "and telling the world a similar knife was the supposed murder weapon."

"A Hotel California steak knife *was* the murder weapon. And I *wasn't* brandishing it. The press wanted it raised so they could get some photos."

"They wanted the Hotel insignia on the front page of every paper in California, and you gave that to them."

"You suggested," Sharon interjected quickly, "that a burglar might have been interrupted in the midst of a theft."

"I did not," McHugh said emphatically. "That is how the media interpreted the information that I passed on to them. What I said was that the female victim's purse had no identification or money, leading us to believe those items had been removed. I also said that there was no cash in the man's wallet."

"What about his credit cards?" asked Am.

"They were left," McHugh said.

"Isn't that unusual?"

"Not necessarily. You can't trace cash. And if you're in a hurry . . ."

McHugh's insinuation didn't sound emphatic enough to Am. "That's the assumption, isn't it? No one's mentioned premeditation."

"And I haven't, either," McHugh snapped. But, with a grudging admission, he added, "The crime scene contains contradictions."

"Contradictions?"

"There are certain discrepancies."

Am to Sharon: "Are you following this?"

"Can you elaborate?" she asked.

"This is off the record, and not attributable." McHugh's pale blue eyes sought Am's and Sharon's, and they both nodded.

"You've probably heard the victims were found in a walk-in closet?"

Cotton had told his story enough so that everyone on staff had heard. They nodded again.

"Well, the murderer took the precaution of cleaning up."

"Wiping for fingerprints?" asked Am.

"More elaborate than that. And less elaborate. He wrapped the bodies in bed linen, and cleaned up where the struggle took place. He worked hard at getting the blood out of the carpeting, but he didn't dispose of the murder weapon, and he didn't wipe off his fingerprints. The evidence guys are having a field day in there."

"Why would you clean," asked Sharon, "if not for the purpose of covering up?"

The detective gave a significant shrug.

"When did the murders take place?" asked Am.

"They're doing tests now."

The same answer he had given during the press conference. "Preliminary analysis?" Am asked.

"Off the record," said McHugh, "yesterday. Late afternoon or early evening."

"Any suggestions," asked Sharon, "on how we handle guest safety concerns?"

Out of habit, Am reached down and picked up some litter

off the hall carpeting. The toilet lid wrap must have fallen off a maid's cart. The Hotel California's strips didn't have the wording Am had seen at other properties, announcements like "Sanitized for Your Protection"; they merely had the Hotel's insignia stamped on perfumed paper. Am had never been able to figure out the innkeeping tradition of using paper wrap for the privy, but it seemed as if fewer places were using them these days. The Hotel, he figured, would remain one of the last holdouts. He stretched the strip of paper with his two forefingers.

"Encourage normal precautions," said McHugh. "Tell guests not to answer the door without checking the peephole, and offer escorts to all your rooms. Instruct the staff to offer simple, reassuring answers to any inquiries, and conclude by emphasizing that the police believe the assailant fled the scene of the crime some time ago."

"And do you?" asked Am, the question offered with extended fingers and the toilet wrapper.

McHugh stared at Am. The look usually worked. "Most murderers don't stick around to improve on their tans."

Am responded to his words, not his eyes. "His cleaning up would seem—"

"Look," said McHugh, "in times of stress you can't expect people to respond rationally. We got a shrink on the department who figures a kid might have done this, someone fourteen, maybe fifteen. She thinks the kid was rifling the room when the couple walked out of the bedroom and he panicked. Afterward he was still thinking like a kid. Hide the bodies, clean up, and maybe no one will notice, sort of like what we all did when we broke Mom's favorite vase."

"Has the woman been ID'd yet?" asked Sharon.

"Negative," McHugh said. "The dead lawyer had lots of lady friends. One of his partners is flying up to do a positive ID on him, and we hope he'll know who she is. In the meantime we're doing our own tracking. Your front office manager, Roger, has been very helpful in getting us whatever we need."

That didn't surprise Am. Casper always enjoyed doing anything but front office work. Am wanted to ask more questions but felt a little silly trying to do so while facing

McHugh with the paper wrap between his fingers. He had thought to slip it unobtrusively into a pocket, but there hadn't been a good moment.

"Since we're all busy people . . ." McHugh's statement tailed off into a question as he stared pointedly at the toilet wrapper.

"Thank you, Detective," said Sharon.

At McHugh's departure, Am ripped apart the strip and looked around for a handy trash can, but he didn't see one. Sharon pretended not to notice, which made the situation that much more ridiculous. Am decided this walking around each other, and being formally polite, had to stop.

"We've got this one guest who drives the maids crazy," he said. "Whenever he's with us, he never seems to use the toilet. The strip is always there. It looks like it's never disturbed. Barb the housekeeper thinks he might have one of those ileostomy bags, but I think he's just a joker who likes to play with people's minds. I'm convinced he slides the wrapper on and off."

"That seems like a pretty silly thing to do."

"Everyone has little tricks that get them noticed. Winston Churchill used to put pins in some of his cigars. During important debates, when the opposition had the floor, he'd light up his stogies. Everyone would watch his ash get larger and larger. They'd wonder, When is that damn thing going to fall? And after a while nobody would be listening to any speeches. They'd just be watching that growing ash on Winnie's cigar. That's how the maids are with this guest. They look at him with a bit of awe and a bit of fear. They see him in the room for days, and they wonder if there won't come the time when he just explodes. He's become quite the myth."

Am stuck the remains of the strip into his pants pocket. A real hotel detective, he thought, probably wouldn't be talking about bodily functions at a time like this. But in a world of the strange there is still the need to talk about the offbeat, to stand back and try to reaffirm what is normal and what isn't. As he had gotten older, Am thought that arbitrating normality had become that much tougher.

"This whole thing reminds me of your saint," Sharon said.

"What saint?"

"Julian. Remember how you said he came home and thought he'd found his wife with another man, and he killed the couple?"

Am nodded.

"There's something baroque about all this. Why would the murderer clean? And why did the murderer kill?"

"Few murderers are saints," Am reminded her.

Then he recalled something that Mark Twain had once written and repeated it aloud: " 'All saints can do miracles,' " he said, " 'but few of them can keep a hotel.' "

# 32

Sainthood was not on Carlton's mind.

It usually isn't on first dates. Carlton and Bobbi had decided that the fraternity of the Bob Johnsons was not as important as their time together. They talked over drinks in the Sandcomber Lounge, a bar whose tropical island motif looked as if it had been inspired by Disney. There were ersatz palm trees that had wind birds perched on limbs. Given a breeze, or even overactive air-conditioning, the birds let out electronic warbles. The sounds delighted visiting tourists, but one bartender had quit and filed a workers compensation claim, stating that the noise was akin to eight hours of hearing fingernails on a chalkboard.

The wall ornaments were consistent with the kind of flotsam designers would want to find on beaches, colorful worn glass, sand dollars, shells, and multihued fish netting. There was no sewage, tar, dead fish, or syringes on display. Most of the drinks were served in coconuts or pineapples. A barnacled dinghy in the corner was home to some musical instruments and presumably a band that had not yet arrived. Each of the tabletops was adorned with sand and driftwood. Bobbi touched her fingertips along the sand and declared that the designer who had thought up the effect was a genius. Those who had to clean the fallen granules, which were supposed to be corraled inside an upraised lip but regularly found their way to the floor, would have disagreed. Little indentations were left in the wake of Bobbi's fingers.

"Footprints in the sands of time," she said.

"That's beautiful," said Carlton.

"Some poet wrote that," she said. "I write poetry, too."

"And I'll bet it's pretty, but it couldn't be as pretty as you."

Her fingers stopped dancing in the sand and reached for his. Their digits twined.

Carlton spoke from his heart: "I wish this was a deserted island, and only the two of us were on it. Like Robinson Crusoe."

"Which would make me what? Friday?"

"Monday through Friday. And the weekends, too."

She giggled at that one. Her Bobby had quite the silver tongue. "I feel like I'm dreaming," she said.

"Me too."

"Oh, look. The sun's about to set. Let's watch."

Hand in hand, they observed the sun being swallowed from their own tropical island. In its wake they were bathed in a red glow.

"Red sky at night, sailor's delight."

"You are a poet," he said.

"Borrowed again," she said. "But I'm going to write a poem about all of this."

"Am I going to be in it?"

She tried to hide her big face behind her big hands, a move that beguiled Carlton, and said, "I'm thinking of slipping you in."

No one had ever included him in a poem before, of that Carlton was sure. He felt reborn, like one of those plants that against all odds emerge out of rock or asphalt, and he tried to express that thought to Sharon.

"That's beautiful," she said.

"Another?"

Intruding on their red glow, and their mutual admiration society, was a cocktail waitress. She was dressed in a sarong of tropical colors. Her rainbow piscine name tag said Rhonda and identified her hometown as Bayonne, New Jersey.

"Let's walk on the beach instead," said Bobbi.

Am signed off on yet another form. Who guards the guards from bureaucracy? he wondered. As interim security director, he had found himself vouching for just about everything.

Lost and found duty was one of his new responsibilities. He had charge over inventorying and locking up all unclaimed items. While most guests were just negligent or absentminded, he knew some deliberately left behind certain articles. The Hotel now sent sealed generic letters to guests, advising them that an item(s) had been left behind in their room and that they should contact the director of security for further information. The lack of specifics was an improvement over the Hotel's previous method of sending out postcards describing what was being held. One man had been advised that a pink nightie was left in his room, but not before his wife, family, the postman, and half the people in his town had been informed of the same thing. The man's wife had threatened to sue him for divorce, and he had threatened to sue the Hotel for breach of privacy. The pink nightie was never claimed.

The pickings for that day weren't as salacious. A dozen rooms had left behind books that Am logged dutifully, though he knew that most guests never wanted them back. In six months they'd either find their way to the Hotel library or to interested employees. One man had forgotten his swimming trunks and another his two ties (though he wasn't fond of neckwear, Am had one of the largest tie collections in the Western world, courtesy of guest largesse). From three other rooms had come an electric razor, a camera, and a wind-up alarm clock. Am was glad that nothing too exotic had been left behind. He'd heard about guests who'd forgotten their pornographic tapes, bondage material, and sexual paraphernalia. Most, but not all, were embarrassed when claiming their losses.

The only lost item not quite run-of-the-mill was a man's wedding ring, which had been left in the Bob Johnson hospitality room. Even that wasn't too unusual, except that most of the time wedding rings were found next to room sinks or in one of the lounges. There wasn't anything distinguishing about the gold band, no inscription or initials. Am supposed that "To Bob" wouldn't have helped him much anyway.

There were numerous reports to write, the usual closing of the barn doors after all the animals had escaped. The keystone report was purportedly for Kendrick, but Am knew it would be copied and forwarded to the owners, as well as to Hotel legal counsel. In it, Am carefully detailed what had occurred. When the Hotel was sued (these days it was never a question of "if"), the report would certainly be subpoenaed. Putting a positive light on murder wasn't easy. Am noted that there was no sign of forced entry and documented that there were no outstanding keys to the room. He included a copy of the Detex rounds, which showed how the guards had conducted a pass of the floor every three hours, a progress recorded by key punches. Unmentioned was how most guards considered patrolling another form of sleepwalking, and that they remembered to open their eyes only when clocking in, if then.

Am documented that there had been no reports of noise from other rooms and nothing untoward seen by staff. He didn't speculate, just included everything that was known about the deaths that didn't put the Hotel in a bad light. Brevity ruled.

There were several supplemental reports. Am wrote of the response teams that had been formed, his conversation with McHugh, and the efforts to ameliorate the situation. He concluded with a brief write-up on the Bob Johnson Society and the goings-on of Murder Mayhem Weekend. For once, the show had lived up to its billing.

Am wasn't yet ready to relax. As he finished up the reports, he tried to make them look all the more official with appropriate titles. He quickly put a heading to all of the accounts, save for the Kendrick summary. Am didn't want to use "murdered" in the title, and he thought "incident" too trifling. Already punchy, he remembered what Sharon had said about St. Julian. He tapped out, "A Visit from St. Julian," and contemplated the heading for a few moments of perverse pleasure before deleting the entry and entering, "The Unfortunate Deaths in Room 605."

Before turning off the computer, Am called up that room number. Looking up the charges of the dead was getting to be a habit of his. The first thing he noticed was the privacy notation. David Stern had requested that he not be bothered with any telephone calls and had asked the Hotel not to acknowledge his presence on the property.

There wasn't much to his bill, except the excessive eating in. Judging by the expensive room service charges, he and his lady friend had dined well. The last charge had been recorded a little before five the previous day. If McHugh was right about the time of their deaths, they wouldn't have had long to digest their last meal.

Curious, Am scratched out a note to accounting. He wanted to take a look at 605's charges. On the signed room service tabs would be a notation of who had done the serving; maybe the waiters had noticed something out of the ordinary.

Am reached out to turn off the computer but at the last moment found himself tapping into room 711. Tim Kelly's death now seemed like a distant memory. Was it only a dozen hours earlier that he had first scanned Kelly's charges and come away with a head of steam? That steam had certainly dissipated. He and Sharon had combined for some beautiful theories that had been belied by harsh facts. He should have remembered one philosophy professor's favorite quotation: "There is nothing uglier than reason when it is not on your side." Kelly hadn't had sex or drugs, and his only rock and roll had happened when his body hit the sand.

For a few moments Am remembered the thrill of the hunt that he and Sharon had experienced and the sense of intimacy that had grown between them. The blood sport had been exciting. He had been forced to reassess his initial impression that she was some stuck-up easterner weaned on private schools. There was still her reserve, though. She was good at reining herself in. He wondered why she felt that need.

Computer screens are this century's gift to daydreaming,

but even in his fog Am recognized something was wrong. There was something disconcerting, something . . .

Tim Kelly's bill. The man had died early that morning, so how was it that he had already been charged room and tax for the night?

Looking for answers, Am found that Casper was still on the job, miracle of miracles. "Roger," said Am, handing him a printout of Tim Kelly's bill, "what's this?"

The front office manager looked over the bill and its charges and could apparently find nothing wrong. "What do you mean, Am?"

"Kelly died at two A.M. How can we be charging him for tonight?"

"Oh, that," he said. "I talked with Mr. Kendrick before he left this morning, and I mentioned that the room might have to be out of service for tonight. He said if that was the case, we should add on the room charge."

And since all the Contractors Association rooms were being charged to the master account, the additional room night would probably never be questioned. And even if it was, the Hotel could counter that the room couldn't be rented because of Kelly's death, and that the group should be liable for the charge.

In disgust, Am said, "I'm surprised Kendrick didn't insist we charge ten dollars to put pennies on the dead man's eyes."

Roger surveyed the list of charges once more. "I don't see that notation anywhere, Am. Should we be adding that to the bill?"

# 33

The staff parking lot, referred to as Outer Mongolia, was on the southeastern edge of the Hotel property. The valets parked guest vehicles in what was called Inner Mongolia, which was much closer to the Hotel. Frequently Am took the bus to work or bicycled from his Del Mar bungalow, but today he was glad he had driven. If only Annette (he wasn't in the New Age habit of naming cars but had accepted her name along with her pink slip) cooperated, he could make his getaway and look forward to a few hours of blessed sleep.

Annette was a vision of a bygone California dream and behaved like something out of "The Twilight Zone." A 1951 Ford station wagon, the car was an anachronism that looked even more dated than her years. Annette was a bona fide woodie, a wood-paneled wagon. Nowadays there are only ersatz versions of woodies, cars with garish plastic wooden veneer. Of course those same sidings don't need the constant attention of oils, lacquers, varnish, and elbow grease, and owners don't have to worry about the sun, elements, termites, and fighting off drunks trying to get toothpick souvenirs. Am knew that woodies were the real thing, and that woodies were history, but more than anything else he knew that woodies were a pain in the ass.

He had never aspired to own a woodie, wasn't one of those Californians who pined for a visual reminder of the beach blanket gatherings of the early sixties. Decades back, woodies were the ultimate beach buggies, ideal for carrying the now-dinosaur long boards. In days of yore, surfers didn't risk only the waves, they risked hernias getting to them.

Am's friend Gerry had forced the woodie on him. When Gerry was tipped off that the DEA was investigating him, he'd decided to leave town in record time.

"You take my baby," he had told Am. "You take Annette."

Am had suggested he call Frankie Avalon.

"Just give me three thousand," he had said. "Annette's worth ten, easy."

Am had told him no. Three thousand times, no.

"But it's not like I'm really going to be selling you Annette," Gerry had explained. "When things settle down, I'll come back and reclaim Annette."

And Am's three thousand dollars?

"You mean your five thousand dollars," Gerry had said with a wink. "You know I could never give my baby up."

Ten years had passed since Am's last conversation with Gerry. His only communication had been a dog-eared post-card sent from Colombia. "How's she running?" Gerry had written. He had signed his name but left no return address. He hadn't even added the usual SoCal greeting, "The weather's here, wish you were fine."

There was a love/hate relationship between Am and Annette. Though her bikini days were long over, Annette still liked to go to the beach. Am was convinced she was a vehicle that Stephen King should write about. If you drove Annette along the coastline, she rode like a Ralph Nader dream, but unfortunately all roads didn't lead to the ocean. Annette invariably balked whenever Am strayed from her approved route.

The ignition started. Purred, even. Am pulled Annette out and drove toward the exit, toward his bed. Through the illu-mination of her headlights he saw a familiar scarecrow figure running toward them. Ted Fellows, the Hotel sous chef, was difficult to mistake. He was tall and thin and dressed in whites. His white hat was bobbing, and his arms were gesticulating wildly. Am knew Ted's apparent neediness didn't bode well. He would have ignored him, save that to do so successfully would have entailed hit-and-run. It was still tempting. Annette slowed to a stop, and Ted jumped onto the passenger's seat.

For a few seconds Ted sucked in air and was unable to speak. "It's Marcel," he said finally, either too short of breath or too indignant to say anything else.

"Marcel's the murderer?" asked Am.

Ted shook his head, sucked in some more air, then said, "This morning he learned the meaning behind road kill. And then we learned the meaning of temper tantrum. Marcel broke a few blood vessels and more than a few plates. The special should have been tossed pans."

His tale begun, Ted started breathing easier. It was Am's turn to hyperventilate.

"After exacting ample revenge for Waterloo," Ted said, "Marcel left for a few hours. When he came back, he didn't say anything to anyone. He just went into his office, closed the door behind him, and drew the curtains."

"He didn't knife anybody, did he?" asked Am. "Tell me he didn't knife anybody."

Ted shook his head. "It wasn't a knife we were afraid of, Am. It was a bomb."

"Oh, God," said Am. He had always thought Marcel was a lunatic, not a terrorist.

"We'd all seen him carry in this big burlap bag, and we couldn't help but wonder what he had in it. Then he started making mysterious trips in and out of his office. He gathered all sorts of ingredients, including a lot of herbs and spices, but he was very quiet about it, very unlike Marcel. Later that afternoon we all felt better when he started shouting orders and questioning everybody's competence. He, Marcel Charvet, wasn't going to look bad in his culinary Super Bowl because of the kitchen's ineptitude."

Am had forgotten about the food critic being feted that night. "What's the menu?"

"It's top secret. That's not unusual. Marcel's done that before. But I had this weird feeling that something wasn't right. Then, about a half hour ago, I overheard him telling the server that his special was Meurtre de la Route. Marcel made the waiter repeat the phrase several times to make sure he got it right."

"I'm not familiar with that dish," Am said.

"Neither was I," said Ted. "I figured it was some arcane dish with a fancy French name, but I couldn't find it in any of my recipe books. I even got out a French dictionary, but I wasn't sure of the spelling."

"So why didn't you just check the entrée out?"

"I did. But his Meurtre de la Route was bagged."

"Bagged?"

"Papillote. Sealed in buttered parchment paper. Sometimes you do that for flavoring and tenderizing."

"Look, Ted," said Am, "this has all been very interesting, but I'm sure you've heard about the day I've had—"

"Not ten minutes ago," said Ted, "Marcel was called out to the floor by some guests. I don't have to tell you that he could teach a peacock how to strut, especially when he has a good audience."

Marcel's next temper tantrum, thought Am, would be when he learned the staff referred to those performances as his "phallic Gallic." When summoned to tables, Marcel always donned his huge white chef's hat, the kind of headware only the Queen Mother should have been allowed to wear. Then he strolled through the restaurant as though he were the feature attraction in an Easter hat parade.

"After getting his hat," said Ted, "Marcel left his office door open, so I decided to close it. I don't know, Am, maybe I went to snoop, too. The place was a mess, littered with all of Marcel's prep work. But in the corner was his mystery bag. It was clearly not as full as it had been. And there was a smell, a reek, I wasn't familiar with. I couldn't help myself; I went over and peeked inside.

"At first I wasn't sure what was in there. You know how Marcel is about cleanliness; by this time the bag was mostly a refuse container. I had to do some sifting, and that wasn't pretty. But it beat what was at the bottom of the bag. There were still a few relatively whole specimens. They were possum."

"Opossum?"

Ted nodded. "And these weren't the kind of possum raised on some ranch," he said. "It was clear these possum hadn't died at the hands of a butcher, or even a hunter. They were sort of squashed. . . ."

"Oh, my God," Am said. "Road kill."

An idling Annette was suddenly floored. Am's driving and her response might have qualified both of them for the Cajon Speedway. He took the back way and parked with squealing brakes at the delivery entrance behind the Hotel.

"Why didn't you stop him?" asked Am.

"You know what he's like," Ted said. "I figured you were the only one he might listen to."

Meurtre de la Route. And one of the most important food critics in the country.

"It might not be too late," Ted said. "It's a five-course meal, Marcel's creations from salad to dessert."

Instead of finishing with mousse, thought Am, he'd probably conclude with Meurtre de la Mouse. He sprinted ahead of Ted, took the back stairs three at a time, threw open the service door, and sidestepped a room service waiter with a tray. It wasn't an open field, but he was able to weave through servers and dishwashers before taking a shortcut through all the cooks working the line. There he gained the passageway to the Hotel's showpiece restaurant, the Trident. And Marcel.

The chef had claimed a vantage point that allowed him to look out to the dining area without being seen. Apparently Marcel was gauging the reactions to his repast.

"Has it gone out?" Am asked.

"Haz wut gun owt?" spat Marcel.

"Your Meurtre de la Route."

"Yez," said Marcel with a wide smile, his eyes defiantly triumphant.

Ted pointed out the table. The epicure was about sixty and looked like a professional critic. His white hair was immaculately combed and parted, his necktie knotted carefully, his pencil mustache perfectly groomed. His companion, a younger man of around forty, also had a persnickety look and air.

"Do they know what they're eating?"

"If zay asked, I told ze server to tell zem zay were eatin' gibier."

Ted translated while Am wiped Marcel's spit off his face. "Wild game," he said.

"Road kill," said Marcel. "That's what everyone say, no? So I make road kill."

San Diego has no "Deer Crossing" signs, and you don't have to watch out for cattle. Few exotic animals, with the exception of migrating birds, are seen within its city limits. Along its roads can be found dead cats, dogs, and skunks. And opossums. Given the alternatives, Am supposed Marcel had chosen his road kill well. The marsupials had made themselves at home all over San Diego. They had few predators, liked trash cans more than sanitation workers, and enjoyed the balmy climate. They were also about as smart as a fur ball. Sometimes they played possum when threatened by cars.

Am thought about playing possum himself but instead found himself walking over to the road kill table. Even when standing in front of the critic and his companion, Am wasn't sure what to say. For a moment he eyed their plates. The papillote had just been opened, and the steam was rising from the dish. From what he could see, the opossum had been carved up and looked like some unidentifiable meat. Maybe the critic didn't know French and had no idea what was in front of him.

"Novel," said the older man to the younger. "How do you think Marcel got the idea to serve possum?"

"Meurtre de la Route," said the other, pronouncing the words as if he had attended the Sorbonne. "Marcel has a sly sense of humor."

"Gentlemen," said Am.

They took their eyes from their plates and looked up. "I'm Am Caulfield," he said, "the assistant general manager of the Hotel California."

They said something back, but Am wasn't listening. He

was still desperately in search of some plan. "We are honored to have you," he said.

It was evident they were used to the royal treatment, but that usually came with the after-dinner drinks. Their forks had been raised in the air long enough. They tried to dismiss Am with a few mumbled words of reciprocal thanks.

"As you know," Am said, "our entrée selection is vast. We are proud of all our dishes, and I was thinking that it might be better if you ordered off the menu so that you can feast on the succulent fare of a representational meal. It hardly seems fair to partake of a dish that our chef so rarely creates."

"The nightly specials," lectured the critic, waving a knife at Am, "are the signature, the trademark, of any quality restaurant."

Am thought about grabbing their dishes and running off with them, or of faking a seizure and falling on the table, but the knife wielder had studied under a basilisk. The critic froze his every intention.

Retreating, beaten, Am said, *"Bon appétit."*

# 34

"The specials—they are my per-og-a-teeve, no?"

PerFrogative, maybe, thought Am.

"What do you think the county health department would say about your per-og-a-teeve?" Am asked. "How many ordinances do you think we violated by serving up your Caltrans special?"

"Ham. How do you zay it? You are ovaryacting."

Twenty minutes earlier, when Am and Marcel had been exchanging screams, each might have been overreacting. Now they were in Marcel's office, and Am was just trying to get the chef to admit he had done something terribly wrong. Marcel's vocabulary was quite limited in that area, and Am was beginning to suspect that the French language didn't include the words *I am sorry*.

"What you have done, Marcel," said Am, "goes beyond a prank. You have put the Hotel's reputation on the line just because your pride was tweaked."

"Tweaked? What is zis tweaked?"

"Upset. Nettled. Bothered."

Marcel shook his head. He was still wearing his ridiculously large chef's hat. "Zis talk of road kill was a very bad thing. In zis kitchen we create wonderful food."

"But just because you perceived an insult," said Am, trying to move in for the kill like Perry Mason, "did that give you the right to serve road kill to one of the most eminent food critics in the country?"

Gastronomic virtue, evidently, was the highest of all courts. "When Marcel Charvet make a meal," he said, taking a deep breath as a buildup to an indignant spit, "any meal, it is somethin' to be remembered."

"And you see nothing wrong with what you did?"

"Have you heard any complanetz yet?"

That was the rub. They say it's not bragging if you can do it. Marcel insisted nothing was wrong with serving opossum. Wasn't it considered a delicacy in some parts of the country? The "spezals" were his domain, and he could serve whatever he wanted. He said he had decided opossum was just the thing, and since his purveyors didn't stock opossum, he quite fortuitously had just managed to—stumble, yes, stumble, that was the word—upon some.

A loud rapping at the office window put an end to their arguing. A busboy was motioning feverishly to Am. "Gunther needs you right away in the dining room, Mr. Caulfield," he said.

Gunther Schneider was the maître d' of the Trident. He resented any intervention by hotel management unless there was a problem, at which point he readily delegated complete responsibility.

"What's up?" Am asked the busboy.

"Older man is down," he said. "He's probably had a heart attack or something."

The stricken man had drawn a standing room only crowd. Am caught a glimpse of the victim's face, which was enough to make him think the man wasn't experiencing coronary problems. One of the servers had decided the same thing. He had already moved behind the man and was applying the Heimlich maneuver.

The blue face had thrown Am off. But after the victim disgorged a chewed piece of meat, and his coloring began to return to normal, Am realized the choking victim was none other than Stanley "Whiner" Weintraub. With some regrets.

Am realized it was he who had insisted that all Hotel personnel be versed in lifesaving techniques.

Whiner had been a thorn in the Hotel's side for years, or at least half a thorn. Estelle "Whiney" Weintraub was the other half. She had the shriller voice. The restaurant was getting the opportunity to hear it.

"Stanley," she said, "Stanley! Are you all right?"

Whiner tried to say something, then gave up the effort. He raised his hand weakly, showed the world he was still alive. Dammit, was Am's unspoken reaction.

No one could figure out why Whiner and Whiney always returned to the Hotel California. According to them, their room was always totally unacceptable, the food was awful, and the service was abominable. Every year the Weintraubs called on Am several times during their stay to report that the Hotel was far, far worse than it had ever been before. They pulled out laundry lists of litanies and woes, and invariably Whiner would end the conversation by saying, "I should pay you for staying here? You should pay me!"

"Murderers!"

It wasn't a good day to hear that ringing announcement. With her husband's voice temporarily impaired, Whiney had the whole floor to herself. Her bony finger was pointed Am's way, drawn, no doubt, to a familiar face to wag it under.

Nils Olsen looked puzzled. He wasn't getting the hero's reception he expected for saving Mr. Weintraub's life. Nils had been in the United States for half a dozen years, had come from Sweden as a student, and had not wanted to return to his country's cold winters. Then again, he hadn't bargained for this much warmth.

"You didn't warn us about the bones! Are you operating with a license to kill?"

While Whiney's attack was heating up, Nils motioned Am over and whispered in his ear. In the middle of her ranting, Am made so bold as to interrupt.

"There were no bones, Mrs. Weintraub. Your husband had the veal marsala. . . . "

Whiney raised her voice a few decibels. It was an old tactic of the Weintraubs. If they ever looked as though they were losing an argument, the hysterics started. "My husband almost dies of food poisoning, and you have to make like a wiseguy. Is that right? Is that decent?"

"Your husband was choking on a piece of veal," Am insisted. "That hardly qualifies as food poisoning. . . . "

"It was dry. He told me that, said it before his throat was land mined. Stanley! Are you all right?"

He waved again, motioned that he was ready to rise to his feet. Nils started to assist him, but that wasn't to Whiney's liking.

"I'll help him," she said. "Stanley! Are you all right?"

He was flapping his whole arm now. Soon, Am knew, too soon, he'd be flapping his mouth.

"Mrs. Weintraub, will you be needing any assistance up to your room?"

"Why do you ask? Do most of your restaurant guests need to be carried out on stretchers?"

"Perhaps Mr. Weintraub would like to sit for a minute, have a glass of water. . . . "

"We'll need a taster before we ever sit here again."

Am shut his mouth. It was either that or bite off his tongue. But rather than having to endure future accountings of how the uncaring staff had left her dying husband to crawl to his room, and instead of delegating the unpleasant chore of accompanying the Weintraubs to another employee, Am decided that he should escort the couple to their room.

Whiney's diatribe never stopped. She was surprised that the Hotel was still in business; why, when they had checked in, they were forced to wait two hours for their room ("But didn't you check in at ten in the morning, Mrs. Weintraub?") and even then hadn't gotten the room they wanted ("As I understand it, Mrs. Weintraub, the room you wanted was a suite, but when it was offered, you wanted it for the same rate as a studio guest room"). And now her husband had been poisoned. Poisoned. Am decided not to argue that point. He wasn't certain he could sincerely object to the idea.

"It isn't enough that people jump from their balconies," she said, "and get murdered in their rooms. No. Now you're trying to kill people in your restaurants. Is this a war zone or a hotel? What? Do you give people the choice of doggie bags or body bags?"

Whiney was still complaining on her doorstep when Am announced, "Thankyouandgoodnight." He suspected Whiner's voice was already back, but even he couldn't get a word in when his wife was on a roll.

Common sense dictated to Am that he should cut his losses and leave, but there was still the matter of making Marcel see that his actions could not be condoned. It would have been nice if a contrite Marcel had been waiting in the kitchen, but the chef had been called to a table. Wonderful. Whenever praise was heaped on Marcel, he was twice as insufferable.

"Am?"

Nils Olsen had an expectant look on his face.

"Mr. Weintraub's fine, Nils," he said.

He nodded. But that wasn't his question. There was another priority. "They didn't sign their guest check, Am. Gunther said I should ask you about it."

Translation: Is it all right if I add the gratuity to their check?

Servers always try to be mind readers. When stiffed, they invariably imagine that the patron meant to leave a gratuity but somehow forgot—that, or they assumed it was part of the guest check. The rule in the Hotel California's restaurants was never to assume a guest's intentions. If they didn't include a gratuity, that was that. Of course that was an edict that had been handed down by nontipped management, and this was an out-of-the-ordinary situation.

"Had the Weintraubs pretty much finished their dinners?" Am asked.

"There wasn't a thing left on their plates," said Nils. "He choked on his last bite of veal."

Am debated for a moment. "Put yourself down for fifteen percent, Nils," he said, "and close it out to their room number."

"Thank you, Am."

He started walking away, but Am called him back. "If you save his life again, Nils," he said, "you're fired."

Nils searched Am's face. Even after years in the country, he still wasn't sure of American humor. "That's a joke, yes?"

"Ask me next week."

There are worse places to wait than in a cavernous hotel kitchen. Rather than go home and open a can of beans and a can of beer and contemplate the longest day of his life, Am decided to take advantage of one of the great perquisites of hotel management and eat a fine meal. Of course, a condemned prisoner gets that same privilege. Am didn't feel like waiting for food, so he wrote out a slip for prime rib. Staff always takes care of staff very well. He was cut off the better part of a cow and given enough potatoes and vegetables du jour to feed three people. As he walked by with his bounty, the pantry chef told him to save room for some fresh puff pastries smothered in chocolate-dipped strawberries "that anyone would die for."

The aromas in a great kitchen are almost meals in themselves. The scents primed Am's appetite even before he sat down. He hadn't known how hungry he was and in short order did the impossible: finished his plate and even had room enough for one of those decadent puff pastries.

Marcel still hadn't returned, and once again Am considered just leaving, but his stubbornness wouldn't let him do that. He decided to go out to the restaurant and look for him. That proved to be a tactical mistake. The chef was sitting at the critic's table. From his rapturous expression, he might as well have been in bed with him. All he needed was a pillow and a cigarette. Am tried to retreat, but it was too late.

"Ham! Ham!"

Reluctantly he walked over to the table. The critic and his friend might have had to eat opossum, but no doubt that was a tastier dish than crow.

"Ham," Marcel said, "zis gentleman zink I am a genus, and I zay, who am I to argue?"

Three people laughed.

"A genus, yes," said Am. "But we're still not sure of the species."

No one smiled, and the critic went so far as to decide Am needed another lecture. "A great chef always innovates, is never complacent. Chef Marcel tells us he never attempted this dish before."

"He gambled," Am admitted.

"He won," said the younger man. "It was delicious. Gamey yet tempered."

Temper did have something to do with it, Am thought.

"I could listen to zis all night," said Marcel.

"Marcel is fond of telling us what he served at the Last Supper," said Am.

Marcel's possum was apparently much better loved than Am's quips. He excused himself, afraid if he watched much longer, Marcel might bloat up to the point of exploding.

Only management was allowed to use the kitchen as a shortcut, probably because management knew that it was rarely a shortcut at all. On his intended way to the parking lot, Am was waylaid by the sight of one of his favorite desserts: double chocolate amaretto mousse. He paused to ask the pantry cook if there was a spoon to lick, and his inquiry resulted in a parfait glass chock full of the mousse. It took Am a few minutes to work through his rapture. He probably shouldn't have stopped by his office, but there was a note he remembered he should write.

He felt oddly content. Having a full stomach might have had something to do with that. For most of the day the world had seemed to be collapsing under his feet, but now that his maw was filled he felt the cosmos had somehow become aright.

Just as Am entered his office, the phone rang. He saw that the call was originating from Gunther's extension. With each ring the phone seemed to ring louder, but Am resisted the temptation to pick it up. It was late, and he didn't have it in him to fight any more dragons. The ringing stopped, and Am praised the Almighty. The note he had thought it necessary to write was becoming less important by the moment. Then the phone started ringing again. This time it was the front desk calling, and again Am wouldn't answer. I can sneak out, he thought. But he had neglected to lock his office door. The Weintraubs had visited him countless times before and knew only too well where to find him. They entered from the lobby, walking inside without knocking and looking like spaghetti western villains out for revenge.

"Went back to the restaurant," he said.

"Returned to the scene of the crime," she said.

"I thought we might get hungry later," said Whiner.

"Midnight snack," Whiney chimed in.

"So I asked what happened to my dinner."

"'Where is it?' he asked."

"And they told me they had thrown it out."

"Threw it away without asking," she said.

They looked at Am expectantly. That was his cue to offer apologies and compensation. He continually amazed guests with his stupidity at not understanding what they thought was obvious.

"I talked with your server, Mr. Weintraub," he said. "He told me that both you and your wife had finished your dinners. . . ."

Whiner held up his right arm and his index finger. "But I hadn't finished," he said.

"The only thing you didn't eat was that last piece of veal that—"

"A man pays for his meal, isn't he entitled to all of it?"

Am looked from one face to the other. He hoped they were joking, but they weren't smiling.

"Mr. Weintraub, I find it difficult to believe—"

"I find it difficult to believe that you charged me for a meal I didn't finish. You did that, didn't you? Authorized that bill to be signed over to our room?"

"When you left the restaurant you weren't in any condition—"

"Now I've returned. And I'm hungry. But my meat isn't there. I don't think I should have to pay for that entrée. Or I should have another one made for me."

"In all fairness, don't you think—"

"Another entrée, or I refuse to pay."

"We'll make your entrée," said Am.

That wasn't the answer Whiner wanted, but it was still victory enough. "Have it sent to the room," he said.

"We wouldn't dine in one of your restaurants again," she said.

"It will be sent up," Am promised.

They walked out of his office, and Am walked back to the kitchen. Marcel was sitting in his office, smoking a cigar. His preferred spot was directly under the No Smoking sign.

Marcel's burlap bag was on the floor. Am reached deep inside it and pulled out a particularly sorry specimen of squashed opossum. Even Marcel, who always seemed oblivious to smells, sniffed disdainfully.

"Weintraubs," said Am.

*"Mon Dieu,"* said Marcel.

The chef had heard displeasing words from those—those—cretins before.

"He never finished his veal marsala," said Am. He held up the opossum. "This," he said, "is going to be the veal marsala."

"But you need to marinate ze possum meat, Ham," said Marcel. "You need to add ze herbs, and stoop it in ze spices, and—"

Am dropped the opossum in front of him. "This," he repeated, "is the veal marsala. They won't eat it tonight. And you know how the taste and complexion of meat can change overnight."

"But what if zay complain? What if zay say eat's not veal?"

"Then we play possum," said Am.

# 35

Most large hotels have resident managers. The perks of such a position are many. A casual observer might consider the job as being the closest thing to royalty. Meals are provided by the hotel, along with daily maid service and laundry privileges. But the sword of Damocles also comes with the job. Am had lived at hotels before but had never much liked it, could never shake the feeling that he was on the job twenty-four hours a day and that doom was always hanging over his head. Whenever the phone rang, he anticipated it to be a problem, not a friend. And there was the fishbowl feeling, the staff monitoring the goings-on of his life as if it were a spectator sport. But had he still been a resident manager, Am reflected, staff wouldn't have had much to talk about lately. Nowadays he was having trouble getting a life separate from work. The antidote for many suffering job burnout is a change of scenery, an escape to some hotel where they can be pampered. But that didn't work for Am. Whenever he visited other properties he felt like a magician analyzing another practitioner's tricks. A getaway would be good, though, maybe a surfing trip down the Baja peninsula or a camping excursion to some secluded canyon in the Anza-Borrego Desert. The desert, located within the boundaries of San

Diego County, was itself larger than some states, while the
county as a whole could claim more square miles than half a
dozen states. Within San Diego County were mountains,
deserts, and the ocean. Anyone with time and money would
be hard-pressed to ask for a more diverse and pleasant locale,
but Am always seemed to be short either the hours or the
cash.

Too tired to read, too numb to move, Am resorted to the
intended soporific of television. His timing couldn't have
been worse. The lead story on the eleven o'clock news was
the murders at the Hotel. According to the report, Jane Doe
still hadn't been identified, and neither had the murderer.
There was a clip of McHugh responding to (or was that
evading?) the reporter's questions. Am thought there was
more to be learned by the detective's omissions than in what
he said. On air, McHugh never mentioned the cleaning up of
the crime scene or how the suspected murderer had gained
access to the guest room in the first place.

For Am, the worst part of the news was having to watch
himself being interviewed. He thought he had the presence
of a cornered fox in a room of baying hounds. The only good
thing about his segment was that it was short. Maybe his unintelligible mumbling had something to do with that. Am
was glad he had listened to the housekeeper's suggestion of
filling the room with flowers. He had sarcastically asked if
she wanted to make it look even more like a funeral parlor,
but Barb had countered that the viewers might notice the
pretty arrangements more than the story being presented. She
had artfully positioned the flowers in front of the dais so as
to obscure the Hotel California display (usually burnished to
a high polish whenever the media was around). Barb's flowers had shown up beautifully.

Murders and festive flowers made for conflicting signals.
The day had been full of those. Things are not always as they
seem, thought Am, words he associated with Conrad, an el-
derly bellman who had worked at his last hotel. Ninety-nine
times out of one hundred, Conrad said, he could gauge his tip
to within a dollar of what he would ultimately receive, but
every so often he encountered a guest who fooled him, who
offered him a hauteur and a smile that all but guaranteed a

substantial promissory note. "The kind of guest," according
to Conrad, "who passes along a folded bill into your palm as
if deeding you the world."

Bellmen know they're supposed to offer a performance
commensurate with their tip. The sure knowledge of a large
gratuity makes them execute bows that come to within an
inch of kowtowing. When receiving a palmed bill, bellmen
must read the signals with which it is offered and then take a
leap of faith. The etiquette of the situation requires the bellman to offer adequate pomp and circumstance even before
knowing the denomination given to them. That moment of
truth comes only after the bellman has exited the guest quar-
ters and is out in the hallway.

"You open your hand," said Conrad, "and you expect
Jackson, but sweet Ben Franklin or handsome U. S. Grant
aren't unheard-of. You'll settle for Hamilton, a fair trade for
your performance, but you know that Lincoln sometimes
comes up.

"But damn," said the bellman, "if there aren't times when
you don't find yourself looking eye to eye with solitary
George Washington. Things are not always as they seem."

Was this one of those times? thought Am. Had the police
offered only a one-dollar explanation to a big-ticket crime?

As if listening for answers, Am heard a voice, then realized it was only the call of the stationmaster. Because his
California bungalow was so close to Del Mar's train station,
Am heard the train announcements often enough to know all
of Amtrak's offerings. This would be the last commuter train
of the night, the 11:05 p.m. run, heading south to downtown
San Diego. Am had set his alarm early enough that he'd
probably hear the 5:47 a.m. train going north.

With stops in Oceanside, San Clemente, San Juan Capistrano, Santa Ana, Anaheim, Fullerton, and Los Angeles, he
thought, stops he had heard announced thousands of times.

One day I'm going to play hooky from work, Am vowed,
and I'm going to take that train north, and get off at every
one of those stops.

And then what? Author Paul Theroux had just kept traveling, finding more and more train lines, rails across conti-
nents. But there is a profound difference between being a

traveler and a hotelier. Am had made his permanence out of transience. He had shared in enough stories and travels as to almost satiate his own wanderlust. Travelers need their ports. That's what they talk about over the next horizon. And there were some things in his port he needed to make right—for the travelers, for himself.

There came a long train whistle, and then there came sleep.

# 36

"I'm just going to work," said Am, using the same soothing tones he would employ if encountering a large, mean-looking, unchained dog. "Just a beautiful drive along the coast."

Annette started right up. She probably would have been scrap years back if it hadn't been for Am's neighbor, Jimbo, who liked nothing better than working on old cars. Jimbo volunteered his time for "parts and beer," neither one of which came cheap. His beer belly (proudly referred to by Jimbo as his "Milwaukee goiter") would have done a sumo wrestler proud; by Am's figuring, he was in to him for a microbrewery.

I'm raising a car instead of raising a child, Am thought. Maybe it was time to trade in Annette for something whose upkeep wouldn't be so expensive—say, the *Queen Mary*. It was not an observation he dared make aloud.

As if to belie her age and temperament, Annette cantered along old 101. The route winds along the coast, and through Del Mar offers such scenery as to make even jaded commuters look twice. On the approach to Torrey Pines State Reserve, there are no buildings to obscure the view of the water; to the west there is only the beach and the expanse of ocean. Am did his usual morning scouting for dolphins (he

did the same in the afternoon but usually spotted more biki-
nis than wildlife) but didn't see any. The dolphins often liked
to gambol along the surfline, sometimes even taking the
waves like seasoned surfers. A storm had passed through
Baja a few days earlier, unusual weather for September, but
it suited the surfers just fine. They were out in abundance,
waiting for their rides to glory. The wind was up, and the
waves were high. Spindrift dotted Annette's windshield,
enough to necessitate turning on the wipers. They worked, if
irregularly: the story of the car.

There is a point in every commute where the workday be-
gins, where you are on company time even if you're nowhere
near the time clock. When Am passed Torrey Pines Beach,
and the cliffs blocked any potential roadside viewing of dolphins and mermaids, he started thinking about work. He
didn't consciously see the Torrey Pines (found naturally in
only two places in the world and distinguished from other
pine trees by its cluster of five needles), or Scripps Clinic, or
the Salk Institute, or the University of California at San
Diego, or even the long pier marking Scripps Institution of
Oceanography. For the last six miles of his drive Am was
planning out his workday and praying that there wouldn't be
any new land mines waiting for him.

On his desk were only two incident-related reports, one of
which was written on cocktail napkins numbered one
through six. The thespians must have decided it was their
turn to make a nuisance of themselves. They had closed
down the Breakers Lounge the night before, and the bartender had reviewed their show. Between drinks, the actors
had taken turns doing scenes from their favorite plays:
Shakespeare in the rounds.

Some of their performances had been inspired by the Bob
Johnsons. The appearance of Bob Johnsons (identified by
their name tags) had prompted denunciatory scenes (Ten-
nessee Williams was evidently a popular selection, as was
Eugene O'Neill), and several times during the course of the
evening the hennaed playwright had, with pointed finger, announced her plight: "It was supposed to be a six-act play,
one for every meal, and red herrings for snacks, but, alas, the
Philistines would not have it." The bartender/critic didn't

think their vituperation as commanding as other performances. The thespians' final curtain call came at two a.m., with closing scenes from *Our Town,* and apparently there wasn't a dry eye in the lounge.

The last of the cocktail napkins suggested employing the actors at the Breakers for just such performances, as they had proved more popular than the usual piano bar. The postscript, which was written around what looked to be the partial remains of a green olive, noted that the actors had run up a six-hundred-dollar bar bill. Am didn't find that tab as frightening as the bartender's suggestion and firmly filed his note away.

The other report was left by one of the Brown's Guards. Included was a Polaroid shot of a Hotel reader board that had been tampered with. Apparently someone had neglected to lock up the display, and the Jackson-Ropenhauser Dinner Party in the Whaling Room had been changed into Jack the Ripper Was Here. Am was sure the alteration was only a prank, but given the circumstances it didn't strike him as funny. Any signboard is a magnet for attempted highjinks. Given the opportunity, people like to play Scrabble with the letters. At most hotels electronic reader boards have taken away that creativity. Entries on an electronic board are typed on a terminal, which eliminates the laborious process of hand-posting the letters, but the Hotel California still eschewed such gadgetry, preferring its wooden letters and large oaken reader boards. Am wondered when tradition would yield to labor costs.

The reader boards were scrutinized by more than group and banquet participants trying to find out where their function was being held. The Hotel was visited daily by sales representatives of other hotels, callers the industry refers to as reader board readers. The readers were there for the sole purpose of writing down which groups the Hotel was hosting. They compiled their lists with the hope that in the future they could lure those same conventions to their properties. One GM Am worked under had vehemently hated reader board readers. He was all too aware of the half dozen or so "vultures" who visited the property daily, and the sight of their "carrion feeding" always incensed him. The happiest

Am had ever seen his boss was the day of the bogus reader board entries. On display were the purported gatherings of a Pornography Making Workshop, a Jim Jones Kool-Aid Tasting, a Symposium on Endangered Faeces, and a Reunion of the Manson Family. What delighted the GM most was how the reader board readers blithely wrote down the entries in front of them, never questioning what was there.

Was Am doing the same thing? Was there something about the murders he was taking at face value? Getting the chance for deep thought in any workplace is a rare event. There was something in the back of Am's mind that wanted to come out, but the thought was driven away by the rapping at his office door. Whoever was doing the knocking had taken loud lessons from a bull elephant.

Shouting, of necessity: "Come in."

Jimmy Mazzelli opened the door. "Problem, Am," he said.

Problem. Why was that a word that usually prefaced his nickname? Jimmy helped himself to an empty chair, his slouch instantaneous.

"What's the problem, Jimmy?"

"Gent's losing his cool at the front desk. Last night one of my boys apparently delivered his laundry to the wrong room. Man didn't notice until this morning. We're tracking it down now."

Jimmy liked to refer to himself as the bell captain and the other bellmen as "his boys," but his was a self-appointed title.

"Man's name?"

"Hazleton."

"Room?"

"Three thirty-eight."

"How much laundry?"

Jimmy handed over two pink laundry slips, and Am whistled. The last time he had seen a similar laundry bill was when the duke and duchess had stayed at the Hotel.

"Who delivered it?"

"Wrong way."

"God. Find it, would you?"

"Like I told the gent, won't be more than fifteen minutes before we get it to him. We already talked to Wrong Way on the phone, and he narrowed it down to half a dozen rooms or so."

"How could he forget where he delivered that much laundry?" asked Am. "How is that humanly possible?"

Jimmy coughed behind his hand. Wrong Way wasn't someone he ever bad-mouthed; he made Jimmy appear the epitome of competence.

"Why don't you send Mr. Hazleton back to me."

"Righto, Am."

As usual, Jimmy had left out a telling part of the story. When Mr. Hazleton walked into the room, Am expected a man dressed to the nines, but Hazleton looked more like he was auditioning as a flasher. He was wearing a raincoat and shoes and apparently nothing else. Am remembered to extend more than his jaw, but Hazleton favored a harangue to his handshake.

"I'd like to know what kind of hotel you're running here?" he asked.

It was a good question, one Am often asked himself. "Why don't you sit down, Mr. Hazleton," he said. "Would you like some coffee or tea?"

The offer calmed the guest slightly. "Nothing," he said. "I just want my laundry."

"Lots of laundry," said Am.

"Yes," he said, "lots of laundry. And the last time I stayed at this hotel the same damn thing happened. This is the second time my laundry's turned up missing in action."

There is a multiplying factor to pent-up rage. It explained why Hazleton was out to shoot bear in nothing but his raincoat. Am let him have his say.

"Why is it," he continued, "that your property can't manage a simple thing like delivering the damn laundry to the right room?"

The situation called for sympathetic noises, which Am offered. Hotel managers are good at soothing sounds. Anyone who works in hotels doesn't need to use a thesaurus for the word *sorry*. They live the listings. Mr. Hazleton continued to bemoan his missing laundry, and Am continued to make sounds. For want of anything else to do, Am also shuffled exhibits A and B, the pink laundry slips. Belatedly he gave them a closer glance and decided they were friendly to the defense. He passed them over to Hazleton.

"I'm just guessing," he said, "but the bellman might have misinterpreted your writing. I happen to know you're in room 338, but from these slips I can see how the items might have been taken to room 328. Or 358. Or 339. Or 388. Or even 329."

At the Hotel, guests fill out their own laundry slips, and Hazleton's writing should have gotten him into medical school. Hazleton examined his own writing and was faced with the numeric indictment. "Hmmmm," he said.

"I'm sure we'll have the laundry to your room in a matter of minutes," Am said. "In the future, though, we'll take pains to make sure this never happens again."

Hazleton nodded, a much more timid man than the one who had entered Am's office. He stood up, paused to give an embarrassed little wave, then started for the door. As he passed by, Am couldn't help but notice that he wasn't wearing any socks with his black shoes. Stockings had been part of his missing laundry consignment.

"Mr. Hazleton?"

He turned.

"Why so much cleaning?"

Am violated his own rule by voicing his curiosity. It's okay to be nosy if you work in a hotel, as long as you're silent about it. Twelve suits, fourteen ties, three sports jackets, and five pairs of pants had been sent out for dry cleaning and the laundry ticket included bags of dress shirts, underwear, and socks.

Hazleton's expression both pleaded the Fifth and told Am to go to hell, but a bending of the Constitution prevailed. "I don't like to travel," he said. "The company knows it. So I save my laundry and dry cleaning and wait for them to send me out. There are per diems on most things, but not laundry. I make them pay."

He shuffled out, black shoes and no socks, Willy Loman gone anarchic. Jimmy Mazzelli met him just outside the door. "Found your laundry, sir," he said. "Delivered all safe and sound to your room now. We'll make sure it don't happen again, you can be sure of that."

"Jimmy," Am called, stopping the bellman before his Boy Scout act got on track. Canadian Mounties can learn a thing or two from bellmen. They not only get their man, they usually get a tip at the same time. An experienced bellman in search of a gratuity is about as easy to shake as a pit bull with a good hold.

Jimmy reluctantly left his game. Maybe he realized a man wearing only a raincoat wasn't likely to be carrying a wallet, or maybe there was something in the tone of Am's voice that activated his self-preservation instinct.

"Yes, Am?"

"Bring me the delivery logs."

Hotels are great believers in signing everything in and out. The rationale behind the paperwork is sound. Whenever a hotel accepts anything through its employees, a bailment relationship is established, which means if a hotel employee agrees to hang up a sable coat on a hanger in the back for a few minutes, and that coat disappears, the hotel is liable for the loss. Be it mail, deliveries, messages, faxes, or laundry, all items at the Hotel were supposed to be accounted for, both coming and going.

With Jimmy watching over his shoulder, Am opened the log book to the laundry and dry cleaning entries. Mr. Hazleton's clothing had been signed in and out. The correct room number had been entered, and Wrong Way had initialed delivery to room 338. The bellman's mistake was that he had trusted to the scrawl of a laundry slip rather than checking off the tag with the room number entered into the log. Incompetence can always beat any system.

More for Jimmy's sake than his own, Am flipped through several pages of the log book, an obligatory reviewing of the troops that was supposed to be a reminder of management's watchfulness. A few initials hadn't been entered, enough for Am to be able to grouse. Not that such shortcomings were ever noticed until a package turned up missing. Or until laundry was taken to the wrong room.

Because room 605 had so occupied Am's mind, he noticed what would have otherwise been an innocuous entry on one of the delivery sheets. Two days ago there had been a delivery to the murder room, a bottle of Robert Mondavi Cabernet

Sauvignon and a wheel of cheese. The delivery had been accepted at 4:40 p.m., and the receiving clerk's initials were T.K. The log showed the intended recipient was David Stern. The signature of whoever had dropped the wine and cheese at the desk looked indecipherable, but T.K. had noted "Card attached." The final notation showed that delivery had taken place at 4:45 p.m. by A.S.

Am tapped at the initials, brought Jimmy's eyes to them. "Who's A.S.?"

Jimmy didn't even have to think: "Albert Slocum. He in trouble?"

Am didn't answer. McHugh had put the time of deaths at late afternoon or early evening, which would have been about when the wine and cheese were taken up to the room. The delivery bothered Am. The murdered lawyer had wanted his anonymity protected. Who had known he was there to send the wine and cheese?

He'd have to talk with T.K. and with Albert. He wondered what they had seen and what they remembered.

And he wondered if the couple had clinked wineglasses together and made a final toast before being murdered.

# 37

"McHugh."

"I have a request," said Am. "Would you please fax me a list of everything that was inventoried in room six oh five?"

Just getting through to McHugh had been difficult. Am had been transferred and put on hold half a dozen times, had been forced to plead his case to one skeptical voice after another. Now he finally had an audience with the greatest skeptic of them all.

"Why?" asked McHugh, sounding even less ready than usual to suffer fools.

"A bottle of wine and some cheese were delivered up to that room just before five on the day the murders took place. There was a card with the delivery. I'm curious as to who did the sending."

"You're curious about a lot of things." McHugh didn't say anything else for half a minute, but Am heard him rustling papers. Finally: "We didn't find any bottle, or cheese, or note in the room."

"Has an alcohol blood level been done on the victims?"

"Jesus. I suppose this couple opened their honor bar and out popped a dwarf hooker whose MO was putting Mickey Finns in the airline bottles."

Am made a dignified attempt at blackmail. "Was it my imagination, or did I hear on the news that the police were interested in receiving any and all information that might be useful to them in the Hotel double-murder case?"

"I'll put it on the list," said McHugh.

He didn't have to say it; Am knew about where it would be positioned on the list. As if defending himself against that unspoken charge, the detective said, "They probably ate the cheese, and drank the *vino*, then stuck the empty bottle outside the door for one of your monkey suits to pick up."

"Probably."

Still, even McHugh couldn't ignore the matter entirely. "Who delivered the stuff to the room?"

"The wine and cheese were dropped off at the front desk and a bellman took them up. I have a call in to both the clerk who accepted the delivery and the bellman who took them up."

McHugh asked for their names and telephone numbers and when they were next scheduled to work. Before supplying the information, Am exacted a price. "I'd still appreciate that inventory. It might help if I knew what was in the room and what wasn't."

"Why, sure," said the detective, his tone unusually conciliatory. "What's your number? I'll fax it right over to you."

Surprised, Am gave him the number and his thanks. As promised, the fax arrived soon after their conversation. There was a long list of inventoried items, but only one entry was circled: condoms. That explained the detective's alacrity. Next to it, McHugh had written: "Do you think there's a connection?"

Out loud, Am announced, "Asshole." To himself he made a vow: I'm going to show that man.

His imprecation hadn't gone unheard. Barbara Terry had walked in on it and now stood in the middle of his office, looking uncertain as to whether she should proceed. "Is this a bad time, Am?"

"Is there ever a good time, Barb?"

She chuckled. Barb had been a housekeeper for more than forty years, had cleaned about everything and seen about everything, and yet she still didn't despair. There are people who reaffirm your faith in humanity. Barb was one of those. One of Hercules' twelve labors was the cleaning of the Augean stables in a single day, a matter of clearing out thirty years of deposits left by three thousand oxen. To Am's thinking, Barb had to perform a similar feat every day. White-haired and round, she didn't look like Hercules, but she wasn't one to shrink from combat, either—if the cause was just. Over the years Am had learned to read her eyes; usually they were a laughing blue, but when joined to battle, there was a fierceness to them. They now carried that look.

"I'm told Mr. Harmon will be checking in today, Am."

The name didn't mean anything to him. "Mr. Harmon . . . ?"

"I'm sure Chief Horton must have mentioned him to you. The Chief was on the case this last year. He said that Mr. Harmon made him, that is, gave him gas like a . . . Well, never mind. Suffice to say, Mr. Harmon put a bee in both of our bonnets."

"What's Harmon's crime?"

"He's an adulterator."

Barb liked her food and her words plain. She was direct, if not always grammatical. Am figured her complaint was a few letters off.

"It's been a long time," he said, "since those days when there were signs in hotels saying that because it was improper to entertain guests of the opposite sex in the bedrooms, the lobby should be used for that purpose. We're not in the morality business, Barb."

"Oh, that," she said, waving her hand to signify the inconsequential. "I said adulterator. Not adulterer."

"Adulterator? Of what?"

"Of our honor bars. It wasn't easy to track him, Am. Oh, no. He liked to drink and then counterfeit all sorts of liquors. If he'd just done the Scotch, or bourbon, or vodka, we might have caught on to him easier. But he seems to have a taste for everything with a proof."

Her outrage finally made sense to Am. One of the first tricks you learn as a child is to replace the gum wrapper in its package after the gum has been removed. You generously offer a stick of gum to any and all and laugh at the apparent chagrin of those duped. Usually the luster of such a prank wears off in adolescence. Usually.

The Hotel California supplies honor bars in all of its rooms. The term *honor bar* is certainly a misnomer. The guest is supposed to fill out a form for all items consumed, thus the "honor." Not that any hotel accepts the word of its guests; there are attendants who monitor and restock the portable bars on a daily basis. Those same attendants are supposed to be checking the seals on the liquor to make sure they haven't been tampered with, a task not altogether easy because of the diminutive bottles. For some guests, there is no honor in honor bars. They do worse than water down a drink; they substitute $H_2O$ for Absolut vodka, Johnnie Walker Scotch, and Tanqueray gin, or cola for Jack Daniel's, or Jim Beam.

"The Chief and I decided we had to wish more than a hangover on the culprits," said Barb. "Whenever we received a report of a tampered-with honor bar, we went back and recorded the names of all guests who had been in the room the previous three months. That's about how fast you can count on most of the liquor inventory turning over. Over the last year the Chief documented more than thirty cases of minibar tampering, and one name can be linked to six of those occurrences. Mr. Harmon's been with us six times in six different rooms during the past year, and on each of his visits someone's fiddled with the liquor in those rooms."

Am had heard from some of those irate guests. Harmon had, he thought, turned water into whine. Tamper-proof systems had recently been established for honor bars, but Kendrick hadn't yet seen fit to switch. At least Harmon got his kicks only from getting free booze. What if he had decided to adulterate the drinks with castor oil, or worse?

Indignantly Barb said, "He'd probably switch water for brandy in a St. Bernard's cask."

"He's a regular, Barb," Am observed. Those were words staff groaned at. Hotel managers tend to forgive the idiosyncracies of regulars.

Barb grimaced. "Am, you're not saying—"

"I just need to know what you're up to. Whatever you do, it's sure to end up on my lap."

The housekeeper motioned for Am to wait a moment, then she walked out of his office, yelled "Pablo," and reentered the room. A tinkle of glassware preceded Pablo's entrance. The houseman's cart was laden with little bottles.

"Some is tea," said Barb, "and some is cola, and some is water, and some is a little bit of everything. It should pass inspection, I think."

Carrie Nation wouldn't have hesitated swinging her ax. To all appearances, the bogus booze looked genuine. Trojan horse payback. The housekeeper looked at Am expectantly.

He knew it violated ABC regulations. He knew it was contrary to city health codes. He knew it meant a guest, a regular, would probably want to chew his ass (or was that liver?) over this. "Okay," Am said.

She reached out a hand and touched his cheek, then remembered her task. The housekeeper had a mission from God. She urged her cavalry forward, and Am listened to the charge of clinking bottles.

It was more fun dealing with adulterated beverages, Am thought, than with murder. Sighing, he returned to McHugh's list and started going over what had been left in the room. When the list started to blur, he leaned back on his chair and balanced the paper on his nose. That's when Sharon walked in. Am was glad that this time he wasn't feeling a bra. His eyes somewhat hidden by the paper, he was able to take a long and not too obvious look at Sharon. She appeared tired, as tired as he did. Odd. The night before she had left a few hours before he had.

"Nose to the grindstone?" she asked.

With the paper still balanced on his nose, a pose that was probably the result of too many visits to Sea World, Am told her about his morning. Then, providing his own gust of wind, he blew the paper toward Sharon, who made a shoestring catch.

"McHugh's inventory of six oh five," he said. "And his dig."

Sharon looked over the list. Her mouth tightened slightly when she saw what Am was referring to.

"I've been wondering how many people knew David Stern

was in that room," said Am, "and which one of them sent the wine and cheese."

Sharon's brow furrowed. "If he was so intent on privacy," she asked, "why would he let anyone know he was here?"

"I don't know," said Am. "That was his business. I only wish we had respected his seclusion. The delivery should not have been accepted. There were excuses, naturally. The desk was busy, and T.K. took in the wine and cheese before he noticed Stern's status. He wasn't sure what to do, so he asked Roger, who put the whole thing back in his lap. T.K. figured that since the delivery had come with a name and an accompanying note, it was okay to have it sent up." Am sighed.

"You don't sound happy with his decision."

"I'm not. The wine and cheese should have been held at the desk just like anything else directed to Mr. Stern. Unless otherwise instructed, he shouldn't have been disturbed. Even his message light shouldn't have been activated."

"Is that common? Guests asking for complete privacy?"

"It happens. And it's not always because some hanky-panky is going on. Sometimes there's sensitive business. Sometimes it's on doctor's orders. Sometimes it's a VIP who needs to find herself and not her press clippings."

"But this wasn't one of those instances, was it?"

Am shrugged.

"And neither one of us thinks this was a case of a burglary gone bad. Which means what?"

His suppositions, if any, were interrupted by yet another visitor, who stuck his head into Am's office. "Morning, Am."

Am introduced Ward Ankeney to Sharon. Ward was an avuncular sort who often pointed to his thinning hair as proof positive that he had been keeping the Hotel's books for the last dozen years. His title was controller, but anyone who asked what he did invariably heard him reply, "Bean counter." Ward never looked comfortable unless both of his hands were occupied. He always had a pipe in one hand, usually unlit, and with the other he was invariably punching away at a computer, or calculator, or a ten-key. This time he had his usual pipe in the one hand, and in the other were some papers. Reluctantly he gave up the papers to Am, leaving his right hand without a task.

"Copies of six oh five's charges," Ward said, his free hand coming to life with operatic gestures and then waving goodbye.

Am had forgotten that he had asked for the room charges. Perhaps subconsciously he was trying to black out as much as possible from the day before. Convenient amnesia. As if attempting a jigsaw puzzle, he laid the charges on his desk and bent over them. Sharon came around behind him and joined in the scrutinizing.

"They sure ate well," she said.

Am didn't comment. He picked up one of the pages, punched it slightly, and said, "That explains it."

"What?"

Without answering, he punched into his computer, called up 605's charges, and handed Sharon a printout. "Last night," he said, "I called up this account. And that's when a room service charge caught my attention. This one."

Am passed Sharon the copy. "I thought it must have been a large order, but it wasn't. Just a solitary bottle. I was curious because of the time of delivery. Death arrived shortly after room service. It must have been some party up there, fine wine, cheese, and, to top it off, Dom Pérignon. Then a double murder. With our staff going in and out of the room, I figure there's a good chance either the bellman or room service waiter saw something."

"Maybe," said Sharon, her excitement ill suppressed.

Her tone made Am turn around. Sharon's face was flushed. "Notice the signatures," she said.

He was prepared to tell her that an individual's signature could vary greatly, the result of everything from a guest's being drunk to their using any handy surface (a server's back was quite often the object of choice) to sign a check. But the David Stern who had signed three other room service checks was clearly not the same David Stern who had signed for the last bottle of bubbly. There had to be a logical answer.

Almost triumphantly, Am announced, "The woman signed for it."

Sharon stared at the writing. "That doesn't look like a woman's signature."

It was Am's turn to scrutinize the scrawl once more. The handwriting did look masculine. "Lots of women have a blocky signature."

Sharon didn't appear to be listening. She handed Am a copy of another charge. "Did she sign for the dry cleaning, too?"

Am looked at the invoice. A man's suit had been dry-cleaned—no, express-cleaned, the one-hour service. The same hand that had signed for the cleaning had signed for the champagne.

"Apparently so," he said.

"That's funny," said Sharon. "According to the time and date when this was signed, she should have been dead for at least twelve hours."

# 38

Am wondered how it was that the dead kept managing to accumulate hotel charges. When he had perused room 605's account the night before, he had assumed the laundry charge had just been a late posting, but that hadn't even proved to be the last of the charges. The updated printout showed that the honor bar had been used. Housekeeping, which only that morning had been given permission by the investigative team to clean the room, had inventoried the portable bar and found that virtually all the food had been emptied out of it. Am supposed it was possible that the investigating team had done the eating, but he didn't think so.

"It's so—grisly," said Sharon. "Can you imagine murdering someone, then hanging around the room? And how could he have ordered champagne afterward? Have you ever heard of anything so sick?"

Am nodded his head, then shook it, both agreeing and disagreeing. "Sick, yes. But the room service waiter said the man hardly looked like he was in the partying mood. Usually when someone orders a pricey bottle of bubbly they're ebullient. Augustin said this man was so subdued as to stand out."

"Explain the champagne, then."

"I can't."

Am and Sharon had compiled a list of everyone they believed had come into contact with the suspected murderer. Everyone agreed he was of average height or less, had thinning red hair, and was on the heavy side. His age was gauged from thirty-five to fifty-five.

Teresa Fuentes had tried to do turndown service in room 605 and had talked with him. Henry Polk, the sixth-floor butler, had picked up the man's suit for cleaning and brought it back. And bellman Albert Slocum had delivered the wine and cheese and had happened to ride up the service elevator with a man fitting that same description. All the employees described him as soft-spoken and polite and agreed that he was withdrawn, perhaps even confused. By description, he hardly seemed to match the profile of a cold-blooded murderer.

"So," said Sharon, "I guess we should call the police?" Her words were more a question than a statement.

This time they had more than a missing rubber. They had witnesses, charges, and signatures that didn't match. They even had descriptions that were in general agreement. This time, she knew, they wouldn't be laughed at.

"They'll probably get one of those police artists," said Am. "They'll put together a sketch. It will be on the evening news, and someone steaming carrots in some town will say, 'I know that man.'" He sounded envious.

"I suppose it's the right thing to do," Sharon said, but not very convincingly.

"A police artist, to go along with the police photographer who's already been here, and the forensic scientists, and the trace evidence people, and the detectives, and McHugh." The last name didn't settle well with Am.

"We don't have their . . . " Sharon was going to say expertise but thought better of it. "Personnel."

"I know an artist," said Am, brightening suddenly.

"But what good would a picture . . . ?"

"He's fast."

"Without a name—"

"I've seen him do sketches in a minute."

"But I still don't see how that could—"

"He's a Hotel guest. The Hotel guest. Wallace Talbot."

Sharon remembered the name. He was the guest who had come to stay. The tour guide had pointed out his artwork around the Hotel and said that he had been a resident for more than fifty years. In her silence, she assented.

"Holden," he said, stretching forth his hand to grasp Am's. "Friends. Come in! Come in!"

Wallace Talbot had checked into the Hotel California for a week's stay in 1942; so far, his reservation had been extended for more than half a century. There was a second greeter at the door, but this one had four legs. Cinder, Wallace's black cocker spaniel, tried to give everyone a kiss. Cinder was happiest when there was a party, and she was convinced the appearance of seven people in her doorway could mean only that.

It had taken arm twisting, juggling of schedules, and pulling employees from the floor to assemble everyone who might have encountered the potential murderer. Am hadn't explained the necessity for the meeting, had just termed it important and made it mandatory. He had advised Wallace of the need for his artistry but hadn't given him any more details than that.

"Coffee, tea, or sodas, anyone?" asked Wallace. He was genuinely delighted to have all the visitors. In any other room, and with any other guest, the staff might not have felt at ease, but everyone knew and liked Wallace. He bore a resemblance to Douglas Fairbanks, Jr., was tall, thin, and urbane, and like the movie actor seemed to manage everything effortlessly and with much savoir-faire. Wallace was one for flourishes, from hand gestures, to opening a door. He never forgot staff birthdays: flowers for the ladies, cigars for the men. Some employees called him "Peppermint" because of his daily promenades around the Hotel, where he handed out peppermint sticks to all, especially small children. Am had never had the heart to tell him he couldn't stomach peppermint.

"If it's all right with you, Wallace," said Am, "I'll take care of the refreshments in a few minutes. But for now, I'd like the rest of you to get to work."

Am took a few minutes to explain why they were gathered and said he hoped a sketch of this mystery man, and perhaps murderer, might help in their investigation. He swore everyone to secrecy. He didn't want rumors and didn't want to involve the police prematurely. Most of all, Am said, he didn't want the Bob Johnsons on the case.

The mood of the room changed. With the purpose of their gathering revealed, an excitement built, ancient hunting instincts brought to the fore.

Wallace seated everyone in front of his easel and brought out a sketch pad and pencils. He usually worked in oils, could often be seen painting from the wraparound balcony of his fourth-floor room. There, he had a panoramic expanse of the Pacific as well as a sweeping view of the Hotel gardens. Fully half of his paintings were seascapes. He truly knew all the moods of the La Jolla Strand and loved to capture the human element at play on the beach, the children at their sand castles, the adults with their pants legs rolled up, walking along the surf. He was a popular artist who commanded high prices for his works, but at the same time he was a very skilled painter, a combination that often doesn't go together.

To many, San Diego is still regarded as a navy town, but that's a designation that is at least a generation removed. It was accurate enough, though, when Wallace arrived in San Diego, maybe even doubly so because there was a war going on. A bad knee had made him ineligible for the service, but his talents as an illustrator were put to use by the defense industry. In 1942 housing was at a premium in San Diego. Wallace was supposed to stay in the Hotel for only a week, but he said that from the moment he checked in it felt like home to him. Rather than move into an apartment, Wallace remained. He could afford to, being the only child of wealthy parents who were long deceased. His ultimate artistic success supplemented his inheritance and deferred the necessity of his ever having to check out. Wallace had never expected to live out his life at the Hotel, but whenever he thought about leaving, thought he should get a home and have all the normal trappings, he always asked himself, "Why? Why leave what I love?"

A local paper had recently interviewed Wallace. He had

said, "Most of my money has gone to the Hotel California. It's an investment I've never regretted." In many ways Wallace paid rent to be a resident manager. He made rounds every day, walked all over the Hotel grounds, and saw that everything was as it should be. He took it upon himself to help guests and act as a goodwill ambassador. Many children had grown up on his peppermint sticks and came to him now as adults with open hands and big smiles. To date, he had never run out of either peppermint sticks or good cheer. This morning he needed the latter.

The seven blind men describing the elephant were more in accord than the four witnesses (the fifth witness, T.K., was early on convinced that the deliveryman could not have been the mystery man) describing whom they had seen. Though everyone agreed to the same general description, finding the common ground of a face proved tough work.

How do you describe a nose? How do you remember the direction of the part of the hair? Were the eyes close set or far apart? And how chubby were those cheeks? Was it really a double chin, or was the chin just not very well defined? Did he wear glasses or not?

A room attendant, a butler, a room service waiter, and a bellman opined, argued, confessed to ignorance, and called each other blind. In between the collaborating and the bickering, a desk clerk inserted attempted comedy sketches and an artist tried to work. Am thought the cast of *Clue* had nothing on these characters. He tried to organize what Wallace wearily called "the artistic charades." Only Cinder seemed totally happy with the situation. She went from lap to lap. In the early 1960s, some twenty years into Wallace's stay, the owners had instituted a "no pets" rule, but they had grandfathered Wallace's black cocker spaniel. How had Cinder managed to live so long? The dog that was happily trading up laps, and lapping up faces, was really Cinder IV. Other GMs had turned a blind eye to the situation, but not Kendrick. He had vowed this would be Cinder the last.

"Holden," said Wallace, "would you mind getting that other pencil? Thank you."

Wallace called Am "Holden," after Holden Caulfield in *The Catcher in the Rye*. He insinuated that Am was the incarnation of Holden, now grown up and gone west. The confusion of youth, Wallace had noted more than once, was translating nicely into Am's midlife crisis. Wallace insisted that Am was the Hotel's catcher in the rye. "You are he," said Wallace, "whose job it is to wait for the innocents to fall off the cliff and be there to catch them." Am had always liked that job description better than assistant general manager.

The bickering gradually quieted. In their mind's eye all of the witnesses had a picture of their man: he was younger, he was older. He had small lips, he had lips like a clown. But an overall description was hashed out, and expanded upon, and agreed to, even if the consensus wasn't quite true to their individual vision. One by one the witnesses came around to the sketch and offered their suggestions. When Wallace finally knew the direction he wanted to go, he banished everyone to their seats and worked out his own finishing touches. Between penciling, he talked.

"There have been other deaths here, of course," he said, shading in a section with a critical eye, "but none like these. I remember, though, two very troubling suicides.

"Very different deaths," he added. "The first victim was a girl. Must have happened thirty-five—no, forty years ago. Dick Murray was the house dick then.

"I've told you about Murray, Holden. He was a tough SOB, a little guy with a big chip on his shoulder. He always had his nose in the *Racing Form*. This was one instance where he took it out long enough to find out about this girl. Real melodrama, that. She was in love with a naval officer, believed he shared her same feelings, but learned differently. When she took an overdose of pills, she didn't only kill herself: apparently she took the life of the young child in her womb."

Wallace stopped talking, chewed on his lip for a moment, brought out the eraser, and delicately removed some of the lead. "Murray went and found that officer," he said. "He called him out. They say he gave up six inches, and sixty pounds, but he still beat the tar out of him."

The artist thought for a moment, then nodded, as if agreeing with a long-lost voice. "The other suicide was a drowning. Man went swimming in the ocean and didn't come back. Guess that happened thirty years ago. Murray looked into that one, too.

"Everyone just assumed it was a drowning. But Murray didn't like something. He made a few calls and found out the man's business was going under and the creditors were moving in. As it stood, it didn't look like he was going to be left with a proverbial pot to pee in. Murray figured he couldn't stand the thought of poverty. The guest lived like a king his last few days at the Hotel. His final meal was chateaubriand and a French wine, after which he went out and took that fateful swim. There were those who believed the rich meal made him cramp up, but after Murray found out what he did, he said it just fueled him on to the deed."

Wallace stopped working for a moment, bit softly on the pencil he was holding. "Murray told me he went to the Del Mar track that day and won a bundle on a horse named Big Splash. Said he never bet hunches, except that one time."

Wallace eyed his effort critically. "I'm almost there," he said. "I must say he doesn't look like one of those faces you see on 'America's Most Wanted,' though."

Am and Sharon both stood up to take a look at the sketch, but Wallace held them off with a hand. "Holden, Miss Baker, I will signal the time for the unveiling."

Impatiently they both returned to their seats. Wallace asked the witnesses a few more questions, and started a few more arguments. He wanted to know about moles, wrinkles, birthmarks, clefts, and dimples. Mostly, though, he wanted a "feel" for the face, an idea of what the man was.

"Don't think of him as a murderer," said Wallace. "If you saw him on the street, you'd probably think he was a . . ."

"Baker," said Augustin.

"Accountant," Henry said.

"Store manager," said Teresa.

"One of those technical kinds of people," Albert said. "The kind who always bring their little computers."

"Pedophile," said T.K., hoping for a laugh but not getting one.

Wallace explored their reasons (except for T.K.'s), and their answers made him alter his drawing slightly. He examined his work with one long, last look and finally decided that it would have to do. He turned around the sketch and held it aloft for all to see.

The four witnesses were the first to respond. Although they hadn't been able to come to verbal terms with the man, they did agree on the result. What was represented was their collective man; or at least a close facsimile thereof.

But it was T.K., Sharon, and Am who were the most vocal. "I know that dude," said T.K.

"I've seen that man," Sharon said.

Am, who claimed to never forget a face, said, "I've seen that face before."

"I know," said T.K., snapping his fingers. "I checked him into the Hotel."

"Yesterday morning," said Sharon, her tone one of disbelief, "he took the Hotel tour with me."

"I saw him," said Am, straining for the memory. "I saw him . . ."

Then, triumphantly, "I saw him in the rumba line."

# 39

The actors were hung over, and most of the Bob Johnsons were hung over. No one had gotten enough sleep, and tempers were short.

Carlton hadn't slept much, either, but he wasn't suffering in the same way as those around him. The night before, he had walked Bobbi to her door. There, they had kissed for the first time. It was the purest moment of ecstasy Carlton could ever remember.

So much had happened in the last few days. He had experienced betrayal, murder, discovery, and passion. It felt as though he had died and been born again. He had stayed up most of the night trying to sort things in his mind. He had never given much credence to those multiple personality types, but at the moment he figured Sybil had nothing on him. Everything was churning inside. He had performed the most heinous crime imaginable. To take those moments back, he would do almost anything. What he had done had destroyed a part of himself. But since meeting Bobbi, he felt like that bird that was consumed by fire, then raised itself from its own ashes. That Tucson. Or was it toucan? No, it was a phoenix. Maybe that's what love was. You burn up inside to nothing. You erase all the sins that were there and become a better person, another person. With Bobbi, it felt as if he had been offered a chance for a new life. There were so many things about her that he liked, from her generous lips to the way she dotted the *i* in her name with a little heart.

She sat next to him, and with her there, all was right. Bobbi felt his eyes on her. She looked up, smiled at him, then returned her attention to what was going on. Damn, now what was happening? Turn your head, and you miss everything. Not like soap operas. She could tune in once a week and still know what was going on. But this here was sure confusing. The actors kept jumping around, and things kept popping up—like bodies. There was a lot of flapping of hands. What she would have preferred was the flapping of more flapjacks. 'Course that didn't make things any easier to follow, what with the waiters serving brunch between all the folderol.

"Herring and sour cream," the server advised, dropping off yet another serving dish for the table.

The herring had been dyed red. Bobbi covered her eyes with a napkin. Fish in the morning. How disgusting. Didn't these people know what real food was? And it was red, mashed fish. Ugh.

Carlton noticed Bobbi's discomfiture. It matched his own. He was tired of the actors serving up murder. It was enough that he had to live with what he had done without their bombastic reminders.

"Are you all right?" he asked Bobbi.

Bob was such a dear, always so considerate. "Fine," she said, but she did wrinkle up her nose at the fish.

"Would you like to leave?" he asked hopefully. "We could go to the . . . "

He almost said zoo. But Carlton didn't want to see caged animals. "Around San Diego. See the sights."

Bobbi thought about it. It seemed a little unfair to be skipping out on her kindred Johnsons, but most of them were acting a bit, well, grumpy. And she did want to be with Bob. Why, last night that kiss of his had made her knees go weak. She had almost invited him into her room.

"Uncle Charles!" screeched one of the actresses.

"Yes, Charlie," said the other actor. "Known as Good Time Charlie!"

She, aggrieved: "But you don't really mean Uncle Charles?"

He, triumphant, raising his eyebrows high for the audience: "Yes, I do."

"Let's get out of here," said Bobbi.

# 40

Before everyone dispersed from Wallace's room, Am reminded them of the need for secrecy. All took a vow of silence, promising to say nothing about the sketch or the possible murderer. The cabal went their separate ways, except for Am and Sharon, who walked together. When they couldn't be overheard, he ventured, "I suppose that gives us an hour before everyone knows."

Sharon had more faith in humanity. She thought it would be two hours.

"We're looking for a man who has murdered," said Am, his tone suddenly very serious. "In the security hut there's a stun gun. I'm going to get it, then I'll meet you in the lobby."

He started off at a trot, remembered something, and ran back, handing her Wallace's rolled sketch as if it were a relay baton. "Better make some copies of this. Who knows, we might need help finding him. Use the copy machine in reservations to shrink it down to a less conspicuous size—say, five inches by five.

"And," he added, "find out where the Bob Johnsons are meeting."

She nodded, and he was off. The idea of Am getting a gun, any kind of gun, was sobering. Sharon wondered, not for the first time, whether she should call the police. Instead she went and made copies. Or at least tried. The copy machine wouldn't have looked out of place in a video arcade. It had lights, flashing arrows, and multicolored trays. There were buttons to designate paper size, the darkness desired, the number of copies needed, and whether collating was in order. Let's see, she thought, trying to determine whether she was in a shrinking or enlarging mode. Wasn't that Alice's dilemma? But this wasn't Wonderland. And Alice would never have gotten there if she'd had to make copies all day.

Typical male, she thought. Given any excuse, they revert to the primordial. Me hunter, you gatherer. I'll get the gun and you make the copies. Or coffee.

Her first effort at shrinking the sketch failed, which didn't make her any happier. She moved her face closer to the key-pad and was trying to make out some impossibly small print when a voice behind her asked: "May I help you?"

Sharon turned around and eyeballed the name, rank, and serial number of the man doing the offering: Roger, Front Office Manager, Racine, Wisconsin. The one Am called Casper.

"Why, yes, thank you. I'm trying to shrink this to a smaller size. About so big."

She motioned, and Roger did his gauging. "About eight inches?"

Sharon had been told that the reason women had difficulty estimating sizes was that they were always being told by men that six inches was a foot. "A little smaller," she said.

Roger confronted the machinery with a knowing air, pressed two buttons (damn, that was my next guess, she thought), and a moment later the miniaturized copy popped out. "Do you only need one?"

"Several, please," she said.

He punched a button. "You're the intern?"

"Yes."

"How do you like it here?"

"Never a dull moment."

The copies were already finished. Belatedly Roger began to think he should have made the process appear much more involved than it was. He was usually expert at doing such.

He handed Sharon back her original and all but one of the copies. Because he had helped, he assumed that gave him the right to analyze the work "they" had done.

"So, what is this?"

Sharon wanted to say, "None of your business," but instead replied with the obvious: "A sketch."

"Do you draw?" he asked.

"I dabble."

"It's good," said Roger. "Who's the guy?"

"Just a fellow."

"Your boyfriend?"

Her first impulse was to laugh. Yes, she always hung around with murderers. Bank robbers, too. Where did this weenie come off asking personal questions?

"I suppose it shows," she said, attempting dewy eyes.

Roger tried to hide his disappointment. He started to pass her the copy, but stopped the hand-off just short of her hand, examining it once more.

"I think I've seen him before," said Roger.

God, she thought. Was there an employee in the Hotel whom this murderer hadn't run into?

"He's not a guest, is he?" asked Roger.

Sharon shook her head. "Of course not."

"Because," Roger said piously, "fraternization with guests is forbidden."

"I would hope so," said Sharon. "And with managers, too?"

Starchly: "Why, yes."

He handed her the copy. With it came another quotation of company policy: "The copy machine is to be used for business purposes only."

Sharon could almost understand why women were known to bare their ass on a copier and anonymously mail (male) the sentiments to their supervisor of choice. She thanked Roger for all of his help and advice, then walked out of the office, doing her best to jiggle her buns like an advertising streetwalker. It wasn't something that she could ever remember doing before, but in this instance it felt damn satisfying.

Roger's attention was held for the length of her passage, then, sighing, he decided it was time to be off. The front desk promised to be busy soon, and he didn't want to be around. But before leaving, he reached down into the recycling bin. Sharon had left her aborted copy attempt, an oversize reproduction of her beau. It was as big as the sketch she had taken with her, eleven inches by seventeen, not the shrunken visage she had wanted. The larger portrait looked even more familiar to Roger. He had seen that face, but where?

While waiting for Am, Sharon had consulted a reader board to learn that the Bob Johnsons were meeting in the Neptune Room for a brunch and "entertainment." The concierge confirmed the reader board listing and was also able to give Sharon a detail sheet of group activities for the day. The Bob Johnsons had a full agenda. Their brunch wasn't supposed to adjourn for another half hour, but Sharon hoped Am would hurry, because after their meal the Bob Johnsons would be dividing up, some going to the golf course, others to the tennis courts, and the rest sailing. And maybe one murdering.

Am arrived breathless, carrying a brown bag. The concealed stun gun looked conspicuously like a fifth.

"You look like a wino," she said.

"I can dream, can't I?"

"Neptune Room," she said.

"Not far," Am said gratefully.

Sharon had already figured out the route and started walking. When you don't like following, you work out those matters ahead of time. She had also tried to work out the murders.

"There was some forethought in what happened," she said.

Am, still short of breath, nodded.

"Our Bob Johnson knew the couple. He sent up the wine and cheese to them. He called upon them. Presumably, he killed them."

Am nodded again.

"Our Bob must have plotted this for some time. He planned a murder, and he also planned to attend a convention. Talk about killing two birds with one stone."

"Don't think so," Am puffed.

"Why not?"

He took a deep breath. "A couple of things. He let too many people see him. If it was as premeditated as you say, everything would have been thought out much better. This strikes me as a crime of passion, a—a . . . "

The analogy came to him. "A St. Julian-type murder." He didn't remind Sharon that she was the one who had originally put that same label to the crime.

"You said 'a couple of things'," said Sharon.

"It may be nothing, but when the Bob Johnsons checked in, they were one over on their room allotment. Now I know that's not uncommon. Sometimes guests who are supposed to double up opt for their own rooms. Or someone who was going to stay with a friend in town decides to check in instead. Or . . . " He didn't finish, just shrugged.

"Or a murderer," said Sharon, "decides to change his name to Bob Johnson and stays around the scene of the crime."

"Maybe," said Am.

"Didn't all the Bob Johnsons guarantee their stays with credit cards?"

"He could have put down a cash deposit."

"It still doesn't make sense. You commit murder, and then you check into the same hotel?"

"You're trying to think logically. Why didn't he immediately flee the Hotel after the murders? Why did he sleep in the same room with his victims?"

Sharon offered what she thought was the only obvious answer: "He's a psychopath."

"Do you really think so?" asked Am. "Did you sense that when you walked and talked with him?"

Would she have ever been able to guess he was a murderer from their time together on the Hotel tour? No. He was an innocuous sort. She had sensed his melancholy but had also been witness to his curiosity. He had asked all those questions. "For someone who'd killed a couple of people the day before," Sharon said, "I find it strange that he would have cared about how many petunias were planted here in the spring."

Her statement implied that the man was mentally ill, but Sharon really didn't think that. The man might have acted a bit odd, but he didn't strike her as being either loony tunes or a hardened criminal. "I don't think he was crazy," she admitted. "I think he was sad. Lonely."

"Penitent," said Am.

As far as she was concerned, that was stretching it. Wasn't this the man he had spotted in the rumba line? "No doubt like St. Julian?" she asked sarcastically.

Am shrugged, beginning to regret his reference.

"But instead of repenting like Julian," Sharon said, "and tending to the needs of travelers for the rest of his days, our murderer joins a convention and goes on vacation."

Am didn't respond to Sharon's barb. "The Jane Doe," he reminded her, "was wearing a wedding ring. And a man's wedding ring was left in the Bob Johnson hospitality room," he added significantly."

At first Sharon had trouble speaking. Am's implication struck her as more than farfetched. "So," she said, "you murder your wife, and her lover, then you check into a hotel for some well earned R and R, and what the hell, you dump your wedding ring so that you can pick up some babes."

Am opted to not defend his speculation. Uttered aloud, it did sound ludicrous.

"It would only be possible . . . " Sharon almost said "in a nightmare." "In a madhouse." "In an opium eater's deranged fantasy." But she thought about it and reluctantly finished her sentence.

"In this Hotel."

Roger was adrift in the Seven Seas. That's what the staff called the collection of seven meeting rooms on the north side of the Hotel, all of which had maritime names. It was a safe spot, far enough away from the demands of the front desk that he could relax and not worry about encountering anyone of rank. Usually there was just banquet staff, tuxedoed men and women running in and out of meeting rooms.

He stopped at a water fountain to spray his lips. He wasn't really thirsty but out of habit paused at virtually every water fountain. Someone had spat out their gum into the bowl. Disgusting, he thought. For the briefest moment he considered picking out the gum and flicking it into an adjacent trash re-

ceptacle but decided to leave that task for the grounds crew.
They needed something to do anyway.

A familiar voice made him freeze. Am Caulfield. Here. He
shouldn't be here, Roger thought. This is unfair. He should
be in his office working. Of all the forty acres to the Hotel,
of the thousand spots he could be, why does he have to be
here? I can say that I'm checking on whether a meeting room
was set up, responding to a guest inquiry. That's it. The moment passed when he thought discovery imminent, and Am's
voice moved past him. Somewhat sheltered by the overhang
of the water fountain, Roger dared a glance. Am wasn't
alone. That intern was with him, the one he'd helped at the
copier. He watched as they disappeared into the Neptune
Room, carrying water pitchers.

The coast was clear for Roger to escape, but his curiosity
was piqued. Something was going on, and it was his job to
keep tabs on the unusual, wasn't it? No one knew about that,
of course. That was his secret. But it pleased him to know
that he had some power over Am and the others who im-
pugned his abilities. They didn't know about his double life.
Still, everything was supposed to be hush-hush. He was just
supposed to pass on what he heard and saw and not be obvious about it. But the only way he could find out what was
going on was to follow them. Uncertain as to what he should
do, Roger walked toward the Neptune Room and cracked
open the door. It was mostly dark inside. What light there
was emanated from the front of the room. Probably a slide
show going on, he thought. That was good. He could scuttle
in unnoticed. His steps followed his thoughts.

From experience, Roger knew there would be a coffee
setup somewhere in the back, a good place, he was sure, to
observe. While making his way there, Roger heard loud
voices. Some kind of strange commotion was going on, but
he didn't dare turn around, not yet. His imagination, and
nerves, amplified the sounds. Roger's hands were shaking by
the time he reached for the coffee, and his pour was un-
steady. The voices hadn't let up. They were louder now, and
there were more of them.

"Intruder! Interloper! Spy!"

They were talking about him. Roger turned to face his ac-

cusers. He had an explanation, he always did, but this time
he didn't have to offer it up. The cries came from the Murder
Mayhem Weekend actors. Deep breath, short thought. That
meant these were the Bob Johnsons. So why were Am and
the intern here?

In the dim light, Roger could make them out. They were
on opposite sides of the room, both proceeding forward
along the far aisles. A few of the Bob Johnsons raised their
hands for water, but neither Am nor Sharon noticed them.
They weren't looking for empty glasses, no, they seemed to
be staring at faces.

Roger wasn't the only one ignoring the thespians. Bull had
been bored from the moment his plate had been cleared away
and the actors had started their prancing. Who cared about
this Uncle Charles? Did anyone really give a fig about how
his family members were dropping like flies? Bull was interested in the story behind David Stern and the woman with
him. Those were real murders, not some fruity characters
mincing about.

What was the Hotel dick/manager/spoilsport doing skulk-
ing around? Was he a busboy in his spare time? Seemed odd
for him to be helping out in this capacity. Bull watched him
for a minute. If his job was to be making with the water, he
sure was stingy about pouring. Must be that drought Californians were always lipping off over. Strange, Bull thought,
how places with the least amounts of rainfall always liked to
sport the lushest vegetation.

He watched the house detective pause and look across the
room. Bull followed his gaze and saw that the dick wasn't
working alone. His lady friend was also making the water
circuit, but she wasn't doing any glass filling, either. They
acknowledged each other, and their efforts, with a shake of
their heads, then both of them started forward again. It was
clear they were looking for somebody. Who? And why did
they keep looking at their trays? There was something they
had there, something other than a water pitcher. Now what
was it they kept consulting? It sure as hell wasn't a dessert
order. They were looking at faces and checking with a road
map. A picture, that's what they had to be carrying.

As for the Hotel dick, it looked as if he were carrying

more than a picture. The bulge in his coat made him look as though he were packing a piece. Interesting, he thought, a hell of a lot more interesting than the play. So what was going down? The busboy detectives were almost up to the stage now, and still they hadn't found their face.

Maybe it was time to call that bellman who always had his hand out. The boy had given him his home number, had said he would help in whatever way possible. His information had been good, even if it hadn't come cheap.

Bull decided to stretch his legs and make that call.

# 41

Mary Mason was lingering outside the Neptune Room, ready to guide the Bob Johnsons to their activities. They would be participating in three of her favorite contests: "big balls," "mixed doubles," and the "paddle boat demolition derby." The object of big balls was to drive a golf ball farther than anyone else. Mixed doubles was similarly misleading, not a pairing of the sexes, but more of a three-legged-race tennis contest, with the players' ankles tied together. As for the paddle boats, the contestants were encouraged to ram into each other and knock the opposing captains into the drink. Mary was glowing. It all promised to be such fun!

And now even Murder Mayhem Weekend was back on track. That made Mary extremely happy. The next act was scheduled in three hours, another episode of murder to be performed over cocktails and snacks. She looked at her watch and hoped this performance would conclude on time. There was so much to do.

One of the doors to the Neptune Room opened. Were they convening already? No, not yet. It was only that rather dour Bob Johnson.

"Where's the phone?" asked Bull.

It doesn't cost you anything to smile. That's what Mother

always said. Mary smiled and pointed. "Right over there, sir."

A minute later, and the doors again opened. But the Bob Johnsons still weren't emerging en masse. How odd! It was Am and Sharon, carrying water pitchers and talking very intently with one another.

"Hello, Am! Hello, Sharon!"

The two of them looked up, but before approaching Mary, they paused for an ocular consultation. Apparently they came to some mutual decision. Sharon pulled out one of the copies of Wallace's sketch and handed it to Mary. "Does he look familiar?"

She examined the drawing. "I've seen him," she said.

This guy has better face recognition than the president, thought Sharon.

"Recently?" Am asked.

"Yes," said Mary, then remembered. "This morning, in fact. He should be inside. He's one of our Mr. Johnsons. I remember he asked for some nonfat milk. He said something about how he was now watching his calories."

Sharon bit her tongue again. There seemed something terribly ironic about murdering and then going on a diet.

"It was dark inside," Am mused. "Maybe too dark to make out red hair."

"We might have missed him," Sharon said hopefully.

Am pointed out how there were only two exits, neither one too far from the other. They agreed to take up positions and wait for the Bob Johnsons to emerge. They talked too cryptically for Mary to understand what they were saying and were so intent that she didn't dare interrupt. It was a shame, though, because she wanted to tell them about the woman the man was with, the one with whom he was so obviously smitten. They looked quite the item.

Roger was glad of his caution. He had paused at the door before exiting the Neptune Room and had heard Am and Sharon talking outside. It was difficult to make out their words, but it was clear they were after one of the Bob Johnsons. Roger decided it would be best to leave when everyone else did. Judging by the building crescendo of the actors' voices, that wouldn't be long.

Bull Johnson was too far away to overhear what the Hotel dick and Miss Marple were discussing, but he was close enough to watch what was going on. The bellman with the Eye-talian name said he'd be right down. In the meantime, Bull would continue with his look-see.

Like a classroom of students waiting for recess, everyone was watching clocks, and doors, and each other. A minute passed, and another. Then the first door was kicked open, followed by the second, and the Bob Johnsons started streaming out. "Big balls here," shouted Mary. "Anyone for big balls, line up here."

One of Mary's assistants was calling for mixed doubles and another for boat people. The stream of Bob Johnsons stalled, and the hallway grew congested. From their opposite vantage points, Am's and Sharon's heads moved side to side, scanning the crowd. Am spied a patch of red hair but couldn't make out the face. He started to push through the Bob Johnsons, but there was gridlock. The lines started moving only when Mary and her assistants took their shouting and followers and headed outside.

Sharon had seen Am's agitation, had watched him try to wade into the crowd, and had looked to see which individual had grabbed his attention. Then she also caught a glimpse of some red hair. The man was on the short side, his features obscured by the shoulders and bodies around him. Sharon figured out his likely route (he was with the big balls group) and made for the exit, beating the body of Bob Johnsons to the door. There she waited for him, watched as his red head bobbed closer and closer to her. She stepped into his path and managed a face-to-face, then expelled a lot of air and a lot of disappointment. He wasn't their man.

It took Am another half minute to get to her. "No go," said Sharon. "Not our carrot top."

Am sighed. It seemed that just about everyone had seen this guy, but where was he? They backtracked, looked inside the Neptune Room and examined the bathrooms, but their Bob Johnson wasn't to be found.

"What if he was wearing a hat?" Am asked. "Or what if he dyed his hair?"

Sharon shook her head. "He just wasn't here," she said.

"What about Mary's remembering his request for skim milk?"

"Are you saying Mary's infallible?"

Am wasn't inclined to argue that point.

"Or, let's assume he was here," said Sharon. "We didn't do a head count, but I'm willing to bet a number of Bob Johnsons skipped out after the breakfast, and our man was one of them."

"Then it's time," said Am, "to figure out what room he's staying in."

For most of the twentieth century registration racks have been a part of every hotel. When the guest checks in he fills out a registration card, and that card is inserted into his room number slot on "the rack." The registration rack is a desk clerk's guide in a glance to knowing which rooms are taken, which are out of service, and which need to be cleaned. Color-coded tabs affixed to the registration card advise the clerk as to which room is checking out or which is being moved. Different properties disseminate information in a variety of ways, often using these tabs to identify who is a cash only customer, who is disabled (in the event of an emergency, the guest might need assistance in evacuation), who is a walk-in, and even who is a VIP. Am had never heard of a color-coded tab for a murderer, but he hoped the registration cards would help him find one.

These days registration racks are being phased out. As hotels have grown larger, as computer printouts have become push-button referrals and front desk space had become increasingly crowded with terminals and machinery, the racks have been supplanted. The Hotel, being proudly behind the time, still hadn't retired its rack. The Hotel guests still registered, if not with a quill pen, then with large desk pens that weren't even attached to chains.

Incompetence, for once, helped Am and Sharon in their hunt. Groups the size of the Bob Johnsons were invariably preregistered, their paperwork processed ahead of time to avoid the kind of madhouse check-in that had occurred. Because each of the Bob Johnsons had registered personally, there were handwritten references instead of the typed handiwork of some secretary. T.K. had checked in thirty-four of the hundred and seventy-six Bob Johnsons staying at the Hotel. Out of that number, five of his Bob Johnson check-ins had opted to put down a cash deposit instead of presenting credit cards. Figures, thought Am. The vast majority of guests usually used plastic, simplifying check-ins and check-outs. And in this case, that might have simplified who was the murderer. Leave it to the Bob Johnsons to make nothing easy.

Am and Sharon pulled the five registration cards from the rack and examined their handful of potential murderers. There was Bob Mayfield Johnson, Bob William Johnson, Bob Carlton Johnson, Bob Thorp Johnson . . . and what was this? Ah, yes, Bob "Sleepy" Johnson. One of the Seven Dwarf Johnsons.

"Bob William Johnson is with his wife," Sharon noticed.

"Still doesn't rule him out."

They compared the writing on the registration cards with the David Stern champagne and dry cleaning signatures. Bob Thorp Johnson and Bob Carlton Johnson looked like the closest matches, but after examining letters, loops, and slants, they weren't able to proclaim an identical match. The comparisons became odious, and the signatures started blurring, similarities emerging with all of the handwriting.

Outside Am's office, Roger wished he had X-ray eyes like Superman. It was something he had been fervently dreaming about since puberty. Roger had stationed himself around the front office for much longer than usual, hadn't left it for almost half an hour, which was a new record for him. He had watched Am and Sharon going back and forth between the front desk and Am's office and had surreptitiously spied on them while they pulled the registration cards from the rack. But for the last five minutes Am's office door had remained closed. Roger had been forced to wait and wonder about what was going on.

Keeping tabs on Am and Sharon had made Roger visible to the front desk staff. The PBX operator flagged him, saying that someone on the line was mad, someone asking for the manager. Usually Roger ran from angry calls. He directed them to anyone but him. But this was one time he agreed to take the call and was actually glad to be on the receiving end of a temper tantrum. The caller insisted that the GM and hotel security be immediately dispatched up to the Montezuma Room, as a major burglary had occurred and immediate action was required.

Roger now had the opportunity to interrupt Am and Sharon's closed-door tête-à-tête. Am would be forced to handle this call, and that would give Roger time to snoop around and find out what they were up to. He went and knocked, rather loudly, on Am's closed door. "Oh, Am," he said. "Sorry to bother you, but you're needed."

# 42

In just twenty-four hours Sharon figured she had progressed up the company ladder. Instead of searching the trash for condoms, she was now just searching the trash. Adriana Dominguez, one of the room checkers, was trying to help her, even if she wasn't sure what Sharon was looking for. But Adriana was also reluctant to ask. As a room checker, Adriana was used to examining guest rooms to make sure everything looked and operated correctly, inspecting how the towels were folded, checking under the beds, testing out televisions, and acting as the last line of quality control between the hotel room and the guests. Adriana couldn't figure out why Sharon was looking in the garbage, in the closets, and in the drawers, but she played along with her game. She also helped translate for Sharon, who kept holding up a sketch of some man and asking staff whether this was the guest currently occupying the room (the rooms changed, but her questions didn't). Nothing she did made much sense, but gringos were always doing strange things, especially this one. She had a reputation already. Some of the men said she was a nymphomaniac, while others said she was just crazy. Adriana had been warned not to talk about condoms with her. It was a subject that was said to fascinate her to no end.

Sharon was glad Adriana was so amenable in assisting her. After Roger had interrupted them and given Am little alternative but to deal with a new problem, he had calmly, too calmly, suggested, "Why don't you get a room checker, Sharon, and look into the situation. Then we can meet here and discuss your findings." His cryptic suggestion to take along a room checker had been a good one; going in and out of rooms, and scrutinizing them, was their job. They would have a feel for what looked right and what didn't.

She was also pleased, even though she didn't want to admit it to herself, that Am had shown some concern over her safety. As she was leaving he had called out to her and said, "Just the facts, ma'am. Nothing else." In his eyes she had seen his care and his caution. It was clear he didn't like her going into a murderer's den without him, but Roger had made the other situation sound like a matter of life and death.

Sharon hoped this was not another wild goose chase. Ruling out two of the Bob Johnsons as murderers had proved easy. The maids said the occupants weren't the man on her sketch. A third Bob Johnson room also looked doubtful. The guest had been tentatively identified by a carpenter as a tall, dark man, which didn't sound like *their* Bob Johnson. The carpenter was sure he was not the man in the sketch. Well, almost sure.

There were still two rooms with unidentified Bob Johnsons. No one had seen the guests, at least no one Sharon could find. Perhaps not coincidentally, they were Bob Carlton Johnson and Bob Thorp Johnson, the two guests whose signatures had most closely resembled the forged David Stern's.

Under Adriana's questioning eyes, Sharon carefully searched both of those Johnson rooms, looked under the mattresses, tilted the lampshades, and felt in the upper reaches of the closets; but she didn't find anything conspicuous. On the face of that, the lack of clues might have seemed discouraging, but in the case of the Bob Carlton Johnson room less seemed to be more, and Sharon was convinced she was on to something. The very absence of items in his room made it stand out. He had virtually no luggage, only a shirt, a three-pack of new boxer shorts (one of which was removed), and two pairs of socks. Both the underwear and the socks looked new. According to Adriana, they were brands sold in the Hotel haberdashery.

"All I can tell you," said Roger, "is that a lot of costly food was taken out of the Montezuma Room."

Like most of Roger's emergencies, a call to 911 didn't look in order. "What food?"

"I didn't get details. The man was so mad that he didn't want to give them. But I said you'd be over right away."

The caller wasn't the only one who was angry. Am was tired of being offered up as the daily sacrifice. He wanted to shout that he was on a murder case, dammit, but he refrained. He would have delegated, but there are times when you know it's a mistake to send a subordinate. But taking along company wasn't out of the question. He gave Roger a speculative look. Maybe he'd need a go-fer, someone to run around and do the busy work while he returned to tracking down a murderer.

"You're coming with me," Am said.

Roger looked apprehensive. Self-preservation, and the proximity of those interesting registration cards on Am's desk, were double incentives for him to try to beg off. "I think the desk is going to be busy, Am. Maybe you ought to call someone from security, someone official."

"Consider yourself deputized. Now you're official."

While Roger mumbled and dissembled, Am called over to sales and catering and asked which group was gathered in the Montezuma Room. Usually only the largest of events were held there. It was a stand-alone hall often touted as the Hotel convention center.

"I should have remembered," said Am, getting an answer to his question. "Thanks."

Am gave Roger a look. A fire this wasn't. "Dessert Festival," he said. "Sampling's set to begin this afternoon. Let's go."

The Dessert Festival was an annual event that featured the confectionary talents of San Diego's chefs, with the proceeds benefitting charity. Every year dozens of restaurants and hotels, and chefs and kitchens, contributed to the extravaganza.

"I think the caller was a chef," said Roger, his memory suddenly clearing up as they walked. "He had the voice of one, at least. I hope he's not carrying a butcher knife. Marcel scares me when he's waving his butcher knife."

Marcel was scary enough without a butcher knife, thought Am. But he didn't say anything. Though still an eighth of a mile from the Montezuma Room, Am was already being seduced. He could smell cinnamon rolls and apple tarts. Gracious winds deposited the delectable aromas of fudge and brownies. And there were other, even better, smells. His nose was bonding with olfactory wonders never before scented but instinctually welcomed. Brothers! Sisters! Where have you been all my life?

The Dessert Festival didn't short-change any senses. The meeting room doors were open, and if what was waiting wasn't the Promised Land, it was at least Candyland. Stepping into the room, Am felt like Dorothy going from black-and-white Kansas into Technicolor Oz. The Montezuma Room had been transformed into a huge candy store for kids of all ages. The entryway was lined with chocolate statues, jelly-bean edifices, and gingerbread houses. There were tortes, cakes, pies, cookies, and candies. The ice carvings looked like giant candy canes. Willy Wonka would have been proud, even if his representatives were not.

The chefs were all wearing their white hats, but they didn't look much like good guys. This is what the West has come to, Am thought. No more cowboys in white hats, just chefs. There were seven of them, and they stood like Kurasawa's seven samurai; their spokesman was the heaviest in the lot. There are still those who believe you can't trust the food of a thin chef. Fortunately, this one wasn't French. He resembled an older Pillsbury Dough Boy, was white, pasty, and rounded, and his yeast was rising.

"We're very upset," he said. "Look—" He swept his arms around. "Look at all that's missing."

In the sea of desserts, Am hadn't noticed the bare patches. But a casual look revealed that some Goldilocks had liberally sampled more than porridge.

"Most of us have worked all night," the chef said. "Thousands of people will be coming this afternoon to witness this showcase and sample our creations."

Am didn't bother to mention the obvious—that some sampling had started a bit early.

"The media will be here. But now we're missing a good many of our designer desserts."

Designer desserts. The next thing you know, thought Am, pastry chefs will be signing their bon-bons. "What exactly is missing?" he asked.

"Between eight hundred and a thousand desserts."

Am took a little stroll. All of the confections were identified by small signs. There didn't appear to be a pattern as to what was missing; all areas showed signs of having been raided. There were bare patches in the creamy fondants, almond paste and marzipan, peanut-brittle creams, truffle pecan squares, maple charlottes (what are those? Am thought), chocolate divinity, penuche clusters, candied kumquats, bittersweet mousse (what was the plural—mice?) with Häagen-Das liqueur, macaroon raspberry bombe, baklava, and caramel parfait. The thirty-nine varieties of cakes (the chocolate decadence looked particularly tempting) and twenty-six different kinds of pies had all been sampled, just as the cookie jars had been raided and the dozen cheesecakes tested. One variety had proved particularly popular: Margarita cheesecake. Only one piece was left. Am picked up the survivor.

"Margarita cheesecake," he said. "Never heard of it."

He looked at it longingly. He hadn't yet eaten breakfast, and judging by the denuded section, it did come recommended.

"Oh, go ahead," said the Pillsbury Dough Boy, sounding more irritable than charitable.

At first bite, Am knew why the dessert had gone over so well. "Delicious," he said. His second bite he announced as "Heaven." Am's third pronouncement was "Sublime." And then, to his disappointment, there wasn't any left. That motivated him. There was the chance that if he caught the thieves quickly, they would still be holding some of the cheesecake and he might wangle another piece.

Am asked for the chefs to assign a dollar figure to their

loss, and after a small consultation they settled on three thousand dollars. He inquired when the desserts had disappeared and was told they could have been taken only between ten and eleven o'clock, the time when they were all at breakfast.

"Worked all night," the big chef said, "and set up all morning, and then this happened."

"And you just left everything here and went to breakfast?"

"What were we supposed to do, take ten thousand desserts with us? We closed the doors, of course."

Which meant that only half the Hotel would have been subject to aromatic seduction. All eyes were on Am. He wished he had a magnifying glass, or a deerstalker cap, or a tic, something odd and eccentric to convince the circle of doubters that a qualified sleuth was at hand. He couldn't think of any other questions, so he pretended to take a great interest in all the spots where the desserts had been lifted. If so many eyes hadn't been on him, he probably would have sampled several more desserts. Walking up and down the aisles, he stopped every so often to imitate the same kind of poses people affect when confronted with modern art. Then he tried a different perspective, got down on his knees, and peered around. A marine white glove test followed. There were papers and crumbs on the floor.

"Were these papers here when you left for breakfast?" Am asked.

The fat chef again consulted the other white hats. Then, together, they all shook their heads. They looked like a religious order, their habits bobbing, the brethren of licked spoons.

Am checked the waste-baskets in the room. It was customary for the banquet crews to completely empty the trash whenever breaking down a meeting room. Most of the containers were half-full, filled with foils, papers, doilies, and napkins. Am pulled some samples out of the trash and examined them. Fresh.

"Your creations aren't missing," he announced. "They've been consumed."

The chefs regarded Am and his announcement as they would someone who had caused their soufflé to fall. "Look," he said, "I am very sorry, and apologize on behalf of the

Hotel California. I intend to find out which individuals did this. But while I'm doing that, I suggest you rearrange the desserts so that the bare areas don't look like Mother Hubbard's cupboard. If you think additional desserts are in order, I'll put an SOS out to our kitchen and have them whip some out."

The Dough Boy became the sour-dough boy. "We have emphasized quality in our creations," he said, "not quantity. And besides, the show starts in less than two hours."

"Then we had all better get busy," Am said.

Roger, who had remained mute around the chefs, found his tongue outside the room. "Probably just some vagrants who walked in," he said, "some beach people who sniffed out a free chow line."

He sounded hopeful. It was a favorite tactic of his to blame anonymous sorts. Am always suspected he did that not for lack of imagination, but to avoid any possible confrontations.

"A thousand desserts?" said Am. "Not likely."

"Employees?"

His second favorite target. "Possible, but I wouldn't bet on it. At least two hundred employees would have had to have a Twinkies attack at the same time."

"What, then?" asked Roger.

"A pack," Am said. "A hungry pack. We need to find our Marie Antoinette."

"What?"

"'Let them eat cake,'" he quoted. "In this case, they did."

The thrill of the hunt didn't infect Roger. "Well, now that it's in your able hands, Am . . . "

Am shook his head and motioned for Roger to follow.

"Where are we going?" Casper asked miserably.

"First stop," said Am, "sales and catering."

There, Am was sure, they'd find answers to the cream-puff caper. The trail of crumbs was already in place, and they had but to find where it led. At least in theory. Along the route Am paused several times, testing the wind and his sense of smell. He sniffed mightily, but he didn't have to. Pavlov's dogs wouldn't have needed a bell to start their salivating. With this kind of scent, they'd probably look rabid.

The call of the desserts was strong. There were four other meeting rooms in the near proximity of the Montezuma Room. Usually neighbors see something. In this case they would certainly have smelled something. A noseful of temptation had drifted down the path, and it wasn't honey bees that had been drawn to the scent and the scene.

Kim Yamamoto greeted Am and Roger with a tired smile. She was in the middle of a desk of contracts, probably trying to make sure no other Bob Johnson fiascoes were imminent.

"If you're not too busy, Kim," Am said, "I'd like a rundown on what groups are meeting this morning in the Sea Horse Hall, the Spinnaker Room, the Starfish Room, and the Sextant Room."

Kim didn't refer to her notes, could have probably named what was going on in all fourteen of the meeting rooms if put to the test.

"In the Sea Horse Hall is the Starving Artists Sale. The Spinnaker Room has the La Jolla Republican Women's brunch, and in the Starfish is Trend-three. The Sextant Room has some Procter and Gamble executives."

The starving artists, despite the nomenclature, were not Am's first choice for suspects. The group booked twice a year and advertised paintings for as low as $39, worth almost every penny. It was amazing how much bad art they sold. As for the so-called starving artists, most of them churned out about twenty-five masterpieces a day and made quite a good living.

Am asked for the prospectuses on the groups and ran down their vital statistics. His first hunch, he thought, was wrong. His primary suspects had been the Republican Women, suspicions based on Teapot Dome, Watergate, and a liberal upbringing. But there were only eighty women attending the brunch, not enough to make away with upward of a thousand desserts.

The numbers were there for the Procter & Gamble execs, but his gut feeling was that they weren't involved in the crime: Fortune 500 types usually didn't commit high jinks without sufficient highballs, and it was too early in the morning for those.

That left Trend-3, whatever that was. According to their

prospectus, there were approximately two hundred participants.

"What's the story on Trend-three?" he asked.

"'Three phases to a new you,'" quoted Kim. "They work on mind, body, and soul."

The body part interested Am. "Special diet?" he asked.

"Starvation diet," she said. "They monitor everybody's caloric intake."

Bingo. "May I look at their file?" he asked.

Trend-3 could just as well have been called Trend-y. There were a lot of New Age buzz words in their brochure. The workshop was aimed at facilitating "a self-actualizing experience": a revitalization of spirit, weight loss, and personal epiphany. Am had seen that troika of promised change bandied about before, what he referred to as happiness, thinness, and godness. Devout mendicants need not apply. Operations like Trend-3 never priced their holy trinity cheap.

Several gurus of the whole-grain set were running the program, had incorporated the Hotel's spa into their own regimen, but the Trend-3 approach sounded a bit schizophrenic: alternate pampering with spanking. Body wraps, mud baths, pore (not to be confused with poor) therapy, acupuncture, haiku, and massage were offset by strenuous exercise, ice baths, Rolfing, and colonic irrigations. The only thing consistent was their diet, or lack of one. Carrot juice, salads a rabbit might declare scanty, and blanched rice were the meal offerings of the day. This was the third day of their four-night, three-day gathering. The joys of fasting, meditation, and physical therapy might have sounded good in a brochure, but Am suspected by this time the participants would have viewed the Golden Arches as the pearly gates. He had his culprits, all of them.

Roger again tried to wriggle out of deputy duty, but Am wouldn't let him disappear. The aromatic offerings of the Montezuma Room were easily discernible around the Starfish Room, lingering like the breath of Satan. Am pushed open the doors to the meeting room, motioned with his arm until Roger preceded him, then walked inside. The group leader was in the front of the room, pretzled on a mat in the lotus position. Her disciples were trying to imitate her serenity and her pose. She had long braided hair, gave the appearance of being a graying flower child. Her eyes were closed. Either her concentration was complete or she was good at ignoring the worldly. She was leading the class in some sort of breathing exercises, but they had stopped their breathing. As surely and quickly as cops are made on the mean streets, the participants, the majority of whom appeared to be aristocratic women, had made Am for the hotel dick.

Like a cop looking out on a barroom of hard cases, Am moved his eyes around the room. Some of those who were gathered blushed, and others looked away, but maybe half were bold enough to give him the "cat who ate the canary" look. They weren't about to repent now. They knew what he was there for and didn't have an ounce, let alone a few pounds, of guilt in them.

Madame Sominex finally acknowledged Am and Roger. She acted as though her vibrations had been disturbed, shook her head before opening her eyes and looking in their direction, then closed them again for a long moment, as if trying to dismiss a mirage. No such luck.

"May I help you?" she asked.

"I'm Am Caulfield," he said, "the assistant general manager of the Hotel. I was hoping I could speak with you."

Her nod managed to involve every vertebrae in her neck and could have been timed with the little hand of a clock.

"Continue your breathing," she told the class. "Search for that place in your being that is the sun, that is warmth, that is lightness, that cannot be touched. Find where nothing can intrude, where all is safe and whole unto itself."

She was limber, able to rise from a position that would have bought most an appointment with a chiropractor.

"I think it would be better if we talked outside," Am said.

She raised an eyebrow but didn't argue, acceded to his wish, but at her unhurried pace. Am held the door for what seemed an eternity, and finally she passed through it.

"This is Roger," said Am, trying to get him to emerge from behind his back.

"Call me Sabrina," she said.

"Sabrina," Am said, "have you been in charge of the Trend-three gathering this morning?"

"I have."

"Including the times between ten and eleven?"

"I was. We were rebirthing then."

"You were with your class the entire time?"

"I was."

That surprised Am. Unless her wards had astral-projected into the hall of desserts, he would have to find another group of culprits. Maybe his initial hunch was right, and the Republican Women were involved. Or the Bob Johnsons. Why hadn't he thought of them?

"That is, I was there in body for most of that time, and there in spirit for the rest."

"What do you mean?"

"I physically absented myself so as to not present a barrier to the participants and their pursuit of their personal Vision Quest. And I had to retrieve a compact disc."

"A compact disc?"

"Las Vissen's 'Ocean Serenades.' Do you know it?"

Am shook his head.

"It's a marvelous piece. We were making breakthroughs, and I sensed that 'Ocean Serenades' would help us even more, would be just the inspirational music to inspire everyone."

"So you were gone . . . ?"

"Perhaps twenty minutes. But I left them with good thoughts, and Berlioz. His 'Symphony Fantastique.'"

Subtitled, no doubt, "Desserts Extraordinaire." It must have been a feeding frenzy, Am thought, everyone snapping at desserts like sharks in blood-filled waters.

"I would imagine you noticed the . . . the aromas this morning?"

"Call me Sabrina" didn't understand what Am was asking. He sniffed for emphasis. "The wafting scents," he continued, "from all of the desserts?"

"Yes," she remembered. "It was a good example for us. I called upon everyone to go beyond that instant of enticement, to reach into themselves for what was truly significant, to draw upon their essence and remember the smells of spring, and pine cones, and flowers, and baby's hair. I showed them how the realm of the physical could not compare with where they could go and where they had been."

"They need a remedial course," Am said flatly.

"I don't understand."

"While you were out, your class consumed three thousand dollars' worth of desserts."

Sabrina wasn't about to believe him and displayed another lesson in vertebrae movement, this time managing to straighten every one in her spine. "You are mistaken," she said.

"I'd like to ask your class," said Am.

"They were *rebirthing*," she said with emphasis.

"Mother's milk apparently wasn't enough."

She turned her back on Am and marched quickly back into the Starfish Room, her dream walk and lassitude at an abrupt end. Halfway into the room she slowed down, remembering herself. She mumbled a mantra for a few moments, found her inner peace again, and then faced the class. With an apologetic tone of voice, she called everyone back from their "other places." Am wondered how many were at Winchell's Doughnuts.

Sabrina assumed a self-righteous pose, and Am almost felt sorry for her. She expected so much from human nature, had obviously never worked in hotels.

"This gentleman," she said, directing her finger at Am but leaving some question in her statement, "has suggested that some of you might have wandered into another meeting room and taken that which did not belong to us."

Sabrina expected denials. They weren't forthcoming. There was only silence.

"He said you took desserts."

More silence.

"Desserts that go against the very principles of our gathering, that shout the triumph of the earthly over the spiritual."

Sabrina held out for one dissenting voice, just one, but the lot of them had fallen.

"Charge our masss-ter bill," she hissed at Am.

Casper fled through the door. Am moved just a little less quickly but did offer a sympathetic look to the class. For their sake, he hoped colonic irrigations were not on the day's docket.

# 43

"So, what'd you find out?"

Bull Johnson wasn't concerned about niceties. He wanted information and was holding a big enough roll of bills to get Jimmy Mazzelli's full attention.

"You won't believe this, Mr. Johnson . . ." Jimmy stretched the sentence for long enough to prove that timing was everything. Bull peeled off several bills of sizable denomination, and Jimmy accepted them as his due before continuing.

". . . but the murderer is a Bob Johnson."

Even Bull was surprised. "You're shitting me."

"No. I got triple confirmation. That's why Am and his helper were scouting your group. They had a sketch of the suspect. That's what I'm trying to get a copy of now."

Bull consulted his watch. "Two hundred bucks if you get it within the next half hour." He reconsidered. "No, three hundred."

Jimmy jumped up, but Bull restrained him. "What else?"

"They were searching some of the Bob Johnson rooms. I'm not sure which ones. That intern was waving the sketch around and asking questions."

Bull looked at his watch a second time. "Tell you what,"

he said. "Before you run off, I need you to get me a few things." Bull recited a list. "Then," he said, "when you find out more, I'll be in the Neptune Room."

It was time, thought Roger, to drift over to the Seven Seas. The last few hours had not been pleasant for him. He'd had to work at the front desk, and confront angry chefs, and be hissed at by a harpy. For all of that, he should have come up with some answers, but he still couldn't figure out what Am and that intern were up to.

That would change. He wasn't going to the Seven Seas, as he usually did, to get lost. The Bob Johnsons were set to reconvene in the Neptune Room for cocktails and more of their murder mystery madness. By traveling around the meeting room incognito—no, better than that, as a Bob Johnson—he was sure he would learn something.

Bull had seen both screen versions of *Invasion of the Body Snatchers*. He could never decide which he liked better. He'd never told anyone, but the flicks scared the bejesus out of him. Imagine having a friend turning up as a kind of alien. And think how horrible it would be if a member of your family, or a loved one, was supplanted by one of *them*.

That's kinda what this felt like, he thought. All around him Bob Johnsons were smiling, and talking, and reveling in their kinship. But one of them was that body snatcher. One of them had murdered. It gave him the heebie-jeebies to think there was a Benedict Arnold Johnson in their lot. That made Bull determined about one thing: he was gonna get that Judas.

He had hoped that Eye-talian bellman would have made it back by now. Having a sketch in hand would sure make things easier, but even without it there were ways.

The good name of Bob Johnson might have been besmirched, but they'd know how to take care of their own. Bull cast a red eye around the room, tried to see if he could identify the body snatcher.

Wearing a *My Name Is Bob Johnson* name tag, Roger was circulating freely around the room. He had decided this was a nice group—as long as you didn't have to be one of the clerks checking them in. Roger heard a lot of talk about golf, tennis, and nautical maneuvers. He was hoping to hear something that sounded out of the ordinary, but nothing did.

He engaged in shop talk with the Bob Johnsons and gave the same in return, with certain embellishments, of course. Roger had heard that people listened more closely if you whispered rather than shouted, so he spoke in a quiet voice, hinting a lot but saying little. He mentioned that he worked for the government and left the implication he was involved with intelligence. It was a favorite fantasy of his.

When not weaving tales, Roger kept his eyes open for Mary Mason. He had wanted to talk with her ever since he had overheard her speaking with Am and Sharon. Maybe she knew what was up. Usually she was running around organizing something or making sure everyone was having a good time. It wasn't like her not to be doing something.

The actors started taking their places, and the Bob Johnsons began to find their chairs.

"Be good," said a Bob Johnson to Roger, "be Bob."

Roger repeated his parting words. The lights began to dim and Roger took a last look around the room. As if on cue, Mary Mason appeared. She was standing at the doorway, looking in to make sure all was well. Better late than never, thought Roger. He started walking toward her when the room suddenly went completely dark. From the blackness came a scream.

Confound it all. That scream was the last straw. Maybe it was one of them fairy actors, or maybe it was the renegade Bob Johnson killing somebody else. Either way, Bull was damn sure he wasn't going to be standing around in a room with a murderer without proper lights.

The actors had started up with their gibberish talk. Bull walked quickly toward one of the exits, knowing what he had to do. That bellman had gotten him what he needed. Hell, that boy probably would have sold his mother if he'd come up with the green.

"He's dead!" shouted one of the actors.

Concealed under a table were two brooms and some rope.

Bull was right handy with knots and felt comfortable with the cord in hand. He angled the brooms through the door handles and sealed the escapes with a little rope tying. It didn't take him more than fifteen seconds with either door.

"Excuse me," said Roger, interrupting Bull in his handiwork while trying to get out of the room.

"Ain't nobody going nowhere," Bull said.

The actors tried to play through the disturbance in the back of the room. They had been trained to continue with their performances even if someone in the audience was having a heart attack or a seizure. But this was worse. This was a pain in the butt.

They tried competing with his bellowing, but he had the kind of carrying voice that drew ballplayers to jump into the stands. And he was approaching their stage. Once again the Bob Johnsons stopped the show. Or at least one of them did.

"Give me some lights," said Bull. "Give me some goddamn lights."

No one stirred at first. Most of the audience suspected he might be part of the show. But when Bull took a preemptory deep breath, a host of Bob Johnsons rushed to do his bidding before there was another roar.

The lights came on. Sharing the stage with Bull were several actors. They didn't have to think up their expressions of fright and dismay. The audience of Bob Johnsons was more composed. They were getting used to the unexpected. Truth to tell, the day's activities had been fun, but they had come to expect a little more juice. Like this.

Bull looked out to his fellow Bob Johnsons. His favorite mysteries were those where all the suspects were gathered in one room, usually a setting with a fireplace, a couple of decanters, a bust or two, and a lot of leather-bound books. He liked it when one by one the sleuth eliminated the possible murderers and finally revealed the real culprit.

At one of the exits, Roger tried desperately to unravel a knot. He had a bad feeling about this.

Thumbs hooked through his belt loops, jaw squared, Bull said, "None of you is going to like hearing this. What'd that little Pogo character decide years back? Something about how we found the enemy, and he is us.

"Brothers, it's my sad duty to tell you that's the case. One of us is a murderer."

The gasps went up; the heads turned around; the disbelieving eyes sought reassurance.

Bull had less to go on than Joe McCarthy, but he had that same kind of talent for quarter truths, insinuation, overstating the case, and pretending, perhaps even believing, he was the voice, and right hand, of God.

"A Bob Johnson murdered," said Bull. "And we're going to find out who it was."

With a stifled shriek, Roger yanked at the door. The broom held, and the witch-hunt took off.

# 44

Am was hoping that Sharon would be waiting for him in his office. He was feeling better about his prowess as an investigator. Now, at least, he had solved one crime (or a thousand, depending on how you looked at it). But it wasn't Sharon who sat waiting. Seated was an older man, heavy, but not portly. He had a dark suit and white hair and looked to be about sixty. His eyes were like Spencer Tracy's, with the same expressive blue that looked alternately inquisitorial and mischievous. The lines in his face were deeply cut, mined almost to his mouth, which gave him the appearance of having a perpetual smile or, if not quite that, a look of bemused whimsy.

"Mr. Caulfield?"

Am nodded, accepting and shaking an extended hand.

"One of the clerks suggested I wait for you here," the man said. "I've had a little problem."

"How may I help you, Mr. . . . ?"

"Harmon."

Am took a seat behind his desk, managing to keep a neutral, if concerned, look on his face. So this was Harmon, he thought. He looked more like a Shriner than a criminal, didn't look like a man who would take candy from a baby, but maybe he couldn't be trusted around a toddler carrying a Shirley Temple.

"Mr. Caulfield," he said, "I'm a business consultant who frequently works for a firm in San Diego. I've been a regular at your hotel for many years, and usually try to mate business with pleasure, giving myself a window of time before and after my work to relax. This afternoon I had nothing on my docket but a good book, an ocean vista, and a cold drink. I checked in a half hour ago and availed myself of the minibar in my room. And the strangest thing happened."

He paused, and then he posed. "I decided on a G and T. I poured myself some tonic, then added what I thought was gin."

Harmon looked at Am closely. Though Am already knew what he was going to say, his delivery was good enough to make him lean forward.

"The gin had been replaced," he said. "Replaced with water."

Harmon stayed seated but still gave the impression he was playing to an audience. "I have to admit to being a bit nonplussed, Mr. Caulfield. But I decided a vodka and tonic would do me almost as well. So I took a sip, and I haven't been so disappointed since pulling Kleenex out from Elsie McFadden's bra, lo those many years ago."

"Well, sir, when twice burned, even old dogs learn. I decided to take a close look at your libations, and upon inspection I found that every single bottle of alcohol had been doctored."

Harmon stopped talking, examined Am's face for signs of outrage. Am didn't have to fake that; Harmon's indignation was his.

"I am very, very, sorry this happened to you, Mr. Harmon," he said. "This kind of incident is very embarrassing."

Am gave Harmon a long look and a good read of his eyes. "It is hard to believe that people would stoop to such measures," he said, "difficult to imagine that they would go so far just to cadge a free drink. It wouldn't bother me if the start and finish of it was one little bottle of booze; it's the rippling effect that is so troublesome.

"First, the guest is unhappy, and they have a way of circulating their disappointment. A guest denied is a guest who calls the front desk. The clerk gets an earful and, after what seems an hour of ire, promises to rectify the situation. The discovery is usually made in the evening, so the bellman ends up getting dispatched to an empty room to get the liquor from another minibar, but the saga doesn't end there. The clerk has to document the incident to management, and the bellman has to leave a note with housekeeping. The inconvenience then rolls over into the next day.

"Housekeeping, which is in charge of replenishing the bottles and keeping an inventory, has to restock the items as well as account for the doctored booze. Management has to be very particular with the liquor inventory, has to make sure shrinkage is not occurring because of the staff imbibing. Unfortunately, the many suffer because of the one, and are treated with less dignity than they deserve because of some guest who was too cheap to pay for the booze. Doesn't seem fair, does it?"

Am's speech, and penetrating eyes, had made Harmon uncomfortable. "It sounds like much ado about a little prank," he said, though rather weakly.

"Once would have been a prank," Am said.

For Am, it felt good to finally confront a guest even if on a diplomatic level, where nothing overt could be stated. This was his moment of getting back at all the guests who had swapped their own twenty-five-watt bulbs for the Hotel's three-way variety, had replaced the batteries in their cameras with those in the Hotel's remote controls, and substituted old linen for new. Most of all, it was payback for every guest who had ever tampered with an honor bar.

Harmon stood up, and so did Am. "We appreciate your business, Mr. Harmon," he said. "Next year we will probably be putting computerized minibars in the rooms, the kind that immediately record a sale whenever a bottle or item is lifted out. That should eliminate any surprises."

Harmon looked at Am and asked sincerely, "No hard feelings, I hope?"

"None," said Am, extending his hand. "I'll make sure your honor bar gets restocked right away."

They shook hands, then Harmon raised up his arm as if offering a toast and said, "Cheers."

# 45

"A little peace, Julian," prayed Am. "I need a little peace."

Without it, Am feared, he would forever be sidetracked from hunting down the murderer. With not a little guilt he remembered that he had sent his partner off without him. Where was she? There were messages piled high on his desk, and he looked to see if one was from Sharon. The calls had come from reporters, concerned guests, friends, purveyors, and the curious, but there was nothing from her. Concerned, he called housekeeping and was relieved to hear that Sharon had taken a room checker along with her. At least she wasn't searching for a murderer by herself.

He was tempted to sweep all the messages into the trash. It was easy to understand why some guests insisted the desk hold all their calls. There is a power in putting your life beyond the reach of the world, in deciding when, and if, you are ready to respond to its knocking. That's what David Stern had done.

Something nagged at Am. Even presidents and rock stars could be reached through the switchboard, bona fide callers being privy to a code name or on an approved list. Stern hadn't been a rock star. He should have been reachable, if only to his secretary. Of course he could have just called into work every day and received his messages that way. But what if there had been an emergency? Or an important business decision that couldn't wait? Perhaps they had worked it out that anything important was to be addressed to the attention of room 605.

Am hadn't checked to see if there were any messages for David Stern. He assumed that if there had been any, the police would have picked them up. Since the lawyer had asked for anonymity, all messages or mail (or deliveries, such as wine and cheese) should have been held at the desk for him. Am's real dilemma was whether it was worth getting out of his seat to pursue yet another dead end. The front office supervisors were supposed to monitor the messages. Uncle Harry's note for niece Jane in room 223 wasn't supposed to extend beyond Jane's check-out, though too many times it did. Any message to infamous room 605 would have been noticed. Or would it? When you have over seven hundred rooms, names and numbers tend to blur.

Out at the front desk two clerks were laughing loudly. "Do it," said Tracy.

"Yes," Sue said. "I dare you."

T.K. looked as though he were on a comedic roll, never a good sign.

"Whatever it is," said Am, turning the corner so that everyone could see him, "I'd advise against it."

The clerks tried to stop laughing, unsuccessfully, and T.K. decided to explain. "I was just saying we should page over the intercom, 'Bob Johnson, please come to the lobby telephone. Bob Johnson, you have a call.' "

Am rolled his eyes, shook his head firmly, and started looking through the messages. As properties have become larger, and rooms too numerous to be accommodated by individual cubby holes, different message systems have been devised. No one will be happier than hotel PBX operators when voice mail becomes the rule of guest rooms throughout the land.

As Am suspected, there were no messages for room 605. Before giving up, he decided to look through the hold box, the Hotel's version of the dead letter office, a repository for messages, faxes, and mail that somehow never reached the guest. For once, the system worked.

Since Stern was no longer a registered guest (the Hotel had already direct-billed his firm in the hopes of collecting on the account), some clerk had redirected his fax to the hold box. Am held off reading the pages until he returned to his office. The cover sheet was from Stern's secretary. She had handwritten, "This man still firmly in the denial stage. Says that you're his only contact with his wife and he needs to hear from you yesterday. Didn't make any promises, of course. Soak some rays for me. Liz."

Then Am slowly read Carlton's letter, words from a man in pain. Carlton Smoltz had implored the lawyer to have his wife call him. He knew their marriage wasn't the best, but he was willing to work to make it better. Have her contact me, he had written, anytime.

What would David Stern have advised his client? Am hoped he would have told her to call her husband. This Carlton sounded sincere. Maybe now that there was no longer a lawyer between them, Carlton and his wife would get back together.

Am dropped the fax into his wastebasket, then thought better of that and retrieved it. He might be Carlton's only chance. Am would have preferred sending the words directly to Mrs. Smoltz, but he decided the right thing to do was to send them back to Stern's firm.

"I know his room number!"

Sharon's traditional reserve was broken. She was all but dancing in his office. "He's in two oh eight. I'll bet you anything."

She couldn't stand still, had to walk around as she excitedly described what *wasn't* in room 208. When she finished, Am had trouble being as enthusiastic.

"Did anyone identify him as the occupant of the room?" he asked.

"Not exactly. . . ."

"And did you make sure he didn't send his laundry out?" Unsaid: If Wrong Way fouled up on one delivery, what's to say he didn't another?

Her face fell. "I didn't think of that."

Am picked up the phone, punched in an extension. "I'd like you to check if any laundry went out for room two oh eight. The name's Bob Johnson. Bob . . ."

He looked to Sharon for a middle name. "Carlton," she said.

"Carlton?"

She nodded, albeit with some surprise. The sharpness of his response hadn't seemed necessary.

"Bob Carlton Johnson," Am announced, both to the phone and to himself. A few seconds later he said, "Thanks," but the quizzical expression remained on his face.

Sharon couldn't restrain herself. "Well?"

"Oh," said Am, remembering the purpose of the call. "He didn't send out any laundry or dry cleaning."

She sighed in relief, then looked afraid once more. "Maybe he's already skipped. There's hardly anything in the room."

Am wasn't listening. He was thinking about the name Carlton. It was a coincidence. It had to be. The faxed letter he had read hadn't contained any threats or recriminations. There wasn't a tone of "reconcile, or else." And yet . . .

He motioned Sharon to sit and passed her the fax. She read it, put it down, then picked it up and looked at it a second time. She was about to respond when Jimmy Mazzelli marched in.

"Trouble, Am."

The bellman threw himself on the chair next to Sharon, gave her a casual nod, and slouched.

"What now?" asked Am. His echo: This better be important.

"Bob Johnsons."

Am covered his face but resisted the impulse to cover his ears.

"They got wind of the rumor, Am. Responded pretty vigorously to it."

"What rumor?"

"That one of the Bob Johnsons is the murderer. The talk is, you guys even got a sketch of him."

Jimmy straightened a little and looked around. He hadn't forgotten about the incentive money offered for getting one of those sketches. Though the time limit had expired, he was still confident he could get some green out of Mr. Johnson. Unfortunately there didn't appear to be a copy sitting around.

Am was afraid to ask, but he did: "What happened?"

"From what I hear, the Neptune Room got closed off to the world, and the interrogations got pretty nasty. Everybody started pointing the finger at everybody else. Some fights broke out, and there were all sorts of accusations. Some confessions, too. Everyone had to provide identification. Turned out there were some ringers, guys with names like Henry Robert Johnson and Daniel Bob Johnson. That's against their rules. The first name's got to be either Robert, Bob, or Bobbi."

The Bob Johnson Society ground rules were of no interest whatsoever to either Sharon or Am. "Get on with it," she snapped.

Jimmy looked at her with a little surprise, then continued. "There were a couple of real phonies, though. One was an actor. He was going deep cover. Guess his part wasn't really supposed to start until the next act. The other actors vouched for him. But Casper didn't have it so easy."

"Roger?" asked Sharon.

"The same. He tried to tell everyone he was the front office manager of the Hotel, but big Mr. Johnson—"

Bull.

"—said that he thought front office managers were supposed to be around the front desk, and he couldn't remember seeing him there. No one else could, either."

"Is he all right?" Sharon had the decency to ask the question. Am was more interested in the method, and length, of the torture.

"Yeah. When he finally convinced them he really did work for the Hotel, they still pressed him on his being a spy at their meeting. Casper told them he wasn't with security exactly, but more with the Hotel secret police, and he was doing undercover on the murder. I heard from a banquet waiter that he whined and cried until they let him go."

"Are they still in the Neptune Room?" asked Am.

"Nope. Broke up a few minutes ago."

"And I suppose," Am said wearily, "they're going around in posses again."

Jimmy shook his head. "For most of them, it's a siege mentality. That's what I came to warn you about. A lot of them have barricaded their rooms. They're afraid to go out or let anyone in. You should have seen them when they left the Neptune Room. They walked out like crabs, scuttling backward, afraid for their backs, afraid of each other. Some of them were holding cocktail weenie skewers, and kept swiveling around a hundred and eighty degrees. Bob Johnson isn't a password for hugs and brotherhood anymore, not by a long shot. You whisper 'Bob Johnson' to them now, and most of them jump."

Good, thought Am. Now we're even.

Jimmy looked around again. He still didn't see the sketch. "So, I was thinking, Am. Maybe if you gave me a copy of that sketch, I could put the rest of the Bob Johnsons at ease. If we don't act soon, the whole lot of them might check out. Most of those that doubled up are at the desk now, either leaving or trying to get a room of their own. They don't trust their roommates anymore."

"What a shame," said Am.

# 46

"I remember the day I gave up on jigsaw puzzles," said Am. "A friend had given me one of those giant ones with a few thousand pieces. I worked on that damn thing for days. It's a scene forever ingrained in my mind, a Yankee Clipper gliding across the sea. The puzzle was a bear. Between the foreground and background were several shades of blue that were all but indistinguishable, and the clouds and sea froth were of the same consistency. I swore that puzzle wouldn't beat me, and yet it did."

"How?" asked Sharon.

"It was short one piece. To me, that hole looked about as big as the Grand Canyon."

Sharon understood his reference and his unhappiness. They had painstakingly put together their murder puzzle and had come up with a face, name, and motive. Their only missing piece was the murderer, admittedly a large piece. It didn't matter that everything else was in place; there remained only that gaping hole.

Reluctantly Am and Sharon had called in McHugh and the SDPD. A cordon of plainclothes police had descended upon the Hotel. Sketches of Carlton Smoltz had been given to all of the undercover officers and sentries posted at all entrances

and exits. Calls had been made and information verified.
Jane Doe was positively identified as Deidre Smoltz. As the
hours passed, different teams were organized and contingencies planned, but Carlton didn't cooperate by returning to the
Hotel. Rooms 207, 208, and 209 now housed San Diego's
finest, with McHugh himself holed up in room 208. The detectives weren't optimistic, though; most were certain that
Carlton had fled the city and wasn't coming back.

Though Am had helped the police coordinate their surveillance, his involvement felt anticlimactic, more busy-work
than anything else. The excitement was gone, and he was left
with the feeling that he had fallen short. He experienced the
letdown of being outside the loop, of being the one who answered the phone instead of making the call.

Sharon had noticed his increasing gloominess. "Hey," she
said, "even McHugh said we did well."

"That's what he tells all the meter maids." Am picked up
his jacket, threw it over his shoulder. "See you."

"You leaving?"

He offered a lackluster nod, which made her angry. His attitude suggested that all their efforts didn't matter. "It's Saturday night," she yelled to his back. His cowardly back.

Her words stopped Am. What exactly did she mean? Anyone who worked in hotels had a calendar and time frame not
in keeping with most of the industrialized world. To Am,
Saturday night meant more functions than usual and a full
Hotel.

"So what?"

Did she have to hit him over the head? "Didn't we talk
about dinner and drinks tonight?"

Surprised: "Sort of."

"I haven't eaten a thing all day."

"Neither have I," he said. Except, he remembered, that
piece of margarita cheesecake.

She threw her jacket over her shoulder, reminiscent of his
posturing. "Shall we go?"

He nodded and hurriedly thought of a plan for the evening
that wouldn't take them inland. It wouldn't do to have Annette break down on their first date. Or would it? He de-

scribed Annette's history and her quirks, but Sharon wasn't sure whether to believe him.

"We could head east," Am suggested.

"No," said Sharon. She wasn't superstitious, but like most people, she didn't walk under a ladder unless she had to.

Several cars passed them, but not without a little rubber-necking and a little smiling. "This car isn't exactly incon-spicuous," said Sharon.

"Twenty smiles to the gallon," said Am. "Even more when we do parades."

"Parades?"

"Annette, and me, and about fifty other woodies some-times tour with the OB Geriatrics. We putter around, long boards in tow, and offer viewers nostalgic Elysian Fields, or at least beaches. Unanswered, of course, is the question of which came first, the beaches or the illusion."

"You're raining on my parade," she said.

"It never rains in Southern California. Sometimes it just mists very heavily."

"Who are the OB Geriatrics?"

She was a careful listener, something he wasn't used to, something that was a little bit frightening. "Official name, the Ocean Beach Geriatric Surf Club Precision Marching Surfboard Drill Team and Gidget Patrol, usually shortened to the OB Geriatrics."

In an attempt at a Rod Serling voice, Am said, "Imagine, if you will, a collection of woodies, followed by a bevy of beach bunny Gidgets, and then the *pièce de résistance,* a group of aging surfers. Boards in hand, aloha shirts on their backs, the Geriatrics show on land what they do on sea: take the big waves. Their skits, choreographed by booming music, and a few lifeguard types with whistles, have them hanging ten, wiping out, and running around like a latter-day collection of Busby Berkeleys. Around them are such props as papier-mâché seagulls, beach chairs, inflatable sharks, one with a human leg in a toothed mouth, and cheering Gidgets in Hula Hoops. Like Indians of old demonstrating their skill at the hunt, the surfers pantomime their ride of the big blue horse, but instead of tom-toms, there are the sounds of 'Surf-ing Safari,' and 'Wipeout,' and 'Surfing U.S.A.,' pushing percussions that have the crowds cheering, singing, and dancing.

"Of course, these days," added Am, giving up on his "Twilight Zone" voice, "most of the Geriatrics probably surf better on asphalt than on the ocean."

"And are they really a precision surfboard drill team?"

"That sort of depends on how many beers they've had beforehand. Another old tradition."

They cruised south along the coastline, proceeding through the Bird Rock area of La Jolla onto Mission Boulevard, then through Pacific Beach and Mission Beach. The lights of Belmont Park's Giant Dipper roller coaster beckoned them to stop. Most of San Diego seemed to be out for a walk or a ride, and Am and Sharon joined the strollers. The crowd was polyglot and diverse, from the dressy set out to dine to the beach purists whose wardrobes didn't extend beyond bathing suits. Two SDPD patrolmen were out on their walking beat. The beach police wore shorts, which looked much more comfortable than bulletproof vests. Skateboards were not yet issued as official police equipment.

Screams are always a good draw. They drifted toward them and the roller coaster, where a long line of people were waiting to have their near death experiences.

"One of San Diego's other landmarks," said Am. "Like the Hotel California, the Giant Dipper is on the *National Register of Historic Places.*"

"Are you kidding?" she asked.

"I am not," he said. "It was built in 1925 and is now the last of its kind."

The carriages slowly creaked up the rails, but though the roller coaster was of age for Social Security, she still knew how to thrill. The speed picked up and with it the banks, drops, curves, and, most of all, the screams.

"Care for a ride?" asked Am.

"Thanks, but I've had enough thrills and chills for the weekend."

They continued their stroll, coming to the Plunge, Southern California's largest indoor pool and a venerable landmark for the swimming set. The huge pool had been put out of the athlete's foot business for a few years but after a face lift had returned grander than ever. Short of the ocean, it offered more liquid space than any other spot in the city. Sharon was particularly taken by the huge mural on the wall, a pod of killer whales. She moved her head up and down and then side to side, never taking her eyes off the artwork. At last she announced, "I don't like it."

"Why not?"

"Those whales seem to be moving, following you around like the Mona Lisa's eyes. It must be disconcerting to swim laps and always feel like you're being pursued by killer whales."

"Maybe that's the idea, to make people swim all the faster."

They moved on, stopping frequently to window-shop. Sharon insisted on going into only one store, a surf shop. Her browsing, Am thought, was reminiscent of a tourist's looking upon quaint aboriginal artifacts. She marveled at the different kinds of boards, the long and the short of them, the body boards, boogie boards, and knee boards. Fingering through the multitude of waxes, wet suits, sunblock, beachwear, decals, and bumper stickers, Sharon almost looked as if she were tempted to go native. When in Rome . . .

"Ready to take up the sport?" asked Am.

"Right after bullfighting," she said.

"Not forty miles from here we could catch a bullfight," said Am. "There are two bull rings in Tijuana."

She shook her head emphatically. "I get squeamish enough watching football."

"Maybe the matador would present you with the ears."

"If he did, I'd probably present him with my dinner."

Her announcing "dinner" put an immediacy to their hunger. In their short drive, they had probably passed a hundred restaurants, every one of which now seemed to be calling. But this was a night, Am thought, for fine dining. Sharon would want finger bowls and menus where English was the second language.

"We better get our name on a wait list," he said.

She surprised him: "Why don't we hold the tablecloth, and the anchovies?"

They ate pizza on the boardwalk, not goat's cheese with

hearts of palm and sun-dried tomatoes, but pepperoni and mushroom with a runny red sauce. Straddling the beach wall, they alternated between watching the tide and watching the tide of humanity. As if to sum up their viewing, Am said, "Freud said the ocean is feminine, and also said a lot of people are nuts."

"Is that an exact quote?"

"Close enough."

She questioned him about where he got off talking about Freud, and waxing poetic, and sometimes sounding pedantic, and Am told her about his philosophical meanderings and how for years he had faithfully scanned the Help Wanteds in the hopes of finding some firm advertising for a philosopher, "a pursuit," he said, "that has proved as fruitless as Diogenes going out with his lantern and searching for an honest man."

"Why hotels?" she asked.

"Why not? A fantasy industry in a fantasy city."

"And what makes this a fantasy city?"

"It should be more desert than not, and maybe because of that, it's difficult to tell what is mirage and what isn't. This is a city where old is measured not in centuries, but in decades, where Yuletide is celebrated by sailors in Hawaiian shirts cruising San Diego Bay in boats draped with Christmas lights, where the change of seasons is measured not by falling leaves or dropping snow, but by the number of convertibles with their tops down.

"San Diego would be a difficult city to invent if it didn't already exist. Some great fantasists have known that. Ted Geisel, better known as Dr. Seuss, lived out most of his life in La Jolla, and L. Frank Baum wrote one of his Oz books in Coronado."

Am opened his arms to all that was around them. "Behold," he said. "Emerald City."

"And that makes you what, the Wizard?"

"Sometimes. Guests come to the Hotel for a respite from the real world. Any great hotel fosters an environment of fantasy, has a staff of magicians, each and every one versed in maintaining illusions. Showmanship is important, and so is sleight of hand. No one wants to see a juggler sweating, or an illusionist positioning mirrors. The guests pay for their fantasies, and they make the staff pay dearly if they don't get them."

"And where does the Hotel California come into your fable?"

"Camelot, you mean. It is the constant among the transience, the castle among the sea foam. The Grande Dame is a personality, a presence, a pronoun, even. The Hotel. Everyone needs their magic places."

"And do you really think the Hotel is a magic place? Or is that just good PR?"

"Ask the pilgrims. They'll tell you."

"That's the first time I've ever heard the traveling wealthy referred to as 'pilgrims.' "

"Shrines must be kept up. And the wealthy aren't the only wayfarers. Sometimes the poor, or the middle class, decide to be king for a day. I think the Hotel is more special to them than it is to the rich. When their cameras come out it doesn't take much imagination to see them years from now thumbing through their photo albums and remembering little details of their stay, and the people that they were, and their memories. The Hotel seems to take on a cosmic significance to many, almost like a trip to Mecca. When staff becomes cynical, I try to remind them that they could be providing the brightest day in a fellow human being's existence."

Am paused for breath but not to consider, not to think of something cute or to be clever, but just to find the words for what was inside of him. In the background the noise from the roller coaster was building, along with the speed of its cars. There were a few screams from the occupants.

"I've watched the magic at work, couples teetering on divorce reclaiming the very room where they began their married journey, and finding their roots again," said Am. "I have seen the bitter and the sweet, a man who traveled with his wife's ashes three thousand miles, a husband who still remembered. He decided what was left of his wife belonged in the Pacific, off the shore of the Hotel, because their fondest memories were of that spot. He checked in with an urn, and when he registered, it was as mister and missus. For a few days, he told me, she was almost there."

As the speed of the Giant Dipper built, so did Am's words.

"I have witnessed the world coming to the Hotel, family reunions from around the globe. I have helped with special events, conferences on the environment, and international treaties, and have seen the world shrink, and become a better place, in front of my eyes.

"For over a century the movers and shakers have come to the Hotel. I know a maid who put a pea under a princess's mattress, just to see if she'd really feel it. I have shaken hands with the father of the atomic bomb and said, 'There—there goes someone who literally shook the world.' And on that same day I helped the doctor who found a cure for polio, and I thought, This is alpha, and this is omega. This is death, and this is life. That is the Hotel."

There was the grand finale of both machine and speech, the last rush of metal on wooden slats, of larynxes being stretched: "I remember helping the first woman astronaut up to her room, and I couldn't help but reflect that she who went to the stars, also went to our third floor. And somehow through that vicarious experience, I have been there to those stars."

Slow, and slower: "There are times when I curse the Hotel, when I hate her, when I wish she had not become such an encompassing part of my life. But I have never doubted that the Hotel is a special place. It is where I belong."

Am was suddenly embarrassed. He could never remember having rambled on like this before. In the madness of a workday it is often difficult to acknowledge special moments. His talk had been personal, introspective, not the usual kind of black humor uttered on the job. Being honest made him feel vulnerable. He looked for an easy joke, or a pat statement, but found himself short of any, so he looked at Sharon instead.

She was trying to hide her tears, but not doing a very good job. Surprised, Am wasn't sure what he should say or do. In the movies, men were always pulling clean handkerchiefs out of their pockets, but Am only had a Swiss Army knife in his pocket, and she didn't need a bottle opener, but a closer.

Still, he attempted chivalry. He carefully wiped some crusted pizza sauce off his napkin and handed it to her. Sharon rather fiercely attacked her eyes.

"They're not really tears," she said. "Just California mist."

# 47

They had drinks at Jose Murphy's, a Pacific Beach club as schizophrenic as its name, and between listening to a band and watching other people dance, they talked. Sharon asked more questions than he did, and Am wondered if she was that curious or whether it was a defense mechanism. She inquired of the loves in his life, and Am explained how he hadn't really dated for six months, but that the time alone had been good for him. Until the breakups, he had been preoccupied.

Breakups?

Almost apologetically, he explained he had been dating two women at the same time. "It wasn't planned," he said. "It just sort of happened. One was eight years older than I am, and the other ten years younger. The older one liked staying at home, and playing Scrabble, and going for quiet walks, while the younger preferred night life, and dancing, and a faster lane."

"So what happened?"

"I went bald," said Am.

Sharon pointedly scrutinized his full head of wavy hair, then questioned him with a look.

"Not literally, just mentally. I relived the Aesop's fable of the red-haired man with two mistresses, the one older and the other younger. When he was with the older one she plucked out his red hairs, while the younger one pulled out his gray hairs. They plucked and plucked until he went bald."

"A hair-raising story," she said. "It must have been terrible having two women fawn over you. What's next? Triplets? And since they'd all be the same age, you wouldn't have to worry about going bald."

"I'm not looking for triplets," Am said, "and it wasn't a case of losing hairs. I just didn't lose my head to either one of them."

His eyes demanded hers, and his message was this: You, I could lose my head to you. And she didn't immediately look away.

They drove back to the Hotel, Am playing tour guide along the way, describing the names of various beaches and the lore associated with them. They parked Annette near Children's Cove and stopped to look for sea lions on Seal Rock; but they didn't see any. The moon was full, and there was a hint of coastal sage in the air. Everywhere there seemed to be something Am wanted to show her: the caves around La Jolla Cove where opium smugglers used to store their wares; the remains of Alligator Head, a rock landmark whose jaws had been taken years back by a storm; the crumbling edifices of "Red Roost" and "Red Rest," reminders of the days in La Jolla when all homes had been identified by names and not street numbers, a practice the U.S. postmaster put a stop to.

They watched the activity at La Jolla Cove, three scuba divers going out for a night dive, and marked their progress by their luminescent green lights. Unsaid, but between them, was the feeling that they too were venturing forward into new depths. They slowly retraced their way along the path, detouring for a time with their shoes off to amble in the grass of Scripps Park, before finally returning to their footwear and the trail. The strong sound of the surf reminded Am of yet another landmark. "Boomer Beach," he said. "When the surf is up, it really booms."

The pounding of the ocean stopped them. They stood close to one another, could feel the impact of the torrents of water. It wasn't a scene out of *From Here to Eternity*, but they found themselves holding each other, and kissing, and coming up for breath.

Sharon finally broke away. "Am—orous," she said. "That must be the secret of your nickname."

"No," he said.

"Am I getting close?"

"It depends." His lips moved near hers, but she wasn't about to be put off—that, or she thought their kissing had gone far enough.

"Give me a hint."

Her single-mindedness was both beguiling and frustrating. "I earned it on the job."

"That's not much of a hint."

They started walking again. Sharon worked at wangling more information, but Am was closemouthed. When they got back to the car neither was quite satisfied with the other. In silence they drove back to the Hotel. Am found a spot next to her car, but good nights didn't immediately follow. By mutual signal they reached for the other and began to kiss once again. Their breathing became short, their flesh warm and sensitive. Again Sharon broke their contact.

"No more, Am—ore," she said, a guess and a plea in her statement.

"I have protection," he said.

"As we know only too well," she said, "condoms break." Then she kissed him on the cheek, patted Annette's upholstery good night, and stepped out of the car. "I had a wonderful time," she said.

"The night's still young," he said, but she laughed. He waited until she drove off, and still he sat. He needed to cool down, but even more than that, there were lots of things to think about. Oddly, her statement kept playing in his mind. Condoms break. That was obvious, wasn't it? But it was something he hadn't thought of. Tim Kelly, the guest who had checked out the hard way, returned to his thoughts. Am decided a talk with the night auditor, and night security, was in order. He wanted to see if a theory of his held water. The notion was a little crazy, but it was something he felt compelled to check into.

It was another two hours before he got home. Am's curiosity might not have killed him, but he was damn tired. As he turned onto Coast Boulevard, the signal lights from the train tracks started flashing, and the barriers moved into place. Freight train, he thought. Too late for the passenger trains. Fighting off sleep, he waited until the train passed by. His hobo spirit was willing, but his flesh was weak. Someday, he thought, yawning, I'll hop aboard. I'll travel north, with stops in Oceanside, and San Clemente, San Juan Capistrano, and sometimes Irvine . . .

He parked Annette in her garage.

. . . and Santa Ana, and Anaheim, and Fullerton, and Los Angeles . . .

Almost sleepwalking, he found his way to his bed.

. . . and with continuing service on to Glendale, Van Nuys, Chatsworth, Simi Valley, Oxnard, Ventura, and, and . . .

The train stops worked better than sheep. He fell asleep before running out of them.

# 48

Whatever happened to those IBM signs, thought Am, the ones that used to say THINK?

In the sixties, there had probably been millions of those placards on walls. It hadn't taken very long for the variations to follow, THIMK being one of the most popular. Now there weren't even any THIMK signs to be seen. Either the country hadn't been into thinking for a few decades (and not just limited to the Reagan era), or thought processes didn't need to be exhorted by signs.

It was early in the morning to have to think so hard, but Am still tried. The results, he feared, were closer to thimk. He decided the best way to try to get one particular answer was to place some personal ads in the local newspapers, as well as post his inquiry around high schools in the area. He worked on the wording, then called in his ad to the newspapers. Judging by the bored voices of the receptionists, they had taken much stranger personals.

There was only one incident report from the night before, and it involved neither Carlton Smoltz nor the Bob Johnsons. There had been several noise complaints stemming from a celebratory party thrown by Ducky Duckworth. The Padres had signed Duckworth, the possessor of one of the best arms in baseball, to a thirty-million-dollar pact. He and his friends had celebrated away over ten thousand of those dollars between the hours of 9 P.M. and 2 A.M. Security had been dispatched several times to quiet them down. The merrymaking hadn't been confined only to Duckworth's room. A dozen of the revelers had ended up swimming naked in the north pool. Am decided two notes were in order, one to the food and beverage director and the other to housekeeping. By running up so much alcohol to the room, the restaurant had fueled the party. What was good for F&B was not always necessarily good for the Hotel, and this was one instance where service should have been slow or even nonexistent. His note to housekeeping included a copy of security's report and a request for them to look over Duckworth's room before he checked out. Am was afraid that the party might have resulted in the kind of interior decoration the Hotel didn't want. If the room was trashed, he wanted Duckworth to pay for the damages. From experience he knew it was always easier to collect payment before a guest checked out. Afterward they were likely to blame any damages on anything from an earthquake to the maid.

The notes written and dispatched, Am decided some coffee and maybe a Danish would taste good. He wandered over to the staff cafeteria but found Marcel Charvet standing between him and his coffee. It was a dear price to pay for his caffeine habit.

"Ham, Ham!" he said, slapping Am enthusiastically on his shoulder. "The myzteree is zolved!"

"Misery?"

"Myztery. Come with me."

Am reluctantly followed Marcel to his office. When the chef picked up a bag, Am was afraid he was going to get a noseful of opossum, but instead Marcel dramatically revealed a bag full of walnut-size balls.

"Ze truffles," Marcel said triumphantly.

The missing truffles. The ones Am had said he would be on the lookout for. He picked up one of the unprepossessing fungi. It didn't seem the thing of culinary orgasms. Am sniffed at it but failed to discern anything more than a slightly musty odor.

"Good, no?" asked Marcel.

Agreeing was easiest. He nodded.

"Would you like to meet ze detective?"

Competition. "Sure."

"Voilà."

Am had thought the tablecloth was covering a food delivery. In a way it was. A pig was in a cage, but Marcel didn't make introductions.

"Zis peeg keep pushing at his box," said Marcel. "He sneef like he smell a sow in heat. So I wonder what smell so good to him. And behind ze door, under a towel in ze corner, I find ze truffles."

"What's the pig doing here, Marcel?"

"Ze luau tomorrow night."

Oh, no, another ersatz Hawaiian dinner. Any other chef in town would have ordered an already butchered pig. Knowing he shouldn't ask the question, Am still did: "Why a live pig?"

Marcel started explaining, throwing in a lot of his spittle to boot. He told Am things about sweetbreads and other culinary concoctions that sounded like endorsements to vegetarianism. The chef had plans for everything from the blood to the offal.

"And ze, how you zay it, curl-le-Q tail, zay are delezious fried. . . ."

So much for the other Hotel detective. "Got to go, Marcel," said Am. "Lots of work."

"Ham," he said, "Ham! One more thing."

The pig wasn't the only one destined for the spit. Marcel moved in close for the kill.

"Ze Weintraubs," he said, liberally spraying on Am, "came in for dinner last night."

Oh, no, thought Am.

"Zay both wanted ze veal marsala. Zay said zay wanted them just like zay had had ze night before, not like at dinner, but like ze one delivered to their room."

It had been a busy morning for Augustin Ramirez. Sundays were always popular for room service, with guests lounging in their beds and reading their thick newspapers.

But this morning hadn't been like most Sundays. Maybe it was a full moon. The guests he had served had acted very strange. Most of them had answered their doors as if deathly afraid, and their acting scared had made him feel the same. Some had even asked to see his identification. And all the strange people had the same name: Bob Johnson.

He felt his pocket. It didn't have the usual full feeling. The tips so far had been disappointing, and Sunday morning was usually one of his best days. The *policia* hadn't helped. All three rooms had ordered enormous breakfasts, but none had tipped worth a damn. And this after their rooms were free, and their meals were being direct-billed to the city of San Diego. But Augustin knew that over the course of a shift the good usually evened out with the bad. Though he'd endured the stinkers so far, you never knew what the rest of the day would bring.

What was this? He checked a ticket waiting for him in the kitchen. Ah, this was more like it. Room 322 had ordered a champagne breakfast, and not just any champagne. Dom Pérignon.

Augustin knocked on the door, always three knocks, no more, no less. The door opened. Some of the room service waiters liked to wheel their carts inside, but Augustin thought it was more classy to carry in a tray or two, to show his straight back and firm arm.

He started inside, paused to bow, and in that moment almost dropped the tray. In his forty years as a room service waiter, he had never dropped a tray. But in front of him was . . .

It was only his lifetime on the job, years of rote service, that allowed Augustin to get through the next few minutes. He stammered and stumbled; he mixed up silverware; and it took him three attempts to uncork the champagne. His hands were trembling, and he spilled the precious bubbly. But Augustin was lucky. The man didn't pay any attention to him, and neither did the woman, so focused were they on each other.

The champagne poured, the table laid out, Augustin readied to leave. There was the matter of collecting the money, or having the check signed, but the room service waiter was too

scared to approach the man. He wanted only to get out of the
room.

"Hey!"

The word stopped Augustin. He was found out.

"Didn't think I'd forget you, did you?"

Augustin didn't look in his eyes. He couldn't. He started
with his silent prayers, and that's when the man slipped three
bills into his front pocket. "Keep the change," he said.

"Thank you," said Augustin. He walked outside and almost collapsed. He had to find Am. There was no time to
delay!

But for all the urgency, the room service waiter still
stopped to peek at the money that had been thrust upon him.
Three hundred dollars! On a bill of a hundred and eighty-five
dollars, that was some tip.

For a murderer, Augustin decided, the man wasn't half-
bad.


It had been a magic evening for Carlton and Bobbi. They
had taken a cruise around San Diego Bay, had dined in a
downtown restaurant that overlooked the beckoning lights of
the city, then had found a nightclub where they listened to
some jazz and ended up swaying away on the dance floor.

Arriving back at the Hotel very late, they had kissed and
held all the way to her room (one of the police sentries was
in the restroom when they passed, and another didn't look
very closely; he was looking for a single man, not a couple).
At her door, Bobbi had invited Carlton in.

And there, the magic of their evening never really stopped.


What Augustin had told Am was impossible to believe. He
was surely mistaken. But after learning that room 322 was
registered to a Bobbi Lee Johnson, Am had dashed out of his
office. Now, almost at the room, he was second-guessing
himself. He didn't even have the stun gun. And wouldn't it
make sense to retrieve McHugh from room 208 and have
him accompany Am to 322? But he couldn't bring himself to
delay. What if Carlton Smoltz disappeared again? No, he had
to proceed alone.

He knocked on 322's door. Loudly. There wasn't an answer. What if Smoltz was jumping out the window? Or worse, what if he had murdered yet another woman?

Am inserted his pass key, but the door opened before he could turn it. There, in only a robe, holding a flute of champagne, was a man Am would have known anywhere.

"What's the meaning of this?" the man asked.

After his run, Am was breathing heavily and looked disheveled. He pointed to a spot on his blue blazer that invariably sported his name tag, only to see that it was missing, a likely victim to his exertions. Like other top management, Am wasn't required to wear the Hotel uniform and wasn't identifiable as an employee. He took a deep breath but even with the wind couldn't come up with an immediate response. Cops were lucky. They always had Miranda to fall back on. Carlton straightened, appeared both protective and authoritative. "Bobbi, call Hotel security."

Belatedly Am had his opening. "I am Hotel security," he said. "My name's Am Caulfield."

"Oh," said Carlton. His "Oh" said it all. He deflated slightly. Now that Carlton thought about it, the man did look familiar. He was the Hotel detective who had given the talk. His being here could only mean one thing. This was the moment of reckoning he had expected. Carlton took a sip of champagne. He had discovered champagne went well with both real and imagined police.

"Won't you come in, then, Mr. Caulfield?"

Am entered very slowly, very cautiously. He followed Carlton into the room and watched him sit down on the sofa. The host motioned for Am to sit on a nearby leather chair. Am did so but positioned himself at the end of the chair, ready to respond if Smoltz pulled a knife or a gun.

"Dear," announced Carlton, "we have company."

Bobbi Johnson was sitting at the table, finishing up her breakfast. She gave Am a big smile. "How do," she said. She was a voluptuous woman, big and meaty, and like Carlton, she had on only the Hotel robe. "Champagne?" she asked.

"No, thank you," said Am.

Bobbi joined Carlton on the sofa. They gave each other a look that had too much significance for Am's comfort, but

Carlton disarmed his suspicions with the question: "Do you have a clergyman in this Hotel?"

Am breathed a sigh of relief. The murderer did feel remorse. Although the Hotel had a chapel, there was no Hotel clergyman on property. "No," said Am, "but I can get you one. As they say, confession is good for the soul."

It took Carlton a moment before he understood. "Oh, not that," he said. The words were uttered with a grimace and what appeared to be all sincerity, but they were words spoken with a finality, the firm shutting of a sad book.

Carlton regained his bearings, took a moment to squeeze Bobbi's arm. "It's just that we want to be married," he said, "and we can't think of any other place we'd rather have our wedding than here."

The couple held hands. Am wasn't sure whether to be complimented or insulted. The man had murdered his wife on Thursday and now wanted to be married on Sunday. In a roundabout way, he supposed, Smoltz believed in the sanctity of marriage.

Bobbi poked Carlton in the ribs and whispered something in his ear. Am tensed again, suspecting they might be plotting something. "That's right," said Carlton. "Perhaps a judge would be better. We were hoping I might legally change my name before the ceremony. I promised Bobbi that I'd become a Bob Johnson. She's kind of partial to that name, and so am I."

The two of them smiled at one another.

"Mr. Johnson," said Am, "I mean, Mr. Smoltz, do you realize the seriousness of this situation?"

"I do," he said. "I have found the woman I love, and nothing is so important as to make things right with her."

Am shook his head. "I mean—"

"If you're referring to what happened the other day," said Bobbi, "Bobby"—Carlton! Am wanted to scream—"told me everything. He said he didn't want to drag me into the mud, and didn't want to woo me under false pretenses. Any other man I know would have done his poking first and his talking later, but not Bobby. He's a gentleman, and what happened was an accident. If you ask me, that two-timer and her no-good lawyer got what they deserved. . . ."

"Now, Bobbi," said Carlton.

They reached for each other's hands. "Bob still accepts all the responsibility like a real man," she said. "But I'm telling you, that strumpet and her Lothario forced him to act as he did. That's the way I'm betting any jury is going to see it, and even if they don't, I'll stand by my man."

In the face of all her clichés, Am was speechless.

"I now have a reason to fight," said Bob/Carlton, "and to live."

His eyes teared up. He tried to rub away the tears, but instead his brushing opened up the ducts, and the dam. "Oh, Bobby," said Bobbi, holding him and kissing his wet cheeks. He returned her kisses, then looked to Am, slightly embarrassed.

"I am not without remorse, Mr. Caulfield," he said. "I will forever be troubled by what I did. There is no justification for my actions, and there will be retribution—my own, and the state's. But understand that I don't want to mourn away the few minutes of freedom I have remaining. There will be time enough for that. For now, selfish as it seems, I want to declare my love."

Bobbi took his hand. "We want to declare our love."

Am didn't know what to say. He worked in a business that had inculcated in him the primary goal of making the guest happy. But what did you do when that guest was a murderer?

"Mr. Smoltz," he said, "a wedding is out of the question. The Hotel cannot condone murder, nor can we cater to murderers."

Bobbi started to cry. Carlton was more understanding. Head bent, he nodded sadly, then tried to comfort his fiancée.

The sobbing eventually got to Am. What the hell, he thought. He cleared his throat, got Bobbi's and Carlton's attention.

"Perhaps an impromptu engagement party," he said, "wouldn't be absolutely out of the question."

# 49

Am tried not to dwell on what he was doing. At odd moments he realized that facilitating the engagement party of a murderer was, well—criminal. But that murderer, at least until the police took him away, was still a guest. Am took some solace in the fact that he wasn't organizing an engagement party so much as a going-away party.

It took him less than an hour to set everything up. In attendance were Am and Sharon, a lawyer Am had recommended for Carlton, a photographer, Philip the banquet waiter, Dorothy from catering, and Wallace Talbot. Carlton was delighted that Wallace was in attendance, saying it was wonderful to have a celebrity in their midst. For his part, Wallace went around and handed everyone peppermint sticks.

The party was bittersweet, tears with laugher. It reminded Am of a bon voyage party he'd once attended, when a friend of his was shipping out to 'Nam. Everyone tried to maintain the fantasy of happiness, but reality arrived with the toasts. Even champagne bubbles can't suspend illusion indefinitely. Carlton left Bobbi's arms for his lawyer's, and Am walked both of them to room 208. McHugh and the police had arranged for a late check-out, ostensibly because they wanted to make sure the murderer didn't show up, but it was the start of the football season after all. When Carlton knocked on the door (late in the third quarter), Am was sorry he hadn't brought along the party photographer to document McHugh's expression. It was almost vindication enough. Sending the detective the engagement party pictures, he decided, would even the score between them.

Am had expected a feeling of freedom to accompany the resolution of the case, but it was more of an emptiness. He had been so involved, withdrawal was hard. He sat at his desk and tried to attend to piled-up work, but he found it difficult, trivial compared to his case. His mood didn't improve when he heard that Kendrick had returned to the property. His impulse was to leave, but he resisted that. Kendrick would only call him at home or, worse, torture him by not calling. Better to face up to him sooner than later. He was sure Kendrick wouldn't have any difficulty finding fault with everything he had done.

The telephone rang. Kendrick, thought Am. But it wasn't. The display showed the housekeeper's extension.

"You were right, Am," said an excited Barb Terry. "We kept a watch on his room, but no one got the chance to go in until just now, what with his half-day rate, and his Do Not Disturb sign up all day, and his not wanting no maid service. But I had everyone watching for him. Soon's he left the room I had one of the room checkers run in. She just called me and said he'd done some serious damage."

"Who?" said Am, then added, "What?"

Barb sounded disappointed that Am didn't know what she was talking about. "Why, Ducky Duckworth," she said.

Just how many straws does it take to break the camel's back? thought Am, not for the first time. "Thanks, Barb."

"Better grab him, Am. He's about to check out."

Am grabbed his coat and name tag; it wasn't quite the statement of a sheriff's badge and his six-shooter, but when confronting a guest he knew it was always best to look as official as possible. He hurried to the lobby, hoping to intercept Ducky before he checked out, but the pitcher was already at the front desk. He was trying to casually read the sports section, the same sports section that played up his signing with a banner headline. How had one sportscaster put it? "How much is the right hand of God worth? About what Ducky Duckworth signed for today."

T.K. was checking Ducky out. The desk clerk looked grim. If T.K. couldn't joke about it, the situation had to be serious. He saw Am and heaved a sigh of relief, motioning him with his head to join him at the desk. It was too late to head off Ducky anyway, so Am made his way behind the front desk and followed T.K.'s finger to the credit card terminal. The word *declined* was flashing.

Ducky's bill was for almost twelve thousand dollars. Most hotels process credit cards for the expected amount of a guest's stay upon check-in. The clerk who had obtained the initial approval hadn't anticipated Ducky's expensive party and had received authorization only for two thousand dollars. T.K. had apparently tried to get the additional amount approved, but without success. So how do you explain to the thirty-million-dollar man that his credit is no good?

There were other guests at the front desk, most of whom had already identified the pitcher. There are celebrities who love being noticed, and Ducky was one of them. He was a big man, about six feet three, with eyes as hard as his fastball. His face was thick and square, which made the bulge in his cheek stand out all the more. Am hoped he was doing his hamster act with bubble gum rather than chewing tobacco.

Whenever a guest's credit card is declined, that news is usually conveyed to the card holder by the clerk in low, funereal tones, but in this instance even a whisper would have been overheard. Am thought it best to spare the pitcher the embarrassment of having his private life made public and decided to steer him quietly to his office.

"Mr. Duckworth, I'm Am Caulfield, the assistant general manager of the Hotel, and—"

"How do you spell your name?" said Ducky, his tone bordering between boredom and annoyance.

Am pointed to his name tag.

"Well, give me a paper," Ducky said impatiently.

"For what?"

"You want my autograph or not?"

"Actually, I was hoping if you had a moment, we could talk in my office."

Ducky's crowd of admirers was getting larger. He yawned and stretched. "Don't really have a moment, son. Got a plane to catch."

The pitcher was probably a dozen years younger than Am. His pronouncement was likely meant to discourage other autograph seekers, but Am still didn't like being referred to as "son."

A little more firmly, he said, "If you'll just step this way . . ."

"Listen, son, I really got better things to do than discuss baseball with you. I'm just trying to pay my bill. That okay with you?"

There were about twice as many rubberneckers as before. Speaking softly, Am said, "It's a matter of your credit, Mr. Duckworth."

"What?"

His shout took in most of the lobby, brought absolute quiet to the entire front desk area. Ducky was looking at Am expectantly. Everybody was looking. Anything Am had to say was going to be heard by all. So be it.

"Sir," Am said, "your credit card has been declined."

At the best of times that news is embarrassing. This was not the best of times. Those who could contain themselves, smiled. Those who couldn't, started laughing. Here was a man who in essence had won the lottery, who had just been signed to a contract, and a lifetime, few could imagine. And now, for a moment, at least, he had to descend from his cloud.

Ducky didn't adjust to gravity very well. He glowered at the laughers and silenced everyone. "What the hell are you talking about? Did you see the fucking headlines today?"

"I did."

"I think I'll buy this Hotel," said Ducky. "It could sure use some changes."

Having announced he was a bigger man than everyone, Ducky straightened, picked up his bag, and started to leave. Calling after him, Am said, "Defrauding an innkeeper is a felony charge in this state, Mr. Duckworth."

That stopped the pitcher. "What?"

"You have an outstanding bill. And I understand there was considerable damage done to your room. If you walk out on those charges, I can only assume you are trying to defraud the Hotel, and I will be forced to call the police and ask them to put a warrant out for your arrest."

Ducky used his famous stare on Am. He gave him a look that would have made a cleanup hitter tremble, but when Am didn't blink, didn't show an inch of give, the pitcher suddenly capitulated. Ducky, after all, was a fine hurler. He was known for his smoke, but he did have an effective change-up. He walked back to the desk.

"Uh, is a personal check okay?" he asked. "How about I just leave it open, and you can figure out whatever's right?"

"That would be fine," Am said.

He ripped out a check, scrawled his signature, and didn't wait for a receipt, or a thank-you, just quickly walked away. Then Am heard an unfamiliar sound. Applause. And it wasn't for Ducky, it was for him. Perhaps two dozen guests and staff were clapping. At first Am was embarrassed, but that feeling passed. He pretended to step out of the dugout, doffed his cap to the crowd, then disappeared from sight as heroes are wont to do.

There was little time for Am to savor his small victory. He was told there was someone holding on the line for him, and the sinking feeling returned. Kendrick. But it was a female voice that returned his greeting.

"Am, this is Kris Carr."

"Ms. Carr. How are you?"

"I'm fine, Am."

She paused long enough to make him doubt that. "Not again?" he asked.

"Afraid so."

"I'll be right up."

Kris Carr was waiting at her door. She was wearing a terry-cloth robe and nothing else.

"He went for the frilled jobs again," she announced.

Am tried to maintain a serious demeanor. "Any idea when they turned up missing?"

"That's the thing I don't like. I wonder if someone's been watching me. I went down to the pool around three o'clock. The pervert must have come in between then and now."

Am looked at his watch. It was a little past five. "And you're sure your door was closed and locked?"

Kris nodded.

Am examined her sliding glass door and the windows and again could find no sign of forced entry. He sighed. "It looks like an in-house theft."

"Any suspects?"

"Two, maybe three hundred of our male staff."

Kris laughed and appeared to relax. She eyed Am speculatively, then altered her pose, leaning toward him, her robe opening up even more. She held the robe's belt in her hand and played with it slightly. By manipulating her clothes she added a new element between them, a tension. It was almost as if she were toying with a ripcord.

"Is one of them you, Am?" she asked.

He didn't say anything, was hard-pressed to find a proper answer.

"What are you thinking?" she asked.

What did most men think when confronted by those Grand Tetons? She had, after all, invited him to ask the question.

"Are they real?" he asked.

"What do you think?" she asked, moving closer.

She was one of those people who had probably picked the right job. Kris Carr was an unashamed exhibitionist. Am couldn't tell whether she was really making a play for him or whether she just wanted him to go weak at his knees.

"I asked you," he said.

She was close to him now. "They were enhanced some," she admitted, "but I haven't heard any complaints. The left one I call MasterCard, and the right one American Express."

Her announcement came with left and right emphasis, and Am was surprised that she hadn't named one of them Diners Club. For a moment he was paralyzed by the sight, but then his hotel training came to the fore. For the second time in a very few minutes he repeated himself: "Your credit cards are declined."

# 50

The UV light operated on batteries. It was portable but not inconspicuous. Am pretended it was a ray gun, and as he went around zapping the staff, he tried to make what he thought were appropriate Martian sounds. None of the employees seemed too surprised. And it was easier, and perhaps more in keeping with his role, to act offbeat and not offer any explanations. If he had played it as officious, he likely would have seen only half as many hands. Though he spied lots of warts, moles, hairs, and broken fingernails, he found no lime-green trace of the fluorescent dust.

He was half tempted to look at Kris Carr's hands. Maybe to get more attention she had faked the crime, but then she didn't seem like a woman who lacked attention. It was better to avoid the room anyway, he thought, as in his own mind he wasn't convinced it was just her hands he wanted to appraise.

By seven o'clock Am decided that he'd been witness to enough five-fingered failures. Tomorrow he'd do some more scanning. The tracer powder would last at least that long. He knew that compared to a murder the case was trivial, but he was both miffed and motivated: this mystery involved not only a theft, but a violation of a guest's privacy. The Hotel was lucky that Kris Carr was more insouciant about the thefts than most guests would have been. Maybe she was used to dispensing with her undergarments, but that still didn't make the thefts acceptable.

He had almost forgotten about Kendrick's return, but the note on his desk jarred that suppressed memory. "Please see Mr. Kendrick before you leave," the message demanded. Am was sure the operator had taken literary license and included the word *please.*

The executive offices were deserted save for Kendrick. He was talking on the phone, a conversation that interested him enough that he noticed neither Am's approach nor his subsequent disappearance. There are few instances where eavesdropping can be condoned, but Am thought this was one of them. By the sounds of it, Kendrick was talking with the company spy.

The conversation lasted almost ten minutes, with the weekend's events discussed in detail. The goings-on of the staff were dwelt upon, in particular the activities of "Mis-tah Caw-field." Being privy to only half the conversation, Am was afraid the spy would remain unidentified, but in the end Kendrick slipped up when he said: "Thank you for your report, Roger."

Casper was the spy. What should have been obvious, wasn't. Belatedly Am remembered that Casper had portrayed Mr. Derry at the Come as a Guest party. Derry was a regular from Langley, Virginia, and the Hotel staff was convinced that he was a CIA operative. Although quiet, there was something furtive about him. Roger had worn a raised, dark trench coat and had carried a walkie-talkie around with him. He must have thought he was pretty clever, coming as the spy guest and being the spy. Those without teeth sometimes find other ways to bite, and Am felt betrayed. He had always thought of Roger as being a scared little rabbit. Somehow that seemed preferable to a back stabber.

He crept back down the hall. It wouldn't do to walk in on Kendrick just now. After five minutes of standing around, Am loudly retraced his route. This time, as usual, Kendrick was well aware of his presence prior to his arrival.

"Come in, Mr. Caw-field," he said.

Am entered the office and sat on one of the GM's uncomfortable chairs. Kendrick sighed loudly, the ten-second variety. "Seems I can't go ah-way without everything going to hell."

Management by second-guessing is the fastest way for an employee to lose confidence, but Am was used to it by now. Rather than comment, he just looked at Kendrick, who stared right back. It was the straight-backed chair more than Kendrick's look that made Am squirm. He couldn't get comfortable, especially with the pressing in his groin and abdomen area. After several attempts at positioning, Am removed the source of the problem, the UV light he had crammed into his right front pocket.

"What is that?" Kendrick asked.

"An ultraviolet light," said Am. He hoped that would be explanation enough, but it wasn't.

"For what?"

Deciding a demonstration was in order, Am approached Kendrick's large desk. "I salted some objects with fluorescent tracer powder," he said. "The dust gives off a glow. This afternoon I was looking for a criminal with glitz mitts."

Am clicked on the light and played it over one of his hands. The light offered only a slightly purple hue. "Although you really can't see much here," Am said, "if I had come in contact with the powder, you would have seen . . ."

Without any forethought, and without any expectations, he swept the light over Kendrick's hands and suddenly stopped talking. It was a scene out of an old science fiction film where the radiation victims glowed. Kendrick's hands looked like a green toxic waste dump. They were phosphorescent, radiating a key lime glow.

"You!" he said, shocked. Amazed.

Then, with a little more thought and a little more feeling: "You son of a bitch!"

Kendrick didn't know his bras were in the wringer. "How dare you—"

"You stole Kris Carr's bras," Am said.

Taking a deep breath, attempting a defensive dignity, Kendrick said, "What are you talking about?"

Am shook his head. Who guards the goddamn guards? he

thought. He kept the UV light on Kendrick's hands. A strobe questioning light never worked so well.

"Maybe you can explain away your company spy and your less than ethical tactics. But try justifying your stealing the bras. I'd like to hear you do that."

Kendrick tried moving his hands, but Am followed them with the light, their dance of hands and light an odd choreographed sequence of spotlighted green beacons. Finally, with not a little desperation, Kendrick hid his hands under his large desk. Given that pose, his protestations of innocence sounded strained. "I have no idea what you are babbling—"

"People don't change their habits," said Am. "You worked as a GM for several prestigious hotels prior to coming here. You were in a position of trust. I'm willing to bet those properties also suffered from some strange thefts and that there were some oversize bras reported missing."

Hands still under the desk, Kendrick asked, "Are you willing to bet your job?"

Am thought about it for a moment. "Yes," he said. "I'm willing to bet my job."

There wasn't any bluff in his answer. Even Kendrick knew that. "Perhaps," he said, "we could work out an arrangement . . ."

Am laughed bitterly, and Kendrick stopped talking. Neither one of them said anything for a minute, both doing their own assessment of the situation. Am kept the light at the ready, and Kendrick kept his hands under his desk.

"I think it's unfair," Kendrick said finally, "that I should lose my career, and my reputa-shun, ov-ah such trivial—allegations."

It was as close as Kendrick could come to a plea and the first time Am could remember him engaging in something approaching a conversation, something other than giving orders.

"I work hard," Kendrick said. "You know that. I put in eighty-hour weeks. I know I am a perfectionist. I know I have the reputa-shun of being difficult. But I make money, and I make opera-shuns run more efficiently than they ever have before."

And you and your kind take the soul out of a place,

thought Am. You take away what made it special by bringing in a cookie cutter design and trying to stamp a uniformity that shouldn't be there. You save a nickel, but you lose a dollar. But you'll never understand that. You can't see that this Hotel needs its quirks and traditions. People come back for those.

"Not everyone wants McDonald's," said Am. "We have an original here, not a lithograph, and you've never treated it as such."

The only thing the two men had in common was the Hotel, but neither one of them knew it as the same property. Kendrick was leaning forward, straining to understand what Am was saying, but he couldn't comprehend. To him, the Hotel was like any other. It was a business formula, not a living and breathing thing. It was dollars and cents. And if there was room for anything else, it was oversize bras.

"I want your resignation," said Am. "Make it effective this evening, and clear out the office tonight. Your resignation letter will announce my appointment as acting general manager, and will recommend me for the permanent GM's position."

"That's blackmail," said Kendrick.

Am shook his head. "No, it's not. I deserve the job. I've earned it, and you know that. Besides, the owners will decide whether I stay or whether they want to bring in someone else."

"If I do as you say," said Kendrick, "do you promise to never men-shun a word of all this?"

"Yes," said Am, "provided you return the bras you stole, and provided you give me your word that you will never steal from any hotel you work for in the future."

"I promise," he said.

"And I, also."

Kendrick appeared relieved, but not completely; he looked like a man torn between conscience and self-preservation. "I am truhs-ting in your word as a gentleman," he said.

"You already have that."

The GM decided he was protected enough to be honest. He didn't act superior, but he didn't look beaten, either. Misery loves company, and he was ready to share. "You will find your victory not so sweet as you think," he said. "Although I am not at liberty to divulge what went on this weekend, you will soon be hearing from the owners. And I'm not talking about the old owners."

"What do you . . . ?"

Kendrick held up his hand. "I am not being coy, suh. I have already said more than was legal, or prudent. There are certain contingencies still being discussed, but I figured I owed you that much warning, at least."

The men regarded one another. There would never be admiration between them, never anything approaching friendliness. There was a bridge to their perspectives that neither had ever spanned, but at that moment they had at least come to some sort of agreement.

"We still un-dah-stand our compact?"

Am nodded. Kendrick could have left without warning him, but he hadn't. A change of ownership would likely mean Am wouldn't have a job, as new owners traditionally bring in their own management teams. It was a lot to take in all at once.

"So my reign will likely be short," said Am.

It was Kendrick's turn to nod. Am expected to feel bitterness, but he didn't. There was some sadness, but more than that was the sense of inevitability. Or was that futility?

"I am reminded," said Am, "of the monarch who asked his counselors to devise a saying that would serve in both prosperity and adversity, and they came up with, 'This, too, will pass.' Tomorrow I will be the GM of the Hotel California, but this, too, will pass."

Kendrick's head was cocked, like a dog trying to make out an unfamiliar sound. It was clear he couldn't understand what Am was getting at.

"I majored in philosophy," offered Am, "not hotel-motel management."

"Ah," said Kendrick, sounding sympathetic for once.

It was the right explanation. "How much time?" asked Am, the resigned terminal patient to the doctor.

"The sale should be final in a hundred days."

Not much time to pursue the Holy Grail, Am thought.

"Then I will have to make those days memorable," he said. "Like Camelot."

If things hadn't changed between them, Kendrick would likely have said, "What does running a hotel have to do with a bunch of silly knights?" But he didn't say anything. The agreement between the two men was not rapprochement. They didn't come away fathoming each other, didn't even shake hands as they took leave of one another for the last time, but as Am left the office, he did volunteer a final "Good-bye."

Looking up and catching his eye, Kendrick said, "Sayonara."

# 51

When he arrived at the Hotel on Monday, Am wasn't sure what he should do. For most of the morning he sat in his office. He wasn't hiding out, exactly—the faster-than-light Hotel grapevine had already put out the word that Kendrick had up and quit and Am had taken over, which had resulted in a constant stream of visitors offering their congratulations—but he really wasn't doing anything. To Am's mind, the high-point of his morning was when he raised himself out of his chair and turned his cartoon of the exasperated clerk and Cassie's drawing of Procrustes around again. Momentarily, at least, that made him feel better, but his malaise soon returned. There were things that needed doing, but he didn't want to do them. He felt deterred by the unpleasant matters yet to be faced up to, realities oppressive enough to keep him immobile. Most visitors saw his chipper face, but Am didn't offer Sharon that same mask.

"I understand congratulations are in order," she said.

"Yes."

Her demeanor was as tentative as his. "You don't sound very happy."

"I suppose I'm preoccupied," said Am.

"Over what?"

"Figuring out what season this is."

"I don't understand."

"I don't, either," said Am. "Some people never get used to this climate. They need leaves to change color. They need the snow and cold of winter, and the green promise of spring. Their lives are regulated around those conditions. But I'm used to January being Miss Elsie, who comes out from Minneapolis to escape the cold, and February is the Burkes, who never miss the golf tournament at Torrey Pines. I'm used to August bringing the extended Stephenson family to the beach, and September being Mr. and Mrs. Chu and their racing coterie for the last two weeks of the season. Every month of the year I associate with one guest or another."

"It sounds like you do know your seasons."

"Used to," said Am, but he didn't elaborate. He opened a box on his desk and took out a Bible.

"Representatives from the Gideons just dropped these off," said Am, "two old men. They wanted to know if we needed any more complimentary Bibles. Strange how Bibles are the only items in hotel rooms that management actively encourages guests to take, but they've never proved nearly as popular an offering as virtually everything else. We only needed one replacement box."

Am patted the carton and let a little quiet build. "We got to talking, and one of the men asked me if I knew the Bible. I told him that as a hotel manager I was well acquainted with the story of Job. They both thought that was pretty funny.

"I guess they were looking for an opportunity to proselytize. The other one said that in every business there was a 'time to weep and a time to laugh,' and then he credited Ecclesiastes. Judging from the last couple of days, that description sounds about right, doesn't it?"

Sharon wasn't sure where the conversation was going. She didn't say anything.

"Ecclesiastes," he mused, then thumbed through the Bible, found the book, and did a little silent reading. When he finished, he looked meditative.

"How about a book report?" asked Sharon.

"Funny. We were just talking about seasons, and that's kind of what's there, a time lesson. It reminds us that there's a time to be born and a time to die; a time to love and a time to hate.

"But what it doesn't tell," said Am, "is what time it is today."

If Sharon knew, she didn't tell him.

It was one of those beguiling days in the hotel business, where guests are effusive about what a wonderful stay they've had, and the staff can do no wrong, and everyone is smiling, and there is no better business to be employed in, and world peace seems not only possible but likely. There are those days.

Am had talked to the owners, and they had taken his ascension lightly, never hinting that great changes were afoot. Almost, he could revel in his new position, could just feel plain good. But even if Kendrick was wrong, even if he had planted seeds of doubt as his final sour grapes, there were still some matters pulling at Am. His puzzle was still missing a few pieces. He knew they wouldn't make the picture look any better, but it was time to put them in their place anyway.

In the afternoon he had gone to Kendrick's former office, had presumed to take over the great man's den. He was sitting at Kendrick's oversize desk when the moving men arrived. They had orders to take away the desk and the chairs. When Kendrick's furniture was removed, Am found himself sitting on the floor in the middle of what was now a cavernous room. The empty office amused him, as did his position. From the floor he made some calls and did some thinking. He didn't like what he was hearing, but he wasn't surprised. Am knew that if it was time for anything, it was time for truth.

There was one call he didn't expect. When you put a message in a bottle and throw it out into the ocean, it's unlikely you will ever hear back from anyone, but the long shot came in. Everything fell into place, but the fit was still lousy.

Room 711 was unoccupied. Am went up to the room and thought about Tim Kelly. He had been wrong about everything except his initial assertion that Tim Kelly had not committed suicide.

Sharon came up to the room a few minutes later. Am thought he owed her that much. "Hi," she said.

"*Hai,* " said Am. "Isn't that Japanese for yes?"

She nodded slightly and looked to him for further comment, but he didn't say anything else, just led her out to the balcony. The tiles had been replaced, and the balcony was well scrubbed. There was no plaque to Tim Kelly, nothing to indicate that he had dropped seven stories to his death.

He breathed deeply of the sea air and felt calmer. He didn't like looking at a death, so he looked at something better, the immutable ocean. Today it had an aquamarine tint, but every day its colors changed, its palette altered by the clouds, sun, tides, and kelp. He looked north, blinked hard as if to remove some motes in his eyes, then looked again and recognized the distant objects. The hang gliders were out in force, plying the late afternoon thermals. Some of the pilots were courting angels, had caught updrafts that made them look small, birdlike. To get to those heights, the pilots had to run and jump off the Torrey Pines cliffs. Am wondered if they made prayers to Daedalus and Icarus. It was a long way down.

"Tim Kelly died a silly death," he said.

Sharon stopped watching the hang gliders and focused on Am. "The other night you reminded me that condoms break. That got me to thinking. How do they break? And why?

"Maybe I was so hung up on the sexual element, I couldn't see the obvious. I forgot that condoms could be used for other things."

"What other things?"

"Water balloons. In my college days that seemed to be their primary use."

Am took a breath. He felt like one of those hang gliders, felt as though he were leaping off a cliff. "Tim Kelly was up on this balcony after a night of drinking and failed romance, and from here he looked down and saw a young couple making love.

"He decided to interrupt their lovemaking, decided to rain on their romantic parade. Kelly filled his condom with water. He couldn't just drop his balloon; he had a fairly long throw to reach them, and not the best vessel for the tossing. Kelly needed momentum. He began his run from the sliding glass doors of the balcony. I think he slipped near the railing."

Am kicked the framework and the tiles. "These doughnuts are more decoration than support," he said. "Kelly was intoxicated. He didn't know which end was up. A few of the tiles gave way. I imagine he panicked when his foot broke through. My guess is that he kicked himself up and over."

Sharon measured the hypothesis and the fall as well. The theory came up short. "That's still only a guess."

"No. Remember how we found water pooled in the bathroom the next day? That was the residue of Kelly's filling his condom. There was also the digs in the wood which marked where he skidded, and the fallen decorative tiles.

"And," said Am, "there's the couple who witnessed his fall. He's seventeen and she's sixteen. Next to the backseat of a car, there's no more popular place than the beach for young couples to go and make out. I placed some discreet ads and posted some notices at local schools. And just a short time ago I heard from a very uncertain young man. He told me about being on the beach with his girlfriend, and their being disturbed by some sound, and his looking up to see a man falling to his death. Tim Kelly got his desired coitus interruptus, but not in the way he wanted. He landed not ten yards from the couple. They didn't dare go to the police because the girl was afraid of what they'd have to say, of what they'd have to testify. Her parents didn't even know she was out. When they left the beach, they were in a panic."

"They left behind the confusing second condom," said Sharon.

"Yes."

"So what do you do with the information?"

"I tell Mrs. Kelly. Dying from a regrettable accident is a far better thing than thinking her husband killed himself."

"It could mean a lawsuit," she said. "Lawyers running around taking depositions, engineers doing decking studies, and the ABC investigating whether too much liquor was served."

"I guess that's something the new owners will have to worry about, isn't it?"

Sharon didn't move. What time was it? thought Am. Almost, it was a time to hate.

"You graduated from Cornell three years ago, not three months ago. Care to tell me what you've been doing since then?"

She didn't back down. "I imagine you already know."

"I do," said Am. "You've been working for Yamada Enterprises. Among their many holdings are hotels. You're one of their top hired guns. I assume you came in here to play Mata Hari, to collect whatever damning evidence you could. Is there some rule that everyone has to have spies these days? Is it de rigueur?"

She shook her head. "It's not like that. I was just supposed to analyze operations."

"Do they pay you in silver?"

"Try not to be bitter," she said. "The acquisition has been in process for some time. Mr. Yamada doesn't like surprises. He wanted me to look behind the scenes."

"I guess you gave him a real eyeful, huh?"

She didn't say anything.

"The murders didn't scare him off?"

"No," said Sharon. "They were leverage to get a better price."

Am laughed bitterly. "So it's a done deal?"

"Yes. I was going to tell you. . . ."

He didn't want to hear it. "The Hotel California is owned by the Japanese?"

"Yes."

It was wrong. You're not supposed to sell national monuments to foreigners. Other San Diego resorts had been purchased by the Japanese, La Costa Resort and Spa, and the Colonial Inn, and Le Meridien just to name a few, but the Hotel California was different. It was a landmark.

Sharon must have been reading his mind. "Didn't Americans buy the London Bridge? It's a global economy, Am. When the Japanese bought Radio City Music Hall, the Rockettes didn't trade in their high kicking for Kabuki theater. And when the Japanese purchased the Seattle Mariners, bought their piece of America's favorite pastime, the world didn't stop."

She was right. She was persuasive. But in his gut her words were all wrong. The Hotel California had always been an American dream.

"Are we going to get futons like some of those other hotels owned by the Japanese? And kimonos in the rooms instead of robes? And will all the Hotel restaurants feature sushi bars?"

"You sound like a bigot."

"Good. Put that in your report."

"I already told you, that isn't the kind of information I'm gathering."

"Take another note: tell them I think sashimi sucks. Tell them we have redwoods in California, and that bonsai doesn't work on them."

"You're not listening."

"You're fired," said Am.

"I'm an intern, you can't—"

"You misrepresented yourself, and you were here on our invitation. That invitation is now rescinded. When your overlords officially take over the place, you may return, but not until then."

"It would seem to be in both of our best interests—"

"Spies aren't welcome here," said Am.

He stared her down and wondered if she felt as sick as he did, but his face didn't reveal his quandary, only showed his disgust. Her face offered more: shame, and anger, and a willingness to talk. But he closed those doors as they showed themselves.

She left, not looking back, probably afraid to. Am watched her walk to the door and out of his life. He stood on the balcony, alone, and tried to find some answers in the ocean. It was talking gently, the surf slow and easy.

Am had always thought a GM was much like a ship's captain. He had imagined that when he became the GM of the Hotel California, he would invite guests over to his table, just like the captain of a ship. He would take them on their voyage, guide them on their journeys. And though he was that captain of the ship now, his ship was going down. Was he supposed to stay with the ship? He wondered what someone who was Japanese would do in his position. Commit hara-kiri? Perform seppuku?

That wasn't his way. Am looked down to the sand. If he had to choose a death, he thought it would be better to die as Tim Kelly had, throwing a water-filled condom down at a thrashing couple below. That was more the American way. If not honorable, it was at least darkly amusing.

# 52

Am returned not to Kendrick's office, but to his own. He closed the doors, turned off the lights, and made himself a cave where he could lick his wounds. On his desk was a bottle of Stolichnaya vodka with a note saying it was compliments of Mr. Harmon.

He wasn't in the habit of drinking on the job. With free-flowing liquor all around, the hospitality business either attracts, or breeds, a disproportionate amount of lushes. Though Am knew it was the oldest excuse in the world to say he'd earned a drink, this was one time he almost felt justified in mouthing that lie. He kicked his legs up on his desk, leaned back, and eyed the bottle. His love interest was gone, his job was going, going, and almost gone, and his dreams were getting maudlin. He felt like fodder for a country music festival.

His hand worked over to a mug that looked fairly free of mold. He unsealed the Stoly with slow, languorous fingers. Almost, he could imagine himself undraping Sharon the same way. He poured three fingers into the mug, stopped, then reconsidered and added another finger.

"To the new general manager of the Hotel California," he said aloud.

He took a long sip, then started laughing. It was a good thing he had closed the doors. His laughter bordered on the hysterical. Harmon had gotten the last laugh, having substituted water for the Stoly.

There were so many toasts Am could make: To illusion; the emperor's clothes; Vanity Fair; the Emerald City; the fantasy Hotel; the human comedy; and to the genie emerging from the bottle.

Am laughed until tears rolled down his face, then collected the bottle, if not his wits, and drove home. That night he slowly sipped away, savoring every drop of the Russian counterfeit, getting drunk on the water and his thoughts. Colorado River water never tasted so sweet.

He knocked at her door at midmorning. Sharon was surprised to see him.

"What you did was wrong," Am said. "And I think it best you not return to the Hotel. But . . . I did a lot of thinking last night, and I finally realized what time it is: it's a time to heal."

His olive branch was disarming, but she also felt it was still damning. "Maybe it's just a time to explain," said Sharon, her words defensive. "I didn't take this assignment to hurt anyone."

"I think I know that."

"I was supposed to get a sense of the property, something beyond a P and L sheet. I was there to help."

"That's usually the greatest sin of all."

"Don't be so superior, Ian Caulfield."

He flinched. It had been so long since Am had heard his real name, it sounded unnatural and condemning.

"You're not the only hotel detective, you know. You challenged me to find your real first name, and I did, *Ian*."

She put gleeful emphasis on the name, as if it were something she should be proud of and he ashamed of. Am responded in singsong kind: "You're just jealous because you're stuck with the name of Sharon instead of being blessed with an exotic nickname."

"What's wrong with Sharon?"

"It's old-fashioned. It exudes this wholesomeness, this picture of some apple-cheeked woman presenting a pie."

"Oh, and now that I'm in Southern California I should be called Moonbeam, or Freedom, or Wave?"

"No. Those are too common. Maybe I'll call you 'Are.' "

"R?"

"I, Am, you, Are?"

They offered each other a smile. It was a start.

"Don't think I've given up on finding the story behind your nickname, Ian Caulfield. I'm sure someone in this city knows its genesis."

"I do," he said.

"Tell me."

He took a deep breath, reminded himself that the genie was already out. "It was my first promotion," he said, "and my first memo. It taught me how important it is to proofread whatever you write. I signed the memo, proudly affixed my new title, and circulated it around. What I didn't notice was how I had abbreviated my title. I shortened assistant manager to ass man, and that's what everyone called me. Of course, in front of guests, they referred to me as Am. That's what stuck."

"Ass man," she said.

"Truth to tell," he said, "I'm more of a leg man."

"And that's the whole great secret?"

"That's it."

"Ian," she said, doing a name comparison. Then, "Am." She sampled the names as though they were food, chewed on them some, then announced, "If the ass fits, wear it."

"I don't exactly feel like I've been knighted."

"Jousting is a part of every knight's training."

"Is that the only way to win a lady?"

"Are you trying to win a lady?"

Instead of answering directly, he asked, "What are you doing today?"

"I'm working on a report," she said. "You just interrupted me. I was describing security at the Hotel California. The interim director, and I think I'm directly quoting, has 'the deductive talents of Sherlock Holmes, the tenacity of Lew

Archer, the charm of Travis McGee, the inquisitive mind of Hercule Poirot, and the inner toughness of Sam Spade.' "

"Don't stop now," said Am.

Sharon suddenly became serious. "Yamada's son is going to take over the operation of the Hotel," she said. "He'll be bringing a management team along with him. There's not going to be a bloodbath, but your old position won't be available. I'm recommending that you be retained as security director."

Angrily Am said, "As if I'd accept that demotion."

"At your same salary."

As much as he wanted to, Am didn't immediately naysay the job. He had always pictured himself as the GM of the Hotel, had never in his wildest dreams imagined himself as its security director. For a moment he played his own devil's advocate, went through the pros and cons of the job, before letting his pride speak: "I don't think so."

"Give it some consideration."

Am shrugged. He didn't want to admit it out loud, but he liked solving mysteries, and there was something romantic about him being named the defender of the Hotel. He could still be that catcher in the rye. "Tell me that part about Sherlock Holmes again."

"Do you want to come in and have some coffee?"

"No," he said. "I want you to come with me."

"Where are we going?"

"We're going to take a train. Every morning and every evening for the last ten years I've lived in Del Mar, I have heard it calling. Today is the day we follow the Sirens."

"What's our destination?"

In a stationmaster's voice, Am said, "Oceanside, San Clemente, San Juan Capistrano, Anaheim, and Los Angeles." Then, speaking normally, he said, "I figure we'll just keep getting off until we find that someplace that looks right. Or we'll just keep going."

"We could find a hotel on the beach."

"We could act like tourists."

"And complain about the service."

"And make a mess."

"And take the towels."

"And palm the silverware."

"And make noise all night."

"I like the sound of that," said Am.

She leaned over and kissed him lightly. He didn't complain.

"I stopped by the Hotel this morning," Am said, "and I told everyone I'd be gone for a few days."

"You were confident."

"I was hopeful."

"Any calamities?"

"No. The mail had already arrived. I thumbed through the guest comment cards and noticed some familiar handwriting."

"No!" she said.

He handed her the comment card. Carlton Smoltz had mailed it from the San Diego County Jail. It was probably the first hotel guest questionnaire ever mailed from a prison. Carlton had judged his stay as excellent and in the comments section had written, "I had a wonderful visit, and can't wait to return."

"I hope," said Sharon, "he doesn't recommend it to his friends."